Reckless Hearts

Rival Bull Rider Cowboy Romance

J Wilder

Copyright © 2025 by J Wilder

All rights reserved.

Reckless Hearts

No part of this book may be reproduced in any form or by any electronic or mechanical means, including information storage and retrieval systems, without written permission from the author, except for the use of brief quotations in a book review.

Cover: Emily Wittig - Emily Wittig Designs

Copy Editor: Sandra - One Love Editing

Copy Editor: Geissa - GP Author Services

J Wilder Reader Group

JOIN J. WILDER'S READERS' Group – The Wild Ones

Love steamy books, chaotic polls, exclusive teasers, and general unhinged reader energy?

Come hang out with us in The Wild Ones—my official reader group!

BASICALLY, all the fun stuff. None of the chill.

Come be feral with us.

WILDER ONES - J Wilder Reader Group

Author's Note

I'm pretty sure I could charge this book with attempted murder.

How can something I love so much be so mean?

Midway through drafting, I somehow destroyed my left arm. It started with a sharp pain in my wrist (which, of course, I ignored), and by that night, it had traveled all the way up to my shoulder. I had a choice: delay the release or... learn how to dictate.

Let me tell you, I have never once thought, "You know what my life is missing? Dictation."

But in the end, it saved the freaking day.

Even if I did learn I mumble everything and apparently say words that are... not the ones I mean.

That said, I am so, so proud of this book.

It pushed me, but these three hold a piece of my heart.

Every now and then, characters come along and steal it entirely. For me, that's them.

Now.

I know.

We all hate miscommunication.

I get it. *I do...*

But also? Sometimes? I love it.

So, fair warning: these boys are idiots. Idiots in love. And honestly? That's kind of my favorite part.

A quick note before we dive in:

I made up my own bull riding organization for this book: The National Bull Riding Association. It does not exist in real life and is not based on the Professional Bull Riders (PBR) organization. Just vibes.

Terms you might see:

Bullfighter – Not the red cape or face paint kind. These are the rodeo athletes who distract the bull after a ride to keep the rider safe. Literal lifesavers.

Wrangler – A cowboy who handles the animals, ropes bulls, and keeps everything running behind the scenes.

Bull Rider – The adrenaline-junkie athlete who rides a 1,500-pound bull for (hopefully) 8 seconds.

Chute – The metal stall where the bull and rider are loaded before the ride begins.

Season – The full bull riding tour year. Events are held in different cities throughout the season, all leading to the championship.

Trigger Warnings

Your mental health comes first, always. Please take care of yourself while reading.

This book includes:

* Death of a parent (past, referenced throughout)
* On-page panic attack, and references throughout.
* On-page bull riding accident resulting in injury

If you ever need to skip a scene or take a break, that's okay. Your well-being matters more than anything else.

Dedication

Dedicated to everyone who's ever looked at two rivals and thought: "Why not both?"

Chapter 1
Colt

Two thousand pounds of raging animosity twists and bucks between my thighs. My body's coiled tight, every muscle locked and straining. I force myself to loosen up, to move *with* the bull instead of fighting him in a brutal ballet of instinct and grit. Each jolt threatens to send me flying, but I hang on.

It feels like flying, falling, and breaking all at once.

For these eight seconds, nothing matters but the connection between us. Every moment is an eternity, stretching and bending under the force of the ride. Sweat stings my eyes, mixing with the grit of the arena, and turns the world into a muted haze.

The best riders know, it's not a fight. It's a dance. And the bull leads.

My thighs burn, and the rope scorches my palm as Rampage kicks high, his rear legs reaching for the sky before he dips hard to throw me. I lose everything except the rhythm between us, fierce and unrelenting.

Time stretches, and the world grows quiet as each heartbeat pounds louder in my ears. Pure instinct takes over my body as I let myself go with him.

I pour everything I have into the final seconds. These endless, glorious, impossible seconds.

Then I see him. Maverick, waiting in the chute, tension crackling through the air as his gaze fixes on me with unsettling intensity. My focus, my determination, my bitterness. It all crashes together like a storm. I ride harder, fire burning in my chest, because I know he's waiting to see if I'll fail.

The bell goes off, marking my victory, but the milliseconds of distraction give the bull all it needs to throw me like a rag doll. My body's weightless for a moment before I slam hard into the ground. The air rips from my lungs, pain sparking bright and white. Years of practice kick in and I roll fast, just in time to avoid a hoof to the ribs. The beast would like nothing more than to kill me, and I left myself wide open.

Hands pull me up and away, dust-coated and breathless. Bullfighters work together, taunting the beast into his pen. They save more lives than any of us can count. They've earned our respect ten times over.

It's not until the gate closes that my senses return. The noise is staggering, the cheer of the crowd a wild, victorious thing that wraps around me. I look up to the sky, panting and alive, and let the triumphant, reckless surge carry me.

Cocky now, I turn toward the chutes. It's chaos, wranglers shouting, riders settling onto their bulls. I don't bother hiding my smirk as I find Maverick, daring him to do better.

He doesn't look worried.

He looks *satisfied*. Like he's proud of himself for getting in my head enough to almost get me trampled.

Heat crawls up my neck. My ears burn. Getting distracted like that was humiliating.

Knowing *he* was the reason? Fucking mortifying.

They announce my name over the speakers, and the bitter twist in my gut is replaced by electricity. Victory pulses through me, humming under my skin.

Bull riding is taunting death and walking away grinning. It's the closest thing I'll ever feel to invincibility.

Dust grits between my teeth as I smile, lifting my wide-brimmed hat high above my head to wave to the crowd.

Half of them cheer. The other half groan. Money changes hands in the stands, some spectators ecstatic, some licking their wounds. The fact that they were hoping I'd get crushed isn't lost on me.

I dip my head to Rampage, still glaring from his pen. His fury earned us forty-five out of fifty points on top my own. In bull riding, both rider *and* bull are scored. Without him, my ride wouldn't have meant shit. Every rider depends on the wildness of the animal beneath him.

I needed these points to rise up in the ranks, now three spots from the top. It's proof that I'm still in this fight, still here despite it all. Annoyance threatens to take over, and I force myself not to search for Maverick, who's ranked one spot above me.

Letting myself get hung up on that bullshit will only screw with my head, when I need every ounce of concentration to move me forward. Anything can happen during the circuit.

Nothing matters but the next bull. The next ride. The next win.

I duck under the railing and make my way through the bustling maze behind the arena, still vibrating from the ride, adrenaline sparking in every muscle. Metal gates clang. Voices echo. Sweat and dirt sting my nostrils.

I spot a kid hovering ahead. A gangly teen, wide-eyed, clutching a rodeo program to his chest. Must be working for a rider. No fans allowed back here.

"Mr. Lawson." He steps forward, his words awkward but hopeful. "Can you sign my hat?"

"Sure thing, kid," I say, feeling the lingering high from my performance seep into my voice, making it warm and easy as I scrawl my name across the brim.

"That ride was *insane!*" The kid's enthusiasm is infectious, pulling a grin from me despite the exhaustion creeping into my bones.

"Keep cheering for me, you hear?" I laugh, tousling the kid's hair, earning a toothy grin from him.

"I will, sir! Maverick Kane doesn't stand a chance against you."

I stiffen, then place the hat on his head, giving it a little squeeze. "He sure as hell doesn't. Stay out of trouble."

The kid beams and nods. "Will do!"

A few more people stop me, congratulating me on my ride. Their voices overlap like a chorus.

"Thought that bull was gonna eat you alive, Colt!"

"You showed 'em!"

"Damn good ride!"

I nod and smile, letting their words wash over me, feeling the exhilaration stretch into a satisfying ache. My body's sore and bruised, each step a reminder of the wild dance with the bull, but I keep moving toward the dressing room, where I'll be able to catch my breath.

Bone-deep exhaustion is settling in by the time I push through the swinging locker room door. My hat's pulled low, my neck too tired to hold my head up. That fall definitely took a toll on my body, and it's making itself known.

Then I hear it, a soft chuckle.

I freeze at the sound of the sweetest voice I haven't heard in years, and my head snaps up, and there she is. "Oh fuck."

She gives me a shy, tentative smile. "Is that any way to greet an old friend?"

Callie Harper.

Her back's against a wooden beam, trying and failing to look casual. Her hands fidget, wringing together as if she doesn't know what to do with them.

Eight years.

I blink, trying to breathe past the punch to the chest her presence delivers.

"Callie?" Her name comes out like a question, laced with disbelief.

She finally looks at me. Those hazel eyes. God, those eyes, warm, familiar, devastating.

The sight of her here, in this world we once shared, knocks the wind out of me more than any bull ever has.

The woman in front of me, because that's what she is now. All curves and seduction. Every inch of her calling to be touched. Her copper hair spilling out from beneath a black Stetson like something out of a dream I never expected to wake up to.

The last time I saw her, she was fourteen in a sundress, disappearing into the back of a black town car leaving a hole in my chest where she used to be.

I understood why she had to leave. Her dad had just died. She needed space.

I just didn't think it would be forever.

"Are you just gonna stare at me, or are you gonna say hello?" Her voice wobbles at the end, like she's not sure she belongs here.

"Hello," I say dumbly.

God, I sound like an idiot.

Reduced to a singular word, still stunned, not quite sure if she's actually here or if I hit my head harder than I thought. I've waited for her over the years, expecting her to come back from school for the summer. But she never did. If those memories of our friendship hadn't been seared into me, I would have thought I made them up. There was a time Callie and Maverick had been like family. Now, even the thought of Maverick twists my stomach and makes me want to throw shit.

Her gaze darts around the room, landing everywhere but on mine, her teeth sinking into her lip. "I know it's been a while... I probably should have let you know I was coming. If you're busy, I get it."

"Busy? Are you kidding me?" I ask, incredulous.

Fuck. I don't know how she got it into her head that I'd be anything less than ecstatic to see her, but I'm going to end that right now.

She smiles, small, uncertain and for a second, I see the girl who used to drag Maverick and me into trouble with nothing but a grin and a dare. It hasn't faded. It's still there, just buried under nerves.

Before she can second-guess herself, I'm already moving.

"Geez, Callie," I mutter, striding over.

I wrap my arms around her and lift her off the ground in a tight, full-body hug. My ribs scream. My shoulder protests.

I don't give a damn.

She's real. She's here.

And I'm not letting go.

I don't even know what I say after that just a rush of words, awe, and disbelief spilling out of me. I can't stop touching her. Can't stop looking.

"I can't believe you're here."

She shrugs like it's no big deal. "Had to finally see you ride for myself."

"When did you get here? How long are you staying? How have you been?"

It's like every question that's been building up explodes from me. Suddenly, that young boy's hurt comes forward before I can stop it. "Why—why didn't you come back?"

Rich hazel eyes glisten. Her hands tremble on my shoulders. But she doesn't get the chance to answer.

Because then Maverick walks in.

And everything changes.

His boots scuff against the floor, halting just inside the doorway.

Maverick's gaze lands on us, on *her* and the sound he makes isn't a word, just a sharp, audible inhale that slices through the air like a whip.

He freezes, eyes wide, locked on Callie like she's a ghost he never thought he'd see again. His steps stutter when he finally moves, cautious and slow, like approaching a wild animal.

His expression darkens as the pieces click into place, her arms around *me*, my hand low on her back, the way she fits against my chest like she's never belonged anywhere else.

And yeah, I smirk.

Petty? Maybe. He's ahead of me in the rankings, but *she came to me first.*

The satisfaction is short-lived.

"Callie?" His voice is rougher than usual, a little raw, a little shaken. Vulnerable in a way I haven't heard in years.

Annoyance flares in my chest.

Of course he has the same reaction. The same stupid, stunned awe. As kids, she was the sun we both revolved around. Looks like that hasn't changed either.

"Hi," she says quietly, like she's not sure she's allowed to say more.

His head tilts as he searches her expression, reading what's left unsaid. A line forms between his brows, as unhappy as I am with the way she's unsure of herself with us.

Then he smiles, soft and full of wonder. "Well, aren't you a sight for sore eyes? What are you waiting for? Come give me a hug."

She doesn't hesitate.

She runs to him.

Runs.

My jaw tightens as he lifts her easily, pulling her into his arms like he's done it a thousand times. One boot slides back to steady himself, and then she's there, wrapped around him. His hand cradles her face, thumb sweeping gently across her cheek before he tucks a strand of hair behind her ear.

I stand rooted, the corridor's noise fading as I watch them. That old dynamic of the three of us tangled up in ways no one else ever quite understood. It's right here. Raw. Real.

We were always like this. Years of running wild on her family's ranch, sneaking into the hayloft, falling asleep in a tangle of limbs after long days in the sun. Half the time, Callie was asleep on Maverick's shoulder or poking at my ribs with her frozen toes, giggling while we tried to push her off the couch. It was messy and close and loud, and somehow, it always made sense.

Maverick shakes his head and pulls back a little but doesn't let her go. His usually guarded demeanor cracks wide open, and the questions pour out of him, just like they did from me.

Callie doesn't miss the similarities, glancing over her shoulder at me with a sparkle in her eyes. "Easy," she laughs. "I will answer all of your questions. For now, I'm just happy to see you."

My muscles lock up again when he keeps his hands on her waist a second too long. His palm spans the whole damn width of her back, and I hate how *right* it looks.

He meets my eyes.

There it is. The unspoken standoff.

No words. Just heat and history crackling in the space between us. What used to be friendship has curdled into rivalry in public and resentment in private. Quiet betrayals. Loud silences. All of it simmers beneath the surface as we stare each other down.

Callie shifts away, her brows drawn together as she glances between us. Her expression pinches. "What's happening between you two?"

That's right. She's been gone so long she doesn't know.

Doesn't know how he threw me away for the sport like our years together didn't mean a damn thing. Like I was just some stepping stone he could crush on the way to the top.

And the worst part? He walks around like he doesn't get why I'm still pissed. Like I didn't bleed for him too.

When Callie left, I lost her. But when Mav chose bull riding over everything else. We lost us.

We've been like this ever since. Two unmovable walls. No point trying to talk through it. Not when he still doesn't think he did anything wrong.

Maverick raises an eyebrow.

I shrug.

"Same as ever," I say, letting the bitterness slip into my tone. It's not subtle. It's not meant to be.

Callie's brow furrows. She looks between us, clearly lost, like she's walked into a story that kept going without her.

"Maverick Lincoln Kane and Colt Wyatt Lawson..." Her voice wavers, less a crack of thunder now, more a quiet plea. "How did it get like this?"

She stands between us, hands on her hips like she's trying to summon the old fire, trying to be the girl who used to keep us in line.

The only one who could tame two reckless boys who thought they were untouchable.

But we fell apart without her.

Neither of us answers.

The silence stretches, thick and uncomfortable, because there's no good place to start.

How do we explain that the boys she once knew don't exist anymore?

That we're men now. Wounded, angry, and competitive to the point of self-destruction?

That we burned the bridge between us and danced in the ashes?

"Didn't you know?" Luke Williams drawls from the open doorway, perfectly timed. "These two *hate* each other."

Chapter 2
Callie

His voice drops like a bomb in the room.

"These two hate each other."

"Bullshit," I say, the word slipping out sharp, reflexive. For a second, heat flares in my chest, anger, frustration but it's gone just as fast, swallowed by something heavier. Confusion. Dread.

"Luke, back off," Maverick says, voice a warning.

Neither of them corrects me. Neither denies it. They just stand there, Colt clenching his jaw so tight it's a wonder he can breathe, Maverick wound up like a live wire. Both of them staring anywhere but at each other.

My heart stutters.

I crossed an entire state for this. For them. And now they won't even look at each other?

"Maverick?" I manage, barely above a whisper. "Colt?"

They still don't answer.

I glance between them, stomach twisting. The two people I trusted most in the world, who used to finish each other's sentences, who used to feel like home but now?

Now, they look like strangers.

"What the hell happened to you two?"

What could have possibly changed in eight years to cause... whatever *this* is? I'm struggling to wrap my head around the fact that Colt looks like he could punch a hole in the wall, and Maverick's shoulders are drawn so tight I'm surprised they haven't snapped.

"I don't know what's going on between you two," I say softly, my voice catching. "But... you're best friends. Aren't you?"

Colt snorts, sharp and humorless, and mutters something that sounds a lot like, *Not friends with that bastard.*

"Best friends?" the guy, Luke, says, shoving his hat back on. His rich black skin and warm undertone contrast sharply with the pale khaki of his rolled-up sleeves. He leans in, his voice low and conspiratorial. "They've been at it for as long as I've known them." His eyes crinkle with amusement, and he chuckles. "I don't think they're capable of getting along."

I don't move. I just stand there between them, between Maverick and Colt as silence wraps around us like barbed wire. I glance from one to the other, and for the first time since walking back into their lives, I see it. Really see it.

The distance.

The anger.

The hurt.

My arrogance smacks me straight in the face.

Did I really think I could just show up after eight years and everything would fall back into place?

They don't look at each other. They don't look at me. Just two statues carved out of old memories and silent resentment.

When I left, they were brothers in everything but blood. Colt with his reckless grin and go-all-in energy. Maverick with his sharp focus and relentless drive. We were a mess of scraped knees and big dreams, each one of us balancing the other two.

Now, they're standing like strangers. Enemies.

They don't answer.

Of course they don't.

Colt's expression is a wall of indifference, but his hands are fists at his sides. Maverick just watches me with that unreadable intensity that always used to scare the hell out of other kids and make me laugh.

I take a step back and cross my arms, forcing them to look at me instead of each other.

"I need one of you to please start explaining," I say, lost in confusion and needing to understand.

They flinch, *both of them*, like they've just been caught breaking a window instead of shattering a ten-year friendship.

Still, silence.

It presses in on us like a weight. I can barely breathe through it.

God, I knew coming back would stir up memories. But this? This is *carnage*.

I can't help but wonder. Is this my fault?

If I hadn't left... would they still be like this? Could I have fixed whatever it is that came between them?

Back then, I packed what little was left of me and buried it under textbooks and dorm rooms and years of silence. I convinced myself it was better that way. Cleaner. Safer.

Telling myself that at least they had each other. That even if I left, even if I missed them so much it hurt, they would be okay. That they'd still be *them*.

But standing here now, watching the tension vibrate between them, I know that was a lie.

They're not fine.

And they don't have each other anymore.

My stomach twists, guilt blooming like a bruise across my ribs.

The only thing keeping me grounded is knowing it's not too late.

My time here is limited, but I'm going to spend every damn minute of this bull riding season making sure they sort their shit out. That they find their way back to each other.

I can't stay, not when I know what staying would do to me.

"You two used to be glued together. Now you're acting like you don't even recognize each other."

Our conversation's cut off when several riders crash

into the locker room, breaking the tension between us. The old wooden door slams shut, causing the fluorescent lights to flicker.

The sudden movement jars me, reminding me of the reasons I came back in the first place.

I've done a lot of work to come back here. Therapy. Time. Distance.

This season is my last window. I just graduated. I've got a job offer waiting in the fall, real life breathing down my neck.

But before I can move on, I needed to come back. To see them. To know they are fine without me. To face the part of myself I left behind when I ran.

I've missed them more than I can put into words.

I have just long enough to say goodbye to who we used to be. To lay it all to rest before I step into whatever comes next.

Because when it's over. When I leave again. These moments are all I'll have.

"Hello, darlin'," a man drawls as he saunters over, the cocky tilt of his mouth all too familiar. I vaguely recognize him from watching events on TV. He's older, a little weathered around the edges, but he's still wearing the same smug grin that seems stamped onto every bull rider's face. "You're not supposed to be in here. Not that I'm complaining."

I open my mouth to reply, but Maverick cuts in sharply, his voice hard as steel. "Watch it."

The man raises both hands in mock surrender. "Sorry, didn't know she was taken."

And just like that, an idea starts to form. A risky one. If I'm going to get these two to start acting like friends again, I need to force them into situations where they *have* to be around each other. This guy just handed me a perfect opportunity.

"I'm not," I say sweetly, flashing my best smile. "We're friends."

The tension spikes instantly.

I'm playing with fire, and I know it. Colt and Maverick have never liked sharing my attention. Not when we were kids, and definitely not now. But maybe they need a little push. Maybe I need to rattle them enough to get a reaction.

Colt makes a low sound in his chest, more growl than breath, but he doesn't argue.

The room goes quiet for a beat, then erupts into rowdy laughter and jabs, the other riders catching on to the shift in energy. It's like someone flipped a switch. I can practically feel the heat of the unspoken challenge: *Who's going to get the girl?*

"In that case," the stranger says, grinning wider, "you should come out with us. We're hitting up a local bar. Wouldn't mind having a pretty face like yours tag along."

I feel a little like prey, but I can hold my own. They don't know I grew up around boys just like them. Boys who think they're all that just because they had a good ride.

I know my plan will work when I catch Colt and Maverick glaring at the guy, arms crossed, jaws tight. Well, at least one thing still brings them together, and I'm going to use it to my advantage.

"I'm in," I say easily, swinging my hair back over my shoulder. "Meet you outside?"

"I don't think so," Colt says, stepping forward. His hand lands gently but firmly on my shoulder, and when I look up, I meet those sky-blue eyes of his, like a punch to the gut. My stomach tightens, but I force myself not to get swept up in it.

Stepping away, I shoot him a mischievous smile. "Well, it's a good thing I didn't ask you."

Maverick goes to say something, but I shake my head, pushing the door open. "You can keep whatever you were about to say to yourself too."

The door swings shut behind me with a satisfying *click*.

I hesitate for half a second, tempted to press my ear to the wood as a flurry of muffled voices breaks out on the other side. They're probably trying to figure out who I am and what the hell just happened.

Instead, I move through the maze of corridors, past rows of gear and echoes of the past, and out the back toward the trucks.

Time to stir the pot.

I lean against the hitching rail, boots scuffing the ground as I set a three-minute timer on my phone. If Colt and Maverick are anything like they used to be, that's all it'll take.

While I wait, my thumb hovers over my mom's latest message.

> Mom: How are you doing, sweetheart. I know this is hard on you.

> Me: All good here. Made it in time to see Colt and Maverick's rides.

> Mom: They did well. Tell them both I say hi.

She still doesn't watch the events live. Instead, waits for the results and then watches a recording. If it were up to her, she probably wouldn't watch at all, but as the owner of Harper Ridge Ranch, it's her job to stay informed.

> Mom: You sure you're okay? I know your therapist said it was a good idea, but I'm still not sure.

> Me: You promised me you'd trust me this summer. I'll be fine.

I'll be fine... I type it with more confidence than I feel. Coming back was something I needed to do, but that doesn't mean it doesn't scare the shit out of me. Not that I'll tell her that.

> Mom: You're right. You're all grown up now. I love you, kiddo. Just take care of yourself.

> Me: Always do. Love you too.

> Mom: Text me when you get back to your motel.

> Mom: Alone.

I roll my eyes, because of course she'd tack that on. She's never hidden what she thinks about bull riders. Nothing but a bunch of reckless, arrogant boys who wouldn't know how to put a woman first if their lives depended on it. To them, becoming a champion isn't just a goal. It's the ultimate high. Nothing and no one will ever come before winning that gold buckle.

She doesn't need to warn me. My dad already taught me what happens when you fall in love with a bull rider.

"*You promised to quit when Callie was born.*" My mom's pleading voice still echoes in my memories. I'd overheard my parents repeatedly having the same argument. Back then, I'd been naive enough to take my dad's side, convinced she was trying to take away something that mattered to him.

"*Just one more.*" Dad cups her chin, drawing her attention.

My mom's gaze searches his, hoping he's telling the truth. "*You've been saying that for years.*"

"This time, I really mean it." He places a gentle kiss on her forehead.

Just like that, all the fight washes out of her. "Do you promise?"

"I promise, sweetheart. One more ride and I'm done. Then you won't know what to do with me. You'll be complaining that I'm under your feet all the time."

I can still hear the laugh she gave, full of relief, like he'd finally untied a knot she'd been carrying in her chest for years.

I didn't understand then, but I do now.

The heartbreak of loving someone who chooses danger over family.

My dad knew she was terrified every time he got on a bull, knew it was tearing her apart. She begged him to stop. If not for her, then for me. And he promised. Over and over, he promised.

But in the end, those promises didn't matter.

In the end, my dad chose the ride.

He kept competing until the day he was killed. Trampled in the arena while we watched it happen on TV.

My mom's gut-wrenching screams as she watched the love of her life bleed out still haunt my dreams.

So no. I don't need to be told what happens when you get too close to a bull rider.

I already know.

When my dad died in the arena, something inside me shattered. Not just because I lost him. But because in that moment, I understood, *really understood* that he never chose us. Not me. Not my mom. Not the promises he made about quitting.

He said *one more ride* a hundred times. He told us he'd walk away after the circuit, after the season. After nationals.

He never meant it.

And when the bull bucked him and he didn't get up, I realized what had always been true.

The bulls came first. The ride came first. *It always did, and it always will.*

I breathe through the ache in my chest until it settles into something dull, manageable. I've had years to practice pushing it down. I decided long ago, I was never going to beg anyone to give up riding. Because how can I expect anyone else to choose me when *my own father* wouldn't?

That's why, when Maverick and Colt told me they were serious about competing, I did the only thing I could.

I ran.

Maverick comes out with Colt hot on his heels, his voice heated as he says, "She's coming with me."

"Like hell she is," Colt responds just in time for my alarm to go off.

"Perfect timing." Smiling at the way matching creases form between their brows, I turn off the alarm and tuck my phone into my back pocket.

"Tell him you're coming with me," Colt says, then instantly backs off at the look I give him. "I mean, will you please ride with me?"

My breath comes out unevenly as I chuckle, taking

them in then it catches in my throat. So much was happening earlier that I didn't get a chance to really look at them. And now, standing side by side under the setting sun, I'm not sure I'll recover from this.

There's *handsome*, and then there's... *this. Them.*

Colt's all sun-soaked charm and magnetism. Those blue eyes and that dimple could coax the panties off a nun.

Then there's Maverick quiet, controlled, unwavering. There's a steadiness in him that makes you feel safe without even trying. When his dark eyes meet mine, half-hidden beneath the messy fall of brown hair, there's depth there, a hint of something that tempts me to dig deeper and uncover all of his secrets.

They're opposites. Sun and moon. Fire and water. Yet somehow, always orbiting each other.

And right now? They're both looking at *me*.

Their attention on me sends an electric shiver dancing down my spine, sparking a tingling sensation.

I always did have a secret crush on them. How could I not when they were... *them?*

It's painfully clear time hasn't changed a damn thing.

"You keep looking at me like that, I'm going to get full of myself," Colt teases.

Heat climbs up my neck, coloring my cheeks, but I can't seem to look away. Their gazes stay locked on me, long lashes lowered just enough to veil their expressions, but not enough to hide the pull between us. It feels like a rope drawn tight, humming in the space between us.

"Like you aren't already," I murmur, swallowing hard. *This is not how we feel about our friends.*

Colt tilts his head, grin deepening, that damn dimple appearing again. "I could be worse."

"Jesus Christ, let the girl breathe," Luke says as he walks out, arriving just in time to break the spell. My relief must show on my face because he turns to me with open arms. "You can hug me as a thank-you."

"Not a chance," Maverick snaps, his voice low and rough.

His whole energy shifts, darker, more intense, as his gaze drags from me to Colt. There's tension in every line of his body.

We're at a standstill, no one moving, like we're all waiting for something to drop.

I nod once, mostly to myself. "Okay. Fine. You hate each other. Great. But I didn't come back to walk into the middle of some pissing contest. I came back to see you. *Both* of you. And while I'm here, you're going to act like you don't loathe each other's existence. Got it?"

They don't respond.

But they don't say no either.

I take that as a win.

This isn't over. Not even close.

But I've got time.

Time to remind them of who we were.

Time to fix what I broke.

And if I can't?

At least I'll know I tried.

Chapter 3

Maverick

Every muscle in my body screams at me, pleading, begging for rest, but Callie Harper still has me wrapped around her finger.

She's out of Luke's truck the second we pull into the lot. Cutoff jean shorts, a black T-shirt stamped with her family's ranch logo, and those long, sun-kissed legs tucked into beat-up cowboy boots. She might've been gone from the ranch, but clearly, she never let her roots go.

All I want is to drag myself to the motel, soak in scalding water until I can't feel my skin, and collapse on the too-hard mattress. My tendons ache as much as the rest of me, a reminder of today's ride. I stuck the eight, but that bull did his best to break me apart.

That's the thing about riding, the high hits like a drug. But when it wears off, you're left bruised and broken. And still... we'd all do it again in a heartbeat.

Coming to a dive bar in the middle of nowhere is my

personal idea of hell, but one look from Callie, and that bone-deep exhaustion turns into a paper-thin excuse.

If I'm not careful, people are going to figure out I'm nothing more than a puppy trailing after her which isn't far from the truth. I've been waiting for her to come home since the day she left.

When it became obvious neither Colt nor I would agree to ride in the same truck, Callie suggested we could both cram into Luke's or stay behind. Damn her for knowing exactly what to say to get us moving.

Even my toes hurt as I follow her toward the bar, two massive barn doors marking the entrance. A heavy dread settles in my gut, begging me to turn around. I'm tired. I'm sore. I just want to crash.

"You coming?" Callie turns back, her smile beaming at me, and my whole world stops for a second, before crashing back into me. She's glowing, lit from within like she swallowed the sun, and somehow, her warmth reaches me from across the gravel lot. The ache in my bones eases.

God broke the mold with Callie Harper. Nothing and no one has ever come close.

I nod. Words are hard when she's near. She reaches her hand back, fingers twitching like she's waiting for mine.

Colt beats me to it.

He grabs her hand and spins her into him, her copper hair flying, laughter bursting out of her. Her wide eyes flick up to meet his, and that sharp twist in my gut returns.

He smirks at me over her shoulder, smug in a way that

makes my fists clench. We've kept our distance for years, like opposite poles of a magnet. And right now? I could punch that look clean off his face.

Callie pauses at the door, waiting for me, and Colt's forced to stop or let her go. He doesn't say anything, but the look he throws me is loud: *Back off.*

She flashes me a mischievous smirk, the same one she used to wear when dragging us into trouble. My childhood was all scraped knees, stolen pie, and summer sun. And every golden memory has her in it.

Luke claps a hand on my shoulder. "You gonna keep staring or follow her in?"

I grunt, half-annoyed, half-grateful for the shove. He's right. She's finally here. No point wasting time reliving the past.

Gravel crunches beneath my feet as I catch up to them, half expecting Colt to argue, but he just keeps his hand on her shoulder, meeting my eyes in a truce that so long as she's around, an agreement that whatever's between us comes second to her.

The pounding twang of banjos makes me wince the second we step inside. A wall of heat and noise hits like a stampede, and my head's already pulsing. Colt winces too, at least I'm not the only one suffering.

He's forcing his signature dimpled smile. The one that makes people believe they're close to him, while he's actually maintaining his distance. Honestly, it's a fucking talent.

Somehow, Callie slipped away from both of us,

wiggling through the crowd. It's packed in here, a mix between not much else to do and people wanting to see bull riders up close. I've been to enough of these to know what to expect. Men looking for a fight and girls with hopes that they may just be the one who ropes one of us in.

Can't help but feel bad for them because I've never seen a cowboy settle down that way. We're a different breed, drifting from one place to another. The idea of being tethered feels more like a noose than anything.

Colt's chatting with fans, putting on that charming grin. Me? I shove through the crowd with half-assed apologies, determined to get to her.

By the time I do, there's a line creased between her brows as she stares down some guy, her arms crossed in front of her. I'm about to step in when Colt materializes beside me, shoulder bumping mine.

"Let's see what she does," he says, almost fond. "Kinda feel bad for the guy."

He doesn't notice my double take, too focused on the showdown.

Whatever she says, it's working. The guy's ears turn red. He's not having an easy go of it. He swipes off his hat and nods a few more times without making eye contact, then spins on his heels and vanishes into the crowd like a scolded dog.

I shake my head. "She always did know how to put someone in their place."

Colt laughs. "We should know better than anyone."

I chuckle, memories bubbling up of her chewing us out while standing a foot shorter, somehow still terrifying.

Blue eyes shift to me, a familiar lightness in Colt's gaze for the few seconds it takes him to remember things aren't what they used to be. The wall comes down again, freezing me out.

I rub my neck, the weight of the day dragging me down. "I need a drink."

"Agreed," Colt says, leading us to a corner booth with a reserved sign propped on the table.

I collapse onto the bench with a groan, resting my head against the wooden back. It's too early for how much everything hurts. Every inch of me hurts. Colt must notice because a bottle of pills slides across the table. I don't like pills; it's too easy to rely on them. Too many riders have gone out that way.

I go to push them back, but he stops me. "Relax. It's just ibuprofen."

Grunting my thanks, I pop a few into my mouth, swallowing them dry. Anything to get me through the next few hours.

"You two look rough," Callie teases, slipping in beside Colt. "Should've left you at home." Her voice is smooth, like bourbon over ice. "Don't worry," she adds with a wink. "I ordered us some drinks."

As if summoned, the waitress appears with a black tray nearly toppling with glasses. "Two steins and a mixer, sweetheart?"

"That's us," Callie chirps, already reaching up to help

her. "Keep 'em coming." Callie slides a tip across the table, and the waitress looks like she's already half in love with her. Our girl just has that effect on people.

Our drinks hit the table with a satisfying thud. The glasses are frosted, and the beer goes down smooth, cold against my throat. Colt and I let out matching groans as the blend of bitter hops and sweet malt hits.

"Alright, you got us here. Now it's time you answered our questions." I meet her gaze steadily. She's not squirming her way out of this.

"What brings you back here, Callie? Why now?" Colt asks the question that's been on both of our minds since the second we saw her.

She takes her time sipping her drink. I hold back my impatience. I've been waiting a long time. I can wait a little longer.

"I've got the summer off. I was planning on staying for the season. Thought I'd tag along with you two," she says finally. "Just graduated. My job doesn't start till the fall."

It lands with a quiet thud. Final. Like she's already marked the day she leaves on the calendar.

Her gaze flicks up. "Is me being here... not okay?"

The uncertainty in her voice slices right through me. No hint of the wild, fearless girl who used to boss us around like she ran the damn world.

"Of course it's okay," I say quickly. "This place is your home too." I leave the rest of my thoughts unsaid. Everything I've been wishing for is sitting right in front of me like a present, wrapped up in a bow.

She lets go of a long, deep breath, her shoulders sagging like the weight of the world has just been lifted off her.

I want to press. Ask why she never visited, didn't call, didn't come home even once. But I don't. Not tonight. I won't risk breaking whatever this is.

Clearly, Colt feels the same because he skirts around the topic, instead asking, "What has our little Callie been up to all these years?"

Callie perks up, talking about her life, and her mood is contagious as ever.

The warm ease between us spreads like the alcohol, a buzz in my veins. We drink, Callie leading the conversation, her stories rolling out and lulling me into the soft cradle of the past. Colt's defenses slip, the fake smile turning real, and I'm just lost enough in this unexpected reunion to let it feel normal. The noise and ache recede, and all that's left is the feeling that the world might've fixed itself.

It's been a long time since I felt like this, like the past didn't wreck everything, like maybe there's still something worth saving. Callie's in the middle, the axis Colt and I still spin around, and when I glance his way, there's a flicker of recognition in his eyes. We both know she's the reason we're even sitting here like this.

"You should see the campus," Callie says, sipping her drink, more talkative than I've ever seen her, more confident than the girl who left. "Half the buildings look like castles. I swear, I kept expecting someone to hand me a wand and a Latin textbook."

Colt leans in, grinning. "Please tell me you wore a plaid skirt."

Callie shoots him a look, sharp but amused. "Gross."

"What?" He throws up a hand. "Just trying to picture you in your natural academic habitat."

"Try picturing me punching you in the throat instead."

Colt chuckles, and she fights a smile, losing quickly. Just like that, the air feels light again.

Drinks go down easily as more of the crew shows up. Other riders I've seen before, faces that come and go with the dangers of the circuit, fill the tables around us. The bar pulses with laughter and shouts, the carefree hum of cowboys too young to know their limits or too wild to care.

Colt and Callie go back and forth, familiar as breathing, and I can almost see the kids they used to be, arguing over who got the last slice of Mrs. Kitty's cake. I watch them together, talking close, and can't shake the feeling that I'm seeing everything I missed, like glimpses of a life I could've had.

Huffing out a breath, I brush the hair off my warm face. Fuck, I must be drunk. I'm getting all sentimental.

"You good?" Luke asks, his voice low enough not to carry. He raises an eyebrow like he's worried about my sanity. I'm worried about it too, but I huff out a laugh. I'm in for a hell of a night.

I give him a curt nod, but push my glass into the center

of the table, not that it'll do any good, considering it's empty.

"Your girl's looking cozy," Luke remarks, nodding his head in Callie's direction.

They sit so close their elbows brush, both of them flushed and happy. I search my feelings but find no trace of jealousy. "Just catching up,"

Luke snorts and leans back. "You're too calm for your own good, buddy."

"It's complicated," I admit, and I scrub my hand through my hair, as if that'll help clear the mental mess Callie has made.

"No kidding. And here I thought you hated each other."

I start to respond, but Callie's laughter cuts through, sweet and sudden, yanking my attention straight back to her. She's flushed and radiant, a little tipsy, and for a second, I forget about the ache in my shoulders, the rivalry simmering between me and Colt, the past that won't stay buried.

He catches her instinctively, hand steadying her lower back, and I'm hit with that same flash of electricity.

I don't know what I expected this night to be, but watching them together like this relaxed and close, like no time passed at all does something to me.

Her cheeks are flushed, her smile loose around the edges, and that familiar spark lights behind her eyes. She exhales like she just made a decision, setting her glass down with a clink. She sways slightly in her seat, bumping into Colt's side.

"I want to dance."

"God, why?" Colt groans like it physically pains him, but I can already see the gleam in his hazy eyes. The alcohol's hitting him hard.

Callie grins at him, all sunshine and challenge. "Unless you're scared of a little line dancing."

"Fuck... you just had to put it like that, didn't you..." Colt drains the last of his drink before grabbing her hand. "Alright, let's go."

She stands, then turns to me with that wild gleam in her eyes, the one that used to get us into trouble.

She leans in, her smile crooked. "Mav..."

"Yeah?"

"Dance with me," she says, playful, teasing.

"I'm not dancing, Cal."

My joints are creaking as it is. At least the beer's kicking in, numbing some of the pain.

"Please."

Well, fuck me. The plea in her voice wrecks me. I'd walk into a fire if she asked.

She pulls me to my feet, weaving us through the crowd like she owns the damn place.

We follow because we always have.

It's in that moment I know:

Callie Harper could tempt the devil with her smile.

Chapter 4

Callie

The air is hot and thick, warm bodies brushing against mine as Colt leads me through the crush of people to the middle of the dance floor. The wood beneath our boots vibrates with the low hum of the music. Everything smells like beer and sweat and cheap cologne, but for once, I don't care.

The beat kicks up, a slow twang with no real structure, and I sway along, loose and easy. The alcohol has smoothed every edge. I'm floaty, grinning for no reason.

Colt leans in close, tipping his head to mine. "Don't think too hard. Just move."

I shoot him a look. "Are you saying I'm bad at this?"

"Never said that." He nudges me with his hip. "You just... think too much. You always did."

"Gee, thanks," I deadpan. But I can't hold the glare. Not with him smiling like that, all boyish charm and dimples I didn't stand a chance against back then.

The song fades out, and a familiar chord progression cuts through the noise, one that makes the whole crowd come alive. Whoops and cheers erupt around us as people break into formation.

I feel it before I even think it, my feet falling into step like they never forgot. It's all still in me. Years of bonfire parties and backroad get-togethers carved this dance into my bones, and suddenly, I'm twelve again, giddy and free.

We fall into place, Colt at my side, and my limbs move without thinking. It's fast, a little clumsy, but fun. All around us, boots stomp and bodies twist. It's a mess, but it's a beautiful mess.

Colt calls over the music, breathless from the steps. "You've still got it."

"I was born with it," I yell back, flashing him a grin.

"Modest as ever."

I open my mouth to respond, but a shooter girl appears with a tray. "Y'all want a round?"

"Yes," I say, maybe too fast. I grab one, knock it back, and grab another for good measure. It burns sweet and smooth.

Colt watches me with a crooked smile. "So this is how tonight's gonna go?"

"You didn't know?" I shoot back, teasing. I twirl back into place, dizzy but high on laughter, and bump right into Maverick.

He steadies me with both hands on my waist, expression suspicious. "You planning to dance me under the table?"

I flash him a grin. "Please. I already know you know all the steps."

He groans. "Don't bring up the 'Cotton Eye Joe' incident."

"Oh, I'm bringing it up. Seventh grade gym class. You went all in."

"I blacked that out for a reason."

"Too bad. C'mon. One dance."

And despite his protests, he follows me into formation anyway. Because no matter how much time has passed, Maverick Kane has always had a soft spot when it comes to me.

I steal a look between them. Colt, bouncing along like this is his natural habitat, and Maverick, biting back a smile as he falls in line. This is exactly what I wanted. Not the dancing, not the drinking, not even the shots. Just this.

All of us together. Like nothing ever changed.

We were always like this touchy, tangled up. Colt used to drape himself across the couch with his feet in my lap, and Mav would braid my hair just to pass the time. It was just... us. A mess of limbs and laughter and loyalty.

And being here with them again, feeling all of that click back into place, it hits somewhere deep.

Somewhere between the third or is it fourth? Round of drinks and the last line dance, my brain starts to fuzz around the edges. I remember flashes. Colt's breath against my ear when he leaned in to joke about someone's bad dancing. Maverick's arm around my waist when the floor got too crowded and someone bumped me too hard.

The bubble of warmth in my chest that wouldn't stop expanding.

I don't remember leaving the bar. Just the vague sensation of being carried, strong arms cradling me against a warm chest. The creak of the motel door. The shift of blankets. The cool slide of a pillow under my cheek.

Then Colt's lips graze my forehead, his voice low and soft as the dark.

"Good night, Wildflower."

I'm glad I came back.

Even if it hurts. Even if I'm scared.

I wouldn't trade tonight for anything.

Chapter 5

Colt

THE AIR's already brutally hot, the kind that sticks to your skin and saps your energy. The breeze doesn't do a damn thing to help as I stand on the motel's second-floor walkway, one arm braced on the railing, the other wrapped around my coffee like it might keep me sane.

My memory of last night is hazy, alcohol smudging the details, leaving behind blurry impressions. But the flashes of Callie dancing between Maverick and me have me in a chokehold.

I told myself she was still the same girl I'd grown up with even as I obsessed over how her Daisy Dukes hugged her ass, how her shirt clung to her curves, the swell of her breasts teasing through the fabric.

The girl who left came back a fucking goddess. Untouchable. The thought feels criminal. Like any second, she's going to come stomping out here and ream me out.

Groaning, I slap a hand to my forehead and drag it down my face. "Jesus, Colt. Get your shit together."

"Morning," Callie says, her voice rough with sleep, and it's the sweetest thing I've ever heard.

I turn and freeze.

Shock punches the air from my lungs. She's standing in the doorway of my motel room, her hair a wild halo around her shoulders like someone dug their hands through it, but that's not what knocks me flat.

She's wearing my shirt.

Only my shirt.

It hits her mid-thigh, covering all the important parts, practically a damn dress but that doesn't matter. Because it's *mine*.

I think I could die happy.

Noticing my gawking, she raises a brow with a teasing smile and lifts the hem to reveal her shorts underneath. I ignore the slight sting of disappointment.

This is better. Of course this is better. She shouldn't be wearing just my shirt... right?

She pads onto the outdoor walkway, snatches the mug from my hand before I can react, and takes a sip.

Immediately, she grimaces. "What the hell is this?"

"My coffee," I manage, still recovering from the visual. "Also known as cowboy fuel."

She lowers the mug, nose scrunching. "You have serious issues," she rasps.

That earns another laugh because she's fucking right.

"You feeling okay?"

"Been better," she sighs, leaning her weight against the doorframe. "I can't exactly remember everything from last night."

"Me neither. Some parts are a blur." Not a lie. Not entirely the truth either.

She gestures toward the room. "So I slept here?"

"We didn't know which one was yours. Figured this was safest." I shrug, biting my lip, because it felt damn good seeing her curled up in my bed... even if I didn't sleep in it.

"You could've shared with me," she says casually. "You must be sore after riding last night."

"Nah, the pullout was fine. Nothing I'm not used to." Which is a lie and a half. There's no way I could've handled waking up next to her. Her warm body tucked against mine, my morning wood digging into her hip. Just thinking about it has me shifting, trying to hide the reaction she always pulls from me.

If she knew, would she hate me? Would she still look at me with those soft eyes?

"Still," she murmurs. "I could've taken the couch. I'm the one who got drunk and passed out."

And what a cute drunk she was.

"You calling me old? Saying I can't handle a pullout?"

She scoffs. "We're the same age."

"Yeah, well, I'm not the one saying you're old and sore." I roll my neck, and it cracks loudly, undermining my point.

Her brow lifts like she's saying, *See?* "I'm just saying—we used to share a bed all the time. It's not a big deal."

Not a big deal? Right. Maybe not for her. She's not the one who is secretly obsessed with her childhood best friend.

I've spent too much time thinking about her over the years, missing the piece she took with her when she left. Now, she's here again, smiling that sunshine smile and lighting up the dark hole she left behind. Anyone would be twisted after that, right?

Knowing she's leaving in a few months has the tender spot beneath my ribs aching at the thought, and my sternum hollows out. It's one of those things that's hard to judge: is it better to have had a taste or to have stayed hungry?

Nah... definitely better to take whatever I can, no matter what happens to me.

It felt good to be with my old friend. One of the only people who's ever really understood me.

"You don't know. I might snore," I say.

Her lips twitch, curling in the corner. "You say that like you didn't always snore."

"Hey, at least I don't drool," I fire back.

Her mouth drops open in faux offense, almost spilling her coffee. "That was one time. And I had a sinus infection."

"Uh-huh. *Sure.* All those other times, too?" I nudge.

She's just too damn cute. Too easy to tease. With

everyone else, I put on a persona. With Callie, I don't have to try. She pulls it out of me. Always has.

"What time are we heading out?" Callie asks, casual as anything, like this has always been the plan.

"Hm?" I blink, still not used to the idea that she's actually staying. That this is real.

She strolls to the railing, dumps her coffee into the bushes, then turns toward me, so close her arm brushes mine. "Next event's what, eight hours? We hitting the road soon?"

"You in a hurry?" Maverick's voice cuts in behind us, and I flinch. Didn't even hear him walk up.

She shrugs, unfazed. "Just trying to figure out if I have time to wash my hair before sitting in a truck all day. Smells like beer."

"You've got time," I say quickly before Mav can scare her off with whatever's brewing in his head.

Maverick studies her. "You sure you're up for this?"

She rolls her eyes. "You two aren't exactly high-maintenance. I think I'll survive."

He huffs out a laugh, but it's tight. "Not what I meant."

She pauses then, just a flicker of something in her eyes. "I'm not here to be careful," she says. "I came to make this count."

The way she says it shuts both of us up.

She glances between us. "Unless you're saying I can't tag along?"

"Hell no," I say.

Maverick echoes, softer, "Not a chance."

She nods, like that settles it, but there's still that flutter of nerves in her posture like she's waiting for someone to tell her she doesn't belong.

She doesn't know we've spent eight years hoping she'd come back.

"You can ride with me," we both blurt out, but I'm faster.

Maverick glares. I wink.

"I'm a better driver. She's safer with me," he says.

"That's bullshit, and you know it," I fire back.

We're already arguing, and I'm gearing up to make my case when Callie cuts in.

"We can't all ride together?"

"Hell no. You're funny." I bark out a laugh.

Her brow knits. "Well, I shouldn't be surprised after yesterday, but I was hoping it was some kind of ego-driven bull rider thing?"

"We haven't been friends in a long time," Maverick says evenly. "Whatever you thought we were... we're not that anymore."

There's pain in her reddened eyes, and she hides it by looking at her feet. She doesn't say anything for several seconds, and neither do we.

We tried to tell her yesterday; she needs to face it today.

Her hands open and clench at her sides, over and over.

Fuck, I want to take them in mine and uncurl each of her fingers.

It's not how it was supposed to be.

But there's no changing it.

She stares at her feet, silent. It's brutal. Worse than any bull ride I've ever taken.

We've been this way for years, and I have no plans to change. Callie's just not used to it, she hasn't been around.

It would help if I explained it to her. Everything that went down, how winning got in the way. How she was the only thing that ever held us together, and once she left, whatever friendship we had cracked, revealing just how fragile it really was.

They say bull riders only care about one thing, and that's winning.

We're proof of that.

There's only one way to win this thing, and that's by beating the other.

When she finally looks up, there's fire in her eyes. That stubborn Callie spark.

"Since you're so determined to fight, I'll ask Luke if I can ride with him. That way, we can keep it fair."

"Like hell you are," we say in unison.

She smirks, smug. But I know we've lost.

"We'll take turns," I say.

"Turns?" Her eyes narrow. "Am I some kind of shareable object?"

My mouth opens and shuts like a fish out of water because wasn't that exactly how I was treating her?

"It's not like that. We both missed you, and we have our own trucks." He glances my way, jaw tight, then says,

"Switching back and forth will give us both time to hang out with you. Don't you want that?"

Hell... did he just agree with me? Did *Maverick Kane* just compromise? I have half a mind to check his temperature. Still, it must've been the right thing to say because she softens.

I think we've won this but then her eyes grow misty, and I know in that second I'd do absolutely anything to make it go away.

"I don't have much time here, and most of it will be spent on the road," she says, voice trembling. "I don't want to waste any of it."

"We'll take my truck," Maverick says. "You ride passenger. He can sit in the back."

"Why do you get to drive?" I grumble.

He grins. "Because I offered first."

Chapter 6

Callie

Hot air blows on my bare feet, perched on the dash, my purple polka dot nail polish looking out of place against the masculine tan leather. The scenery is repetitive, all smooth roads and open plains. And I love every moment of it.

The baking sun, the dust kicking up from the sides of the road, the prairie flowers lining the ditches. There's beauty in its simplicity, something a city could never have.

Things worked out okay. Colt bribed some ranch hands to drive his truck to his parents' place, leaving no more excuses for why we can't all go together.

It would be perfect if it weren't for these two sour idiots.

The silence between Maverick and Colt holds an underlying tension that's impossible to ignore. When we stopped for gas, Colt's shoulder brushed Maverick's arm, and you'd think they'd been burned for how fast they jerked apart.

This was not what I was expecting when I'd finally made the decision to come back. Maybe I was naive to think everything could be the same, the way I'd frozen it in my mind. It's not the first time I've realized that my fantasy about their happy life was more about my comfort than reality.

I had to believe it so I could keep living without them.

My gaze traces the side profile of Maverick's face, the rough arch of his nose, likely broken more times than he can count. His brows are heavy, a five-o'clock shadow covering his sharp jaw, and the purple bruises under his eyes revealing his lack of sleep.

He's wearing that stoic expression he likes, one that makes him appear unbothered. It probably works on everyone else, but the prominent tendons running along his throat give away his agitation.

You never know what you had until it's lost… That thought threatens to defeat me, but screw that.

I still have time to fix this before I go back.

"I can't fucking take this anymore," Colt groans, head hitting the back of my seat. "At the very least, turn on some music. Do you always drive in complete fucking silence, man? Are you a masochist or something? Is this some new form of torture?"

Colt sounds so miserable I can't help the smile that spreads across my face. Maverick glances at me from the corner of his eye, and I shrug.

"He's not wrong. Any more of this and I'm going to overthink my entire life."

Maverick gestures to the radio with his chin. "You choose."

Pure static fills the speakers when I twist the knob, and Maverick gives me a knowing look.

"Please tell me you don't drive in complete silence every trip?"

"Of course not... I listen to true crime podcasts, but I didn't think you'd like it."

There's rustling from the back seat, and Colt pops his head through the center console.

"You too? Have you listened to the one where she faked her own kidnapping to escape her abusive husband and then helped take down his whole trafficking ring?"

"Yeah, that one's pretty good, but the *Backroad Butcher* series had me hooked. The way he stayed under the radar for two decades? Terrifying."

"I bawled like a baby listening to the kids addicted to fentanyl. Fucking travesty."

The oh-so-reserved Maverick replies, "Same. Those kids didn't deserve that."

Mouth open, I sit in awe as the two of them go back and forth about their favorite cases.

Maybe I won't be the one to bring them back together after all. Clearly, true crime's doing a good job on its own.

There's a glint in their eyes as their competitive spirits rear again, getting into their own theories about who did what in unsolved cases.

Both of them have decent arguments, neither really backing down, but at least they aren't going for each other's throats for once.

"Come on, man. You've got to admit that note makes her look guilty as hell," Colt says, hanging over the console so far he's practically in the front seat. You'd think these two were professional investigators for how into it they are.

Maverick's laugh fills the cab of the truck, and it hits me in the chest.

I haven't heard that laugh in years and forgot how sweet it is. It's almost a giggle, which should seem out of place on such a serious guy, but it's so pure and true it's impossible not to get caught up in it.

By the way Colt jerks back, no longer shoved between us, it's clear I'm not the only one affected by Maverick's laughter.

I twist to look at him. His dark hair covers his eyes, shielding his expression, but a rigidness has replaced the relaxed stance from seconds ago.

I catch Maverick glancing in the rearview mirror, his expression darkening as he takes it in. His mouth pinches tight before he turns forward again, like none of it happened.

Just like that, a wall falls between them, and we're back to silent resentment.

Well, I can't take it.

I yank out my phone, shuffling through all my songs.

There's a giddiness forming in my chest when I spot one I know they both like.

We'd belted this song out at the top of our lungs back then, so loud my mom yelled at us. That didn't stop us from replaying it over and over like it was our summer anthem.

I hit Play, and both guys groan the second the first chord starts.

They're so alike that it's hard not to tease them. I'm positive they'd hate it, but come on... the temptation is so freaking real.

Stubborn. That's what they freaking are when the lyrics start and neither sings.

Fine, then.

I belt the song out as loud as I can, throwing all the same ridiculous emotion into it as I did back then.

I do the stupid hand gestures we made up, not caring how ridiculous I look, and squeeze my eyes shut, letting the nostalgia wash over me.

My head snaps up when Colt joins in on the second chorus, a look of pure exasperation on his face, but he sings with me.

His voice is rough and deep, nothing like the boy I remember, and tingles race down my spine, raising goose bumps in their wake.

Women must be falling at his feet... I'm struck by a jealousy so sharp my voice cracks on the next word.

But Colt doesn't look away.

His blue eyes are locked on mine, piercing into me, holding me in place.

I'm being pulled toward him, like he's tied a rope to my heart. I'm drifting across a distance I hadn't realized we still shared.

It's the way he's staring that has me holding my breath.

He's still singing at the top of his lungs but it's directed at me.

It had always been just fun before, but now, the meaning of the song sinks into me.

A girl too wild to tame, who he aches to ask to stay.

A boy who watches her among wildflowers, knowing he loves her enough to set her free but still hoping she'll choose him.

It's a whispered promise and a plea that has blood rushing in my ears.

The emotions rolling through me take over, and I'm frozen, unable to make a sound, my chest tight.

Then, Maverick's voice joins in.

Strong and steady, wrapping around Colt's in a way that steals my breath all over again.

The two of them, once so fractured and sharp-edged, are suddenly singing together like they never fell apart at all.

The sound fills the truck, fills my chest, until it's hard to tell where the music ends and the feeling begins.

It's everything I missed. Everything I thought was lost.

Unlike Colt, Maverick's not looking at me but every word feels aimed at my heart.

My eyes sting as everything we've left unsaid bubbles up between us.

The guilt that's been twisting my stomach slowly untangles with every word.

Chances are I'm reading too much into it... but it feels like they're telling me they understand.

That they don't hate me for leaving.

I'd been holding that fear deep inside that I'd show up and they'd want nothing to do with me.

And it would've been fair.

I walked away.

I broke what we had, and they only know half of my reason.

This isn't forgiveness.

But it's a start.

It's *understanding*.

For the first time in a long time, my breaths come easily.

Colt's smiling at me now, his grin wide, laughter in his voice, and it calls me back to life.

Maverick too, singing beside him.

Their voices mix, reaching for me.

Calling me home.

I catch the final chorus, singing my heart out, laughter bubbling up until I'm breathless, my chest light and full.

I didn't know how badly I needed this.

But somehow, *they* did.

Being read this easily should be terrifying.

But with them?

I don't want to waste a single second on misunderstandings.

I'm still riding the high when Maverick pulls into a familiar-looking motel.

A carbon copy of the one we were just in.

The entire parking lot is jammed with pickup trucks, all bearing some version of a bull-riding logo.

A laugh bubbles out of me, half disbelief, half wonder. This is my life now, dust and grit and a million battered trucks. Rough men with rougher dreams. A world built out of eight seconds and broken bones. And somehow, I fit here. I belong here again.

Colt and Maverick unload our bags, back to acting like the other doesn't exist, even while working together.

Maverick brings my bag over but doesn't hand it over when I reach for it.

"Come on. Let's get you checked in."

Nerves twist in my gut, not knowing how this is going to play out.

I'd been a little too excited when I flew in... "Yeah, about that—"

"Woah, you made it alive," Luke says, coming up to us looking mischievous.

"Thought for sure one of you would kill the other."

He circles Colt, who shoves him lightly.

"Holy shit... not even a bruise."

"Get the hell out of here," Colt mutters, but there's a red tint at the back of his neck, and I don't miss the way he glances at me.

He knows damn well I don't like them fighting but I'm not naive.

They've made their distaste for each other loud and clear.

Luke examines the three of us and nods like he's figured it all out.

"It's because of you," he says.

"Tell me, how did you get these two whipped so fast? Do you know how long I've been trying to get them to get along? Do you have any idea how awkward it is to have my two friends hate each other?"

He says it in a way that's half joke, half truth.

I shrug. "They clearly like me more. You should work on that."

Luke rocks back on his heels, a slow smile forming.

"I'm starting to understand why."

Biting back my smirk, I reply, "You know, you're growing on me too."

"Sounds like Luke's banned from hanging out now," Colt says, stepping between us, arms crossed, staring down his friend.

Luke laughs. "Hey now, I'm just being friendly. Not every day you two bring a girl around."

I don't have time to process the idea of them bringing a girl around any day when Maverick cuts in.

"Knock it off."

He places his hand on my lower back, warming me through the thin fabric as he guides me toward the motel office.

I'm not ready to move, but I follow him anyway.

Everything about Maverick screams he's in charge responsible, dominant, possessive.

His gentle touch promises he'll take care of me if I follow his lead.

I'm swallowing hard as my thoughts turn somewhere they don't belong.

His near-black hair that's normally pushed off his face falls into his eyes, giving his already broody look even more heat.

I'd be a millionaire if they ever let me turn them into a thirst trap.

There's a line coming out of the office door, and I stop when Maverick's hand tightens on my waist, pulling me into his side so he can drop his mouth to my ear.

"I'll talk to them about getting your room moved beside mine."

My cheeks heat, and I can practically feel the blush taking over.

"I know that look. What did you do?" Colt asks suspiciously.

"I didn't... I didn't book a room."

I barely get the words out before both guys are turning on me, shouting in unison:

"*What?*"

Chapter 7

Maverick

THIS LITTLE HAZEL-EYED devil has the nerve to attempt to look innocent, like she didn't just drop a bomb the size of Canada on us. I search her eyes for a sign that she's joking because there's no way my girl flew across the country and has no place to stay... Fuck, even the idea is giving me heartburn. Throat tight from holding back a barrage of questions, I do my best to lock my shit down, but before I can say anything stupid, Colt beats me to it.

"What the hell were you thinking, Cal?" His normally easygoing tone is nowhere to be found. He's all business right now, talking down to her like she's a kid, and from the way she's toeing up to him, this is not going to be good... for him. It's certainly going to be fun for me.

"Who do you think you are?" she spits back, any sign that maybe she should have booked a room before showing up nowhere to be found. It's as if the second Colt opened his mouth, she'd disagree with whatever he says.

Which is his own fault for going after her that way. Callie's never responded well to authority, and she's definitely not going to take being reprimanded by him. She'd go down in a fiery grave of her own making before she'd ever admit she's wrong.

A twisted, hidden part of me wants to see what happens when Callie gives in. When she stops fighting and starts wanting to listen. Would she still have that fire in her eyes as she does what she's told? What the hell am I thinking? There's a pole beside me, and I'm tempted to bang my head against it, knock some sense back into myself. I'm saved from my personal downfall when the woman at the counter calls us up.

"Hello, ma'am. Colt and I have rooms, but we're looking to book another one." This isn't the first time we've been here, so she recognizes him and me easily enough, printing off our room keys. As she hands them to us, she gives us a customer service smile, while her tone calls me an idiot.

"We're all booked up. With the rodeo in town and all."

Of course they are. The entire parking lot's full with riders.

"If that's all, I have a line here," the woman says, already looking at the person behind me.

Entwining my fingers with Callie's, I maneuver us through the small, crowded space, using my larger frame to make a path, all while she and Colt are still going at it.

I know this place. The next motel's a county over, and it'll be as packed as this one. Small towns like this aren't designed for an influx of visitors. Just a stop on the highway, except for once a year when the rodeo comes to town. My teeth are sharp against my tongue as I run through our options. If we can't get her a room, she can have mine, and I'll sleep in my truck. I can already feel the backache, but like hell she'll be the one sleeping out there. A glance at Colt... never mind, I don't want him in my truck any more than he already is, leaving his germs all over it.

My fingers drum on my thigh as a glimmer of an idea infiltrates my mind, growing more enticing by the moment. Something I shouldn't entertain, but it's impossible not to. She's set off a possessiveness in me, unique to her, from the second she'd turned back up.

"You'll stay with me."

It's a command, and I expect her to balk at it. Instead, her head tilts to the side, the corner of her lip curling like she got exactly what she wanted.

Colt, on the other hand, is going off.

"The fuck do you mean stay with you? She's staying with me."

His voice is several octaves too loud, a vein ticking in his forehead. He's been working himself up this entire time, going back and forth with Callie, and now he's about to detonate.

Callie, always the peacemaker, raises her hands between us with a gentle smile pointed at him. "That's fine, I'll stay at yours—"

"Not going to happen." I stomp on that idea before she can get it all the way out.

I should stop there, but I can't help but push Colt's buttons. He's so fucking easy to push off the edge. It has nothing to do with the thrill I get whenever he confronts me, all that rage focused firmly on me, cracking that perfect image of his is like an addiction. It's so enticing that I take it way too far.

"You going to bring her into your bachelor pad? Wake her up when you bring back a fucking buckle bunny?"

Callie gasps, and Colt stumbles back, his face contorting with betrayal, and I wish I could pull those words back and swallow them.

"It's been a long time since I've been near anyone, and you fucking know it, asshole." Colt's hurt shifts to anger, and he's shoving me hard.

"Fuck. Listen..." I stop, not sure how to go forward. Apologizing to Colt is not something I do, and it's caught in my throat.

"No, you fucking listen," Colt says, shoving me back.

I barely move in time and stumble backward.

I have to apologize before this gets out of hand, but Colt's already on his next throw. This time, I see it coming and dodge out of the way.

"I'm sorry—fuck."

"That's enough."

Loud, sharp, and leaving no room for argument, Callie turns on her heel and walks away, leaving Colt and me to chase after her.

"I've got an idea to fix this shit. Give me a minute," I tell her, and she hangs back, letting me take the lead.

I make my way up the stairs to the second floor of the motel, Colt yelling at me the entire time that we haven't settled who Callie's staying with yet, and I better fucking stop... I tune him out, making my way down the hall until I reach the room next to mine.

It takes five bangs on the wood before it swings open, a wiry rookie yelling, "What the hell do you want—"

He cuts off the second he recognizes me, but I'm not here for fan service. I need something from him.

"Switch rooms with Colt."

"What? Hell no. I'm all settled in."

I rest my arm on the top of the doorframe, looming over him, but first, I'll try the easy way.

"I know you're lugging your gear around. I'll pay your season transit fees."

Transit fees are the cost of having the company pack up your gear for you instead of hauling them around yourself. Normally, rookies wouldn't get this kind of opportunity. By the way he's smiling, I hit the nail on the head.

"You serious?"

I nod. "Now, get the fuck out."

Surprised but happy, he says, "It's all yours."

The railing cuts into my hips as I cross my arms, waiting. Colt's still coming at me with questions, and now Callie's even getting into it, but they'll just have to wait and see. I figured this shit out, and they're going to accept it.

The guy's stuff is half falling out of his bag as he drags

it from the room, handing over his key card and taking a confused Colt's.

It's less than five strides from me to the adjoining room doors. I unlock it with a click. The one from the other side's still closed, and I hand my key to Callie.

"What are you waiting for? Let me in."

There's a glimmer in her eyes as her fingers brush mine, taking the card. "You're a smart one, Kane."

My brow arches. "You're just realizing this now?"

"Why the hell are you calling this asshole smart?" Colt jumps in. It's like he's compelled by muscle memory more than anything.

Her head tips back, and she shakes it with a laugh as she makes her way into the room. "Boys."

Within seconds, the door swings open, and Callie's staring at us, hand on her hip.

"There. Problem solved." I gesture between the rooms.

"You'll sleep in there, Colt will take the pullout, and I'll take the bed in here."

"Hell no. Do you have any idea how fucking sore I was the last time?"

Callie laughs. "I knew it!"

"You offering to sleep with me again, Sunshine?" His grin's salacious. A glimpse into his thoughts.

That's not fucking happening.

"If you're going to be a pussy, I'll take the sofa."

Colt scoffs. "What, so you can say that's the reason you had a shitty ride? Screw that. We're both men. We'll share the bed. Just stay on your fucking side."

Never in a million years did I think I'd hear those words out of Colt's mouth.

I'll dig your grave? Yes. Sleep next to you? Not a chance.

From the look on his face, he's going through his own personal crisis.

The only one with an ounce of sense left, I say, "Not a good idea."

"Who's the pussy now?" he presses, never one to back down, his blue eyes piercing into mine, daring me to push back.

Never could resist him. He has a way of gnawing at me until I'm as immature as he is.

I square up, shoulders back, ready to take him on, when Callie's laugh breaks through the room.

Colt and I turn simultaneously toward her with matching glares.

She's practically doubled over, the doorframe the only thing keeping her standing as she snorts, laughing so loud.

"Find this funny, do you?" I'm unable to hide my amusement, and that just encourages her more.

She's shaking her head no, but her teeth sink into her growing smile.

This fucking girl.

I bend and easily catch her middle with my shoulder, lifting her in the air, one arm firmly bound around her thighs. I walk her through her room and drop her on her bed.

"Stay."

It's a miracle she doesn't jump up the second the word leaves my mouth, but she's looking at me with so much amusement she damn near steals my breath away. Callie's bathed in soft evening light, glowing up at me from the middle of a bed.

Jesus Christ... I'm never going to survive this girl.

I turn on my heels before I can lose whatever's remaining on my mind. Between the two of them, I'll be admitted by the end of the season.

With her out of the way, the adjoining door clicks behind me, and I crowd Colt.

He doesn't budge, his smugness fully in place, a challenge written all over him.

For once, I give in. Hope he enjoys it. It'll be the first and last time.

"Neither of us are in any shape to sleep on that couch, and you know it. And I'll be dead before I let you sleep next to Callie. You feel the same?" I question, getting right to the point.

"Damn right," he shoots back, quick as a whip.

"Then suck it up, buttercup, because you're sleeping with me." I say it like it was my idea in the first place.

He eyes me up and down, that dimple appearing in his cheek, but he doesn't call me out on it. Instead, he dumps his bag on the corner of the bed and starts pulling shit out.

He's bent forward, muscles visibly flexing beneath his thin Henley as he rolls his shoulder, a movement I've seen him do countless times before. A reminder of the night he went down and I was crowned Rookie of the Year.

He strides out, clothes scattered across the floor where he left them, some piled on the comforter. It's like he opened a can of confetti and then left to take a shower.

The reality of what I just did smacks me in the face with instant fucking regret.

I really am an idiot.

Chapter 8

Callie

THE NOISE HITS ME FIRST, the door clicking shut behind me as I step out of my room, quickly followed by the fatty smell of barbecue frying nearby. The parking lot's full of rowdy bull riders, lost without their adrenaline fix. They're causing an absolute ruckus, taking over the entire space, each one yelling over the other. These are some of the most competitive men in the country, and it doesn't stop just because they've left the arena.

I make my way down the stairs, scanning over faces, searching, until I spot them, breath catching in my throat. Maverick and Colt are both leaning against Maverick's truck just to the left of the stairs. They're silent, arms crossed, looking anywhere but at each other. Their brows pinch in the middle, feet tapping on the ground in the exact same cadence. I wonder if it's being so alike that's kept them apart, both too stubborn to ever let anything go.

I take them in while they aren't looking, and there's a

soft, electric current humming under my skin. The sun's setting, casting them in golden light, highlighting the sharp edge of their jaws, the scruff from the day's travel giving them a rugged appearance. Heat pools in my stomach, a low ache I force myself to ignore. After years of being surrounded by city boys, these two are really showing off what I've been missing.

Maverick's wearing a long-sleeve, deep blue shirt that complements his deep tan skin from hours spent in the sun. The sleeves are pushed back, revealing thick corded forearms that lead up to substantial biceps. He's all wide shoulders and lean muscle, his thick quads filling out his jeans perfectly. There's something about his closed-off expression, the utter calmness, that sparks something in my chest, because I know he can't maintain that mask with me. He never has. For him—for me—for us, there's never been a need for a mask.

Colt's physique is harder to make out under his jean jacket, but no less tempting. His hair falling over his eyes, casting them further into shadows. His teeth gnaw on his full lips, and I have the overwhelming urge to bite them. It's easy to see why the girls hover around him. If Maverick's rigid, Colt's his mirrored opposite flexible, easygoing, with a quick smile. That glint in his eyes, the one he normally shows the world, is missing as he stares blankly somewhere in the distance.

"Don't you two look handsome." Tied to them by an invisible string, I skip down the stairs, my pulse quickening with each inch closed between us.

Their heads snap up at my approach, and the force of their attention lands solidly in my chest. There's always something a little wild about cowboys, but that's not what this is. There's something untamed about them, like there's something hidden within just waiting to get out and it's fixed its attention on me. It's a heady sensation to be their sole focus, equally thrilling and terrifying. Getting too close to men like this is like standing too close to a fire and begging to be burned.

I force a smile when Colt wraps an arm around my shoulder, tugging me close.

"You look gorgeous tonight, Sunshine." He leans in, mouth inches from my temple, so close it ruffles my hair. He's warm and welcoming, like a soft spot to curl into, and I have to fight the urge to pull him closer. My mouth is bone-dry, my throat raw, as I breathe in his woodsy scent. I can't help but crave him like a cool glass of water after a month in the desert. With each inhale, his scent envelops me more, filling my lungs until my head grows fuzzy and my body tingles. It doesn't take long for the feel of him to turn that sensation into hunger, a gnawing ache deep inside me that only they can fill.

I'm barely toeing the line of friendship as it is, and I'll forever be grateful that telepathy isn't a thing. Strong fingers catch my jaw, tilting my chin up until I'm faced with sharp blue eyes. I'm captured, unable to look away as he searches for answers. The slow smile curling his lips tells me he found exactly what he wanted.

Maverick saves me, tugging my arm, freeing me from a

reluctant Colt's hold. The moisture is sucked from the air as an electric charge sparks between them. Cold eyes glare into each other, neither willing to back down.

Spinning out of their reach, I use my best mom voice. "Don't freaking start. We've been on the go all day, and all I want is a cold beer and a warm burger. Whatever silent dick-measuring contest you're playing at can fuck right off."

Color washes over their cheeks, both looking abashed for being caught. Is it weird to call two grown men adorable? Because they totally are.

"I promise to be on my best behavior," Mav says, then points at Colt. "Can't say the same for this one."

"You can fuck right off with that," Colt clips out.

I give them my back, walking into the crowd, counting in my head. They'll fight all night if I let them, and we don't have time for that. It's less than five seconds before they're right behind me, like a solid wall.

Maverick's chest brushes my shoulder as he says, "Stay close tonight. These assholes can be a real handful once they get drunk."

I spin on them, despising that misogynistic rhetoric. "And that means I should change my behavior because they can't control themselves?"

"No." Colt's head tilts to the side, and he replies like it's obvious. "You do whatever you want. We'll take care of anyone who's stupid enough to get close to you."

Why do those words send a thrill down my spine, triggering a primal want? I've been fine taking care of myself for a long time... but I have to admit, the protectiveness radiating off them is hot.

"And what if I want them to get close to me?" I don't. Any of these guys come within a two-foot radius and they're in for a bad night, but for some reason, I want to see how Colt and Maverick react to this. Friends wouldn't have a problem. Hell, they could offer to wingman... but what will they do?

A low, deep rumble vibrates through the air, a warning if I've ever heard one, sending electricity arcing across my skin. Their reactions are instantaneous, the tension coming off them palpable as they crowd me.

"Fuck that," Colt says, then freezes when I raise a single brow. I wasn't planning on going anywhere near the men here, but the challenge in Colt's voice is just enough to motivate me.

"Try again," I say, giving him one more chance.

Maverick looks like he wants to strangle him, knowing exactly what he's set off. Colt inhales, runs his hand through his hair, pulling at the ends before meeting my gaze. "Please, hang out with us tonight. I just... I'm not sure I can handle these guys being anywhere around you."

He's almost desperate, like it really would hurt him, and any remaining defiance I'm feeling washes away with his words.

"That was the plan all along." I smirk.

Colt looks equal parts relieved and frustrated.

Maverick sighs, his patience with us already running

out. "Luke's truck is set up over there. Take a seat, and I'll grab you some food."

"Me too?" Colt asks.

"Get your own food," Maverick answers instantly.

"Come on, man. I'm going to stay with Callie."

"Not my problem." Maverick gives me one last look, completely ignoring Colt, before heading off.

A muscle ticks in Colt's jaw, his brows pinched as he stares a hole into Maverick's retreating back.

I slip my hand into his, entwining our fingers, and just like that, his attention is back on me. His eyes are warm as he looks down at our hands, then back at me, giving them a light squeeze. Any anger simmering has been doused by that simple gesture, and he's now almost giddy, guiding me, a wide smile on his face.

"Hey, there you are," Luke calls out. "I was half expecting the three of you to hole up in your rooms."

"Trust me. We thought about it," Colt answers, helping me into the bed of the truck. "She wanted to come out."

"Why are you saying it like that?" I say, scooting on my butt until I can lean against the cool metal.

"Yeah, man." Luke's grin turns mischievous, an all-knowing glint in his eyes. "There's food, music, and drinks. Who'd want to miss this?"

Colt climbs in and takes the spot next to me, his hand finding mine again. He holds them up between us, examining how my small palm fits in his. "Yeah... it's not so bad after all."

Warmth fills my stomach at the awe in his voice. He sounds like he finally found something he's been looking for.

Luke clears his throat. "Man, you are so screwed."

Colt snorts. "Tell me something I don't already know."

They aren't subtle, and it's easy to decipher the undercurrent of what they're saying. There's a small flame lit in my chest, one I keep protected from the outside, and he's stoking it. Hope and want are two of the most dangerous things. It's not fair for me to hope he wants me as much as I'm starting to want him.

The thought ricochets in my head, bouncing off the walls until I'm forced to acknowledge that there's no amount of resistance on my part that could prevent my reaction to the two of them.

"That buckle bunny's hot. You think they'll take turns?" The guy doesn't even bother to lower his voice.

Colt stiffens beside me, his muscles pressed against the side of my thigh tightening. "What did you just say?"

"Fuck." Luke's already pushing the guy backward, shaking his head in warning. "Why does everyone around here have a death wish? Save it for the arena."

"What? I'm just stating the obvious."

It's Colt holding *me* back as a current of rage stokes a fire in my gut. Guys like him are scum of the earth. They think they're better than everyone meanwhile, they're whining when they can't get a date.

Colt's laugh lacks any amusement. "You better watch it. You have no idea who you're talking to."

"What, she your girl?"

"She's the heir to Harper Ridge Ranch," Luke says.

The idiot's face pales in recognition. "You're... I'm sorry."

My grin is sharp as I lean forward. "You keep fucking around like this and you're about to find out. I'll make sure you'll never ride on one of our bulls again. Do you know what that means? Hmm? It means you'll have a very short career."

I'm bluffing. Just because my family breeds them, once we've sold the bulls to the league, we have zero control. But this guy doesn't know that. Everyone knows Harper Ridge Ranch produces the rankest bulls, and without them, a rider doesn't stand a chance.

If you can stick the eight, you're guaranteed a good score.

The guy removes his hat and bows his head. "I... I didn't know who you were. I'm very sorry, ma'am."

"If I hear you whisper the term *buckle bunny* again, you are done. Do you understand? You might as well pack up and head home."

Colt tries to muffle his snort, enjoying this exchange entirely too much.

"Yes, ma'am. I'll never say it again. Promise."

Now that his hat's off, I can see he's younger than I thought. Hopefully, he takes this to heart.

"Let's get you out of here before you say anything else stupid," Luke says, wrapping his arm around the kid's shoulder.

He looks relieved, staring at Luke like he's his savior.

A laugh bubbles up from my chest, and I tip my head back to rest on the metal. "That felt good."

"I bet it did. I thought he was going to piss himself. He'd have probably preferred I punched him."

I huff. "He deserved it."

"Oh, definitely." Colt's amusement is clear in his voice, tinged with pride. "I'm pretty sure that kid's never going to talk again, let alone say shit like that."

The breeze picks up, lifting the hair on the back of my neck, and I shiver. Colt shifts beside me, shrugging off his jacket, laying it over my shoulders. The fabric is still warm from his skin, soft against the goose bumps rising along my arms, then tucks me into his side.

"If you're cold, we can go in," he says, his lips brushing the shell of my ear, and I'm anything but cold, shivering for a whole new reason.

"Ketchup and mustard, right?" Maverick says, his hands full of an assortment of food.

I nod, mouth watering as he passes me my burger, a red cooler placed in front of me filled with ice and beer.

Colt's eyes widen when a burger's tossed at him, the tin foil wrapper barely holding it together. "You got me a burger—"

"Not a word," Maverick cuts him off, hurling himself into the truck and taking the spot on my other side, sandwiching me between them.

To my surprise, Colt obeys, only unwrapping his dinner and taking an enormous bite.

There's no room, their legs pressing against mine, the heat of their bodies seeping into my skin, but I'm not complaining. Not when my nerves are lighting up, coming alive with every brush of their arms. My skin's hypersensitive wherever they touch me, the simplest movement making my thighs rub together.

Maverick's hand circles the spot just above my knee as he leans over to grab the cooler, bringing it closer to us.

There's a low hum in the back of his throat, and his hooded eyes are molten when he faces me. Thick, humid air fills my lungs as I struggle for each inhale. We stay like that, time frozen around us until Colt breaks the moment, popping the cap off a beer and handing it to me. "You look thirsty."

I snap my gaze back to him, searching for the double meaning and it's right there, clear as day, painted across his face with a wide grin.

"Shut up," I hiss.

"What? I never said it was a bad thing."

It's a dangerous, slippery slope, and my feet are skating right along the edge of a very steep cliff. Every fiber of my being calls me to let go and fall into it.

He's back to his burger, and my stomach twists into a tight knot. What if I'm reading way too much into this?

Both of them are relaxed, enjoying their food, while I'm so wound up I can't even taste mine.

I pound back my beer, then lean over to grab another, hatching a very dangerous plan. Somehow, things are going exactly how they should and nowhere near what I want.

Chapter 9

Callie

AN HOUR and a few beers later, our food's long finished, the garbage already disposed of, and my buzz hums under my skin. A few riders I don't recognize have gathered around, and it's easy to see Colt and Maverick have known them for a while. The conversation flows from topic to topic, laughter coming out easily.

I stretch my legs out, letting the buzz lull me into something close to contentment.

But under the laughter and the glow of the truck lights, something unsettles in my chest.

It's nothing. Just nerves. Just being here.

I shove it down like I've gotten so good at doing, not willing to let the worry steal this night from me.

I rest my head on Colt's shoulder. It feels good just listening to them, to be a part of their regular lives.

"Did you hear about Jimmy?" a guy sitting on the tailgate asks in a low voice.

"What are you doing? Trying to bring that kind of bad juju here?" another guy cuts in.

"Relax… if that were true, we'd all be screwed. It's sad what happened, but it's part of the sport. He got a raw deal landing like that. Spine didn't stand a chance."

The world compresses around me until it's impossible to take a breath.

They're talking about it like it's nothing like someone didn't just die. Their only concern is that they may jinx themselves.

"I heard he had a kid."

"His mistake for having a family while riding. Should have known better."

My nails dig into my palms as I pull my knees up to hide my face. The edges of the world blur and tilt too loud, too close, too fast.

Did they talk like this when my dad died? Sorry about his kid, but he should have known better?

The worst part is…they're not wrong.

He should have known better.

They risk their lives every weekend, and you don't do that when you care about someone.

You don't risk your heart like that.

Because it's the person left behind who has to deal with it, who loses a piece of who they are.

I count my breaths like my therapist taught me. Five in, three out but it's shaky, useless.

"Hey, Cal, you should see the scars these two have. Must have made a deal with the devil to still be alive."

They're laughing while I'm falling apart.

Blood rushes in my ears, muffling the noise around me as their stories bleed together.

"Remember when Colt got stomped on?" someone says, and the words cut through too fast for me to block.

I shudder.

"You cold?" Colt throws an arm around my shoulders, mistaking my reaction for a chill.

I nod, not trusting my voice.

Maverick tips my chin up, searching my face, and I try my hardest to lock it down. I don't want them to see what it does to me.

I don't want them to know I left because I couldn't watch them anymore.

Whether he figures it out or not, Maverick knows something's wrong.

He cups my cheek, rubbing his thumb along the edge. "You want to go in?"

I want to run.

I want to get as far away as possible.

Pretend none of this is happening.

Pretend they aren't risking it all.

It's tempting to go back to the safety I've lived in for years.

I force a smile. There's plenty of time to hide later.

Right now, I'm not willing to give up a single second with them.

Because what we have, *the three of us*, it's rare.

The kind of bond people spend their whole lives searching for and never find.

These memories are precious, sweet enough to last a lifetime.

Strong enough to keep me sane when I'm no longer near them.

I knew coming here would be hard.

But I'd regret not having these moments the rest of my life.

I've given myself this time to memorize everything about them every laugh, every look, every reckless, beautiful thing so I have something to hold on to.

Something no one else could ever replace.

Something to warm me later when they're just a memory.

Something to dull the ache when they aren't around.

I just need to hide my panic attacks.

Need to push them down like my therapist taught me.

They can't know what it costs me to be here.

"Are you alright?" Maverick's voice is edged with concern, a deep crease between his brows.

"I'm just tired. It's been a long day."

Colt's already getting up, holding out his hand to me. "You should have said so. I've wanted to go back for hours. These guys are boring."

"Screw you!" someone shouts, but I miss who it is, still unable to meet their faces.

Statistically, at least one of their careers will end in a grave. If they're lucky, a wheelchair.

Colt winks at me. "Don't hate me for telling the truth."

I don't even remember getting down from the truck, the walk back, or climbing up the stairs, my body fully on autopilot.

I manage to make an excuse to call it a night, then collapse against the door the second it shuts.

My breaths are ragged, my back sliding down the wood until I'm curled at the base of it, holding the glued pieces of my heart together.

I don't care how much it hurts.

I'm not giving up the short time I have with them.

Chapter 10

Colt

My beer's bitter on my tongue as I crush another one, adding it to the small pile at my side. I've hidden myself behind the building, not feeling up to playing my part. The playboy, boy next door, always ready with a smile.

Nights like these make me wonder why I ever put on this mask at all.

Not that I don't know. Half the money in bull riding is in sponsorships, and the TV loves the guy I show them.

I don't have it in me tonight, too many thoughts flying through my mind. How good Callie looked in my jacket, her warm thigh pressed against mine, so cute I just wanted to bite into her. My head drops into my palm, holding me up when I start to sway.

There'd been something else... As the night went on, her smiles grew brittle, and she stopped meeting my eyes. I let her play off her shudder as just being cold. It was easy to see she didn't want to talk about it but it took everything in me not to ask.

While Callie wasn't looking, Maverick lifted his chin in an upward nod, asking if I knew what was wrong. All I could do was shake my head.

The silent language we used to speak came back easily.

If there's one thing we still agree on, it's her, and if anything's wrong, we're going to fix it.

The years of not knowing what she's been doing have twisted protectiveness into outright possessiveness.

That's not quite right though. I don't want to own her. I want her to own me. I want her to let me do everything for her. To let me be the one she relies on.

She's playing it off, but I know her too well not to see it that she's guarded. Holding herself back. Still got one foot out the door, ready to walk away at any time.

The knowledge sits under my ribs, cutting into me when I breathe. A permanent ache, chewing away at my sanity.

Surviving her leaving once was hard; doing it again would be impossible.

Not that I'd let her get away. There's nowhere she can go that I won't follow and bring her home. And as much as it kills me to admit it, Maverick belongs with her too. So long as he keeps his distance from me, we'll work it out.

I want her so tied up in what we have she won't even think about going back to the city.

Maverick may be the biggest asshole around, but I don't hate him enough to want him gone.

It pisses me off, but I have no intention of getting between them.

Callie wants to go back to how we were as kids. I can't give her the impossible, but I'll do my best not to kick his ass while she's around.

I tell myself it'll be easy enough that if she's happy, I can live with it. But a sick feeling's already coiling low in my gut, warning me it's going to be a hell of a lot harder once reality slams into me.

A slow, crooked smile twists my lips. Fuck, it's been a while since we had a good fight. Wonder if we can set that up while she's asleep.

Sleep... fuck.

The back of my skull connects with the stone wall, and I wince. It's numb now, but shit's going to hurt in the morning.

I do it again, trying to rattle the thoughts loose, but it's no good.

Sooner or later, I'll have to crawl my drunk ass back to our room and face him head-on.

I haven't seen him in a few hours. With any luck, he'll be out cold.

We sprang apart the second Callie's door closed behind her, so fast you'd think we were contagious.

Whatever little truce we had going while she was around terminated the second she was gone.

He watched me from a safe ten feet away.

The moment stretched between us, and when his mouth twitched, I thought he was going to say something. Instead, he turned on his heel and walked away.

I'd take being buried six feet under before I admit I stood there, gaze locked on the flex of his shoulders as he left.

It would be a lie to say I've been able to ignore him.

No...he's always there, buzzing at the edge of my sight, a little alarm going off: *Look at me.*

Blaming it on us both being bull riders would be easy, but it's bullshit.

I've never been able to ignore that subtle electric hum that pulses through me whenever he's near, like he's some kind of live wire I should know better than to touch.

I hit my head against the wall one more time for good measure, then peel myself off the ground, stumbling to get my balance.

I don't usually get tanked like this, but something tells me I'm better off blacking out tonight.

Rounding the corner, I'm relieved to see most of the guys are already inside.

It's after 2:00 a.m., and even cowboys have to sleep.

My stomach twists the closer I get to my room and I know it's got nothing to do with the alcohol.

I can only pray that bastard's asleep.

Like a prisoner walking to the chair, I take my time making my way to the door.

Come on, Colt. Pull yourself together.

You're a grown-ass man. This isn't a big deal. Just get in there and pass out.

The pep talk barely helps, but combined with the liquor in my system, it's enough to get me inside.

It's dark.

The only light comes from the moon, casting soft shadows through the window, making it hard to see but there's no mistaking the large shape on the bed.

I bend down, pulling off each boot slowly, dragging my feet as I make my way to the edge of the mattress.

The air catches in my lungs as I strain to listen, hoping for the rhythmic sounds of breathing.

But I can't hear anything over the pounding of my own heartbeat.

Hell, I'm more nervous now than getting on a bull.

The couch looks ancient, the cushions sunken like battle scars from a thousand asses.

Just looking at it makes my back hurt.

"Don't be a child," Maverick rasps without rolling over.

I curse under my breath. "I thought you were asleep."

"I was. You aren't exactly quiet. How much did you drink?"

"Judgmental fuck. I wouldn't be wasted if you hadn't suggested this stupid sleeping situation."

Or was I the one who suggested it?

"Get in or fuck off, but stop hovering over me like a psychopath."

He yanks the blanket up higher, effectively ending the conversation.

"Don't fucking kill me in my sleep."

Grumbling, I crawl into bed, not even bothering to change.

Normally, I sleep butt-ass naked, but like hell that's happening now.

"Don't give me ideas."

"You always couldn't wait to be rid of me."

He grunts. The fact he doesn't even reply pisses me off more.

I picture booting him out of bed and wonder how badly he'd kill me.

I shift so my back is facing him, trying to get comfortable, but it's no use.

Every molecule in my body is tuned to him.

The rough sound of his breathing.

The faint cologne still clinging to his skin.

The covers rustling when he moves.

Everything has my pulse racing and my heart clawing at my ribs.

What the absolute fuck is happening to me?

"Your thoughts are too loud," he huffs like I'm an annoying dog.

He shifts again, and this time, the sheet pulls low across his hips.

Something about the movement is lazy, and unguarded makes my mouth go dry.

"You're breathing too loud," I mutter under my breath.

Real mature, Colt.

He doesn't answer. His favorite move: complete, infuriating silence.

I'm listening so hard I hear the exact second his breathing deepens into sleep.

He's relaxed.

I'm trapped, choking on his heat traveling the distance between us.

He makes a low sound in his sleep, something between a sigh and a growl, and it shoots straight into my brain, flipping all my circuits.

I don't know what I'm feeling and I'm too drunk to figure it out but I know I don't like it.

And I know it's his fault.

Smothering my head with the pillow, I force myself to breathe slow and deep.

Mav's right.

It's going to be a long-ass night.

Chapter 11

Maverick

Colt bursts out of the gate, riding Diablo, the top-ranked bull of the season. Both a lucky and unlucky draw. A make-or-break situation.

He can earn the top score if he sticks the eight, but on that animal, eight seconds might as well be eight hours.

I woke up with his face inches from mine. Like the world had hit pause, I froze, letting myself use the quiet to take him in. The sharp edges of his features had eased in sleep. He looked soft. Like someone I'd want to hold on to. Kind of cute, actually... when he wasn't busy glaring at me.

My fingers tighten on the cool steel bar, leaning into the fence for a better view.

As much as I hate it, I've got to admit Colt's a beautiful rider. Graceful, pliant, moving with and not against the bull.

His arm swings high into the air, earning more points

for style as nearly two tons of muscle twists and bucks beneath him.

My brows pinch together when he leans back a millisecond too late and just like that, he's tossed off as easily as throwing a baseball.

Colt rips off his helmet, cussing under his breath, and disappears through the gate.

My cheeks puff out on a sigh.

It ended exactly how I thought it would. Time left on the clock, and his ass in the dirt.

Colt doesn't know, but I haven't missed a single one of his rides since we started.

I've tried not to watch, tried to stay with the other riders.

But without fail, my gut twists, and my heart races until I can see him.

A gnawing sensation that if I'm not there, no one's looking out for him.

It's ridiculous. There's an entire team out here taking care of us.

But I can't stay away, and I've given up trying.

Which is why I can read him like a book.

Just by the way he sat in the chute, I knew he was in for a tough go of it.

It's his own fault, coming in drunk off his ass the night before an event, stumbling around the dark room loud enough to wake the dead.

Not that I'd been asleep.

How could I be, knowing any second, Colt fucking

Lawson was going to swagger through the door and lie beside me?

Every creak from outside had my ears perking up, wondering if it was him.

Goddamn hours of that shit until the sound of sloppy steps approached, followed by the beep of our door.

The sound of his heavy breathing filled the air, blocking out everything else.

It was visceral, having him that close, but I kept my eyes shut, muscles locked tight, the hair on the back of my neck lifting under the weight of his stare.

Finally, I couldn't take it anymore.

I snapped. Pushed his buttons, made him give in.

Maybe if I had time to think it through, I would've wondered why I cared so much about him sleeping on the sofa.

It's not like it's my problem if he's sore. If anything, it's better for me.

But every second he stalled burrowed deeper under my skin, until I found myself taunting him, until he climbed in beside me.

I wasn't ready for the heat of his body radiating across the few inches that separated us.

Definitely wasn't ready for the way it pulled at something low and hungry inside me.

With the last grains of sanity, I turned away from him, faking sleep.

He didn't need to know my thoughts were racing a

million miles a minute and I still don't know what they mean.

He settled quickly while I stared a hole in the wall, just trying to sort out where the fuck everything went wrong.

"Hey, you're up next," a bullfighter hollers at me, voice annoyed enough it's probably not the first time.

Damn it.

I run my palm down my face and bust my ass to the staging area behind the pens.

I'd been daydreaming so hard I nearly missed my own ride.

Whatever the hell Colt's doing to my head, it's gotta stop. And it's gotta stop now.

Two familiar men wait at the top of the chute, one leg braced on the rail and the other safely on the deck in case they need to bail fast.

"How's it looking?" I ask, cracking my neck as I prep to mount.

The bullfighter smirks. "You've got yourself a live one. He's ready to kill."

As if to prove the point, the bull rears in the pen, nearly crushing Colt. He only just manages to dodge it.

The other one lets out a low whistle. "Gonna be a pretty ride."

These two have helped countless riders, and they make it easy.

Within minutes, the gate opens, and the clock starts ticking.

Muscles flex between my thighs as the devil beneath me bucks, hungry to kick me off and take a piece of me.

He's wild, but I've ridden him before.

I release the tension in my body and move with him on instinct.

Forward when his feet go up. Backward when he rears.

Leaning into his turns instead of away.

Seconds counting down.

I make a rookie mistake and look at the clock.

Just like that, the bull slams his skull into my face.

The bone-shattering crack reverberates through my head.

Thank God the whistle blows, and I manage to dismount with help from the bullfighters.

Blood pours over my mouth, down my chin, soaking through my shirt.

I don't waste time waving at the crowd instead head straight for the medics.

The medic area's tucked away behind the building.

Most riders consider it bad luck to even glance at it, like getting hurt is contagious.

It's set up to handle common injuries. Get you stitched up, pop in a separated shoulder... realign your broken nose...

And no bull rider steps foot in a hospital unless absolutely necessary.

I've seen guys with sideways ankles swear they just need to walk it off.

That's where the medical team steps in and forces them.

"You're making a hell of a mess," Doc greets me, bushy brows pulled together as he gives me a once-over.

Quick as a whip, he pinches my nose between thumb and finger, and there's a sickening pop that has bile rising in my throat.

"Jesus Christ." I hiss, covering my nose with one hand, nails digging into the other.

Bastard didn't even warn me.

"That fucking hurt, you know." I glare at him.

"Wouldn't hurt if you quit breaking it."

He tosses me a cloth to wipe my face, clearly done dealing with pissed-off cowboys for the day.

It's stained red by the time I toss it in the trash.

"Thanks, Doc," I mutter, then head for the locker room, hunting for the extra-strength painkillers I keep stashed.

I stay away from the prescription shit.

Seen too many guys go down that road.

Blood dries, sticking my shirt to my skin, tearing out hair with every step.

Staying up all night has me operating at barely human levels.

One more corner, and then I'll change, crash, and forget today ever happened.

Ah, fuck.

Colt's waiting there, arms crossed over his chest,

tendons straining at his neck like he's seconds from snapping.

I groan. "Whatever the hell you're pissed about, it'll have to wait. Now's not the time."

I move to sidestep him and the bastard blocks me, turning himself into a goddamn wall.

"Fucking reckless out there. Does winning mean that much to you?"

It takes my pain-addled brain a second to catch up to what he's saying.

Almost seems like... he's worried.

Nah. Can't be.

"What's it to you?" I mutter, because really, I want to know. Normally, he'd be laughing his ass off, not looking like he's about to deck me.

"Callie saw it. Turned white as a ghost. I thought she was gonna pass out."

He glares at me, voice rough and cracking.

"You can't fuck around when she's here."

Guilt slashes through me, sharp and ugly.

I tell myself she's not new to this; she knows injuries are part of the game.

But it doesn't fucking help.

"At least I finished my ride," I snap, a bastard move I can't stop.

Anything to wipe that look off Colt's face.

His whole body jolts like I slapped him.

Without warning, he throws a punch, nearly missing my already broken nose.

Before I can think, I shove him back, rage boiling over.

He stumbles a step then comes at me.

That's when Marco charges up the hall, fist cocked back like he's about to end Colt right there.

Instinct takes over.

I grab Marco's arm mid-swing, yanking him off-balance before he can land the hit.

"Who the fuck do you think you're swinging at?" I snarl, voice low and lethal.

Marco's mouth opens and closes uselessly.

"Fuck, man, I was just trying to help—"

I shove his arm away, shoving him back a few feet.

"Didn't fucking ask for your help," I snap. "Whatever's between me and Colt stays between us. Touch him again and you'll wish a bull stomped your goddamn face in."

Marco backs off fast, hands raised like I'm a live wire.

Colt stares at me, breathless, chest rising and falling.

"You just defended me?" he says, like he can't believe it.

My pulse hammers in my throat. *Shit.*

Sanity starts to seep back in, leaving me raw and exposed.

What the hell was that?

I don't have a good answer. Don't want one.

I turn away, voice rough.

"Forget it."

"Fuck you," Colt snarls, then walks off down the hall, Marco following several few feet behind.

Grateful the locker room's empty, I strip down, take a lightning-fast shower, and pull on clean clothes.

At least now I'm partially human.

Mind still racing, it turns to Callie.

I hadn't seen her watching.

Hadn't seen her face drain of color.

But the thought has me on edge.

And from the way she didn't check in at the medics, I'd say she's avoiding me.

I owe her an apology.

She's not responding to any of my texts.

I almost message Colt but if she wanted him, he'd be with her, not yelling at me.

That leaves the old-fashioned way.

I start checking every room.

No sign of her.

Nobody's seen her either.

A few offer to help me look, but something tells me Callie wouldn't want that much attention.

That being said, if I don't find her in the next five minutes, I'll have every damn person in here searching.

The longer it takes, the worse the feeling in my gut gets.

Something's seriously wrong.

Chapter 12

Callie

Trigger warning: On page panic attack.

Maverick's face colliding with the bull's skull.

The crack loud enough to reach me in the stands and then... blood. Crimson pouring down his nose, covering his lips, soaking his shirt. Darkness crowds the corners of my vision, static filling my ears as my heart bangs hard enough in my chest to break my ribs.

I know this feeling. Rapid breaths, coming out so fast I can't speak, growing more light-headed by the second. The only thing breaking through is my overwhelming need to get as far away from here as possible.

The daughter of the great Harper Ridge Ranch passing out on live TV is not something I want to experience. Not when I promised my mom I'm okay. Not when Maverick and Colt don't know.

My fingers skim the walls as I take the hallway corners too fast, feet racing to escape before everything goes black.

Pressure builds behind my eyes as I search through rooms, finding them all occupied.

I need somewhere quiet. Somewhere hidden. Somewhere no one will find me.

I nearly miss the plain wood door to my right, so inconspicuous it blends into the wall.

The sign says Custodian.

If I could breathe, I'm sure relief would flood me at the sight of the empty space. Instead, my knees give out the second I close the door behind me.

Weak and scared. Two words I never want to describe myself.

From experience, this will end eventually whether by passing out or simply time, I can't be sure.

Red fills the back of my scrunched lids... blood... Maverick's blood.

That vision morphs into an old one, locked away, shoved deep inside me.

It shakes and rattles loose, the binding not strong enough to keep the memories sealed anymore.

All I can see is my dad on the stretcher.

Blood covering his head, soaking his copper hair until it turns blood red. His white face, unmoving hands.

My lungs scream, but I can't fill them, panting over and over but getting no real breath.

A deep, instinctual fear shudders through me.

Rationally, I know it'll be okay that once I pass out, my body will take over for my broken mind.

Because that's what it is. Broken.

But nothing can overpower centuries of primal instinct.

The less oxygen I get, the more I panic, trapped in a vicious cycle.

I pull my knees to my chest, tucking my forehead against them, and try to count like my therapist taught me.

Each number is supposed to slow my breathing... but it's too late.

I'm too far gone, the numbers spilling out faster and faster.

I don't notice the door opening.

I barely register the light filtering in.

Vaguely, I hear my name whispered, then shouted but it's too far away to reach me.

I'm so deep inside myself the world is distant, muffled.

Someone shakes my shoulders, but it barely registers above my shuddering.

I want to say, *Just leave me alone... don't look at me*, but all I can do is gasp.

This time, my name comes clearly.

My head is captured in firm hands and then lips press hard against mine.

They're warm and soft, and my body responds on instinct, opening to them.

"Breathe with me, Wildflower," Maverick commands, and I follow.

Inhaling his exhale.

Exhaling into him.

In and out.

In and out.

He's steady. Grounding. Controlling the pace until the static grows fainter and my senses start returning.

Touch. The feel of his lips grazing mine, the warmth of his steady breath, the firm press of fingers cradling my head.

Smell. Hints of forest and leather filling my nose.

Sound. His calming words coaxing me back to the present.

"That's it. Breathe, baby. Come back to me. You're doing so well. Just like that."

Sight. Dark brown eyes filling my vision.

Maverick.

His eyes are wide as they search mine, his thumbs wiping away my tears.

"You scared me," he says, his voice breaking around the vowels.

"What if you died," I rasp, my throat raw.

He drops his forehead to mine, trying to reassure me.

"I'm okay. Just a broken nose nothing that hasn't happened before."

I shake my head, tears stinging. "It could've been—"

Maverick shifts against me, easily lifting me onto his lap, securing me sideways against his chest.

The heat of him chases away the lingering chill from my panic attack.

Unsteady, I rest my weight on him, trusting his hold.

"Look at me," he says, his mouth grazing my temple.

When I don't immediately move, he guides my chin up with his thumb until he's all I see.

"It's a little crooked. Gives me a more rugged look, right?"

The always serious Maverick attempts to cheer me up with a shaken smile.

I can't help but give in.

"It's distinct, I'll give you that."

His brows pull together as he tucks a loose strand of hair behind my ear.

"I'm not sure that's a compliment."

Even teasing, his voice stays low and gentle, like he knows I'm not ready to return to normal yet, and he'll give me all the time I need.

He's created a bubble around us, and I want to live in it forever if he'll let me.

It's my turn to really look at him.

Besides the small cut across the bridge of his nose, there's no trace of blood. His hair's wet, drops falling from the ends, like he rushed to find me.

He's showered. Changed.

I must've been out of it longer than I realized, time losing all meaning while I fought to hold on to consciousness.

The cool strands of his hair slip between my fingers as I rake them back soothingly.

Maverick leans into my touch, a soft hum vibrating in his chest.

I know I should explain, he deserves to know what he just witnessed.

But the words catch in my throat.

If he knew, he'd worry every time he got on a bull. His attention would split.

And the most dangerous thing a bull rider can be... is distracted.

I don't want to be the reason Maverick gets hurt.

I've stayed away so long.

Worked so hard.

Was I naive to think I could come back here? To think I had control over this?

First injury... and I'm already a blubbering mess.

I rest my head against his chest, letting the steady beat of his heart soothe me.

I know it's not fair to keep this to myself.

I know I should have told them years ago.

Even knowing that, I still don't want to.

"I can feel your thoughts spinning," Maverick murmurs, rubbing circles into my back.

He falls silent, letting me rest while he works through his own thoughts.

Then, always giving me exactly what I need, he says, "You don't need to explain. I don't need that from you."

My grip tightens on his shirt, then loosens as his words settle into me.

One day, I'll tell him.

Tell them both.

But for now, I'm okay.

I don't know how I survived without Maverick's steady, unshakable support.

Even as a kid, he was my anchor.

He still is.

My neck stiffens.

Oh.

He definitely knows.

Someone who understands me this well couldn't *not* know.

And his willingness to let it go, to not dig, has my heart aching.

As my head clears, mortification creeps in, heating my cheeks.

I know he'd never make fun of me... but that doesn't stop the embarrassment from flooding in.

Oh my God.

He kissed me.

I jerk away, ready to flee, but his arms band tighter around me, keeping me in place.

That was the only way he could snap me out of it.

What if he hated it?

If I thought I was embarrassed before, it's nothing compared to now.

His thumb runs over my bottom lip, freeing it from my teeth.

"There you go again, thinking too much."

"I didn't... you didn't have to. Thank you."

The words tumble out in a messy contradiction.

"Oh my God. I'm so sorry you had to do that—"

He cuts me off, his tongue slipping past my still-open mouth, sending a full-body shiver through me.

His kiss is soft at first, exploratory, his tongue brushing over every inch like he wants to memorize me.

I'm slow to respond, brain still struggling to catch up, but when I do, it's all-consuming.

My tongue tangles with his.

A low groan rumbles out of him, vibrating into my side.

I whimper when he pulls back, breath panting against my lips.

I move to chase him, but he brushes his nose along mine instead, smiling.

"I've wanted to do that for a very long time," he says, voice rough. "I've pictured it a million times. What you'd taste like. How you'd respond. If you'd make those soft little sounds."

Tingles race over my skin, heat pooling low in my belly.

"I... I shouldn't have kissed you without asking. That's not how I wanted this to happen... I just couldn't think of a different way," he says, so vulnerable my chest aches.

I grab the sides of his face and yank him down hard enough for our teeth to clash.

This time, my kiss isn't soft.

It's fast. Messy. Overflowing with everything inside me.

He answers with a low growl, wrapping his hand in my hair and tilting my head to the side for more access.

It's hunger.

It's need.

It's everything we've been bottling up for years.

Eventually, our movements slow, turning soft, tender, almost reverent.

Maverick eases me down, his hands gentle as he touches me like I might shatter.

I let him.

I trust him.

Fourteen-year-old Callie would be losing her mind right now.

Giddiness bubbles up my throat, escaping in a giggle.

Maverick beams at me a real smile, full of wonder and possibility.

The kind of smile I'd do anything to keep there.

Noise filters through the door.

"We should probably head out. Colt'll be looking for you."

Colt.

My heart stutters.

How would Maverick feel if he knew I wanted to kiss Colt just as badly?

That I've always been greedy and want them both?

He holds my chin lightly and says, "He and I may not like each other, but you'll always come first. We want you to be happy."

"Freaking mind reader," I mutter under my breath, internally freaking out.

"You shouldn't make yourself so easy to read," he teases, pressing a kiss to my temple.

Then he twines our fingers together and leads us out.

This man found me at my darkest.

Lit my way out.

And somehow made me as happy as I've ever been.

Everything about this moment is perfect.

I want to freeze it in time, hold it tight forever.

An ache twists in my chest.

I know it's temporary.

But I push that thought away, refusing to taint this memory.

One day…

It will be all I have left.

Chapter 13

Callie

14 Years Old

THE HEAT HASN'T BROKEN, even though the sun's been down for hours.

We lie sprawled in the bed of Colt's dad's rusted truck, a tangle of limbs and dust-streaked skin, staring up at the stars.

"This is the life," Colt says, stretching until his boots thud against the side panel.

Maverick grunts in agreement, one arm folded behind his head. He's chewing a piece of straw he picked from the rodeo grounds earlier, like a caricature of a cowboy.

I shift, propping my chin on my hands, watching them.

"I'm gonna be the best bull rider in the world," Maverick declares, too casual to be kidding.

Colt snorts. "You mean if you don't get your head knocked off first."

"You're just jealous 'cause you know I'll outscore you."

"You wish."

They bicker lazily, no real heat behind it, just the kind of jabs they've traded since they could talk. I close my eyes and let the sound wash over me, familiar, safe.

"No matter what," I say quietly, cutting through their teasing.

They both fall silent.

"No matter what happens... we stick together."

I don't know why the words feel so important. I just know they do. Like a promise bigger than any of us.

Colt's hand finds mine in the dark, rough and calloused even at fourteen. Maverick bumps my shoulder with his, the movement easy, unconscious.

"We will," Maverick says, like it's obvious.

Colt presses his palm flat against mine. "Always."

I don't know it yet, but this is the moment that will stick. The one that will come back to haunt me later.

When everything falls apart.

When the promises we made feel like splintered glass in my hands.

But for now, it's perfect.

Colt hums something tuneless under his breath, and when I glance over, he's drawing shapes in the dust coating the side panel. A crooked flower blooms under his fingertips. A wildflower, fragile and stubborn and real.

Maverick sees it too. He smirks and nudges Colt.

"Figures you'd pick the only flower tougher than you are."

Colt just shrugs, not looking up. "Seemed right."

When Maverick glances at me, something shifts in his eyes, something too big for either of us to name.

The heat, the stars, the feel of their bodies bracketing mine. It all weaves together until it's impossible to tell where one of us ends and the others begin.

We fall asleep like that, tangled up under the endless summer sky, believing that nothing could ever pull us apart.

I didn't know then that some promises are meant to be broken.

And some are meant to be shattered... just so you can rebuild them stronger.

Chapter 14

Colt

Counting the cracks in the motel ceiling for the last hour has become a new form of torture. I've lost track and restarted at least three times, and I'm pretty sure that last time nearly caused an aneurysm. It still beats the alternative, counting every one of Maverick's steady breaths.

Last night was pure hell, coming in late, hoping he'd be asleep, only for us both to lie awake beside each other. Not that he had a problem falling asleep. Unlike me, he passes out like I'm not even there.

It really shouldn't be a big deal. We're sleeping next to each other. So fucking what? We're adults.

So tell me why I came to bed first, thinking I'd be passed out before him, only to end up faking sleep when he came in an hour later and then he just knocked out instantly?

It's late, really late. After being flung off the back of a bull and slammed into the dirt, my body's heavy with exhaustion, but my traitor of a brain is flying a mile a minute.

I've been lying here for four hours, each minute ticking away making me more stressed.

Eventually, I give up. I swing my legs over the edge of the bed one at a time, choking back a groan. Fire rips through my side. The bruising is worse than I thought.

I brace both hands on my knees, jaw clenched, trying not to make a sound.

The bed shifts behind me. I freeze.

A second later, I feel it. Maverick's hand, warm and slow, sliding over my lower back. Just a touch. Just enough pressure to ground me.

"You okay?" he murmurs, voice thick with sleep.

I should shrug him off. I should say I'm fine.

But I don't.

I just nod once, still staring at the floor. His hand lingers for another beat, then slips away like it never happened.

And God help me, I miss the contact the second it's gone.

My stomach knots, my chest too tight, my brain a mess of static. He's already rolled back over, breathing deeply again like it meant nothing.

Maybe it didn't.

Maybe it did.

I press the heels of my palms to my eyes and exhale, quiet and shaky.

Sleep's not coming anytime soon.

I pull on a thin shirt. The shorts I wore to bed will have to be enough. I absolutely refused to sleep next to Maverick in nothing but my boxers.

Speaking of that asshole, I slip on his sandals because there's no chance I'm bending down to put on boots and head outside.

Cool air lifts the hair on the back of my neck, chilling my sweat-damp skin. Maverick's basically a furnace, heat wafting off him in waves.

Our air conditioner's broken, which isn't a surprise in this run-down motel, but it does have one thing going for it.

One thing that might help me survive the next few hours until the world wakes up and I'm trapped in Maverick's truck for one of the world's most awkward drives.

The glass door unlocks with a swipe of my key card, and I'm instantly hit with the pungent ammonia smell of chlorine.

It's a million times more humid in here and feels like it's coating my lungs with each inhale.

The sound of jets has my head snapping to the side. They're on a timer, so the hot tub should be silent right now.

Two walls are lined with floor-to-ceiling windows, and the soft moonlight illuminates the silhouette already lounging in the water.

My breath whooshes out as my head drops forward.

The odds of someone else being here are next to zero, but it perfectly fits with how my night's going.

"You're up late," the sweetest sound I've ever heard calls out from the shadows.

I'd recognize Callie's voice anywhere. It's elongated with sleep, lazy vowels coming together to form the question.

My eyes adjust to the dim lighting, and I can make out her features, the contours of her face and neck above the water.

For one wild second, it's like we're fourteen again, climbing the fence rails with her chasing after us, shrieking about muddy boots and broken promises.

God, she used to love us so much it hurt.

My throat's thick. I grunt, but it doesn't clear my voice, rough like gravel as I say, "Couldn't sleep. What's your excuse?"

"Hmm. Same. If I'm honest, I don't get much sleep."

I don't like the sound of that. I want to dig into her every thought until I know what's bothering her.

We'd known each other better than anyone else once, but time's built walls between us. Blank spaces I can't fill.

Clearing my throat, I approach, heart racing with every step. Equal parts driven to get in and knowing it's such a fucking bad idea.

Simping doesn't begin to describe what I've been doing since she showed up.

Lusting. Gawking. Fantasizing.

I'm not sure how long I stare at her, but it's long enough for her to laugh, amusement bubbling up.

"You coming in, or are you just going to keep staring?"

Thank God she can't see my blush. She'd never let me live it down.

I grunt again, not trusting my voice, and close the distance.

All the things I absolutely should not be doing and getting in this tub with her is at the top of that list.

The air's heavy with bad decisions and the lack of inhibitions.

So of course, I get in.

Hot water envelops me as I dunk myself, popping up and taking a spot across from her, as far away as possible.

The position also gives me the perfect view.

Her stretched-out arms support her on either side of the rim, head tilted back, neck exposed, vulnerable.

"Fuck me. Get your shit together before you creep her out," I mutter under my breath.

"Did you say something?"

I could kiss the jets, loud enough to cover for me.

"Ah... just..." Shit. "Just bitching about my ride tonight." Good save.

"I still can't hear you."

I go to repeat it louder but choke when she moves, sliding along the curved side until she's right beside me.

"What was that?"

Her copper hair's pulled up in a messy bun, strands escaping at her temples, curling with the humidity, perfectly framing her heart-shaped face.

She smiles brighter, lighting up the night, and soft giggles escape her plush lips, drawing my full attention.

"Are you laughing at me?" I ask, still unable to look away.

Her giggles turn to laughter, and she bites her bottom lip.

"You should see yourself right now."

My gaze flicks up to her eyes. Even in the dark, they're blown wide.

Her cheeks are a rosy pink, and I want to know if it's from the heat or me.

"You should see yourself." It escapes before I can hold it back, my filter missing in the dark.

Her mouth parts as she sucks in a slow inhale, and I'd do anything to taste it.

Time freezes like an unturned hourglass.

Tension builds between us, steam blocking out the rest of the world.

I dip my head lower.

She tilts her chin up.

I want her more desperately than I've ever wanted anything.

Not a win. Not a championship. Not the gold buckle I've spent my life chasing.

None of it compares to her breath warming my lips.

"Do you really hate him?"

Her words are a slap, reality crashing in.

I shift away from her.

Hell. Did I just read her wrong?

She'd been so close we shared the air between us... and

while I'd been consumed by the need to taste her, she'd been thinking about Maverick.

My gut curdles.

Acid claws up my neck.

I have to count to ten before I can answer.

"I knew this was coming eventually," I say lowly. "I just didn't think it would be now."

"Is that what's keeping you up?" I ask.

"Part of it."

She hums. "I need you to help me understand. Because no matter how I look at it, I can't make sense of it."

I'm not as fast with a response as I should be.

An immediate yes should spring from my lips, a restatement of how much I hate him. That nothing could make me like him again.

But the words are thick in my throat.

When I search myself, I don't find the same conviction I once had.

It's not as hard to be around him as it used to be.

Sometimes I catch myself laughing at something he said.

Sometimes I catch myself understanding him.

Things are changing and I fucking hate it.

Hate that my walls are cracking.

But I can't hate who's breaking them.

I let out a long sigh.

"Sometimes I miss what we were," I admit. "Wishing

things turned out differently." That he hadn't chosen a buckle over our friendship. "Back then, I'd have said what we are now was impossible. I trusted him more than a brother."

Bracing myself, I take a steadying breath.

An ache thrums in my chest, the kind that hates how everything turned out.

If I could go back, would things be different?

No. That's not the problem.

I know better than to put this blame on myself.

Fuck, a part of me died that day when he held that trophy high.

And that's the part that fucks with me every time I look at him now.

Because sometimes just sometimes there's something hidden beneath his lashes that I can't read.

Would he do it again?

Would he leave me in that hospital to chase his dreams?

Or would he follow me, hold my hand while I lay there terrified?

I couldn't feel my legs.

The doctors couldn't tell me if it was permanent or temporary.

And I was all alone.

I really thought he'd be there.

That I was more important.

But I wasn't.

Callie left.

And Maverick didn't come.

And ain't that a bitch.

"There's no fixing this, Callie," I say, not sure if I'm reminding her or myself.

It hurts more than I want it to.

The feeling of losing everything good in my life, like an old wound freshly reopened.

My voice is raw, guttural as the words force their way out.

"Why did you disappear?"

She flinches, then drops her head so I can't read her face.

Hiding from me.

I can't let that happen.

"I'm sorry."

Her cheeks are wet when she lifts her head.

And it's not from the water.

It punches the breath from my lungs.

I want to take it all back.

I want to tell her to forget it, that she doesn't need to explain, but I need to know what made it so easy to leave me.

"I want to... I really do... but I don't know how to."

Her voice wobbles, broken.

"I can't stay here. I can't live this life. I belong far away from here, somewhere no one knows anything about bulls, rides, or championships. Somewhere none of that matters."

She looks at me, eyes full of regret. "But *you* belong here. This is your dream, the thing that drives you."

Her hand lifts, gesturing to the trucks lined up in the parking lot, the logos, the gear, the unmistakable life of riders.

"I didn't leave *you*," she says softly. "I left *this*."

Her words slice me open.

My spleen's been ruptured.

Bones shattered.

Organs bruised beneath a one-ton bull.

None of it compares to the tearing sensation ripping through my chest right now.

It's hard to breathe.

Impossible to think through the agony.

Anger's always been there for me but this time, it can't mask the hurt.

Because I could never stay angry with her.

It's torture, having her this close.

Knowing the season will never be long enough.

I want to shake her until it knocks some sense into her.

I want to fall to my knees and beg her to stay.

Over everything else, I want her to choose me.

"Do... do you want me to go?"

Fuck.

She sounds broken, cracked, just like me.

I take her face in my palms, holding her steady, making sure she knows I mean it.

"Never."

She tastes like heaven as I crash my mouth into hers.

Nothing I imagined, no dream, no fantasy comes close to how soft she is.

How sweet the sounds she makes are.

In the back of my mind, a voice yells that I shouldn't have kissed her without asking.

That I'm a greedy bastard, taking advantage of her guilt.

But the way she's kissing me back, nails digging into my shoulders, her other hand yanking me closer by my hair. Callie needs this just as much as I do.

She takes from me.

And I give her everything she needs.

No holding back.

I'd give her everything if she let me.

Each brush of her tongue stitches me back together.

Her whimpers better than any painkiller, numbing my shredded heart.

We part just long enough to breathe, then crash back together again.

I eat her whimpers like a starving man, pulling her onto my lap, the sensation of her slippery skin shorting out my brain.

Nothing else matters but the feel of her in my arms.

I let her wash everything else away.

The door beeps open.

A startled grunt cuts through the moment. As much as I want to keep making out with Callie, I force myself to look.

Maverick's standing there. His mouth opens, then shuts. His fists clench at his sides as he takes in the scene.

Callie's straddling my lap.

Her hands in my hair.

Mine wrapped around her, possessive.

The sour taste of guilt burns my throat.

The way Maverick stiffens, stepping one foot back like he's been punched.

I should be happy.

I should feel like I won.

But hell if I don't want to wipe that look off his face.

If she'd chosen him and not me...

That's not something I could come back from.

Callie inhales sharply.

Her eyes go wide, frantic as she looks between us.

There's a desperate way she's clinging to me, like she's terrified to let go.

I draw a half-moon on her lower back with my thumb.

"Hey, what's wrong?"

"I... I don't want..." Callie chokes out, tears spilling into her lashes.

Dread sinks in my stomach.

Whatever this is...It's bigger than I thought.

"We can figure it out together," I promise.

"It's alright, Callie," Maverick says, softer.

He's studying her every twitch, every flicker of emotion.

His voice drops into something raw, something real.

"He's right. We'll figure it out."

I don't have time to ask what the fuck that means because Callie's already pulling herself off my lap and climbing out of the hot tub.

"I... I don't know what to do," she says, voice shaking. "Because I... I want you both."

Realization slams into me.

I should be raging.

Should be pissed that she kissed me that she's mine and now she's asking for both.

That's what any sane person would do.

But she looks gutted.

Like she's already bracing for us to say no.

Like she's about to lose something she loves.

The words claw up my throat, and I shove them into a chokehold.

Instead, I force a smile that feels like it's tearing something loose inside me.

"Alright, Sunshine," I murmur, voice soft but steady. "We'll figure it out."

She looks between us, teeth sinking into her bottom lip, like that's the only thing holding her together.

I want to pull her into my arms.

But she steps around us, leaving a gaping hole behind her.

I'm left standing there.

Maverick standing there.

Both of us.

Fuck.

Chapter 15

Maverick

The door swings shut behind Callie with a hollow thud, leaving nothing but the wet slap of water against the hot tub walls and the ragged sound of our breathing. For a second, neither of us moves. The whole fucking world tilts, spinning off its axis. I stare at the door like maybe she'll come back, like maybe this isn't as bad as it feels, but the empty stretch of space between us says otherwise.

The memory of the heat of her mouth still lingers, the ghost of her touch clinging to my skin like static. It's not enough. It'll never be enough.

Colt scrubs a hand down his face, water dripping from his jaw, his shoulders tight. "Great fucking job," he mutters, voice sharp enough to cut.

My head snaps toward him, the burn rising in my chest before I can think better of it. "Me?" I bark out a humorless laugh, bitterness coating every syllable. "You're the one she was straddling, man."

His eyes flare. A muscle jumps in his jaw. "Fuck you, Kane."

"Right back at you, Lawson."

The anger between us isn't new. It simmers, thick and hot and tangled with everything we never said. Not just about tonight. About everything. Years of distance. Misunderstandings. Watching her walk away and neither of us stopping her.

Colt hauls himself out of the hot tub, water pouring off him in angry sheets. "What the hell do we do now? Because I'm not letting her go."

My stomach twists, sick and hollow but there's no hesitation. "Yeah. Same."

He scoffs, grabs his shirt and my sandals, already storming off. "Still trying to leave me behind. Still only thinking about your goddamn self."

That tears through me. I lunge after him, grabbing his arm and forcing him to turn. "What the hell is that supposed to mean? You got some great idea?"

He yanks free but doesn't keep walking. His chest heaves, jaw clenched. "Yeah. I do."

I brace for a fight.

Instead, his voice drops, rough but sure. "I always knew."

I blink. "Knew what?"

"Back when we were kids," he says. "Before everything went to shit. It was supposed to be the three of us."

I stare at him, breath caught somewhere between my lungs and my heart.

He meets my eyes, steady now. "It's both of us, or we lose her."

My jaw ticks, but I don't look away. He means it. Every damn word.

And God help me, I don't hate it. Not the way I should.

My chest is heaving, brain spinning out but one truth cuts clean through the noise:

If it means she stays...

If it means she's happy...

Then I'll live with it.

I nod, once. "You're right."

Colt's eyes flick to mine, sharp with disbelief. Testing.

I shrug, breathless.

"It was always supposed to be us."

I stay long after Colt leaves, eyes closed, jaw tight, letting the sting of chlorine burn through the fog of what just happened.

He said it out loud. The thing I didn't even know I was holding on to. The thing I didn't think we were allowed to want.

Both of us. With her.

It's not something I ever imagined Colt Lawson saying. Not without a fight. Not without blood.

But he said it.

And now the world's off its axis, like gravity has shifted, and I can't tell which way is up.

The heat outside is stifling, thick against my skin, but it's nothing compared to the pressure behind my ribs. Not guilt. Not relief. Just this hollow, echoing awareness that nothing will be the same after tonight.

I make it back to the motel somehow. Still moving, but barely processing.

Inside, I strip off my shirt and slide under the covers slowly, trying not to wake him.

He's stretched out on his stomach, half-covered by a sheet, the neon motel sign casting sharp lines across his back. His muscles are tense even in sleep. Like he's bracing for something.

I lie on my side, staring at the ceiling, every nerve wound tight.

Then my knee bumps his hand.

A quiet rustle. A low sound from his throat.

His fingers brush mine.

We freeze.

Not breathing. Not moving.

Just skin touching. Just heat shared between two people who haven't been okay for a long time.

He doesn't pull away.

Neither do I.

It lasts a second. Maybe two.

Then I shift. Roll to face the wall.

And lie there in the dark, wide-awake, every second stretching longer than the last.

Not sure what this means.

Not sure how to want something you were never supposed to have.

Not sure how to survive it.

Chapter 16

Colt

After last night's decision, there's a truce between us.

Something's shifted. The sharp edges are still there, but they've dulled. At least for now.

The bathroom door creaks open, steam rolling out.

Maverick steps into the room, towel slung low on his hips, hair dripping down the sides of his face.

Still half-wet and fully smug, like walking around half-naked is normal at seven in the morning.

"Used up all the towels, didn't you?" I mutter from where I'm still half-asleep in bed, sore as hell and already irritated.

He smirks and tosses a damp one at my face.

It hits dead-on. Warm. Wet. Disgusting.

"Shoulda gotten your ass up earlier, Lawson."

I rip the towel off, jaw tight. "Real fuckin' considerate."

He shrugs and starts toweling off his hair like nothing's wrong in the world like he's not standing there looking like that, all lean muscle and loose confidence, water sliding down his chest in rivulets that I definitely shouldn't be noticing.

I drag my eyes away, mutter a curse, and grab the half-wet towel off my chest as I push out of bed.

His low chuckle trails behind me as I stalk to the bathroom, seething.

I slam the door harder than I need to.

And it still doesn't drown out the image of him standing there in just that towel.

Chapter 17
Callie

THE SWEET SMELL of fresh hay is the first thing that hits me when I walk into the arena, followed quickly by manure. It's impressive how fast I get used to it the smell disappears into the background, becoming just another part of what makes this place special. With the growing attention on the sport, most buildings have been updated, but this one has that old charm from my past. Wood-planked walls faded with time. A dirt floor leading through multiple hallways lined with empty stalls. They won't bring all of the bulls in here until the last minute. The animals are too dangerous to be left unattended in regular pens like this. Without the sound of their grunting, it's almost peaceful. The calm before the raging storm that'll happen tomorrow night.

I've been anxious since dropping that bomb on Maverick and Colt. They told me they'd figure it out, but I have no idea what that means.

They're unloading their stuff, no doubt meticulously checking it. Just like skydiving, one tear in the cinches could lead to disaster. A loose rope could be a death sentence if it catches around their boot.

A horse whinnies, kicking its hooves, and throws its muzzle over the gate, huge black eyes staring right at me. Hot air huffs from wide nostrils, as if to say I'm annoying him. Animals are sensitive to emotion, especially horses. Centuries of being prey have ingrained their flight response, tuned to read the rest of their herd for any signs of danger. It's unsurprising that my anxiousness sets him on edge, making him restless, head swinging back and forth, tail whipping his sides. If I unlatched the gate, he'd be a mile away in a minute.

"Shhh. It's okay," I croon, cautiously moving closer, not wanting to spook him more than I already have. "I'm sorry. I didn't mean to cause such a fuss."

The stunning black stallion watches my approach, breaths filling the space between us, but his demeanor settles, giving me the confidence to move closer. "That's it. I made such a fuss, didn't I? Worrying about things that haven't happened yet. Good thing you're here to snap me out of it." The more I speak, the lighter I feel, as if it's the horse soothing me instead of the other way around. I hold my hand above his nose where he can easily see it and wait, letting him decide if he wants to be touched. He nuzzles into my palm, and his smooth, short fur glides under my touch.

"You're such a good boy."

His wet nose nudges my hand as if agreeing and pushes it harder into me. His huff of frustration is easy to read. "You're right. You deserve a treat."

Recognizing the word *treat*, he whinnies again, this time pleased. I search my pockets, already knowing they'll turn up empty. "Had I known I'd meet you today, I would have brought you something." I stroke his nose again. "I'm sorry. I promise I'll bring you something when I come back."

Snorting, he whips his head to the side where there's a bucket hanging from a post. Inside, it's half-full with powdered oats.

"You like this?" I ask, and I swear he nods yes. "Alright, just a little though. Too much sugar's bad for you."

Does he look disappointed, or am I losing it?

"Okay, okay. Easy." I scoop a handful of oats from the bucket, stretching my hand completely flat beneath him. Flexible lips travel over my fingers, funneling his treat into his mouth. Wide, flat teeth are visible with each bite, but he's extra careful not to nip me. Sniffing my hand when it's all gone, he nudges again, and I can't help the laugh that bubbles up my throat. Moments ago, I was heading into a downward spiral, and this guy's got me giggling.

I used to think horses were magic.

When I was little, my dad would lift me up onto the saddle, hands steadying me, voice warm in my ear.

"Hold tight, baby girl. Trust your seat. Trust the animal."

Maybe that's what I'm still doing now, trusting something bigger than me to hold steady when I can't.

"Just one more," I whisper. "I shouldn't be doing this without your owner's permission, so it'll be our little secret."

He nickers as I grab another handful. The bucket being right by his pen at least lets me know he's not allergic. A little extra snack will be alright for such a charmer. His lips smack together as he cleans every morsel, and then he takes a step deeper into his enclosure when it's clear I don't have any more.

"Oh, I see how it is. Using me for food, huh?" I muse, watching him relax and feeling the tension leaving me.

Nothing like a sweet horse to make all your worries go away.

The metal bar separating us tings with the rhythm of my nails. "I'll be back tomorrow."

I press my hand to the wall, feeling the vibration of distant hooves thudding against the ground. The wood under my palm is warm from the sun, and it feels solid, real, grounding.

A memory flickers me, Colt, and Maverick at fourteen, sneaking into the arena after hours, daring each other to climb into the empty chutes.

"One day," Colt said, grinning that wild, fearless grin. *"We're gonna be legends."*

And Maverick, lounging against the fence like he had all the time in the world, just said, *"We already are."*

I squeeze my eyes shut against the burn rising in my throat.

I want that back.

I want this summer to stitch us back together. I want it to erase the years we lost.

With that, I leave the handsome animal, needing to breathe fresh air after so much time in the depths of the building.

I make my way through the tunnel to the open arena, and it's not long before my sight catches on Colt. He's leaning over the fence next to the bucking chute, wearing that same excited expression my dad always wore.

From the second Colt stuck his first ride, I knew he'd never give it up. No one brushes with death like that without coming out changed on the other side.

His excitement was contagious that overwhelming high, electricity racing over my body and humming in my veins. It felt like he could touch the sky. When Maverick rode just as well, the entire town talked about them. You'd think they were local celebrities. I'd been ecstatic for them, living in the exhilaration of it all. We'd spent our entire lives in arenas, in and out of places we weren't supposed to be, constantly getting yelled at, and narrowly escaping. Now, my boys would be a part of it all.

They shined so bright it was hard to look directly at them as they placed event after event. Quickly, they were good enough to skip age brackets and move to higher-level bulls. They were flying high and taking me with them.

I've lost so many moments with them, so much time. They've grown into men and I wasn't there to witness it.

The deep scent of forest envelops me moments before I'm caged in by thick, corded arms, strong hands gripping the bar in front of me. For the short time I'll allow it, he feels like home. Security wrapped in warmth, a steady place to rest. Maverick's chest rises and falls against my back, steady and sure, syncing up with my own uneven breaths until the tightness in my chest eases. He doesn't say a word, resting his chin on top of my head as he scans to see where I've been looking. His low hum vibrates into my back, and I drop my head into his shoulder. From this angle, I can just make out his eyes, still focused on Colt.

The thick ridge of his brow stands tall as they pinch together. There's none of the heat they normally glare at each other with. It's replaced by something pained, maybe even regretful. As the seconds tick by, an intensity takes over, and his eyes grow impossibly dark, lids hooded as he peers through his long lashes. Goose bumps pepper my neck and arms as the air grows thick, heavy around us. He's still watching Colt, and I'm still watching him, unable to look away from the way he reveals the depth of something more. A banked fire, firmly held under control. He squeezes my shoulder absentmindedly, his thumb massaging into my neck, which is sore from the drive. I should feel like an outsider, coming back into this world after so long, but his reassuring presence, steady at my back, washes any worries away. Colt does the same in his own way, instead of steady, he's playful, his smile welcoming me, telling me I'll always belong here.

It's heartbreaking to see them both want things to be different while being equally stubborn. Their past stands in their way, but so does the way they react to each other. More than rivals, more than friends. They haven't figured out that some of this pent-up aggression they have going on is actually coming from somewhere else, somewhere deeper, more primal.

A place you can't rationalize away.

The longer they suppress it, deny that they don't hate each other as much as they claim, every confrontation between them stokes the flames, compressing the emotions that tie them together until the pressure becomes too much to bear.

How the hell did they end up this way? So blind to what's happening right in front of them and what's building under their own skin.

Heavy attention settles over me as Maverick takes me in. "What are you thinking about now?"

"What happened back then? What happened to make you stop being friends and turn into whatever this is?"

Maverick drops his head to my shoulder and groans, resigning to the fact that I won't let this go. "We got into a fight before the last event of our rookie season."

I twist my shoulders to look at him, eyebrows pulled together in confusion. "That's not unusual."

"Yeah, well, this time was. He was shoving my chest

before our ride, telling me all about how he's better than me. How I never thought he was good enough. That I'm just jealous because he was ahead of me in rank and was going to win Rookie of the Year. He was real fucking snarky about it too. I told him to have a good ride, and he told me not to choke. Bastard. When I heard he landed hard, I asked around. The guys said it was nothing major. Same shit as always. He had a shitty-ass ride, I won the Rookie of the Year trophy, and we've been like this ever since."

I hum, processing the information. "Okay... so what happened next?"

"Nothing happened. I saw him two days later, and he iced me the fuck out. All I got from him was the middle finger and his back. He messed up his ride. It happens but I never thought he'd be that pissed at me for winning."

I watch him, the way his jaw ticks, and he closes off his expression, making it clear I won't get anything more out of him.

It's official, boys are idiots. These two still have a lot to work through. Luckily, I'm here to help make that happen.

"Can you just drop it? It's all in the past now. No use bringing it up. This is what it is... even if we're sorta getting along now."

That's the first time one of them has admitted things might be changing, and warmth shimmers in my chest. They may think it's all in the past, but I'm ready to dig all of that up.

I go to ask another question, but he whines. Literally whines to avoid it.

My mouth splits into a grin I can't hold back because I'm about to cause so much trouble. The good kind though. Well, hopefully.

"Fuck. How fucked am I?" he groans, not even trying to talk me out of it.

Shrugging, my shoulder blades brush against his solid chest, and my ass shifts against the front of his jeans, heat washing over me, making me shiver.

He grunts, a pained sound, his fingers gripping my hip bones, holding me in place.

His attention pinpoints where my tongue wets my lips. "Oh, I'd say you'll be really fucked."

I'm pulled backward, his hard cock slotted against my ass, and he groans into my neck. A whimper escapes my lips, and I'm about to rock into him when Colt shouts, running across the dirt arena toward us.

"We done here?" Colt says, breathless. "I've got somewhere I'd like to take you. Somewhere I think you'll like."

Maverick stiffens behind me, a displeased rumble in the back of his throat.

Colt rolls his eyes at him. "Don't worry, asshole. You can come too."

"Really?"

"Yeah... we need his truck."

That has me laughing, and I can just make out the subtle sound of Maverick's chuckle.

They can try to hide it all they want. But I'm onto them.

What's a little meddling for old time's sake?

This is going to be fun.

Chapter 18

Callie

Sun baking me, the sound of gravel crunching under tires, and the feel of wind between my toes draped out the window make for a picture-perfect moment frozen in time.

Maverick's been driving the last forty minutes, Colt in the back shouting directions over the music, between singing his heart out. Well... more like shouting the words.

It's hot.

Head-in-an-oven hot.

Inferno-of-hell hot.

Sweat slicks the back of my neck and drips down my collarbones to where it disappears into the V of my dress.

Even with the air conditioner cranked on full blast, it doesn't stand a chance when our windows are open, letting the cool air escape and the hot air enter.

I'll take the heat if it means I can keep my legs hanging outside, crossed at the ankles. Time moves slowly here, all dirt roads and narrow lanes.

The country girl in me hadn't realized just how much I missed this.

My life's the polar opposite of this, all honking cars, impatient drivers yelling at each other as they follow the racing pace of urban life.

I adjust the hem of my skirt, holding it firmly in my fist as the wind tries to push it higher.

Pretty sure, having my dress fly up would give them the show of a lifetime.

Colt hits a particularly high note, making me wince, but that's just who he is.

Impossible to embarrass when he's having a good time.

I've always been envious of his ability to not care what other people think and just lean into his happiness like it's the most natural thing in the world and the rest of us aren't being pressured to conform to society.

Although that's not true for him anymore, is it?

He wears his own mask now, an aw-shucks smile that gives nothing about his opinions away. The perfect country boy, never disappointing his fans.

When did he start hiding himself like that?

The way Maverick keeps glancing in the rearview mirror pulls me out of my thoughts.

I turn my head, but there's nothing back there but open road. He wouldn't expect a car to come out of nowhere, and I wouldn't be surprised to hear we're the only ones who've been out here for days.

The song changes, and Colt's head rests on the back seat, voice lower but still lost to the world.

Turning back, I'm just in time for Maverick to check that mirror again, gaze lingering a little too long.

My neck tingles, a thrill skating over my skin, when the corners of Maverick's lips twitch, a hint of a curl tugging at the end.

My chest constricts as his expression melts from stern, revealing that boyishness I remember.

Whether he knows it or not, something's changing between them.

"Fuck! Turn right there!" Colt shouts from the back, the turn only feet ahead.

Maverick slams on the brakes, causing the truck to lurch with the change of momentum.

I'm flung forward, my seat belt ready to catch me, but Maverick's faster.

His arm shoots out, catching my sternum and holding me in place.

Reminding me that feet out the window is a bad position if we get into an accident.

I've seen enough ER nurses make posts warning about this to have me pulling my legs in, placing my feet firmly on the floor.

"What the actual fuck?" Maverick growls, and there's enough menace in it to have me shuddering.

As if sensing my response, his hand drops to my thigh, his calloused thumb arching across my bare skin in calming strokes.

I'm tingling for a whole new reason, his touch sending heat licking up my inner thigh.

I choke back a moan when my clit pulses in response.

"Sorry, man, I didn't see the sign," Colt says sheepishly, leaning over the console. "We're almost there."

"Better be," Maverick grunts out, that boyish look nowhere to be found.

If it wasn't for the fact that he's left his rough palm on my thigh, I would think he's firmly back in stern old man mode.

My nipples harden, and it has nothing to do with the cold air pumping out of the vents, and my breath grows shallow.

If he notices, he doesn't show it.

Instead, his focus is straight ahead.

He almost looks cold while he's setting me on fire, and I want to punch that look off his face.

It's not fair that I'm going through this while he's calmly unaffected.

"Turn left up ahead."

Maverick's forced to release me to turn the wheel.

Good, because any longer and my panties will be soaked.

His hand doesn't return, and I refuse to admit that I'm just a teeny bit disappointed.

Throat thick, I swallow hard and force my attention to the scenery passing us by.

A canopy of trees lines the road, leaving splashes of sunlight peeking through between the leaves.

The truck slows as we roll up to a dead end.

Getting out, it feels like the world ends right here, in this quiet, nowhere spot.

Colt's already ahead of us, arms filled to the brim as he walks right through the trees.

"Come on, you two," he calls back over his shoulder, not slowing his stride.

Maverick falters, brows rising, before going after him.

The space opens into a wide-open field that looks like it goes on for days.

My breath catches as I take it all in.

Wildflowers of every color grow so crowded they overlap each other as they fill the air with their sweet scent.

They stop where the ground grows sandy, only a light covering of grass as it leads down toward a lake.

The water's a deep blue, sparkling where the light catches the surface, and a long wooden deck reaches out into the center.

"It's good, right?" Colt asks from where he's spreading a large blanket in the shade of an old oak tree.

"More than good." I can't help but smile at him.

He really outdid himself with this one.

If he keeps up, I really am going to fall for him.

Who wouldn't?

Maverick helps him lay everything out, popping open the cooler and holding out a bottle of water to me.

I swipe it from his hand, cracking the top and drinking over half of it in one go.

It goes down easy, cooling my dry throat.

Both boys are frozen in place as they watch me.

Colt holds a tray halfway in the air, like someone hit pause on the world as he went to put it down.

Maverick's own water is hovering where he stopped midway to taking a sip.

The weight of their attention is hot against my skin, a smothering intensity that makes it hard to breathe, like being submerged into a bath.

Colt clears his throat, and the world spins again, all of us jolted back to the present.

My chest rises and falls as I get myself together and take my seat on the blanket, legs crossed ahead of me, elbows supporting my back.

The shade provides just enough shelter to cut through the blistering heat, providing bliss on a summer day.

Something drops on my stomach, and I peel my eyes open to find a container filled with fruit, the plastic sides wet with condensation.

"Thought you might be hungry."

Colt's charming the socks off me right now, and I don't know what to do about it.

I fall back on the safety of our usual teasing. "Is this how you seduce all the ladies?"

His brows shoot up. "I'm insulted that you think I have to seduce them."

An exasperated breath huffs out of me. "Oh, sorry... I've yet to witness this magic of yours."

"You'll know when I seduce you."

When.

Sparks start at my toes and race upward until they buzz in my entire body.

He goes back to pulling stuff out of the cooler like he didn't just rock the foundation I'm sitting on.

It's Maverick who pulls me out of it.

He's standing at the end of the blanket, only a few feet from me, when he lifts his shirt to wipe sweat off his face, revealing stacks of carved muscle.

Deeply tanned skin from days spent in the sun shines with the sheen of sweat.

Mouth watering, all I can think about is how he'd feel beneath my tongue as I ran it along the hollows between his abs.

I crisscross my knees in an attempt to ease the ache building between my thighs.

Maverick's dark eyes roam over me, devouring my reaction, a devious smirk slicing his lips just before he removes his shirt completely.

I inhale sharply, lungs constricting at the delicious view he's given me.

Muscles seem to multiply as I progress from his large chest, down his abs, and follow the corded line that disappears into the waistband of his jeans.

All I hear is static, as every inch of him is displayed.

"Y... you're hot?" I stutter unintentionally, my brain completely melted.

Maverick huffs out a laugh, looking altogether too pleased with himself. "Yeah, that's why I took my shirt off."

"You're not playing fair, asshole." Colt reaches back and pulls his white T-shirt over his head in one fluid movement.

He's only inches away, beside me on the blanket.

He flexes under my attention and leans in close enough that I can feel the heat wafting off him.

Frozen in place, I can't look away. Any rational thoughts have left the building, and I'm seconds from spontaneously combusting.

He reaches over me, his arm brushing mine, and it feels like he's branded me with his touch.

The bastard just smiles, sitting back in his place.

It takes me a second to realize he's grabbed the container of fruit, and now he's pulling out a triangular piece of watermelon.

I close my eyes and groan when his teeth sink into it in a last-ditch effort to maintain any sense of sanity.

There's rustling, but I refuse to look.

These dickheads know exactly what they're doing to me, and it's so not fair.

Damn their competitive nature.

What happened to harmless teasing?

When did it change to who can cause me to soak my panties first?

"Alright, leave her alone for a bit. She looks like she can use a break," Maverick says, amused.

I glare at him through slitted eyes, not trusting whatever he's up to.

Colt rises first, grabbing two fishing poles and a black rectangle that I recognize immediately.

"Where did you find it?"

"Stuck under the back seat."

I gasp, cradling my missing Kindle to my chest like a lifeline. Not having it during the long drives has been a special form of torture. Grateful that I got it back, I kiss the device. It's the best chance I have to dissociate enough to ignore the fact that these two are halfway to being naked.

Thank you, fictional hot hockey players. Thank you.

Even with my book to distract me, I still can't help but look up.

They're fishing, but I'm not sure you could use the word *together*.

Each of them are on opposite sides of the dock, facing away from the other.

At this point, I can't imagine spending that much energy just to hate someone.

Not that I think they do.

They've made it entirely too obvious that wanting to hate someone and actually hating someone are two completely different things.

Which is why seeing them try so hard has amusement bubbling in my chest and a soft chuckle escaping my lips.

Colt glances toward me, his head tilted to the side as if asking what's so funny, but I shake my head.

Not a chance I'm explaining any of this to him.

Calm settles over us as time disappears. The only

sounds are the birds singing in the trees and the leaves rustling overhead.

When I finally look up again, the sun's warm evening light dips around their silhouettes, making them glow.

I groan into my palms, dropping onto the blanket, eyes squeezed firmly shut.

How the hell did they manage to look like gods out here?

Meanwhile, my hair is stringy with sweat, sticking to my skin where it's escaped my hair tie.

My dress is rumpled from hours lying on the ground, and I can't be sure, but it's likely my makeup is doing its best to wander in the heat.

I'm just grateful for waterproof mascara since it's the only thing stopping me from looking like a raccoon right now.

I don't look, even as Maverick and Colt's footsteps grow closer, until they're standing over me, causing my senses to come alive.

At this point, I'm not above begging them for mercy.

I've kissed them both, and it would be so easy to fall into them.

God, I want to.

The ground practically shakes as they collapse on either side of me, their proximity so close it raises the hair on my arms.

It's entirely too awkward to lie here with them sitting so close, and I know there's zero chance I can pretend to be sleeping.

So I pull myself up to a seated position.

There's a pop and hiss of a can opening, and then Colt's head lands on my shoulder, hair tickling my neck.

I squirm, but he catches me around the waist.

"Stay still. I'm enjoying this."

Maverick hums in agreement, long, thick fingers entwining with mine.

"What?" I choke.

Colt chuckles, lifting so that his breath brushes my ear, sending goose bumps prickling down my neck.

"Thank you."

Molten heat brands me, stealing my breath.

It takes several moments before I'm recovered enough to process what he said.

"U-uh, but you're the one that brought me here."

Maverick circles my jaw with his fingers, turning me toward him.

"Yeah, but it wouldn't have happened if you weren't here."

He's so close, nose brushing mine.

My mouth opens slightly, and I desperately want to close the distance between us, to feel those hot lips on mine.

It's like being dropped into a volcano and then asked to swim.

It would be so easy, simply lift my chin and let him take me...

My nipples tighten as I fight the temptation, and I know if I don't do something now I won't be able to stop.

I gulp in a lungful of air, ignoring the delirious mix of their scents, and thrust myself up to my feet, jostling the boys from their positions.

"Last one in is a loser!" I yell over my shoulder, knowing I need every inch of a head start I can get.

I smirk, the guys quick on my heels, unable to withstand a challenge.

My lungs burn as I run at full speed, nearly tripping as I rip my dress over my head, tossing it to the side.

Matching groans and the stumble of someone behind me follow.

"So not fucking fair, Callie."

"Who said anything about playing fair? I want to win."

And with that, I unclasp my bra, the wood planks of the dock digging into my soles as I clear the remaining few feet.

Air rushes by me, followed by splashes of water. My forward momentum doesn't allow me to stop, so I jump into the water after them.

I splutter as I come up, frustration coating my voice. "Oh, come on."

"Loser!" Colt sticks out his tongue, and I snap out a hand, nearly fast enough to catch it.

His mouth snaps shut, eyes wide on me in shock.

Maverick's laugh echoes in the wide-open space, the sound so free it has my chest aching.

I'm not the only one affected. Colt's staring, his mouth dropped open as he treads water.

Warmth takes over Colt's features as he watches his

friend like he hasn't seen him in a long time like he missed him.

Colt catches me and dunks me under the water, holding me down as I pinch his sides.

We've done this countless times before, but I'm older and sneakier now.

I twist his nipple, hard, and he flinches back from me.

"Who are you calling a loser, loser?"

It's probably the most immature thing I've said in my adult life, and I welcome the laughter that breaks free from my chest.

It takes over me, filling my veins with coursing electricity, making me feel alive.

I'm still smiling when I open my eyes, finally getting myself under control.

I laughed so hard it hurt not from the laughter but from how badly I knew I'd miss this.

When I open my eyes again, I'm met with matching hooded expressions.

I swallow hard. Not even the spring-fed water cools me down as they circle me.

"Stay back," I warn, palms smacking against the surface, spraying them as I kick my feet, swimming into deeper water, putting some space between us.

"Chicken?" Colt calls out, but I don't rise to the bait.

Instead, kicking my feet, I lean backward until the lake cups the back of my head.

The last rays of sun cling to the sky, painting it in deep reds and oranges.

A calm weight settles over me, making my limbs feel heavy as I tread water, even as the cool depth calls me under.

Maverick's a few feet ahead of me, his body haloed in the fading amber light.

His mouth is parted, chest rising and falling like he's trying to steady something unruly inside him.

I follow his gaze.

Colt's floating on his back, the water lapping softly around his waist, hips just beneath the surface.

Every movement is effortless, slow and deliberate, like he knows he's being watched.

Like he *wants* to be.

The tension crackles across my skin like static before a storm, humming through the space between them.

Colt turns his head, locking eyes with Maverick.

There's no animosity, no challenge.

Just something slow and charged. Curious. Open.

Something that makes it hard to breathe.

Maverick glances away, and I can't tell if the pink covering his cheeks is from the sunset or him blushing, but for the first time since I've been back, I think they really will be okay.

Colt swims up to me, a lazy smile curving his lips, as he grips my foot under the water and tugs me to him.

I gasp as skin touches skin from my hip bones along my side, pressing into the curve of my breast.

My entire body ignites, flames branding where we touch.

Maverick cups the back of my neck with one hand, startling me, and splays his fingers along my stomach with the other.

Unable to stop it, I moan, turning into a whimper when their hands begin to move. Realizing where we're heading way too fast. I'm not quite ready for lake sex.

That doesn't mean I can't have a little bit of fun.

Shoving them backward, I use the force to propel myself to the dock, gripping the edge, and pulling myself up and out of the water before they can do anything.

I don't look back as I lean over and grab my thrown-off clothes from the ground, giving them a nice view.

"Fuck," echoes from the water, the sound rough and wanting.

My grin grows into a smile, so wide it takes over my face.

Who's the loser now?

Chapter 19

Maverick

Am I dead? Did I finally get stomped by a bull and this is the afterlife?

Water trails down Callie's back, along the ridge of her spine, leading straight to her see-through panties. The thin fabric clings to her ass, the tan of her skin showing through. If that wasn't enough to drown me, one side is riding up, revealing the entire curve of one cheek.

My rock-hard cock's the only thing stopping me from chasing after her, forcing me to tread water if I don't want Callie to see exactly what she's doing to me.

Her ass is so fucking delicious I want to sink my teeth where it creases into her thigh. Fill my palms with the smooth globes, spread them apart

She bends over to pick up her dress, and a whimper catches in my throat.

The pink outline of her pussy's displayed through her translucent panties...

"Fuck," Colt grunts, his eyes hot on her, mouth open wide enough it's a miracle he's not drooling.

That settles the afterlife question.

Clearly, I'm in hell if this asshole's beside me.

He's too distracted to notice the way he's edging closer, how his arm keeps brushing mine again and again, like he's testing how much I'll take.

Each graze lights me up, a pulse of heat chasing every nerve ending, my skin prickling like it's starving for more.

I wait for the disgust. The revulsion.

Wait for the urge to shove him off, dunk his smug face under water, and hold it there.

But I don't move.

I can't.

The sinking sun throws shadows across his face, his wet hair slicked back, droplets carving slow trails down his neck, over his collarbone, disappearing into the water.

And his eyes... even in the dark, I can feel the intensity in them fixed on her like she's the only thing tethering him to the surface.

That hunger, that desperation. It's radiating off him in waves, and his own hard-on's the only thing keeping him submerged.

"What the hell are you looking at?" Colt jerks back, face scrunched up in disgust.

My stomach twists, turning my gut into knots as the revulsion I was looking for finally settles where it belongs.

"Get your moaning under control," I mutter, turning back to Callie.

She's pulling her dress over her head, and I enjoy the way Colt sputters.

From his lack of response, he must not be sure if he really was moaning.

What would that even sound like?

A low, guttural groan, or would he release a high-pitched keen, the kind that begs to be fucked?

The hem of Callie's dress drops to her thigh, and I can finally inhale.

She knocks the breath from my lungs without even trying.

She's always stunning, but when she turns back my way, her beaming smile slams into me, punches straight into my ribs, and grips my pounding heart.

She's practically glowing, pouring her warmth into me, filling me up until it feels like I'm going to explode.

Eight years ago, I'd been too young and stupid to understand what these feelings meant.

What it means to feel empty when someone's not around, then complete the second they walk into the room.

When they're having a hard day, so your sole goal becomes making them smile. Not because you pity them, but because it physically pains you to see them sad.

I didn't know back then that everything I was doing was because I was in love with Callie.

I hadn't figured out how to separate what we had from friendship.

Fuck, I've spent all this time miserable, thinking I missed her.

It's so much more than that.

Having her here feels like earning the gold buckle while winning the lottery at the same time.

It's such a one-in-a-billion impossible opportunity that I'm not fucking it up.

This time, I'm going to tell her how I feel.

I'm going to convince her to stay after the circuit's over.

Or whatever.

We'll figure it out.

I can go where she is and commute during the season.

Anything, so long as I don't lose her again.

This time she's going to know exactly what she means to me and if she still wants to leave…

Colt groans. "She's doing this on purpose."

I laugh, my dick still rock-hard. "Definitely."

Chapter 20

Colt

"You hit the dirt hard last week but looked locked in out there today. How much sweeter does this ride feel after the last event?" Jimmy from *Pro-Rodeo Magazine* asks from the front seat.

I lean into the microphone sitting on the table in front of me, plastering on my best country boy smile. I can't count the number of post-ride press events I've been to, and I know exactly how to give them what they want.

"I'll tell you, Jimmy. It sure hurts a lot less," I joke, earning a few chuckles. "In all seriousness, it felt great up there tonight. Like that bull was made just for me. Couldn't have been sweeter."

It's a lie. It felt like my shoulder was being torn apart the entire time, but I keep that shit to myself. No fan wants to hear their rider whine. They see us as something inhuman. Unbreakable. I catch movement at the back of the room. Callie slips in and leans against the wall, arms loosely crossed. She looks tired, not used to the constant days on the road moving from one place to the next. I'll make sure we stay another night here, let her get some rest before heading out.

But she still looks damn good in those jean shorts, cut high up on her thighs, revealing inch after inch of golden skin that has my mouth watering and my cock growing stiff. The table is the only thing saving me from embarrassment. She smirks when I nearly miss the next question I'm so stuck staring at her.

"A few points behind Kane, momentum on your side, feels like blood in the water. Do you think this rivalry brings out your best?"

Kane... they're never going to get over asking me about Maverick, always looking for that juicy sound bite, and I'm here to give them what they want.

"There's no slacking off when going up against Kane. He's a good opponent. He's smooth on the bull and works hard, but I work harder. I don't need him to show me how to be the best. I'm already the best," I answer, giving them the cocky bull rider they expect.

Does Kane bring out my best? Yeah, he fucking does. Competing against him, crushing him, has been my main motivation for a while now. Not that I'm admitting that to anyone. He knows exactly how to piss me off and drive me harder to kick his ass the next time. Rinse and repeat.

My fingers drum against the table as time drags on while they run through the standard questions. I haven't been able to pull my attention away from Callie this entire time. A rider I'd like to kill has been leaning in close, whispering in her ear for the last five minutes. He brought her a water, and the smile she gave him damn near had me off this stage. Jealousy is not a good look on me, but at this point, I'm so far gone I've accepted it.

"Be honest are you sick of hearing Maverick Kane's name yet?"

Chuckles fill the room.

The next reporter cuts me a break and tees me up with an easy one. "After everything your body's been through, has there ever been a moment where you thought, 'This might be the last one'?"

"Never," I reply instantly. "Injuries are another part of the sport. Hell, can you call yourself the best if you've never ridden with a few broken bones?" I pause for the laughter, then continue. "You don't become a bull rider if you're not prepared to come face-to-face with death. It's staring the reaper in the eyes and telling him 'not today' that makes you a winner."

I perk up when Callie waves the guy off, clearly broken hearted. That's right, asshole. She's already taken.

Callie's arms cross tightly over her chest, and her head bows low. She looks like she's protecting herself from something. If that asshole said something to her...

The reporters lean into questions about my injuries. Always a fun topic for them, less for me.

"Just how many broken bones have you had?"

"Counting when my ribs pierced my lungs?" I smirk. "Too many to count."

They eat this shit up. The more gruesome we get hurt, the bigger the high when we win. Fans get to feel the rush without the pain, but they love hearing all about it.

The room laughs, but Callie's not laughing. My gut clenches when the last of her color drains from her face, like she's just come face-to-face with a ghost. The more they ask about my injuries, the worse she gets, until I'm starting to climb out of my seat for real.

"I think that's enough for tonight. I've got to go and ice some of these aches before they settle in."

"One more question."

I pause.

"When it comes down to Vegas, do you really think you can beat Kane?"

My molars crush together, and I take three calming breaths before I can answer the question. He's really digging into me with this one.

"The championship comes down to who's willing to put the most on the line, and it's going to be me."

My satisfaction with my answer disintegrates when Callie disappears from the room like she's being chased. Even from here, her movements are frantic, jerky as she pushes through the crowd and escapes out the back.

Maverick's standing at the end of the table, up next to take the hot seat, but his eyes are firmly fixed on where our girl disappeared.

My shoulder brushes his when I walk by, and he shifts closer.

"Find out what's wrong. Text me, and I'll be right

behind you," he rasps, a low rumble edged with concern. It holds a weight that says, *I'm trusting you.*

"I was going after her whether you asked me to or not," I hiss but then soften my tone. "I'll text you when I find her."

Finding Callie isn't as easy as it should be. She's not in the halls or our locker room. By the time I search out back where our trucks are, my heart's starting to drum in my ears. Where the hell did she go? She looked sick as hell by the time she took off. Thoughts of the worst flood over me. She could be passed out somewhere, needing me. Fear and frustration course through my veins as I turn on my heels and make my way back inside.

"Fuck, what's gotten into you?" Luke stops me with a hand on my chest before I can make it through the door. "Easy, killer. Your girl caught a ride back to the hotel with some of the guys."

"What the fuck? And you just let her?"

"Let her?" he scoffs. "Oh, you're funny."

I've got nothing to say to that because he's right, but that doesn't piss me off any less.

"Listen, I'll take pity on you and not drag this out. I checked. She went with Samson. You know how much he loves his wife. He'd never let anything happen to her."

Luke's words have some of the tension uncoiling in my shoulders. Samson's a good guy. Even if one of the other guys is an asshole, Samson won't put up with that shit.

"I would have held her off. Come up with some excuse. But she didn't look good though."

My skin itches with the need to get to her, to see for myself that she's alright, to take care of her if she isn't. I'm scanning the parking lot for my truck when reality slams into me. Fuck. I don't want to waste time waiting for Maverick's interview to end.

"Give me your keys." I hold my hand out to Luke.

"What the hell, man?"

"I'm serious. Give them to me." I can't hide the growl in my voice, and his brows shoot to his hairline.

"I still have my interview. How am I supposed to get back?"

"Catch a ride with Maverick."

"Fuck... fine. But you owe me." He shoves the keys in my hands.

"Yeah... whatever you want," I say and register his surprised look before hauling ass to his truck. There's no way he could ask for something that I care about more than getting to Callie as soon as possible. Just thinking about her alone in the motel room while not feeling well is eating me alive.

I pull up Maverick's number while waiting at the longest damn red light on the planet. There's a maximum of four cars traveling on this road a day; what the hell do they need a light for?

I haven't used his number in a while, so I forgot I named him Buttlicker.

> Me: Callie went to the motel with Samson. I took Luke's truck and on my way.

> Buttlicker: What's taking you so long.

This fucker. I shove it into my pocket. It buzzes again, and a muscle twitches in my cheek. *This fucking asshole.* It keeps buzzing until I finally can't take anymore.

My thumb slips over the Accept button before I can even register it's a call.

"Listen to me." Maverick sounds dead serious, and shivers crawl up my neck, raising the back of my hair. "There's something going on with her that she's not telling us. I found her in a rough way after the last event."

"And you're just telling me this now?" I grit out, knuckles white on the steering wheel as I take the next turn too fast, tires squealing in my wake.

"She doesn't want to tell anyone."

"Oh, but she told you?"

"No, she didn't tell me. I found her having a fucking panic attack."

He might as well have punched through my chest. "What... what do you mean?"

"I mean she was gasping for breath and didn't even know I was there. So yeah, hurry your ass up and get to her."

The truck bounces as the tire rolls over the curb, too impatient to drive to the entrance.

"I'm at the motel. Get here. Now."

Grateful we keep our adjoining door open, I walk right into her room, my mind still reeling from what Maverick just told me.

"Oh my God," Callie squeaks, hand squeezing the top of her towel. "You scared me."

"I scared you? Why did you run off like that?" The words flow on their own, my only focus getting to her. Once I'm close enough, I can make out the pink swelling around her eyes and the red tinge to her nose. There's a tearing sensation in my chest, and I wrap my arm around her back, pulling her against me. I run my thumb under her lashes. "Have you been crying?"

"Just a little dust in my eye. You're overreacting." She struggles to break free, but I don't let her.

My girl is lying to me, and I want to know why.

"What's wrong? I can't fix this unless you tell me."

"I'm not asking you to fix this," she whispers, then takes a deep, jagged breath and does her best to smile. "Just don't get hurt."

"You worried about me?"

She flinches, facing down, a slight tremble running through her, ripping me apart. I've been such an idiot. Of course she's scared after what happened with her dad. And I'm out here saying I'll put it all on the line to win the championship. That facing death is a part of the sport with my full fucking chest. Guilt's a twisting rope, knotting my gut.

All of this is because of me.

"I'll be more careful. I won't get hurt anymore," I promise.

"Tell that to the bull," she says with a hollow laugh.

"Yeah, those Harper Ridge Ranch ones are vicious." I

try to make a joke, but I'm so far off the mark. She jerks in my hold. I might as well have hit her.

I'm not good at this. I can play the crowd as the cocky rider, but these soft moments?

I'm lost. I cup her face in my palms, conscious of how delicate she feels in my hold.

"Hey, I'm really going to be okay. I'm good at this. I know when to bail when things get sticky."

Even as I say it, it rings false.

Winning in bull riding means to be bold, reckless.

"You can't bail if you want the championship," Callie says, voice soft and understanding. She knows. Of course she does.

"I..." Fuck. Can I win and ride cautiously? Is that even possible?

There's a spread between me and the guy below me, but I won't catch Maverick.

"That's what I thought." Her soft lips meet mine, snapping me out of my thoughts.

"I'm not asking you for that. I will never ask you to give anything but your all. Riding is your life. It's everything you worked so hard for. Every torn muscle, blood, sweat, and tears you've poured into this have been to win."

"Fuck." I kiss her hard, teeth clinking against hers as I frantically pull her closer. She's handing me the whole damn world, and I don't even know if I deserve it.

We break apart, each gasping for breath, and I grit out, "This isn't over."

Her fingers dig into my hair, nails scraping my scalp, as she tries to take control of the kiss.

I'm barely holding on as is. I know there's still more left we need to talk about.

"Callie," I pant, straining to keep my shit together.

She smiles at me, and it's so devious I already know I'm fucked before she lets go of her towel.

The white fabric hits the floor, and suddenly, it's her skin pressed under my palm.

I groan deep in my throat, blood pulsing to my cock, making it so hard it hurts.

I've never claimed to be a saint, so I take what she's offering, let her distract me away from what she doesn't want to talk about.

I run my hand up and down her back in a slowly growing arc with each pass.

My fingers travel from the base of her neck all the way down to the swell of her ass.

Goose bumps rise under my touch, and it's hard for me to take my next breath.

She's so sensitive, body responding to my every move.

I shift lower, cupping her ass, and *fucking come apart* when she whimpers against my neck, pressing her hips against mine.

"Asshole. You were supposed to text me." Maverick's yell can be heard from around the corner, seconds before he walks through the adjoining door and freezes in place.

Callie stiffens in my arms, trembling fingers curling

into the fabric of my shirt, holding on to me. With shallow breaths, she waits for Maverick's reaction.

I hold her firmly in place when she squirms, flight instincts kicking in. There's no way I'm letting her go now.

He takes his time, soaking in Callie's naked body, pressed against mine.

His gaze stalls where her fingers clasp me to her, then where I'm still gripping her ass. "Well, don't stop on my account."

"I... I... uh," Callie starts but stutters, not knowing how to go forward.

"I'm going to need you to tell me what you want," Maverick says, taking a step closer. His large frame fills her entire vision.

"I want... I..."

Callie's heart pounds into my chest, and her chin trembles as she tries to come up with an answer.

I glare at Maverick. He better hurry the fuck up he's scaring our girl.

"Do you want me to leave, Wildflower?" Maverick rasps, throat raw, pain audible in his question.

It's his turn to stiffen, jaw clenched, arms crossed over his chest like he's bracing for her response.

I've seen him stare down bulls and not look this terrified. The tendons in his neck are pulled taut, and a muscle ticks in his jaw from the force of keeping himself in place as he waits for her answer.

"I don't want you to." She sucks in a ragged breath. "I don't want either of you to go."

I dig my fingers into the soft rounds of her ass, squeezing it hard in approval.

A soft whimper escapes her lips, and my cock jerks in my pants, straining to escape.

If we don't hurry it the hell up, I'll embarrass myself by coming in my pants.

"Just keep it fair."

It's a low command, Maverick's tone firm, but even he can't hide the heat, the desperation to get to her.

Fuck.

We're really doing this.

"I will."

It's a whispered promise, nearly impossible to hear, but Maverick must know what she said because he pulls his shirt off with one hand, revealing a chest carved from years of riding, of holding on through every twist and buck.

The shadows catch on every line of him.

He's not just strong but he's built for control, for endurance.

And fuck me, I notice.

My mouth waters. I swallow it down, but it lingers, thick in my throat.

I shouldn't be okay with this.

I should be jealous. Angry.

He's my rival. The one person who knows exactly how to push me over the edge.

But instead of fury, I feel... calm. Settled.

Like some missing gear inside me just clicked into place.

Because watching him move toward her, toward us feels right.

Undeniably, gut-deep right.

Callie holds her breath between us, her eyes wide and glassy, searching mine for an answer.

And she's going to get it. Every fucking inch of it.

"Keep it fair, Callie," I say, low and rough, just to see her tremble.

Her breath stutters. Tears bloom at the corners of her eyes overwhelmed, beautiful, desperate and I catch them with my thumbs, never looking away.

She's here. With *us*.

And even though we're seconds from wrecking her in all the best ways, I feel the wildest need to *cherish* her. To make sure she knows this isn't just about sex.

It's about *finally* having her. The *three* of us. All in.

Her lips ghost against mine, her voice just as shaky as her hands.

"I promise."

Then she kisses me again, making it clear just how much she means it.

She wants us both, needs us both, equally.

There's only one girl in the world who could handle us both, and she's right here in my arms.

I kiss her back, breathing in her eager moans as she rubs her hips into me, directly into my swollen cock.

My gaze meets Maverick's dark one as he presses against her back, wrapping her hair around his palm, tugging it to the side, and whispers into her neck:

"*Good girl.*"

Chapter 21

Callie

Maverick uses his grip on my hair to tug my head to the side, revealing more of my neck. He takes advantage of the space he created, his hot breath sending shivers sparking down my spine and leaving embers in their wake. Colt captures my moan, growling into my mouth as I dig my nails into his shoulders.

I vaguely process the fact that I'm doing this with my childhood friends. That's not why I came here, and I shouldn't be doing this. It's selfish, and greedy, and everything wrong with me. I'm getting too close, and we're all going to get burned. But the heat of their mouths, the roughness of their calloused palms traveling over every inch of me, the way their clothes rub against my naked body have pleasure pushing out every other thought, grounding me into this moment until nothing else matters.

I bare my throat, and it's all the permission Maverick needs. His burning tongue strokes me, open-mouthed kisses traveling from my collarbone to just below my ear. He hums, the vibration reverberating through my bones.

"Are you ready for this, Wildflower?"

Colt pulls back, blue eyes piercing mine, lust pulling his lids low. Their touch stills, waiting for my response, and I want to scream.

A flush crawls up my neck and floods my cheeks as embarrassment threatens to take over, but the way they're looking at me, like I'm their entire world, gives me the confidence to ask for what I want.

"Yes. I want you."

Matching growls rumble through me, heading straight to my core. Two sets of greedy hands stroke my arms, ribs, thighs, stoking an ever-growing heat within me. Thumbs graze the underside of my breast at the same time a touch ghosts over my clit, drawing out a low whimper from the back of my throat as they deny me the friction I need.

If these two keep teasing me like this, I'm not going to survive. Frustrated, I whine, gripping Colt's shirt, hating any barrier between us, and try to rip it off. The fabric stretches around his neck in my uncoordinated haste.

Colt's forehead drops to mine, his chuckle fluttering over me. He runs his nose along mine. I bite into his full bottom lip, and he laughs harder.

"You never could be patient, Sunshine," he says, removing his shirt in one smooth movement.

Hot skin connects to mine, and I moan, the sound coming from deep within.

The sensation of Maverick's bare chest branding my

back, pressing me harder into Colt, has pleasure rippling under my skin. I could stay between them just like this for eternity, living off their heat, but it's not enough to dim the thrumming between my thighs.

The accumulation of every graze, look, and near touch over the last week explodes into desperation. I'm yanking at Colt's pant button, reaching back and blindly doing the same to Maverick's. He takes over, shoving his pants and boxers down.

The weight of his cock sears into my ass as it slaps against me, followed by Colt's wet tip coating my stomach.

I hiss, sucking in air, fingers digging into their hair, pulling at the roots. I'm lost to the haze; all I want is for them to feel the same torment I do.

"More. I need more," I plead, unable to stop myself from rubbing into them, soaking in the way their lengths grind against me.

"You hear that, Colt?" Maverick reaches around, cupping my breasts in his palms. "She sounds so sweet when she begs for us." He squeezes hard and commands, "Do it again. Beg for it, and I promise we'll make you feel good." He bites my earlobe before sucking it. "So fucking good, Callie. All you have to do is beg."

I've never begged for anything in my entire life, never wanted to, but his command tightens low in my stomach, my clit pulsing in response. I want to for them. I want them to know just how much I crave them.

"Please." My voice is shattered, but it's enough.

"That's it, my girl," Maverick praises, rolling my

nipples between his thumbs and fingers. He doesn't stop kissing me, sucking, biting.

His cock presses against my tailbone in short thrusts, like he doesn't even know he's doing it. It's so primal it feels like he's going to eat me whole.

Lips press to mine, a wet tongue running over the seam. I open my eyes to see Colt's, the blue almost completely swallowed by black. It's a heady feeling to have those lust-filled eyes focused solely on me, and I get lost in them.

He's still holding my gaze when he shifts, his cock aligning with my clit. I gasp with the contact, but it cuts off in a ragged inhale as he rolls his hips forward in a slow, languid motion, dragging his length against me.

Each stroke presses into my aching clit, providing the friction I desperately need.

My hips move on their own, chasing the pleasure he's stoking, each glide drawing me closer to the edge. I'm gasping for breath, tension building and building, my core pulsing. Whiny, greedy sounds pull from my throat, pleading for whatever they'll give me.

Pain radiates where Maverick pinches my nipples, twisting them before pressing his thumbs hard. It sends a shock straight to my core, and I arch into him for more, closing my eyes as he alternates between painful touches and soothing ones.

I reach back, sinking my nails into Maverick's shoulder while scratching lines into Colt's chest, leaving my own marks on them.

Colt pulls back, the head of his cock circling my clit before delving between my legs. He growls through clenched teeth as he slips easily through my thighs.

Maverick's feet kick mine inward until they're crushed together. Colt's strokes stutter, a curse under his breath as I'm compressed around him.

"Jesus Christ," he hisses, gripping my hips and thrusting against me.

My pussy clenches every time the head of his cock nudges my entrance, desperate to pull him inside.

I keen in a desperate cry, the need so intense it scares me.

Maverick hums into my ear, sending shivers erupting over my skin. "You're okay. I've got you."

Kneading my breast with one hand, he dips the other between where Colt's and my bodies connect, instantly finding my clit.

"Right there," I rasp, no longer caring what I sound like, rolling my hips into Colts's cock, where it leaves a slick path of precum.

Colt loses control, fucking against me, his strokes frantic as he chases his release. He grips my jaw in his hands, gaze piercing into mine, guiding me higher.

Maverick's expert fingers swirl and twist.

I'm so close it hurts. Every muscle in my body contracts, begging to be released. I'm a trembling mess, legs giving out, counting on them to catch me.

My orgasm builds and builds and builds, that pulsing heat tightening until it feels like I'm going to crack. My eyes close, but Colt's grip keeps my head from falling back.

"Look at me." His voice is ragged, breaths coming out hard. "I want to watch you come."

His words slam into me at the same time Maverick rolls my clit, shattering me into a million pieces.

Colt pulls out, stroking his cock in his fist, and groans as he spurts cum all over my stomach and the back of Maverick's hand.

I don't have the energy to worry about his reaction, laying my weight against Colt's chest, quivering with the aftershocks of my orgasm.

My head's buzzing, filling my ears with static as I gradually come down.

Maverick's controlled thrusts, slow and lazy against my ass, relight the ember low in my stomach.

His palm leaves where it's been resting on my lower stomach, and his weight lifts from my back.

Still breathing into Colt's chest, I try to clear my mind to focus on Maverick.

I can feel his wrist ghost along my hip, then back in an up-and-down motion.

I shift my hips back, trying to press into him, earning me one of his rare chuckles.

"My needy girl."

His cock presses into the seam of my ass before gliding through it easily.

The movement I'd felt earlier was him lubricating himself. Holy shit.

I bite back my moan with the realization that he used Colt's cum to coat himself.

He's using my ass to fuck himself, pressing the halves to mold around him harder with each roll of his hips.

No one has ever touched me like this, and the newness of the feeling has me arching into it, resting my head against Maverick's shoulder.

Colt drops to his knees, his firm grip on my waist the only thing keeping me upright as he looks up at me with hunger, his warm breath puffing against my skin.

The sinister curve to his lips is the only warning I have before he sucks my clit in hard.

Still sensitive from my recent orgasm, I scramble to get away, but I'm caught between them.

Maverick continues to fuck himself against my ass while Colt devours my core.

I squirm against the pressure they're building, not ready for what they're giving me.

"I can't… I can… I need to stop…I need." I huff.

My words don't match the way my body's reacting, rocking into both of them.

"Please," I beg, no longer sure what I'm begging for, suddenly feeling empty.

Maverick groans, pushing two fingers against my lips until I open for him.

He pushes them so far back I nearly gag. "Suck."

I moan around him as their tastes fill my mouth.

I lose myself, sloppily following his orders, not caring how I look. I roll my tongue, sliding it between his fingers and around his knuckles, sucking him deeper into my throat.

Maverick's thrusts stagger, then grow harder as he ruts into my ass.

"Fuck, Callie," he murmurs into my neck, then sinks his teeth into it.

I whine, searching, and Colt reads me easily, sliding his fingers past my entrance and filling me completely, pumping them in and out at the same time as Maverick.

My head tilts back, straining my core, as my body goes white-hot, fire rippling through my nerves as I come again.

Maverick's groan is guttural, coming from deep within his chest, as hot liquid covers my ass.

The room swirls, and Colt stands just in time to catch me, banding an arm around my back, holding me firmly against his chest.

His lips run soft kisses along my forehead, temple, cheek, crooning nothing but mindless praise, while Maverick trails his fingers down my spine, ghosting across the skin until he reaches where he's marked me with his release.

His fingers swirl before dipping between my cheeks.

He hums low in his throat and releases a ragged breath.

"You look good covered in our cum."

Chapter 22

Colt

The thick strap cuts into my palm as I haul the heavy bag over my shoulder and carry it the twenty feet between Jimmy's door and his truck. When the guys knocked on my door promising beer in return for help loading their trucks, I was all for it. Have some drinks, joke around, and maybe even stretch out some of my sore muscles. Instead, it feels like I'm being baked alive by the sun.

This area's normally dry, but the oncoming storm has the air heavy with humidity. It's that uncomfortable feeling where everything clings to your clothes, hair, sweat mixed with dust. It feels like there's a film of dirt coating my skin.

Normally, any rider who's not set up with people to haul gear is in charge of getting their own equipment in and out of their room. It would be nice if they could leave their trucks loaded, but even in these small towns, it's easy to get your stuff stolen that way. I hate to admit it, but it's the other riders you've gotta watch out for.

It's been a long time since I've had to worry about it. My gear's now controlled by the company, and I don't miss lugging around my shit. Let's face it, the real reason I'm out here helping is because I still remember how much it sucked when nobody helped me.

The truck shakes as Maverick dumps a large gray steel box into the bed. Speak of one of the devils who never helped me out. I may not like him, and he may not lift a finger for me which probably just pissed me off more but he's a good guy to the rest of the crew. So I wasn't surprised to see him already out here helping by the time I came down.

This is how it is now, our truce firmly in place, both of us wanting Callie to be happy.

We've got a routine going where Maverick's asleep before I get into the room and gone before I wake up in the morning. It should be like sleeping alone with him firmly on his side and me on mine. It definitely shouldn't be keeping me up at night.

The way my heart races, threatening the structure of my ribs, is because of the upcoming rides. Definitely not his soft, steady breaths or the heat that always seems to seep from his side, invading mine.

Cheeks hot, I look anywhere but at Maverick. That's how I notice the large black smear running from the hem up the side of my shirt.

"Motherfucker..." I hiss under my breath and grab the

edge, pulling it over my head. Scrunching it like a makeshift towel, I wipe it along the top of my shoulders to the hollow of my neck before flipping it over and using the other side to mop my brow, cleaning the dirt and sweat that stings my eyes.

Another large bag is dropped into the truck. Maverick's looming presence at my side has me pulling my shirt away.

Dark, hooded eyes brand my chest. I suck in a breath, only to have Maverick turn without meeting my gaze.

There's a tingling electric current where I can still feel the weight of his stare. It has my chest growing tight and my breath shallow.

Shake it off, man. You're losing it.

I use the physical task of lugging gear, loading each rider's truck, to keep my mind blank. Not that I have any reason to think of someone... nah, no reason at all.

My shoulder aches where the two thin straps cut into my muscle, and I start to regret all my life choices. The short distance to the truck might as well be a mile.

Stacking it on top of the rest of the equipment, I sag in relief, pressing my palms on the tailgate while I catch my breath.

I don't notice Jimmy approaching from behind until he shouts, "Oh shit."

I turn in time to see the large box he's barely got control over, barreling toward my chest. I brace myself, muscles tensing for the inevitable collision.

Fuck, this is gonna hurt.

A wall shoves in front of me. Maverick grunts, stomach caving in and shoulders hunching over as he takes the full force of the impact. He clutches his side and winces from the strain.

"Be careful," he snaps, more like an accusation than a warning.

I glare at him, a smart retort on the tip of my tongue. My pride wants to keep its footing, wants to snap back with venom, but damn if it's not hard to stay angry at the guy who just saved my hide.

I swallow a sharp breath and mutter, "Give me a break, man."

"Oh my God. I am so sorry," Jimmy says, running his hands through his hair, his shoulders dropped low.

Maverick doesn't even look at him, still focused on me. "If you were paying attention, it wouldn't happen."

"Whatever," I murmur under my breath, having no idea what to say to the guy.

Jimmy's face is an open book, confusion scribbled all over it. He runs a hand through his hair, the wild red tangle falling back into place as if used to the abuse.

"Oh my God," he blurts, eyes jumping between me and Maverick. "I am so sorry. Wait...what the hell is happening here? Are you guys getting along? I never thought I'd see the day."

"Just because I'm not yelling at this asshole doesn't mean I don't still hate him. We're coexisting. That's it."

I ignore the way my voice is a little too defensive, a whisper at the back of my head saying maybe we're doing a little more than coexisting. There's been a shift between us, and I'm not sure how I feel about it.

Maverick ignores him, not bothering to waste words on what should be obvious.

Jimmy throws up his hands, backing away with the same helpless gesture he uses in poker games right before he folds.

"Fine, fine," he says, palms out like he's holding off a stampede. "I'm not getting in the middle of this. Again."

Several moments of heavy silence pass after Jimmy's gone before Maverick cuts in.

"What? No thank you?" His words are sharp, cutting.

It's all the reminder I need to snap me back to reality.

"You can fuck off," I spit out, still not sure what just happened but happy to go back to ignoring each other.

Curtis approaches, three beers in his hand, condensation sweating down the bottles.

I swallow hard, my throat dry just looking at them.

"That's it. All loaded up. Thanks for helping out."

Gratefully taking the beer he's holding out to me, I don't waste time popping the top and chugging the first half.

The shock of earlier hits me again: Maverick putting himself in danger to haul me out of it.

Why? Why would he risk himself like that, for me? After everything?

Confusion trickles in, weaving its way through the new cracks that have been gradually forming since Callie's arrival.

Maverick's already walking away by the time I lower the bottle from my lips, leaving me stranded in the thick of my own confusion.

"Hey," I yell after him, my voice raw and insistent. "It's fucking hot out here. Just get over yourself and hang out for a minute!"

He doesn't turn around, just keeps going, each step deliberate and infuriating.

I toss back more beer, a desperate attempt to cool down the fire inside me.

Why the hell would he do it? What makes him care so much?

My mind reels, spinning a dozen ways to make sense of what I can't seem to.

I could chase after him, confront him with the questions that are gnawing at me, but I don't.

The anger and confusion crash against each other, leaving a muddied wake of something far more unsettling.

"What crawled up his ass?" Curtis shakes his head.

"I don't know how you haven't laid him out over the years. He treats you like shit."

My nerves snap.

"That guy just loaded your truck for you," I shoot back. "You should worry about your own asshole tendencies."

"Hey, I was just saying... 'cause I know you two don't get along, and he just left without saying anything..." He stutters like he just realized he stepped on a land mine.

"Yeah... he's like that."

The bottle's empty when I go to take another sip, and I groan under my breath.

This guy's right. Maverick does normally treat me like shit. That's the norm between us. So why did he take a blow for me?

Sparks prickle along my skin, the unfamiliar feeling out of place when thinking of him.

Grabbing the back of my neck, my fingers come back sticky with sweat.

But first, I need to shower.

"Thanks for the beer," I mutter.

Curtis gestures toward where the parking lot wraps around the other side of the building.

"There's more where that came from. You helped a lot. I owe you. The rest of the guys are around the back."

"Nah, I'm good. I've got to wash the scum off me."

My face twists. "I'm fucking disgusting."

Just thinking about taking a shower has me almost forgetting about my unwanted roommate. Almost.

I insert my cordless earbuds, turning the song up until my mood starts to shift to match the raging beat as I make my way up the stairs to my room.

Nothing says *don't talk to me* like music at full blast.

Key card lifted at the ready, I hesitate at the door.

The last thing I wanna do is come face-to-face with Maverick until I know what I'm gonna say to him. Thanking him will be like eating sand, and it's gonna take more than one beer in the shower for me to be up to it.

He didn't have to take that blow for me. It would've been easier, safer for him to just let it happen.

Instead, he jumped in front of me, pushing me out of the way like some kind of fucking hero.

Fuck it.

The lock beeps, and the door clicks open. I take a long, slow inhale, bracing myself, then walk inside.

The room's small enough that a quick glance is all I need to know I'm the only one here.

I shouldn't be this relieved, but that doesn't stop my breath from flowing out with enough force to puff up my cheeks.

I kick off my boots, letting them land wherever they damn well please.

It's a rebellion of sorts, though not much of one, considering how many times I've gone through this same routine.

Shirt, pants, boxers. They all come off in a careless heap, my skin glad to be free of the day's grime.

I should be ashamed of how I've let the place go, but Maverick's quiet, orderly presence has always been enough to goad me into a small, defiant disaster.

The thing that gets under my skin is I've been acting more like a slob than usual, but he hasn't once given me shit for leaving my stuff on the floor even though I know it must bug him.

Every time I see that he folded my clothes and put them on the table, my gut twists.

He doesn't even have to say anything to make me feel guilty.

I pinch the bridge of my nose.

At least he's not here right now.

Thank God for small mercies and all that.

This way, I can take my shower and get the hell out of here.

Maybe even drink those beers the guys were promising.

I haven't taken out my earbuds yet, which is why I don't hear the sound of the shower until it's too late.

I freeze, feet planted to the floor, gripping the doorknob so tight my knuckles bleach white as I'm met with a view of water rushing over Maverick's naked body.

His back's to me, giving me the perfect shot of his broad shoulders, wider than mine, weaved with thick, corded muscles.

I follow the way they taper in at the waist and swallow hard.

I've never really looked at a man's ass before. It curves down, connecting with wide, thick thighs.

I've seen him a thousand times, more than that, but not like this.

Never like this.

He's leaning into his palm, braced against the shower wall, head dropped down.

My mouth grows dry, and I run my tongue along my bottom lip, biting the corner.

I know it's wrong.

I should say something. Should call out, turn away, anything but stand here, frozen.

But I don't.

I can't.

Time stops as the world tips on its axis.

The muscles in Maverick's back begin to tense and flex. His arm movement is slow and deliberate, and my eyes follow with a kind of dread fascination.

All of the blood abandons my brain, and it short-circuits.

Fuck.

He's fucking jerking off.

And I'm fucking watching him.

I can't look away. It's like I've been physically tied to this place.

My heart is thundering in my chest, bashing into my ribs, which heave with each of my shattering breaths.

I feel it then, the sharp stab of something primal and unwanted, and it hits hard, sending a jolt lancing down my spine.

Maverick's muscles contract, spine arching, chin tipping to the ceiling.

His low, guttural groan rips out of him, shattering the haze that's kept me chained here, replacing it with horror.

I stagger out.

The door closes behind me with a soft click as I sag into the wall, feeling it cold and unyielding against my skin, but inside...inside, I am molten and reeling.

The house I built in my mind. The one that keeps

everything securely in its place threatens to ignite and burn to ash as I process what I just saw.

Each breath is ragged and unsteady, and my body, fuck, my body is reacting in ways I never saw coming.

There's an overpowering need coursing through me, my abs flexing so tight they hurt.

This cannot be happening right now.

I am not turned on by that asshole.

I am not turned on by that asshole.

I am not turned on by that asshole.

I look down and an unrecognizable sound breaks from my lips and I thank God no one's here to hear it.

My cock's hard, the head pointed directly at me.

Precum pools at my tip, a visceral, humiliating confirmation that leaves me shaken.

All my walls, all my defenses, obliterated in an instant of naked, unwanted truth.

I'm fucked.

Utterly, completely fucked.

Chapter 23

Maverick

Livestock haulers kick up dust as they approach the venue where we'll be riding tomorrow night. Being first to see the bulls is a ritual I've kept up since I was a kid. Colt and I used to hang out for hours behind buildings, the smell of cow shit seeping into our jeans, just to get a glimpse at what riders would be up against. Callie never understood. She'd spent plenty of time dealing with ornery animals already and teased us mercilessly. She never got it. Not like Colt did.

The first truck pulls in, gravel crunching under its eight tires as the driver fluidly backs it into place. I whistle under my breath, impressed at how it lines up with the venue doors on the first try.

Grunts and kicks echo from inside, less than five feet from me. Not sure what they're pissed about. The NBRA's come a long way in making sure the bulls are comfortable. One of these beasts is going to try to kill me tomorrow, and it's traveling in better conditions than I am.

A small crowd gathers as the crew sets up rails leading from the truck to the stalls. I'm not the only one with this idea. Wranglers keep the crowd at a distance while they get ready to unload.

Sweat runs down my neck, pooling between my shoulder blades. I pull my hat lower and lean against the cool metal of the arena, watching as more trucks pull in like clockwork, lining up in a neat row. Spurs jingle on concrete as riders drift over to scope out the scene. They're not doing much different from what I'm doing, hanging around, seeing if they can guess the temperament of a bull before it's out of the chute. Some of them will get it right; some of them will end up in the hospital. Makes no difference to the bulls.

"Mr. Kane!" A high-pitched shout comes from across the parking lot. A boy who can't be older than ten races toward me at full tilt. His smile is taking over, bright and shining, when he skids to a halt.

A card with my face on it flutters in his hand. "Can I please get your autograph?"

I glance over, double-checking the safety rails are secure and they haven't started unloading yet.

"Real quick," I say, taking the card from him. I pull a pen from my back pocket, scrawl my name, and hand it back to him. I'm supposed to say something encouraging, something he'll remember. But Colt's the one who's always been good at that. So I hand the card back and point my chin to the lady with a camera phone standing across the parking lot. "Now, run back to your mom."

A chill slides up my spine as I hear the clanging of steel hitting the ground.

The safety rails.

A black bull barrels over them like they're made of air, its head low and turning left to right, hot gusts shooting from its nose. It's out for blood.

The kid. He's still standing halfway to his mom, frozen as the bull charges toward him. My body moves before I can even process, boots slamming against asphalt, arms outstretched and waving as I try to close the distance.

"Hey!" I yell, desperate to get the bull's attention. My voice is a raw scrape, my heart an electric jolt. "Over here!"

I'm too far, and the bull is too fast. My legs burn with each stride, fire igniting in my muscles, spreading through my chest as I push myself harder.

The bull's massive body looms like a nightmare on steroids, and I'm still ten feet away, still too far, brick wall coming for him. The boy's screams mingle with the cries of the crowd. White noise, just noise. His eyes are glued to the beast, feet stuck like he's sunk in quicksand, and I'm sure this is the last moment, the last second Colt comes out of nowhere, shoving the boy out of the way, knocking him to safety, and rolling like hell to avoid the hooves that snap the air where they've just been. He comes up, arms wide, hollering at the bull, trying to tempt it away.

Without slowing my momentum, I use the distraction to lift the boy into my arms and bring him to his mother.

Tears stream down her cheeks as she takes him, sobbing into his hair, her arms wrapping around him while he clings to her like a toddler.

Not meeting my gaze, her repeated grateful words blur by as I hear wranglers shout, "We've got it, Colt. Head out!"

I turn just in time to see the bull rush toward Colt. He spins desperately, not the first time coming so dangerously close to a steer, though he should have gotten to safety by now.

"Get the hell out of there!" I instantly regret yelling, his eyes meeting mine in a moment of distraction that he can't afford. The bull seizes its chance, charging in with its head bowed low, horns aimed straight at Colt's stomach.

Stomped bones and torn shoulders can be healed, but a pierced gut is deadly.

These days, we wear protective equipment under our vests, but there was a time when bulls would impale riders and thrash them, tearing apart their intestines. Colt's not wearing any kind of protection, leaving him vulnerable.

Time freezes, each second as heavy as a broken hourglass, as all I can do is watch.

The horn grazes his stomach as he twists away at the very last second, his ass slamming against the dirt with a dull thud. He scrambles, his hands retreating as he puts enough distance for the bullfighters to take over.

They quickly corral the one-ton beast. I don't breathe until it disappears into the building.

Then, Colt's laugh bursts from him, loud and untethered echoing as he tilts his head back, a smile taking up his entire face as he looks up at the sky.

He's grinning when he gets up, dusting the dirt off his pants, as if he didn't just brush against death.

He's smiling and joking around, casual as ever, whereas I'm still not in control of myself, my hands shaking from the residual adrenaline, and he's out here fucking laughing?

He waves off the guys, saying something I can't make out through the static filling my ears as he disappears into the venue.

My feet move on their own, eating the distance between us. He's in the locker room by the time I catch up to him, and the smirk he gives me has my teeth grinding into each other.

"What the hell were you thinking?" I grit out, my hands fisted at my sides, the only thing stopping me from sending my fist through his face. Somewhere inside, I know that this has nothing to do with me, that I shouldn't be reacting this way, but there's nothing rational about me now.

"What was I going to do, let the kid get crushed?" Colt shrugs, so fucking casual.

Something snaps inside me, breaking the only thing holding me back. I slowly stalk toward him, each step deliberate, the distance between us shrinking.

"You know damn well that's not what I'm talking about." The conflicting surge inside me, a twisting knot of frustration, exasperation, and the remaining anxiety from watching him nearly die, propels my words.

Colt's hands are up between us, the same as he'd done with the bull, his eyes wide on mine as he takes a step back with every one of mine.

His throat bobs as he defends himself. "Like you'd just walk away from that."

I snap back, "You're sure as hell right I would. I'm not a fucking idiot out here risking my life for no reason. The second that kid was safe, you should have backed down. Do you want to get knocked out of the circuit? Because that's what will happen if you get a major injury right now."

"It was fine. I had it," he says, his confidence less steady now, hesitation hollowing the words.

"You did not fucking have it." Seizing his shirt, I slam him back into the locker, the metal rattling with the force.

He curls his fingers into my shirt and yanks me forward, the toes of our boots touching. I can make out the lighter streaks in his blue eyes. The world grows small, crackling electricity sparking between us as our ragged breaths mix together.

Years of fighting accumulating into this moment has the hair on the back of my neck standing. Agitation prickles under my skin, a rawness in my chest that shouldn't be there as I stare him down.

Colt's bitter laugh brushes my lips as he stares into me,

accusation and betrayal written in his eyes. "I don't know why you care now when you sure as hell didn't back then."

His words punch through my ribs, stealing my breath.

"Didn't care? I didn't fucking care? Is that what you think?" My voice rises until I'm nearly screaming. Flames lick up my skin as fire boils inside me. How could he be so fucking wrong about everything? I clench my trembling hands into fists.

I want to yell. Scream. Rage at him. I want to slam him into the locker until I knock some sense into him.

"I fucking cared," I growl.

"Not more than you wanted that rookie title." His voice cracks, and everything boiling inside me bursts out.

"Fuck you." I crash my mouth into his. I've lost my fucking mind, and I don't intend to find it.

Palms press into my chest, attempting to push me back, and I bite his bottom lip in response. The world explodes when he opens for me, his tongue thrusting between my teeth, rubbing mine. He tastes like mint.

I groan deep in my chest when he grabs my hair and kisses me harder, our teeth clanging together. Desperate, needy sounds escape him, and I grip his waist, pulling his hips forward until he's lined against my hard cock.

His head jerks back, breaking the kiss, and he stares at me with eyes so wide the whites are visible on all sides. It takes a second, but once I recognize the emotion playing out in his expression, my hands snap away like they've been burned.

Mortified. He's fucking mortified.

The second I release him, he's gone, the door slamming behind him in his wake, leaving me heaving. My forehead presses into my arm, braced against the locker. A million thoughts swirl in my mind, each overtaking the other, but one stands out more than the rest.

I liked kissing Colt Lawson.

I wanted him.

I want him.

Chapter 24

Callie

"I didn't expect to see you here, boy." The stallion looks up and whinnies, jostling the gate to grab my attention, then swaying his head like an impatient child. I laugh, his wide, dark eyes so close to mine I can see my reflection in them.

A large black nose nuzzles into my palm, short hair tickling me as the black stallion searches for more treats, snorting, hot air shooting through my fingers when it comes up empty.

"Don't worry," I laugh, digging into my pocket. "This time, I came prepared."

He nudges against me and eyes the apple. I hold it out on my flat palm, and he chews on it with a wet crunch, his lips working deftly, leaving my fingers damp.

"I think I just made a new best friend," I murmur, scratching along his jaw where he can't quite reach, the short hair prickling against my skin.

The bull in the next stall grunts, and the horse swings his head, exhaling through his nose in what seems to be equine exasperation.

"Must be hard being stuck beside these beasts," I hum, comforting him.

He dips his head in confirmation, then nuzzles into my hand again, but I pull it away, holding it to my chest to show that it's empty. "I'm sorry. I can't give you too much sugar, and I don't know who your owner is."

This time, his annoyance is directed at me. My lips purse around a hidden smile. Whoever owns him is lucky.

Distinctly familiar voices yell from down the hall, and I groan low in my throat. "See? You're not the only one who has to deal with problems."

He huffs his agreement, my ally in this. I rub my palm along the bridge of his nose one last time before making my way to the locker room door, prepared to stand between these two.

Closing the short distance, I go to shove the locker room door open but freeze when I peer through the crack just in time to see Maverick grab hold of Colt, kissing him hard. My mouth drops open as the air catches in my throat. A buzz hums underneath my skin. Mesmerized by what's playing out in front of me, I can't look away.

Their kiss turns desperate, clinging teeth, biting lips, sounds of pleasure escaping them.

Colt's fingers wrap around Maverick's neck, drawing a low groan from him. Maverick leans in, pressing Colt's back into the locker, the two of them lost to their own world, running on instinct.

My legs are weak, but I keep watching, everything spinning wildly out of control. The edges of the world blur as I slide my hand downward.

The soft ridge of my pants grazes my fingers as I move lower, cupping my core. Each sensation echoes theirs.

Wet heat pools between my thighs as my fingers slip down the inseam, every stroke like electricity through my nerves.

Watching them attack each other is the hottest thing I've ever seen.

The dam they've been holding back, buried under brittle anger, explodes with each brush of their lips. Maverick's growl fills the room as he pulls Colt closer, pressing their hips together.

Suddenly, Colt rips away, shoving Maverick back. Emotions flash behind his eyes, but I'm too far away to make any of them out. Colt escapes from behind him, his large strides coming directly at me.

Oh shit. I scramble back, nearly knocking over a bucket of feed, and land on my ass in front of the stallion's stall. My heart is pounding in my chest, pulse flooding my ears as Colt walks straight down the aisle. All he'd have to do is look to the right, and he'd spot me.

I have nothing to worry about. Colt's stunned like a deer caught in headlights as he walks forward on autopilot. A pink flush crawls up the back of his neck and colors the tips of his ears. I can just make out the slight tremble in his hands as they open and close before he forms fists at his sides.

I kick my feet as giddiness rises in my chest and clamp both hands against my mouth to stop it from bubbling out.

Well, I mean, a girl can dream.

The stallion neighs, his lips nuzzling my hair gently, and I look at him, beaming. "Right?"

He's my partner in crime, and I can't help but feed him another apple. It crunches between his teeth while my mind swirls as I try to process what I just saw.

Sure, it ended with Colt shoving Maverick back and storming off, but it wouldn't have happened if, on some level, they both didn't want it.

Plus, Colt was shaken when he left. Not angry. He'd been blushing so hard it would be impossible not to notice.

My lips curl at the corner as an idea takes shape. They've always been stubborn. Once they dig into something, it's almost impossible to get them to change their minds.

They thought one kiss wouldn't change everything? Cute.

I just need to give them the right push.

Chapter 25

Colt

It's late, and the other guys have gone to get enough sleep for the event tomorrow, but the fire in front of us is still roaring.

I'm in no hurry to head back to our room with Callie sitting in my lap, her head against my chest, hair tickling my chin. Her legs are thrown over Maverick's chair. Her hum travels through me as he massages his thumb into the arch of her foot.

She's stunning, the glow of the fire flickering over her features. I could stay just like this forever. Thinking about her heading back to the city has an ache forming in my chest. She belongs here with us. Always has.

And I'm going to do everything I can to convince her.

Maverick's hands travel up her calves, and a soft moan escapes her lips, licking down my gut. I've been trying to think of anything else since she curled into me. Little old ladies, reciting the alphabet backward. The disgusting smell of manure. It's not fucking helping. My cock's already half-hard under her ass, and if she keeps moving like that, she's definitely going to notice.

Maverick's deft hands aren't helping, and I'm unable to look away as they move up her thighs. Her chin tips up in response, warm breath panting on the underside of my jaw.

Fuck me. I'm losing it.

She moans again, this time deeper and more desperate. Maverick skims his thumbs under the rough hem of her cutoff shorts; her hips grind into my cock. I groan, my fingers digging into her hips.

"Do you have any idea what you're doing to me?" I murmur into her hair, and she rolls her hips into me in response.

Maverick groans as he kisses up her thigh where his hands just left. Thanking God for the sturdiness of Adirondack chairs, I lift her ass, positioning her to give him more access.

I can't help but watch him, the way his tongue licks her, and his teeth graze her skin, raising goose bumps in their wake. It's been a week since the locker room, and I've been desperately trying to block all thoughts out.

If trying to distract myself during the day wasn't bad enough, it haunts me at night. I lie awake in the too-small bed, and I swear every molecule of my being is aware of him. The fact that we haven't been able to change our reservations to double beds this entire time makes this a special form of hell. More than once, I've contemplated moving over to the sofa. No matter how uncomfortable it is, it has to be better than lying next to Maverick. But I never do, and neither does he. Something tying me in place, holding me there, that I don't want to think about.

Watching him drive Callie insane like this. Her body trembling against mine, mixed with the whiskey we've been drinking and the cover of night, has my resistance lowering. I'm transfixed on his mouth and the memories of how it felt, the way he gripped me closer. How it felt to be the one in his arms. I shouldn't be thinking about this. Can't think about this.

I focus on Callie, who's reaching back, cupping my neck with one hand, the other raking through Maverick's hair. She's perfect like this. Stunning. Seductive.

Everything I ever wanted, needed, craved.

I trail my hands under her shirt, grazing her quivering stomach, and do long strokes from the underside of her breast down to the waistband of her pants. Her hips shift into my touch every time my fingers dip below her panties. But I don't go deeper. Instead, I draw it out. I want her insane in our arms, losing control. I want her to beg for it. To need it as badly as I do.

She's got other plans, and a growl escapes my throat when she pulls back from the kiss and stands. I don't miss the way her chest heaves or the goose bumps that cross her skin. She's not as unaffected as she's trying to make it seem.

Maverick leans forward, his hand reaching out to her, a muscle ticking in his neck as she jumps out of his reach.

She tsks, shaking her head. "Not so fast."

"Fuck." Maverick drops his head into his hand, groaning, as he rubs it over his face. "You can't do this to us."

"Are you sure about that? Because I'm pretty sure I can." Her eyes twinkle with mischief.

"You're a demon." I groan.

"Aw, come on. I just want to have some fun." She says it so innocently you'd never believe she's in the middle of torturing us.

"What kind of fun, Callie?" Maverick's voice is dark, low, impatient. Strained, like he's barely holding himself back.

"I thought we would play a little game."

"Are you trying to fuckin' kill me?" I say through gritted teeth.

She tilts her head. "I dare you—"

"You've got to be kidding me," Maverick says.

"You either play, or no more touching, and I go to bed." She places a hand on her hip. "*Alone.*"

She emphasizes the word, and I damn near beg Maverick to cooperate. At this point, there's nothing I wouldn't do to get my hands back on her.

"Hurry" is all he says.

"I dare you." She draws it out, and it's almost painful. "to kiss each other."

She could have slapped me, and it would've shocked me less. I whip toward Maverick, who's already looking at me. I expect to see anger, confusion, shock, anything but the heat that's darkening his gaze. The way his eyes trail down to my lips has them parting in response. My throat bobs with my swallow. My throat is dry with a different kind of thirst.

I'm not disgusted. I'm not turned off. Instead, my cock's achingly hard, pushing against my jeans. I've hated him so long. Carried that betrayal. But the way he's watching me and the way I'm responding undermines all of those feelings.

I don't want to think about it. I don't want to think about anything. So I use the excuse of the dare to lean in closer to him. His breath is hot, branding as his nose grazes mine, and the dark pools of his eyes seem to peer into me. Like he can read every hidden thought. My fingers grip the armchair so hard I think it may crack. Tension radiates through me as he moves closer with each breath, giving me the chance to pull away. I don't move. I can't deny that I want this.

Maverick closes the distance between our mouths. He catches my groan, opening for me, sliding his tongue over my top teeth, sending fire sparking down my stomach, going straight to my cock. I meet him stroke for stroke, tasting the whiskey on his lips, wondering if I taste the same. My ass grinds against the seat, needing to move when his hands dig into my hair, holding me firmly in place as he deepens the kiss into something wild, untamable.

His low, deep growl nearly has me coming undone. Soft, delicate fingers stroke down my neck as Callie lowers herself into my lap. I break the kiss, loving the whine coming out of Maverick at the loss.

I capture her mouth with mine, needing to taste her. I don't notice Maverick moving until he cages us, hands firmly on the armrests.

Callie goes to turn to him, but I cup her jaw, not ready to end our kiss, and tilt her head to expose her neck. Maverick licks up the thin column, and a shiver rolls through her when he presses a kiss to the sensitive spot under her ear.

"Don't forget you started this," he murmurs. It feels like a threat.

I love the way she's responding to him, her sensitive body rolling against my hard cock. He grips her hips and pushes her harder into me, rocking her until it feels like I'm going to explode. If he keeps this up, I'm going to come in my pants.

He pulls her onto her feet and then sits in the chair beside us, holding her so her back is against his chest.

"Get up," he commands. A ripple of defiance courses through me, but I do as he says, wanting to know where he's going to take this.

I walk in front of them, standing between her thighs. She gazes up at me through lowered lashes, watching eagerly, her head resting against Maverick's shoulder. I go to close the distance between us, but Maverick cuts in.

"On your knees." I'm not sure if he's daring me to do it or daring me to find out what will happen if I don't.

I don't want to admit what that last thought does to

me. They watch me, gaze steady as I lower myself to my knees. The dirt and rocks press into my skin as I wait for what happens next.

Being submissive goes against everything inside of me, but I don't complain when he tells me to remove her shorts. I groan deep in the back of my throat when her pink lace panties are the only thing covering her, a dark spot in the middle where she's soaked through the fabric. I'm panting, cock begging, but I don't move on my own. Instead, I look to Maverick.

"Go ahead, touch her, but steer clear of her clit," Maverick instructs, his voice smooth and commanding, eliciting an exasperated sigh from Callie.

"That's totally unfair, Maverick," she protests.

He smirks, radiating leisurely control, as if savoring the chance to tease us.

His eyes linger on Callie, a glimmer of something deeper flickering behind them an unspoken promise that if we follow his lead, it'll be worth it.

I run my hands over her curves, slipping my fingers under the waistband of her underwear to start pulling them down.

Maverick rakes his fingers through my hair, holding me in place. "Did I say you could take those off?"

A surge of defiance races up my spine, causing my chest to tighten like it's bound in a vise, but I ignore it as Maverick steps back and adjusts her position. The new angle provides an even better view.

My fingers dig into the firm, smooth skin of her ass, spreading her apart.

There's satisfaction in going slow, in taking my time. My fingers trace the gentle contours of her hips, the smooth expanse of her thighs, and linger at the delicate lace trim of her underwear. She lets out soft, needy whimpers. I finally understand why Maverick is so into patience as a low growl rumbles from my chest, fueled by the warmth that surges through my veins, igniting every nerve with anticipation.

I push my face into her cunt, running my nose along her warm seam, breathing in her sweet scent. Maverick doesn't stop me, and I take it as the go-ahead to continue. A tremble runs through her as my hot breath sinks into her tender core. Each gasp, each moan from her lips is a spark, a lit match held to a fuse. Her panties damp with wanting, I push them aside, my fingers tracing the edge of her heat before slipping inside, testing just how far I can push the boundaries of Maverick's command.

"You will regret that," he says, a threat and a promise wrapped into one, and my cock strains against my pants, throbbing, begging for friction.

This is so much more than I anticipated.

I can no longer ignore the insistent pull that's been growing inside me, breaking open the vault where I've hidden all my emotions.

This feeling, having them, being this close, feels right, like it's always been how things are meant to be. The void

Callie left behind, a gaping chasm that only widened with the loss of Maverick, fills drop by drop.

Maverick's breaths come in rapid, shallow bursts, and his eyes glint as they lock onto mine. A magnetic pull toward him, every logical reason to keep my distance crumbling under the weight of this charged moment. The air between us thickens, charged with an undeniable tension that draws me closer to him.

He releases his hold on my hair, his fingers trailing down to grasp Callie's hips firmly, spreading her apart to grant me better access. I take this as an unspoken invitation, wasting no time as I lean in and let my tongue glide through her slick heat. She's intoxicating, and I hum, savoring her.

My fingers tremble on her thighs as I stroke my tongue from her clit, along through her seam, stopping just before her back hole. Then I do it again.

Her body sags into my hands as her legs give way, and she moans louder, filling the air as I thrust my tongue into her core, fucking her over and over with it.

Maverick lets out a deep, resonant groan that seems to vibrate through my entire torso.

I can't see what's happening, but the air around is charged with an intense energy, almost crackling with anticipation.

"Colt," Maverick says, but I don't stop to look, his fingers pulling her even wider. "She likes it right there."

Callie mumbles in agreement, her voice muffled. "So good."

Holy shit. That's hot.

She rides my tongue, setting her own rhythm and quivering in my hold. Her sounds grow more desperate with each thrust. I flatten my tongue over her asshole before circling it, loving the way it makes her quake. Her cry is cut off, strangled, when I thrust two fingers deep inside her pussy.

"You're doing such a good job, Colt, pleasuring our girl." Maverick's praise shivers across my skin.

I thrust my fingers deeper inside her, scissoring them, preparing her for my cock. She responds immediately, taking everything I give her. My tongue circles her rim, pressing without entering while I fuck her hard with my fingers.

She tenses, arching upward, opening herself even more to me. I doubt she realizes what she's doing. Her body is in control now, searching for release. I sink a third finger into her, and she pulses around my knuckles in response. Her pussy clenches, squeezing them tight. I groan at the thought of feeling her heat around my cock.

"That's it. Come for us. Let Colt know what a good job he's doing."

Trusting Maverick to hold her, I fuck her until she's breaking apart around my fingers. She's tightening so hard I can't move them as she comes.

It's so fucking satisfying to be the one to make her feel this way, but it's not enough to satiate the building need driving me.

My hips move on their own, desperate to sink inside her; there's no way I can stop.

I pull my fingers out slowly, loving the way she whimpers, shivering in my arms.

I take deep inhales, exhaling in a count of five, trying to slow my heart rate to get myself under control. My head buzzes from the lack of oxygen. I'd given up trying to breathe, focusing only on making her come.

Her pussy's glistening in front of me, wetness soaking her thighs, and I can't help but suck her taste into my mouth. The overwhelming need to devour her thrums through me.

Maverick tugs my head back, forcing my chin up to look at him.

A growl, more animalistic than human, rumbles in my chest from him taking away my meal.

"Stand."

His one-word command ignites my frustration, and I'm tempted to snap. To tell him to back the fuck off, that I don't have to listen to him, that I can do whatever I want. I grind my teeth, ready to fight... only to realize the thing I want to do is whatever he tells me.

I'll figure that out later. I rise to my feet, completely motionless, my body buzzing with anticipation.

"Take off your pants and feed her your cock," he instructs with a steady gaze.

"Fuck." The word drags out under my breath as I make quick work of the button and slide the zipper down, pushing my jeans and boxers to my feet, where they pool around my boots.

Maverick lifts Callie as he gets up and maneuvers her until her back is pressed against me. Her arms circled around his neck for support. I watch over her shoulder as he cups one of her breasts, rolls her nipple between his fingers, and lays his other palm flat on her stomach, dragging it downward, painfully slow.

Jesus, she looks stunning draped over him, legs parted, ready.

I run my cock along her ass, then between her thighs, coating it with her wetness, loving her soft whimpers. Maverick really has the right idea; the longer I take, the more she loses her mind. But there's only so much I can take. Fisting my cock, I circle the head around her entrance, I'm barely holding on to my sanity enough to ask, "Are you on birth control?"

She nods, nudging me, and that's all it takes to make me break.

"Thank fucking God," I growl, sliding into her completely in one swift motion, fitting perfectly as if she was meant for me. Careful not to hurt her, I pause for her to adjust, but she pushes back against me impatiently.

"So good. Feels so good." Words spill out of her in a continuous stream.

"Harder," she pleads, and I give her what she wants, skin slapping against skin as I slam into her. My eyes roll back as she clenches around me in response. Fuck, I'm not going to last.

Callie's head slams into my collarbone, a cry on her lips when he stops without touching her clit. He's a fucking sadist. He catches her moan with his mouth, shoving his tongue between her teeth. The indecent sounds they're making have me pumping recklessly.

"Come on his cock," Maverick murmurs without pulling back, encouraging her. "I know you can do it."

She huffs. "You better be right." She's all sass now, the need for release cracking through her voice.

Maverick chuckles. It's a deep, rough sound that tightens my balls. He's still smirking when he takes her nipple in his mouth, sucking it hard, teeth sinking into the tender flesh. He pulls away, licking the marks he's left, only to do it again, effectively cutting off her complaints.

Listening to her every moan, every sound, I focus on what makes her feel good. Her breath hitches when the head of my cock presses against the front of her inner wall. I do it again, harder, and she whimpers in the back of her throat.

"You like that, don't you?" I murmur, brushing my teeth lightly over the delicate shell of her ear, hitting that spot over and over again.

Her cries grow louder, filling the air around us, and Maverick clamps a hand over her mouth to muffle them. She's completely lost, head thrown back, eyes closed as she grinds into me, giving me all her weight, trusting me completely.

My cock throbs, tingles climbing my spine as my orgasm threatens to take over.

"Come with me, Sunshine."

Callie sinks her teeth into Maverick's hand as her pussy pulses around me. A groan rips from my chest as I fill her with my cum, marking her as mine.

Voices come from around the corner, shattering the moment and slamming me back to reality.

How the hell could I forget we're outside?

I pull out quickly as Maverick's already pulling her shorts into place, covering her, and I yank my pants up just in time for unfamiliar faces to come into view. I don't bother acknowledging them, already annoyed they've interrupted us.

Callie makes a surprised sound when Maverick lifts her into his arms, cradling her under her knees and supporting her back. She visibly whitens at the sight of the intruders, clearly still a little lost in her own world.

Her eyes widen as she scans the surroundings, and then she hides her flushed cheeks with her hands. "That wasn't fair," she says.

She looks absolutely adorable like this. "You started it," I tease, brushing a strand of hair behind her ear and gently moving her hands away from her face, amused by her embarrassment.

"I'd never let anyone see you," Maverick assures her, drawing her focus back to him. I search my feelings but find no jealousy, just comfort in knowing he cares for her as much as I do.

As the intruders leave, she relaxes, and the three of us silently head back to our room.

"Wait," Callie says, turning to look Maverick in the eyes. "What about you?"

I hadn't even thought about the fact he didn't get to finish. My eyes involuntarily drift down to the noticeable bulge in his jeans. Damn, if he feels anything like I did, it must be torturous.

The man has the self-control of a saint because all he does is kiss her forehead and say, "Next time."

Next time.

His words echo in my head, bouncing off the walls as they light a flame in my chest because, without a doubt, there will be a next time.

Tonight was the most intense experience of my life. I came so hard I thought I was going to pass out.

I know I *should* have hated it. Should have fought Maverick's dominance. In no world should I be turned on by him telling me what to do.

But I've never been so desperate in my life. Suddenly, none of the things I *should* do matter anymore. Every scrap of his praise drove me harder as we both worked toward Callie's pleasure.

I fall behind them, watching as Maverick's back flexes under his shirt. When did he become such a man? All thick thighs and broad shoulders wide enough to block Callie completely. My cock betrays me, already half-hard just looking at him.

But to hell with it.

If this is how it's going to be, I might just start enjoying being told what to do.

Chapter 26

Maverick

CALLIE'S WARMTH rises and falls in the hollow of my neck with each soft breath she takes. Her head is tucked beneath my chin, her naked body pressed against mine, one of her knees slipped between my thighs like she belongs there. Like she's always belonged there. Colt is curled around her from behind, his arms looped tightly around her middle, like letting even an inch of space come between us would be unbearable.

She was barely standing in the shower, her body swaying between us as we washed her, exhaustion pulling at every limb. By the time we carried her to bed, she was already drifting, sleep swallowing her whole. She didn't even stir as we tucked her between us, didn't wake as Colt pressed a kiss to her damp hair or I wrapped an arm around her waist.

Without saying a word, Colt and I made the same choice: stay. Sleep beside her. Keep her safe.

I stroke a strand of her copper hair through my fingers, twirling it softly between the pads of my thumb and forefinger, memorizing the texture. This... this moment, this closeness, this *peace*, feels like coming home. Like I've been waiting for this exact shape of love my whole damn life and didn't know until now.

Colt's nose is pressed into the back of her neck. His eyes are closed, but his breathing is off, uneven. He's not asleep. He's feeling this too.

It took me too long to realize I haven't just been waiting for Callie. It's the three of us. *Together*. That's what makes everything click into place. That's what makes it right.

That first kiss with Colt in the locker room. *Jesus*. It wasn't planned. It wasn't calculated. It was instinct, years of pent-up tension and frustration bursting like a dam. By the time my brain caught up, he was already gone. Bolting.

I can't forget the way he fled. Panic carved into every line of his face, like the ground had given out beneath him.

It's haunted me ever since.

Now, I know. He *liked* it. Whether he's ready to admit it or not, Colt wants this too. He wants *me*. Or, at the very least, he wants Callie enough to explore what this could be between the three of us.

Tonight was different.

Where our first kiss had been rushed, frantic, tonight I took my time. I kissed him like I meant it because I *did*. I devoured him, slow and thorough, learning what made him shiver. He likes having his tongue sucked. Likes when

I scrape my teeth along his bottom lip. And the way he responded to my voice, to my hands... he took direction so well it made my chest ache.

I could *see* the war inside him. One part ready to fight, the other aching for more.

And God help me, I want them both. So badly it's eating me alive.

If I expect them to trust me, to *follow* me, I have to go slow. I have to be steady. It's my job to make this feel safe. To take care of them so completely that they never have to question how much I want them. How far I'll go to keep them.

They were so good tonight. They listened. They trusted me.

But I was walking a tightrope, and I knew it. We're past the point of pretending this is casual. We crossed a line, and there's no way back.

I don't want to go back.

This is what I've been missing. Not just Callie, not just Colt. *Us.* The three of us. This wild, messy, beautiful thing that only works when it's all three pieces together.

I used to think I hated Colt. I used to wear that hate like armor.

But it was never hate. It was fear. Loss. Longing. Everything I didn't want to admit.

Callie said she's leaving at the end of the season. Colt probably thinks we'll go back to being rivals the moment she's gone, but they're both wrong.

Because now that I've had this—*them*—I'll burn the whole damn world down before I let it go.

The thought of losing them splits something open in my chest. The ache is sharp, brutal. Unrelenting.

I press my lips to the top of Callie's head and whisper the truth into her hair, barely audible.

"I love you."

She doesn't stir. Still fast asleep. Still unaware of the weight I just handed her in the dark.

But Colt hears it.

I see it in the sharp inhale he tries to hide. The flush that creeps up his neck, spreading across his cheeks and all the way to the tips of his ears.

I keep my eyes on the ceiling, voice a raw rasp. "Don't leave me."

Chapter 27

Callie

THE FIRST THING I feel is warmth, then the heavy weight of bodies, sinking me deeper into the mattress.

The last thing I remember from yesterday is Colt and Maverick drying me off, then one of them carrying me to bed and sliding me under the covers. I must've passed out cold because I don't remember anything after that.

Hot breath fans across my forehead as a nose nuzzles into the nape of my neck. My eyes flutter open to find Maverick watching me, his deep brown gaze soft and full of something that makes my chest ache.

"You look cute all groggy like this," Maverick murmurs, his voice rough with sleep.

I bite my lip hard. I'm not the only one who looks cute. His hair's a wild, tousled mess, sticking up in every direction. There's something softer in his face now, something unguarded. It wraps around my heart and squeezes until it aches.

This is the boy I grew up with. My best friend. My shadow.

Colt's lips brush against my shoulder, his breath warm on my skin.

"Morning, Sunshine," he mumbles, his voice warm with sleep and something that curls low in my chest.

I turn to him, and his gaze locks onto mine, heavy with memories of last night. His smirk deepens, a dimple flashing.

"Alright, get up, you two," Maverick says, swinging his legs off the bed.

Colt groans, pulling me tighter into his chest. "I don't wanna."

I laugh, slipping out of his hold and following Maverick until I realize I'm completely naked and squeak, grabbing the sheet to wrap around myself.

"Don't tell me you're shy now." Maverick chuckles as he buttons his jeans, not bothering with a shirt.

There's a massive difference between being naked under the cover of night and standing bare in the harsh light of day, every shadow gone.

"Just look away," I say, still clinging to the sheet.

"Totally unfair," Colt mutters, grabbing his shirt and pulling it over my head. It swallows me whole and smells like him... like *home*.

Maverick laces his fingers with mine, helping me up. "Better?"

The hem hangs a few inches above my knees, more

dress than shirt. He gives me a once-over, a frown tugging between his brows. "I'm a little jealous."

Colt laughs behind me, getting out of bed. "As you should be, fucker."

The tension that existed when I first arrived is gone. What remains is something playful. Teasing. Easy.

"What are you thinking about?" Maverick asks.

I dodge him, walking past and hiding my face. He reads me too well. Thankfully, our rooms are connected, and I flee to theirs, locking myself in the bathroom.

My reflection catches me off guard. Flushed cheeks. Wide eyes. Hair curling at the ends from last night's shower. I look... wild... *happy.*

I wash up, borrow a toothbrush, figuring if we're making out, this should be fine, and return to my side of the motel.

Colt and Maverick are already dressed. I stumble at the sight of them both watching me like I'm the only thing that matters. Heat slides down my spine and settles low in my belly. My mouth waters as I'm momentarily lost in the thought of lifting their shirts. I can almost feel the smooth, warm skin beneath my fingertips as I count each defined abdominal muscle they have.

Then I notice what Maverick's holding: a sundress.

Two thin straps dangle from his fingers, the baby blue fabric dotted with little flowers.

My nose scrunches. "Where did that come from?"

Maverick's laugh is a low rumble.

"I bought it for you. You really think I'd just have some random girl's dress lying around?"

"No," I say, but it's only half-true. Jealousy apparently comes easily for me.

Now that I know he bought it for me, warmth blooms in my chest, bright and sudden, like sunlight breaking through a storm. I reach out, opening and closing my hand in a silent *gimme*.

He grins as I snatch the dress from his fingers and scurry into the other room, their laughter chasing after me. I tug off Colt's T-shirt, immediately missing the way it smells like him, all clean sweat, leather, and something unmistakably *him*. But then I slip the dress over my head, and that ache is replaced by something else entirely.

The fabric is light and soft, gliding over my skin like a second thought. My hands trail down to my hips, pausing where the skirt flares out just enough to feel flirty. It hugs every curve like it was tailored for me, like he knew *exactly* where to cinch, where to drape. There's even a built-in bra that fits *perfectly*.

A thrill races through me, sharp and sweet, at the realization of just how closely Maverick's been watching me. Not just looking... noticing. Every inch. Every detail.

I step around the corner slowly, nerves fluttering in my chest. I want Maverick to like it. Need him to. The way his eyes darken when he's pleased, the way his smile curls just for me... it does something dangerous to my heart.

Two pairs of eyes find me instantly. They track every inch of the dress, every inch of *me*, slowly scanning upward until they meet my gaze. The weight of their attention steals the air from my lungs.

My breath catches at the heat simmering in their stares, wordless, hungry. A silent promise of what they'll do once this dress is no longer in the way.

"You like it?" I manage, voice soft but hopeful.

Colt's throat bobs with a swallow. His voice is a low rasp, barely restrained. "Sunshine, 'like' doesn't begin to cover it."

"It's perfect," Maverick says, the words a quiet praise, but they light a fire in my belly all the same. I didn't expect to crave his approval, but I do. God, I *do*.

He steps closer, eyes still locked on me. "Let's get out of here," he murmurs, a smirk tugging at his lips, "before I ruin that pretty little dress."

Chapter 28

Callie

FULL FROM BREAKFAST, I sit on top of the picnic table outside the motel while the boys load the truck. The sun is warm on my skin, but all I can feel is the slow unraveling happening inside me.

It's impossible not to watch them. The sweat gathering at the napes of their necks, their T-shirts pulling tight across their shoulders with every easy movement. Every little touch from them last night has branded itself onto my skin. I still feel the ghost of their hands, the weight of Colt inside me, the rasp of Maverick's voice telling me what to do.

I don't know if remembering it is a form of torture or salvation.

When I came here, I thought I could handle it, thought the crush I had faded with time. That I could be near them and still keep my heart safe. That friendship would be enough.

I came here to soak them in. To memorize every look, every laugh, every brush of their shoulders. I came to collect pieces of them I could take with me. To live off the memories when I go back to my real life.

I told myself I'd be fine. That I had to be.

Because I know I'll never feel this way about anyone else.

I don't remember the exact moment the crush turned into love. Maybe it always *was* love, and I was just too young to understand. Everyone always said we were too close, too intertwined. My parents tried to pull me away. Said it wasn't healthy. That I needed other friends.

But I always found my way back to them.

My phone buzzes beside me, rattling against the sun-warmed wood of the picnic table. I don't need to check who it is. I already know.

It's from the city.

From the job waiting for me.

From the life I promised I'd go back to.

Without looking, I flip it face down.

They've followed up a few times now calls, emails, increasingly eager messages with phrases like *final offer* and *looking forward to having you on board*. It's all perfectly polite. Enthusiastic, even. The kind of attention someone would kill for.

It's everything I worked toward. Everything I fought for.

And I'm still going.

That hasn't changed.

But I'm not ready to face it. Not today. Not while the sun's still warm on my skin and Colt's laugh is cutting across the parking lot. Not while I can still feel Maverick's voice in my ear, low and possessive.

I'll answer them eventually. I'll pack my bags. I'll get on that plane and return to the version of me I had to become after everything fell apart.

Just... not yet.

Because this little pocket of time, this quiet, golden *before*, is all I have left. And I'm not ready to break the spell just yet.

There's a sharp ache in my chest, like my heart's clenched in a fist and twisted tight. Every part of me is screaming not to go. Screaming that *this*, *they* are where I belong. That no matter where I live, no matter what title is under my name, this is the only place that's ever truly felt like home.

I don't look away from them.

I just watch.

I memorize the curve of Colt's jaw as he laughs at something Maverick says. The way Maverick's eyes squint against the sun. The ease in their bodies. The peace between them that finally feels almost healed.

It's hard to breathe knowing I only have a little time left before I walk away.

Colt's shoulder bumps Maverick's in a playful, easy way. They're joking while they work, and for a second, it's like I've been thrown into a time machine. All they need is dirt on their faces, and they'd look exactly like they did as kids.

Maverick's laugh booms out, splitting the air, and something torn inside me stitches itself back together. My heart aches, but at least, *at least* they'll have each other.

Luke appears beside me, settling on the table and handing me a cold soda. Condensation beads along the can, and the ice-cold metal feels like heaven in my hand. I take a sip, and it soothes the tightness in my throat.

I tip the can toward him with a quiet smile. "Thanks. I needed this."

"Thank *you*," he says, nodding toward where the boys are still working, smiling, laughing, shoulders looser than I've seen in days. "I think this is the happiest I've ever seen them. Hell, I didn't even know Maverick could laugh like that."

"I can't take the credit," I say, watching them. "This is how they always should've been. I just gave them a little nudge."

Luke raises a brow. "I'm not sure about all that. These two wouldn't have come back together if you hadn't shown up."

I smirk. "All right. Maybe I'll take *some* of the credit."

His tone shifts, quiet and serious. "They're both in love with you. You know that, right?"

My chest tightens, like someone just handed me wings and broke my ribs in the same breath. I don't know if I want to fly or fall apart.

Luke studies me, really studies me like he's trying to read the pieces I haven't laid bare.

"You don't look as happy as I thought you'd be," he says gently.

I let out a breath of a laugh. "Easy to read, am I?"

"Easy? No. But I can tell you've got some secrets." He leans back, palms pressed behind him for support. "I've been told I'm a good listener. If you want to talk."

It's tempting. If I wasn't sure I'd fall apart right here and now, I might take him up on it.

"Wouldn't make a difference," I say quietly.

That gets his attention. "Wouldn't it? Those two seem to think something's changed."

I curl my fingers into the fabric of my dress, not exactly sure what to say. I've never lied to Maverick or Colt. Not once. I told them from the beginning that I was leaving after the season.

But I can see why they think something's changed. Why they think maybe, just maybe, I might stay.

All they know is that I left because my dad died... that it broke me.

They don't know that I left because of *them*.

Because I couldn't watch them chase the same fate that took him.

In the city, I've gotten good at keeping my distance from all of this. The bull riding, rodeos, the risk, the glory. Once I'm back, I'll rebuild that wall. Pretend I don't know what they're doing. Pretend I don't still love them.

Bull riders don't just love the ride. They love the high.

The rush. The roar of the crowd. That's not something you walk away from. Not for anyone.

And I love them too much to ask them to try.

That's the reason I'm leaving. That's why I have to.

Luke pulls off his hat and groans up at the sky. "Fuck. You're going to break both their hearts, aren't you?"

Not as badly as I'm going to break my own.

"They'll be okay," I say, eyes still on them. "Now they have each other."

Luke looks doubtful. "I'm not so sure about that. But I'm not about to get into other people's business."

Grateful he lets it go, I take another sip, letting the cold drink burn its way down.

I'm the one who's going to be alone.

So I have to believe they'll be okay.

Because that's what I'll survive on, knowing they're together, even when I'm gone.

Luke throws a wink over his shoulder as he heads for the motel.

"Better hurry up, Lawson. Pretty sure Kane's stealing your stuff again."

I shake my head, watching my boys disappear up the stairs to their room, already arguing.

Chapter 29

Maverick

THE MOTEL ROOM is a chaotic mess when we get back.

Boots kicked into corners, half-zipped duffels slumped against the wall, clean clothes tangled with dirty ones.

Colt's digging through his bag for a clean shirt when he suddenly freezes.

"Is that my shirt?" he asks, voice suspicious.

I glance down.

Yeah, it's definitely his.

Soft and worn, clinging a little too tightly across my shoulders.

"You left it on my side of the bed," I say, tugging the hem down, pretending like my heart isn't beating a little faster.

"You coulda folded it, not stolen it."

"Folded it?" I bark out a laugh. "What am I, a fuckin' laundromat?"

He crosses his arms, eyes dragging over me way too slowly.

"I want it back."

I shrug, cocky. "Too late. Smells like me now."

Something shifts in his expression, a flash of heat that makes the air between us spark.

He stares a beat too long before snapping his duffel closed a little too hard.

"Whatever," he mutters. "Looks better on you anyway."

I swear the whole room tilts a little under my feet.

Neither of us moves for a minute.

Not until he shoulders past me on his way to the bathroom, knocking my arm with his rougher than necessary.

Not that I mind.

Chapter 30

Colt

THE CROWD'S going crazy tonight. The city's gone all out, fireworks booming in the sky, lighting up the arena in a kaleidoscope of colors. There isn't a single spare inch in the stands. Everyone's getting hungrier the closer we get to the finals.

The finals.

In all my years riding, it's the first time that word hasn't made my pulse spike for the right reasons. Used to be the only thing I cared about points, rank, that gold buckle at the end. Winning was simple. Predictable. The one constant in a life full of chaos.

Things are different now.

Now, all I can think about is Callie. About the countdown I'm on that has nothing to do with standings and everything to do with the day she packs up and leaves.

She told us from the start just the season, then she's

gone. And the closer we get to the end, the more impossible that feels.

The only win that matters now is finding a way to make her stay.

I've already had my ride tonight. Scored decent. Enough to hold my position, maybe inch a little closer to the top. Normally, I'd be coming down off the high right now, back in the locker room, icing whatever's bruised and watching the rest of the event from a screen.

Tonight, I'm back here, tucked into a shadowed corner near the bucking chutes, watching from behind the chaos as Maverick gets ready. The space is a mess of nerves and movement. Riders pacing, bullfighters shouting instructions, the low, restless snorts of the animals as they're loaded into place.

Callie... well, she's not here.

Said she wanted to visit a horse out at the stables. It's not a lie, but it's not the whole truth either. I know what this place brings up for her. What it cost her.

She never talks about it directly, but I see it in her eyes every time the gate opens how her whole body tenses like she's bracing for impact. I know watching us ride isn't easy.

Lately, I've started wondering if there's more to it.

Not just fear. Not just grief.

Something deeper. Something she doesn't want to say out loud.

I didn't press. Not yet, but I will.

I don't watch rides from this close. The sounds, the

smells. It winds you up again, but I couldn't resist coming to see him.

But fuck, I wasn't prepared for how good he'd look.

He's tall, at least five inches taller than anyone else standing here. He's wearing a light blue button-up, the sleeves rolled up just enough to show the lean strength in his forearms. His leather vest covers the protective gear we all wear. Chaps lined with fringe fall over his jeans, swaying slightly with each step.

I don't know when I stopped looking at him with hate, when I started noticing everything else, the creases by his eyes, the way his brows knit together as he takes slow, calming breaths. His fingers flex, already running through a dozen scenarios in his head. He's always been one step ahead of me, my rival, the one I had to beat.

For once, I don't hate it.

For the first time, I want him to ride the full eight.

The announcer's working the crowd into a frenzy. A bullfighter taps Maverick on the shoulder. It's his turn. He hasn't seen me, and I want to keep it that way. I don't want to be the reason he loses focus.

Bull riders are creatures of habit. We all have our rituals, our superstitions.

I know the bull he drew. Carnage. He's one of the wildest in the circuit, famous for throwing riders within the first two seconds and then trying to stomp them into the dirt. That's what makes it so valuable. The more dangerous the bull, the higher the score. Drawing this beast is the best thing that could've happened to Maverick, if he can hold on.

While the other riders look anxious, Maverick moves like he's in complete control. Calm. Focused. Like he's mounting an old horse, not straddling a grenade.

He nods along to whatever the bullfighter is saying, listening closely. They run this part of the show. We just ride the eight.

One grabs Maverick by the vest and helps lower him into the chute.

The bull reacts instantly, thrashing hard. The wrangler yanks Maverick out just before he's crushed against the metal. Most people think the danger's out in the arena. They're wrong. The chute is just as dangerous. You're trapped with the beast, relying entirely on the men around you to get you out in one piece.

A lot of riders would bow out right now. Bulls this wound up aren't worth the risk. That's why those riders aren't ranked like Maverick is.

It's fear that ruins a rider. This sport demands recklessness.

Maverick knows that. He waits for the bull to settle, then gives a nod. He's ready.

I hold my breath as they lower him in again. This time, the bull doesn't fight, just stomps and huffs like usual.

I've ridden some of the nastiest bulls on the circuit, taken hits that rattled my bones, earned hospital stays that blurred into each other, but I've never felt like this.

It's a tight, coiling pressure in my chest that won't let

go. My boots are planted, but everything inside me feels unsteady.

Maverick's lowered into the chute, calm as ever, running his palm over the rope to heat the resin, working with the same steady focus he always does. It should settle me, seeing him in control. Seeing him do what he's trained his whole life to do.

It doesn't.

I know what this bull is capable of, and for some reason, I can't shake the feeling that something's off.

That light relief I felt earlier? Gone, replaced by a sharp, gnawing edge of anticipation that's more dread than excitement.

The next eight seconds are going to feel like hell.

It's only because I'm watching so closely that I notice it.

The rope.

The one thing anchoring Maverick to the bull, the thing that keeps us from flying, is frayed right beneath where his boot presses down.

Terror slams into me like a freight train.

I'm moving before I can think, feet pounding across the dirt, lungs burning.

No one else has noticed. Not yet.

The only reason bull riding feels even remotely safe is because we know what we're getting into. Every risk is calculated. Controlled. Maverick is about to step into that chute with a rope that's about to give and has no idea what's coming for him.

My throat burns as I scream, yelling at them to stop, to close the gate, to check the rope, but the roar of the crowd swallows it whole.

One of the bullfighters steps in front of me, probably thinking I've lost it. I dodge him. I won't let anything stop me. Not now.

This fear isn't like what I feel when I ride. This is different. This is cold. Crippling. It sinks into my bones.

I plant my feet and grab Maverick by the vest, hauling him backward just as the chute door groans open. We crash hard, my back slamming against the dirt with him on top of me. My lungs seize, gasping for air.

I don't even realize I'm still clinging to him, arms locked around his middle, pulling him tighter just to make sure he's real. He's safe.

The arena explodes into chaos.

No one knows what just happened.

Maverick doesn't try to get up. Somehow, he knows I'm not ready to let him go. A wrangler's yelling above us, but I can't make out a word. My ears are ringing. My mind's gone blank. I just need another second.

Need to feel his heartbeat under my palm.

Then I'll deal with the consequences.

The boss steps into view, the man who runs this whole show. Thirty years in the game, and everyone listens when he talks. He surveys the scene with quiet authority.

Before Maverick can move, the boss reaches down and grabs the rope still dangling from his hand.

The frayed edge swings in the air.

A quiet, horrible beat of silence.

The wrangler who'd just been yelling at me stumbles back a step, ghost-white. It had been his team's job to check that gear. He starts apologizing, stammering to Maverick, face stricken.

I want to yell at him. Want to scream that he should be apologizing to me. That idiot nearly cost me everything. I can feel the fury building, swelling inside me, threatening to boil over.

Better the rage than everything else.

Because the alternative is kissing Maverick right here in front of everyone.

The boss helps Maverick to his feet, then reaches a hand down to me.

I take it, trying not to wince as he squeezes. I'm a big man, but this guy might as well be a bear the way his hand dwarfs mine. He lets it go and slaps me on the back. "Damn fine job you did there. Risky, but damn fine job."

I didn't even think about the risk.

Running into a loaded chute, grabbing a rider mid-mount, risking being thrown off balanced into the dirt, crushed or tossed or trampled. None of it registered. All I'd been able to think about was getting Maverick the hell out of there.

A shaky laugh bubbles up in my chest, the adrenaline still roaring through my bloodstream. I can't believe I actually pulled it off.

Maverick's not smiling. He's not grateful. Not relieved. He's glaring at me.

His eyes are wild, jaw tight, and some emotion I can't name is flickering just beneath the surface.

He grabs my arm and drags me out of the arena, through a hall, slamming the door of a vacant room behind us.

His breaths are ragged, eyes wide. You'd never know by the way he was looking at me that I just saved his ass.

"What the fuck were you thinking?" he snarls, shaking me so hard my teeth rattle. He doesn't even give me time to respond before he does it again. "You could've fucking gotten hurt."

"Me?" I snap, grabbing his forearms. "What about you?"

I try to push him off, but he doesn't budge. My fingers tighten, and I realize he's shaking, full-body trembles rolling through him.

He doesn't stop searching me until he's satisfied I'm okay.

"You could've gotten hurt." His voice cracks, shattered and raw like the words tear straight out of him.

My words are choked off as my ribs constrict, thoughts thrashing around my brain uncontrollably. I've never heard him sound like that. I never want to hear it again.

I grab his collar, yanking him forward and crashing my mouth against his.

It's not gentle.

It's not tentative.

It's heat and panic and every raw, unspoken thing

that's been building between us since the second we stopped pretending to hate each other.

Maverick freezes just for a beat. Long enough for my stomach to bottom out, for that flash of terror to grip me.

Then he exhales into me.

And kisses me back like it's the only way to survive.

His hands fist in my shirt, dragging me closer until there's no space left between us. Until the tension, the adrenaline, the fear, it all combusts into something feral. Our teeth clash. My fingers twist in his hair. I want to feel every part of him, want to mark him, want to brand this moment into something permanent.

Because I almost lost him.

Because I didn't even realize how badly I wanted him until the thought of him dying nearly tore me in half.

Maverick growls low in his throat, one hand sliding around the back of my neck, the other gripping my waist like he doesn't trust the ground not to disappear under us. His kiss is all fire and frustration, all unspoken confessions he hasn't figured out how to say.

I kiss him like I mean it.

His mouth opens under mine, lips slick and demanding. I lose myself in it in him until I'm drunk on the taste of him, on the sound of his breath hitching against my jaw.

When we finally break apart, it's not because we want to.

It's because we have to.

We stand there, chests heaving, foreheads pressed

together like the only thing holding us upright is each other.

His voice is hoarse when he speaks. "You scared the shit out of me."

"You scared me first," I whisper back.

He swallows hard, like there's too much he wants to say, but before he can, there's a sharp knock on the door, followed by a shout.

"They're asking for you, Kane. You good?"

Maverick doesn't answer. He just steps back, still holding my gaze like he doesn't trust himself to turn away.

I nod. "Go do your job."

He hesitates, then presses his forehead to mine again for the briefest second before pulling away.

"I'll come find you after," he murmurs, voice still rough, still wrecked.

Then he's gone, the door swinging shut behind him, and I'm left standing in the quiet, breathless and shaking, knowing nothing between us will ever be the same again.

I'm not breathing right.

Not because I'm out of air, but because I don't know how to take in anything that doesn't taste like him.

My lips still tingle. My chest is still cracked open. I feel exposed and full and hollow all at once.

For the first time in my life, I think I get it. What people mean when they talk about being undone by someone.

A soft knock pulls me back to earth, and then the door eases open.

Callie steps inside, her eyes landing on me immediately.

She takes one look at me, hand still covering my mouth, hair a mess, probably looking like I've just been run over by an emotional eighteen-wheeler, and her expression softens.

She doesn't ask what happened.

She doesn't need to.

She just closes the door behind her and walks straight to me, arms wrapping around my middle like she's done it a thousand times. Like this is where she belongs.

I sink into her without hesitation.

"Hey," she murmurs into my chest, her cheek resting over my heart.

"Hey." My voice is rougher than it should be, but she doesn't flinch.

Her fingers trace soothing lines up my spine, grounding me. And when I tilt my head to rest against hers, she shifts just enough to press a kiss beneath my jaw. Gentle. Familiar. Hers.

"Luke told me what happened," she says softly, no accusation in her voice, just concern. "Said you went tearing across the arena like your life depended on it."

I nod, but it's shaky. "It felt like it did."

She pulls back just far enough to look at me, hands sliding up to cradle my face. Her thumbs brush along my cheekbones, eyes scanning mine like she's checking for damage.

"He said you got there just in time," she murmurs,

voice almost reverent. "That you hauled Maverick out like a man possessed."

"I was," I admit. "That rope was frayed. If they'd let him out—"

Her eyes widen slightly, understanding dawning in the way her hands still against my skin.

"Oh," she whispers.

"Yeah."

We fall quiet, the weight of what could've happened still thick in the air.

I lower my hand from my mouth, finally, and her gaze follows the movement. Her brows tug slightly, curious.

"You okay?" she asks again, more pointed this time.

Instead of answering, I lean in and kiss her slowly, grounding, nothing like the desperation I had with Maverick. This one is all comfort. All warmth. All the ways I love her that I still don't know how to say.

She melts into it, arms tightening around me, her fingers finding the back of my neck and anchoring me there. When we finally break apart, she rests her forehead against mine.

"You're kind of a mess right now," she says with a little smile.

"Yeah, well," I mutter. "You try saving a guy's life, kissing him breathless, and then immediately getting wrapped up by a girl who smells like heaven, and see how you do."

Chapter 31

Callie

"Olé, Olé, Olé, Olé... O-lé... O-lé."

Beer sloshes over the edge of Luke's glass as he belts out his fifth celebration chant of the night. He's clinging to Marco for support, though judging by Marco's equally wobbly stance, neither of them is doing much stabilizing. Luke landed the best score of the night, and he's decided to celebrate with the full obnoxious joy of a frat boy who just discovered tequila.

I laugh along with them, the silly chant catching like wildfire across our corner of the pub. I'm pretty sure the song's from soccer, but no one seems to care. It works.

We managed to land ourselves in a proper pub tonight, not a country bar, for once, and it's a nice break from all the twang and two-stepping. Not that I mind cowboy bars, but after weeks on the road with the same crew, the change of scenery feels like a vacation.

Well... not much of a break, considering this place is

still packed wall-to-wall with riders from tonight's event. Luke's a wild staple of the circuit, and the loyalty shows. The way people have gathered around him tonight, it's clear he's earned their respect. He's magnetic when he wants to be and surrounded by a rotating orbit of friends and fans.

My eyes drift toward Maverick and Colt.

Colt's been practically glued to Maverick's side all night, not that either of them would admit it. There's still a hint of nerves clinging to Colt, like adrenaline hasn't fully let go yet. Their gazes keep catching, lingering longer than usual. There's a weight to the silence between them. A shifting.

Then Colt's shoulder brushes Maverick's, and Maverick doesn't pull away.

Instead, he leans in to say something, closer than he needs to be, voice low against Colt's ear. My chest tightens not with jealousy but with something quieter. Warmer. The resistance they've clung to for so long is dissolving right in front of me. Not all at once. Unraveling.

They catch me watching.

Their attention slides to where I'm sitting with a few of the guys, laughter vibrating through the table as empty glasses pile higher. I don't break their gaze as they approach. Something about this moment feels important.

Maverick reaches me first, hand outstretched. "Come here."

Before I can ask what for, he tugs me gently to my feet, only to switch our positions. He drops into my spot on the bench and pulls me down beside him, dragging me close until our thighs touch. Colt slides in on my other side, the wood creaking beneath his weight as he brackets me in.

Neither of them says anything.

They don't have to.

They just sit there, one on either side of me, shoulders brushing mine, chatting casually with the rest of the group as if this is normal. As if this is always how it's been. Warmth builds in my chest, slow and steady. This moment mirrors that first day I saw them again. But now, the tension that once simmered between them is gone.

In its place: ease.

Familiarity.

Like something old and beautiful settling back into place.

They've still got things to work through, things I'll make damn sure they talk about but tonight? Tonight, we're just us.

I press my palm to the center of my chest, trying to ease the ache that's been creeping in more often lately. Time's speeding up. When I first got here, it felt like I had all summer. Now, it's slipping through my fingers like sand.

Colt leans closer, his breath warm against my ear. "What're you thinking about so hard, Sunshine?"

His voice wraps around me like velvet, and the ache in my chest is instantly replaced by something hotter. He doesn't wait for an answer. His hand is already sliding beneath the table, warm fingers wrapping around my knee, then moving slowly higher.

Not casual. Not comforting.

Intentional.

I take a sharp breath, my thighs tensing. We're surrounded by people, music pulsing, glasses clinking, laughter all around us, but all I can feel is Colt.

His thumb traces the soft skin just above the bend of my knee, back and forth, slow and steady. The kind of rhythm that feels practiced. That makes my stomach flutter.

Then, he drags it higher.

Up, over the curve of my thigh. Just under the hem of my shorts.

He's not touching me, not really. But it's everything. Every pass leaves me twitching, breath shallow, hips angling ever so slightly toward him. The ache in my core builds with every stroke.

I grab my drink with both hands, hoping no one can see how flushed I am. How hard I'm gripping the glass. How much I'm trembling.

Colt leans back like nothing's happening, like he's not slowly unraveling me in front of a crowd. He's still chatting with the guys across the table, voice smooth and steady as ever.

Maverick notices. He always notices.

His eyes track Colt's hand beneath the table, then flick up to mine. I'm caught in his stare, dark, unreadable, and I swear I stop breathing. His gaze drops to my parted lips, then lower to where Colt's hand still rests, stroking slow circles against the inside of my thigh.

Maverick's jaw flexes... and then he moves.

His hand slides beneath the tabletop and wraps around my other thigh.

A full-body shiver races through me.

His grip is firm, anchoring me in place as his fingers inch higher. My legs are trapped between them now. Colt's heat on one side, Maverick's steadiness on the other. I can't move. Can't hide. All I can do is sit still and try not to come undone in the middle of a packed bar.

When I shift just slightly, chasing the pressure, their knuckles brush.

Colt's breath catches, and Maverick's hand freezes in place.

I watch Colt's fingers twitch, a faint tremble betraying the tension in his hand. He doesn't pull away.

A pause. A heartbeat.

Maverick doesn't move. Doesn't breathe.

Then gently, like he's afraid to startle him, Maverick slides his finger along the seam between Colt's.

A silent question left hanging between them.

I don't dare breathe as I wait for what happens next, my skin tingling beneath their palms and my chest tightening with anticipation.

Kissing is one thing. It's fire and heat and lust. It can be blamed on the moment, on instinct.

Holding hands is sweet. Caring. Tender.

Maverick's left himself wide open, vulnerable as the

moments tick by. But he doesn't push or pull away, just keeps running his knuckles over Colt's, making his intentions clear.

Giving Colt the room and the power to decide what happens next.

Colt stays frozen, caught in the moment, then *slowly* opens his fingers.

Welcoming.

The air catches in my lungs as Maverick threads his fingers between Colt's.

No teasing. No swagger.

Just quiet, trembling closeness.

It's somehow more intimate than anything we've done.

Maybe I'm drunk. Maybe the alcohol has made me too soft, too open, but I swear the whole world shifts in that moment.

Because I know what it cost them to get here.

And even more. I know what it means that they're reaching for each other now.

Not because of me.

But because of them.

Because maybe, somewhere deep down, we've always wanted this.

Their hands move in tandem now, trailing higher, deeper. My head tips back as their pinkies sweep up, grazing the sensitive seam of my shorts pressing into me.

I choke on a breath. My eyes dart to the crowded room. No one's looking, not really, but we're far from alone. Marco's laughing with someone two tables over. Luke's still shouting victory songs at the bar.

But under the table?

They're ruining me.

I squeeze my legs together, trying to contain it to hide the frantic pulse building between my thighs, but it only makes it worse. Their hands bump again, this time fully pressed against either side of my heat. The pressure, the contact, the heat of their fingers so close to each other. It's unbearable. *Intoxicating.*

Then Maverick presses in, deliberate, certain, sliding his thumb down the line of my core.

Colt follows suit.

When their thumbs meet over my clit, pressing lightly, dragging together in unison, I break.

A quiet gasp escapes before I can stop it, too soft to carry but loud enough to draw Marco's eyes.

I still. Colt's hand stops. Maverick's too, their gazes hot on the sides of my face.

I grip the edge of the table so hard my knuckles go white. I should stop this. I should push them away. I should say something. Anything.

"Let's dance!" Luke yells, slamming his empty glass down on the table like a gavel, his face flushed with alcohol and triumph. The sound snaps through our little bubble, shattering the spell with all the grace of a car crash.

Reality hits hard.

The bar comes rushing back, laughter, music, the

crush of bodies. A dozen pairs of eyes that could turn this secret into something public.

I'd been so lost in their touch, so caught up in the slow, torturous buildup, I forgot where we were. Who was watching.

Forgot I was two strokes away from a full-blown orgasm in the middle of a goddamn pub.

"Yes!" My voice shoots up an octave, loud and too bright. I lunge at the opening, desperate for a reset. "Dancing. Great idea."

I shove Colt's shoulder, nudging him out of the booth, my hands shaking just slightly. He lets me, thank God, because there's no way I could've moved him otherwise. Maverick slides out right behind us, gaze heavy on my back.

I don't dare look at either of them.

Because if I do, I'm not sure I'll be able to walk straight.

And I really, really need to.

I break for the dance floor, escaping the booth like it might catch fire behind me, because if I stayed even one second longer, I'd have climbed into their laps and begged.

Colt's on me in an instant, catching my hand and pulling me into the pulsing crowd. The beat drops, some twangy remix that shouldn't work but absolutely does, and I throw my head back on a laugh as he spins me around.

My skin's already flushed, my limbs loose. I'm warm and drunk and dizzy in the best way. The alcohol has pulled all the tension from my muscles, and I let myself fall into the rhythm.

I glance over, and sure enough, Maverick stands off to the side, arms crossed, half-shadowed. I can't read his expression, but the weight of his stare hits me like a body shot. It slinks across my skin, electric and hot, and makes me stumble right over the next step.

Colt catches me. His fingers tighten at my side, one hand skimming under the hem of my shirt like he doesn't even notice he's doing it.

The DJ cranks the volume, and the whole place shifts. Dance music kicks in louder, messier, a little dirtier. Less line dancing, more grinding. A low, rhythmic thump that goes straight to the base of my spine.

"Well, this is unexpected," Colt mutters, and his mouth is at my ear, his breath skating across my neck. A shiver rolls through me, and I don't even try to hide it.

I laugh and let my hips start to move, my hands lifted in a rhythm that could only be called drunk white girl chaos. Colt keeps pace with me, close but not pressing, and I let myself feel it. The heat of the crowd, the scrape of denim, the pulse of music humming through my blood like a second heartbeat.

I spin.

Colt's there to catch me again, hands sliding down to my hips.

My body's buzzing, my thoughts a slow molasses drip.

And I know Maverick's still watching.

I can feel it.

That low hum beneath my skin? That's him. That tension stringing tighter with every second he stands off to the side.

I shoot him a coy smile over my shoulder because if he refuses to dance, that's on him. But he's the one missing out.

Colt draws me back in, his hands stroking absentmindedly across my waist, through the thin cotton of my shirt. I let my forehead drop to his chest, soaking in the solid press of him, his heartbeat thumping against my cheek like a war drum.

Then Colt stills.

Just for a second before I feel the new heat at my back.

A hard chest presses against me. The scent of pine and leather surrounds me. *Maverick.*

"Fuck," Colt breathes.

"Fuck," Maverick echoes, voice lower, rougher.

I don't move.

Can't.

Colt's hands flex at my waist. His pinkies brush the curve of my ass, and it punches the breath from my lungs. Behind me, Maverick grips my hips.

The three of us lock into place like we've always belonged this way. I'm not just standing between them. I'm cradled. Supported. Surrounded.

I try to shift for balance, but there's nowhere to go. Colt's chest to my front, Maverick's thighs framing mine from behind. I'm caught, suspended in heat and muscle and want.

My fingers curl into Colt's shirt. One hand drops to Maverick's thigh, splayed wide across the muscle. He's so solid it makes me ache.

Maverick lets out a hum that vibrates through my whole spine. I feel it in my teeth. My hips shift forward on instinct.

Colt groans, and suddenly, his hands are tightening again, grounding me as I rock between them. The air crackles. My skin buzzes. The crowd blurs and vanishes.

Maverick leans forward, lifting the hair off the back of my neck and blowing a soft stream of air there. I jolt like I've been touched with fire. My legs squeeze together instinctively, chasing friction, but Colt's thigh slips between mine, holding me open.

My breath stutters. A whine escapes before I can stop it.

Colt's mouth finds my ear. "Fucking adorable."

Chapter 32

Callie

MAVERICK'S MOUTH is at my neck, breath hot, chest flush against my back as Colt fumbles with the motel key like his hands forgot how to work. The second the door unlocks and clicks shut behind us, Colt turns on a dime.

He grabs Maverick over my shoulder, one fist in his shirt, the other braced against the wall, and slams him back hard, taking me with him.

I gasp, caught in the middle as Maverick grunts behind me from the impact. He doesn't loosen his hold on me, just tightens his arms around my waist, keeping me pinned between them.

Colt's mouth is on mine instantly, claiming me with heat and hunger. His fingers cup my chin, tilting my head up as he deepens the kiss, his thumbs stroking my cheekbones. I moan into him, grip his shirt in both fists, twisting it to pull him closer.

My head drops back to Maverick's shoulder as Colt

rocks his hips against me, grinding his cock against my center. Behind me, Maverick presses into my ass, and I can feel every inch of him hard, ready, straining. Colt bites my bottom lip, sharp enough to sting, then soothes it with a lick, tasting me like he's starving.

Maverick's hands leave my hips. I open my eyes just in time to see him thread his fingers into the hair at the base of Colt's neck, pulling him closer. I twist in their arms, watching as their foreheads connect, noses aligned, sharing each other's ragged breaths.

They're unsteady and broken, like every inhale is harder than the last.

Tension coils between them, their bodies going rigid against me with every second that ticks by. The spark in the air turns electric, crackling across my skin.

I don't move.

I don't make a sound.

I don't dare breathe.

The sound Colt makes bleeds into a groan as their mouths meet. My hands splay against his chest, feeling the tremble beneath my palms.

Maverick's grip tightens in Colt's hair, pulling him closer in silent approval.

Colt sucks Maverick's tongue into his mouth, and Maverick moans, deep and guttural, his hips jerking forward, cock grinding into my ass uncontrollably.

The sound of them, the taste, the heat, the way they fall into each other has need clawing through me. Colt's hips thrust into my clit with every grind. The pressure from both sides is dizzying.

A frustrated sound tears from my throat.

Clothes.

Too many goddamn clothes.

I want their bare cocks rubbing against me, sliding through my wetness, giving me the friction I'm dying for. As if reading my mind, Maverick breaks the kiss just long enough to yank my shirt over my head and unclasp my bra.

Colt's already shedding the rest of his clothes, boxers kicked off with a grunt. Maverick bends to peel my shorts and underwear down in one smooth motion, tossing them aside. Colt groans, deep and raw, as my naked body presses into his, his cock sliding against me.

He reaches for Maverick next, grabbing the front of his shirt and pulling him away from me just long enough to tear it over his head. Desperation clings to every motion. Maverick hums, pleased, as he allows Colt to take the lead.

Colt walks backward toward the bed, his hand fisted in my hair, keeping my mouth on his. I catch the faint rustle of Maverick's remaining clothes hitting the floor. His hands are splayed across the small of my back, palms pressing into the top of my ass as his fingers curve around my waist.

Maverick uses my hips to guide us to the bed. Colt's sucking in a breath when the mattress hits behind his knees, and he topples backward. Maverick holds me steady so I don't fall with him.

Colt's laid out before us, golden skin flushed, every muscle defined, his abs leading down to where his cock throbs against his stomach, thick and ready. Precum pools at the tip, dripping down his length.

Maverick leans in, biting my neck, sucking a line up to my ear, and I moan, half from the sensation, half from the anticipation. His fingers slide between my legs, stroking through my soaked core.

"Fuck," he murmurs, voice like gravel. "You're dripping, Wildflower. Desperate for him to fill you up?"

I nod, no words left in me.

Maverick lifts me, positioning me so I'm straddling Colt, one hand on my waist, the other gripping my thigh. They work in tandem, Maverick supporting me as Colt holds himself steady, the tip of his cock nudging my entrance.

He fills me, stretching me over his length as I'm slowly lowered, inch after agonizing inch. I quake, chin tipping back, eyes closed, unable to breathe as Colt fills me completely.

Colt grips my thighs, holding me in place while I adjust, his cock pulsing inside me. The fullness is nearly too much, but it's everything I want.

When I finally nod, Maverick lifts me as Colt thrusts up into me.

My teeth clench, hands wrapping around the back of Maverick's neck for stability, nails digging into his skin.

I'm quivering, unable to do anything but take what he's giving me. He shifts his hips, finding the angle that makes stars burst behind my eyes.

"There," I rasp. "Right there."

His chuckle is rough as he grips me tighter, holding me in place while he drives into that spot again and again, building pressure. Each thrust sending shocks through my core, straight to where my clit aches for more.

Colt and I moan at the same time as Maverick reaches between us, sliding his fingers through my soaked core, not stopping until they're on either side of where Colt's buried inside me. I feel the exact moment they touch. Colt's thrusts falter, a broken groan slipping from his lips before he fucks me harder.

The two of them drive me closer to the edge as Maverick slips his fingers forward and back, pressing and circling my clit with each pass. My skin comes alive, every molecule of my being, singing as the tension builds between my thighs.

His other hand comes up to my breast, pinching and rolling my nipple between his fingers, while he swallows my cry, lips hot against mine, tongue plunging deep as if to match Colt's thrusts.

It's like being fucked twice, and I lose it. My pussy clenches, pulsing with the force of an orgasm, shattering me as I sob into Maverick's mouth.

Colt curses and slams up into me one final time, spilling inside me, heat flooding my core.

I collapse, gasping, trembling as Maverick eases me

down onto Colt's chest. My thighs are shaking, my lungs burning as Colt's cock slips from me, and I whimper at the loss.

Maverick presses kisses to my shoulder, humming low in his throat. "You are such a needy girl," he murmurs against my ear, nipping it with his teeth.

It shoots straight to my core.

And I know. I'm not done.

I don't care if it's needy. I don't care if it's too much.

I want more.

Maverick cups my ass, spreading me open. His cock slides along the seam, teasing, tempting.

His voice is a growl, low and dark and full of promise.

"We're not done yet."

Chapter 33

Colt

Maverick's promise reverberates through me, goosebumps rising in its wake. Heat from Callie's soft gasp and response to his touch curls against my neck. She shivers, and I totally get it. There's something in his voice, the way his command leases his words without raising it. I just came, but my cock still twitches in response.

His hooded eyes meet mine, dark with swirling lust, barely banked behind his lashes. He hasn't gotten a true taste of our girl yet. A level of patience I could never match.

Callie presses harder against my chest, making an incoherent sound when he gives her a gentle squeeze and then lets go.

"Take care of her," Maverick says before exiting the room, not waiting for my response, already knowing that I'll do it, with or without his command. But there's something so much hotter with him directing me.

I graze my fingers along Callie's back over the ridge of her spine in a long, smooth movement before descending. She settles into me, splayed out naked, her knees on either side of mine, leaving her completely exposed. Her deep breath did nothing to cut through the anticipation for what Maverick has planned.

He comes back into the room, cock rock-hard, flushed so red it must be aching. I swallow, throat dry, wondering just how many times he jerked off in our room to make it this long. This is the first time I've really gotten to look at it. I've known him for years, and sharing the same locker room made it impossible not to catch glimpses. But his length and width have me shuddering. It twitches under my gaze, and I snap to Maverick, who's already looking at me. His thumb runs along his bottom lip, which is curved in a slight grin. He doesn't look away as he reaches down, gripping his cock and moving in long, slow strokes.

Fuck. My heart's going wild, thundering against my chest, heat flushing my skin as I watch. Callie trembles when Maverick runs his hands along her back, starting at her shoulders and making their way all the way to the globe of her ass. They brush across me in their descent, and I groan at the barest touch.

I shouldn't be able to get hard right now, but I can already feel myself getting stiffer where I'm pressed into Callie's soft stomach.

That's when I see the plastic bottle he set on the bed beside her knees. When the fuck did he have time to get lube? I barely register the thought before Maverick's guiding Callie's hips into the air so that she's kneeling, upper body still pressed into me.

"You are so fucking beautiful," Maverick growls while his hands are still running all over her. She shivers every time he gets close to her core. Slow and torturous, he takes his time, in languished movements. He's stoking a fire, building it ember by ember, listening to her every breath, watching her every response.

Her nails dig into my chest as his hands travel up her thighs. She sucks in a breath, quivering as he reaches her pussy, this time not moving away. I follow the curve of Callie's arched back until where Maverick's cock is visible above her ass. He's dripping in precum. The beads run down the length of him. A low hum forms in the back of my throat, knowing he's just as turned on as we are.

Callie shifts, pressing back into his touch in a steady rhythm. Her voice turns needy, frantic, desperate as he fucks his fingers inside her.

"That's three fingers, Callie. Look how well you can take me after taking Colt's cock."

My cock jerks at the mention, angry that Callie is no longer pressed against it. She whimpers when he pulls out, hips rocking back as if chasing him. He grips her ass, holding her steady. A low chuckle forms deep in his throat.

"I need you to trust me, Callie," he says as he grabs the bottle from the bed and pops the cap. "Can you do that for me, Wildflower?"

She nods against my chest, and I can feel the heat of her breath when she rasps, "Yes."

He growls, pleased, and it goes straight to my cock.

His now lubricated fingers travel up her seam. Her head lifts, gaze snapping to mine as she lets out a surprise squeak. I can't see what's happening, but I can guess. Callie's nails are digging crescents into my skin as Maverick starts to press against her tight rim.

"I want to take you here, Callie."

A shiver rolls through her, and my cock weeps at the image of her taking him into her ass.

"You want that too, don't you?"

"I-I want it." Her voice breaks.

"You are such a good girl Callie," he purrs.

She's trembling in my arms as I hold her in place, breaths coming out in shallow pants.

"That's it. You're doing so well."

She whimpers and moves into his fingers

Holy shit, that's so fucking hot.

I reach between us, stroking my cock, and press the tip into her soft skin, leaving wet trails over her navel.

"Kiss her, Colt."

She tastes good on my tongue as I take her mouth. The tension drains from her limbs as she relaxes, letting me have all of her weight.

Maverick removes his fingers, drawing a whimper from our girl as he lines his cock up with her pussy, slowly entering her. A low growl grits through his teeth as he waits for her to adjust before he carefully begins to roll his hips.

The sound she makes has me stroking myself faster. I grunt, going fucking cross-eyed when Maverick slams into her and her belly strokes my cock, my precum making her wet as I slide against her.

I capture her mouth with mine again, loving the way it has her relaxing into me. Like my mouth, my kiss, my tongue is the only thing she needs.

I stroke my length in time with Maverick's thrusts. The rhythm he's setting has my breath hitching in my throat. He leans forward, his presence looming over us. His teeth are clenched together as he wrangles himself, keeping each of his movements controlled, drawing every last ounce of pleasure out of her.

It's clear that, for him, his partner takes priority. He gets off on it. His teeth sink into his bottom lip when she presses back, asking for more, and he gives it to her, going harder and faster, drawing out her moans until she's making nothing but incoherent, needy sounds.

Maverick leans over us, palm pressed into her back, keeping her in place as her soft skin rubs against my length with each roll of his hips.

What would it feel like to be the one receiving that kind of care? To have him pay attention to my every reaction. A ripple runs through me, and my cock grows impossibly harder. Now that the thought's there, I can't shake it. I groan, and Maverick catches me watching. His eyes search my face before darkening. He thrusts, gauging my reaction. My mouth opens, cock slamming into Callie.

She feels so fucking good, her body wrapped around mine, holding on to me fiercely as she takes her pleasure. Maverick's attention is burning itself permanently into my skin. With every roll of his hips, it feels like he's fucking himself into me.

My teeth clench together, eyes shut, and my head presses back into the mattress as I work myself closer and closer to the edge. It feels like every muscle in my body is stretched taut, begging for just a little more. My eyes snap open when Maverick's firm grip encloses mine, guiding my hand from root to tip.

I come with enough force to knock the air out of me, moaning through gritted teeth as I uncontrollably fuck into his hand. Callie grinds into us, calling our names. She's shaking, trembles rolling through her as she follows me over the edge.

Maverick's growl fills the room as he ruts into her, his head thrown back with his release.

He arches over her forehead, resting into her back, taking long, deep breaths as he slowly gains control. Several moments pass before he groans and lifts off us and walks out of the room.

Callie doesn't notice, lost in her own little world of bliss. She shows no signs of movement as I lift my hips slightly and tug the pillow out from under me and shift my way up the bed to rest against the headboard. With a firm grip on her waist, I bring her with me. Maverick walks back in, holding two bottles of water, and places them on the nightstand, along with two wet cloths. He holds one out to me. It's warm but not hot, like he took the time to set the perfect temperature. He takes extra care as he slides it down through her legs. She makes a muffled sound but doesn't protest, just snuggles in deeper to me. Once she's clean, he helps me roll her to my side, where I keep her tucked against me with an arm wrapped around her waist. I swallow hard, seeing the mess I made of her stomach, coated in my cum. If I didn't know it was about to turn sticky, I would keep her like that. A little disappointed, I wipe it off, then move on to myself. Maverick takes my dirty towel from me and hands me an open bottle of water.

Warmth flushes through me, contracting my chest, where there is a dull ache. It's hard to process exactly what I'm feeling right now.

Content.

Happy.

Right.

Callie's eyes peel open as I lift her face, and she takes delicate sips of the water. There's a smile in her eyes as she hums, then returns to snuggle into my side. The water feels good on my raw throat. Mav's pulling on his clothes as I finish the rest of the water. It's late, but I don't ask him where he's going. There's a tug in my chest as the door closes behind him.

I move Callie and lower her onto the bed, resting my chin on top of her head.

What the hell am I doing?

Chapter 34

Maverick

The clock glows 2:14 a.m.

The room's quiet except for the occasional hum of the fridge.

I shift on the creaky mattress, trying to find a position that doesn't ache.

Colt mumbles something.

I freeze, ears straining, and catch the end of it, just a whisper.

"Thought you hated me."

It's so soft I almost think I imagined it.

He shifts again, deeper into sleep, his breathing evening out.

I stare at the ceiling, throat tight, then pull myself out of bed, needing fresh air. The door clicks behind me, and my breath whooshes out. My hands shake slightly as I grip the balcony railing for support. The metal bites into my palms, grounding me when everything else feels like it's sliding out from under me. My racing heart pounds in my ears as I sort through my thoughts. I wanted him. When his blue eyes looked up at mine through his dark lashes, I fucking wanted him as much as I wanted her. And that realization scares the shit out of me.

I'd been turned on when we kissed, but this was something more. Like the lock broke on a box that I have buried deep inside of me, and all of those wants, needs, and feelings came rushing out. My fingers tighten over the railing until they turn white as I process what just happened. Callie warm and clutching around my cock, her tight ass gripping my finger. Colt moaning every time I fuck her. The realization that he felt pleasure with each roll of my hip, sending my mind reeling. I listened to both of them, chasing every breath, every tremor, wanting to see how much I could push it, how much pleasure I could draw from them. I wanted the moment to be seared into them until it couldn't possibly be replaced.

The second I came, the post-nut clarity hit me hard.

I could have been totally misreading this entire situation. Of course he was fucking turned on. He was grinding against Callie. That doesn't mean he wants to have sex with me. It definitely doesn't mean he wants more.

I groan, dropping my head to the railing. "I am such a fucking idiot. What the hell am I thinking?"

But no matter what I do, I keep coming around to the fact that I wanted it, and now, I want more.

I want her moans and whimpers, but I want his too.

"Fuck." I rake my hand through my hair, gripping the ends, and look up at the sky. I am so fucking screwed.

I take deep inhales, the cool night breeze bringing thoughts of fall with it. I'm running out of time. Time to convince Callie to stay. Time to fix this thing between Colt and me.

I'm done fucking ignoring it. Done letting this anger between us fester. I'm not giving up until we sort this through, facing it head-on. But I need to take it slow. If I pressure him too hard, he's just going to push back. But I'm done letting him be silent.

I thought stepping on the podium and taking the buckle for Rookie of the Year would taste sweet, but instead, it was hollow.

I wanted him to be proud of me.

I won something we were both fighting so hard for.

We trained together, lived and breathed ranking higher in the sport.

I thought we were the same. That no matter what, the only thing that mattered was reaching the top.

After that, he never looked at me the same. Brushed me off every time I tried to talk to him.

Eventually, a bitterness grew inside me, one that was fed every time we competed.

Our very competitive nature drove a rift right between us.

I had been a cocky, arrogant idiot, so full of myself, thinking I understood what was important.

I was so fucking wrong.

I was chasing the win, blind to everything else.

Had I realized what was happening. How fragile it all was, how close we were to losing each other, I would've done everything differently.

It shouldn't have taken Callie coming back for me to see it clearly.

To recognize that all the animosity, all the resentment, was nothing but a frail cover for hurt.

A young kid's selfish pride.

The belief that the world revolved around me.

It didn't matter to me why Colt was upset because *I* was upset too.

Every time he pushed me away, it only proved what I wanted to believe: that he was wrong.

That his unhappiness was his failure, not mine.

Had I taken my head out of my ass for a single second, I would've realized I was being an immature idiot.

I miss him. God, I've missed him so much.

Colt would never not be happy for me unless something deeper was broken.

And I should've pushed to find out what.

I can't go back.

But I won't make that mistake again.

Fall is coming.

But I'm not losing them.

Not this time.

Not ever again.

Chapter 35

Callie

I slept like the dead last night.

Somewhere between the whiskey and the dancing and the slow, heated looks that said everything words couldn't, the three of us tilted off axis.

Somehow, when the morning comes, we don't tilt back.

The room feels too quiet afterward, like the silence is alive.

Colt shifts beside me, his fingers trailing lazily down my arm, tracing invisible lines like he's mapping me into memory.

Maverick's breathing is slow and steady behind me, his chest pressing into my spine with every rise and fall.

Nobody says anything.

We don't need to.

Every nerve in my body feels raw, scraped clean and

left open to the air, but it's not a bad feeling. It's the kind of rawness that means you transcended something.

That you *earned* it.

I blink up at the cracked ceiling, counting the fading shadows from the broken blinds, and wonder if this is what peace feels like.

Colt's hand finds mine, his thumb rubbing slow, lazy circles over the back of it.

I squeeze back, just once.

Maverick lets out a quiet, contented sound, half sigh, half hum.

It drags a sleepy smile out of me, and before I know it, my whole body is sinking deeper into the mattress, into their touch, into this impossible, perfect thing we've built between us.

Luke bangs on the motel door just after sunrise, yelling something about breakfast burritos and the best coffee west of Texas.

Colt groans, and Maverick flings a pillow at the door without even lifting his head. Colt shifts behind me, sleep-warm and heavy, his arm tightening instinctively around my waist.

Maverick's hand finds mine in the tangle of sheets, his fingers curling around mine like a promise he doesn't know he's making.

The motel hums around us, distant traffic, the low thrum of an ice machine down the hall.

I close my eyes and pretend the world outside doesn't exist.

Sitting cross-legged, fresh from the shower, I braid my still-damp hair. Maverick yanks one loose as he passes, grinning when I curse at him. Colt steals the last clean towel, and Maverick steals Colt's hat in revenge, jamming it onto his head backward and smirking like a satisfied cat.

It's ridiculous and messy and chaotic.

And it's perfect.

We pile into Maverick's truck because none of us trusts Luke's sense of direction or his sense of speed this early in the morning.

The windows are down. The air smells like dust and sun and the faint sweetness of hayfields baking in the heat.

Maverick props his boots on the dash despite Colt's half-hearted threats to break both his legs. I curl into the seat between them, my bare knees brushing theirs, too content to care where we're going.

"This is dangerous," Colt says, lazily draping his arm over the back of the seat behind me. "Three idiots, one truck, no supervision."

I glance at Maverick. "When have we ever needed supervision?"

He huffs a laugh, tipping his head back. "Good point."

We find a breakfast joint that looks like it's been

standing since the sixties, tucked on the side of a dirt road nobody uses anymore.

Inside, it's all cracked vinyl booths and faded photos of rodeos past.

Luke's already there when we pull in, a donut in each hand, powdered sugar dusting his black T-shirt like snow.

"'Bout time you idiots showed up," he calls, flashing a sugar-drenched grin.

Colt flips him off. Maverick steals one of the donuts without slowing down.

Luke just laughs like he's got all the time in the world. Like he always has.

Colt orders enough food for five people. Maverick steals my bacon the second I look away. I retaliate by stealing his toast and dumping hot sauce on it when he's not paying attention.

He nearly chokes, and Colt howls with laughter loud enough to make the waitress snort behind the counter.

We sit there way too long, drinking refills of coffee, listening to the old-timers at the next table argue about bull stats from twenty years ago like it's life and death.

I can't stop smiling.

Neither can they.

Later, after we're full and lazy with sun, we end up down by a river we spotted on the drive.

It's wide and slow and sparkling like a mirror under the afternoon heat.

We kick off our boots and wade in up to our knees, the water shockingly cold against our sunburned skin.

Maverick starts a splash war that ends with Colt tackling him straight into the mud.

I try to slip away, laughing so hard my sides hurt, but they're faster. Maverick grabs me around the waist and hauls me backward with a triumphant roar.

Colt comes up behind us, hands steadying my shoulders just as Maverick lets go.

And for a breathless second, sandwiched between them, laughter ringing in my ears, I swear the world stops spinning.

We dry off in the sun, sprawled out on the grass like stray dogs.

Colt lies flat on his back, arms flung wide, flooding in the heat. Maverick sits cross-legged, one knee bent, tossing rocks into the river with half-hearted aim.

I end up between them without even thinking.

My head finds a spot against Colt's chest, the steady rise and fall of his breathing slow and solid beneath my cheek.

One hand curls loosely around Maverick's ankle where it juts toward me, his skin warm and rough under my palm.

The sun beats down, soaking into our clothes, drying the river water clinging to our skin. A faint breeze stirs the scent of wet grass and river rocks into the air, crisp and clean and sharp with the coming change of seasons.

It reminds me of those endless summers we thought would never end before life got complicated.

Colt would climb the trees by the river and leap out

with no warning, sending Maverick into a panic trying to fish him out.

I'd sit on the bank with my knees tucked to my chest, pretending not to watch them, pretending not to care but secretly hoarding every laugh, every wild, reckless second.

"You remember when you fell in trying to show off?" I murmur, nudging Colt's boot with my toe.

He cracks one eye open, grin lazy. "I was demonstrating advanced river-crossing techniques."

"You lost your shorts," Maverick supplies helpfully, chucking another rock toward the water.

"Strategic," Colt says solemnly. "Kept me aerodynamic."

I laugh, free and full, and Colt's chest shakes beneath me.

Maverick just shakes his head, lips twitching, but there's a softness in his eyes that's impossible to miss.

We were kids then. We're not now.

But somehow, lying here in the sun, it feels like we found our way back to something we thought we'd lost.

After a while, Maverick's fingers find their way into the ends of my hair.

He twists a few strands together, the movements slow and sure, like he's done it a hundred times before.

The tug is gentle, a comforting pull that has my eyes drifting shut without meaning to.

I can feel the occasional brush of his knuckles against the nape of my neck, cool and calloused, making my skin prickle in response.

He works quietly, threading my damp hair into a simple braid, and ties it off at the end with a blade of grass he plucks from the ground.

I smile into Colt's shirt, feeling the faint rumble of his laughter beneath me, even if he doesn't make a sound.

No one says a word about it.

We were always like this, touchy, tangled up.

Colt used to drape himself across the couch with his feet in my lap. Maverick would braid my hair just to have something to do with his hands.

It was never romantic.

It was just... us.

Now, it's more.

Now, there's a charge under the softness. A slow, simmering ache that tightens my chest and twists low in my belly.

But the bones of us. The heart of it. It's still there.

Solid. Familiar. Home.

I shift slightly, leaning my shoulder into Maverick's knee in silent thanks. His fingers linger in my hair a second longer before letting go.

The sun warms our skin. The river murmurs beside us.

And for one perfect moment, everything is exactly the way it should be.

On the way back, I lean my head against the window, and listening to the two of them, a feeling of rightness, contentment, and familiarity hums under my skin as they bicker back and forth.

"You drive like a pissed-off raccoon on meth," Colt says.

"You drive like you're ninety-five and blind."

Later, we find a diner that serves greasy burgers and milkshakes so thick you can stand a spoon upright in them.

Colt demolishes his food like he hasn't eaten in a week. Maverick methodically dismantles his burger like he's studying it for weaknesses. I steal their fries and pretend to be innocent when they glare at me.

The waitress calls me "sugar" and flirts shamelessly with Maverick, who blushes so hard I have to duck my head to hide my laugh.

Colt catches my eye across the table, his grin lazy and full of some secret only we know.

My heart squeezes so tight it's almost painful.

As the sun sets, we end up back at the motel parking lot.

Someone hooks up a speaker to the back of a pickup, and before I know it, half the circuit's out there, boots stomping dust, music spilling into the evening air.

Colt holds out his hand without a word.

I take it.

And he spins me into a two-step so smooth it steals my breath.

We dance until the stars come out. Until the crickets sing loud enough to drown the music.

Maverick leans against the truck, arms crossed, watching us with a look in his eyes that makes my stomach flip.

When I hold out my hand to him and say, "Come on, cowboy, I know you know the steps," he gives in. He joins us.

And for the first time in forever, it feels like nothing is broken.

Nothing is lost.

It's just the three of us, spinning under the stars.

I don't know how long we stay out there.

Long enough for my cheeks to ache from smiling.

Long enough for my feet to blister inside my boots.

Long enough to forget there's a clock ticking down somewhere out of sight.

When we finally stumble back toward the rooms, Maverick's arm slung around my shoulder and Colt's hand warm against the small of my back, I think if this is all I get, it'll be enough.

Even if it tears me apart later.

As we reach the steps, I glance at them, laughter still clinging to my ribs.

Colt tips his hat low, smiling in that soft, crooked way that wrecks me.

Maverick catches my gaze and holds it, something raw and unspoken flashing between us.

I turn back around, pretending I don't feel the way the world's about to tip again.

Because tonight is ours.

Tonight, the world is gold.

And tomorrow... Tomorrow can't touch us.

Chapter 36

Callie

14 Years Old

It's the first time I've come out to the pen in the week since my dad's funeral. I've been locked in the house this whole time, and Maverick and Colt finally convinced me to come out.

Maverick's trying to rope a young steer that's too wild, too fast for him, and even from across the arena, I can tell it's not going to end well.

"Maverick, don't," I call, but he just grins over his shoulder, reckless and golden and fourteen years old, like nothing bad could ever happen to him.

The rope sails through the air, a perfect arc.

And the moment it catches, the steer jerks sideways, harder than he's ready for.

The snap yanks Maverick off his feet, slamming him sideways into the dirt. His body folds awkwardly, shoulder crunching under the full weight of his fall.

For a second, everything freezes.

Then he's gasping, and the sound punches the air from my lungs.

I'm running before I know it, boots skidding over dry grass, heart hammering like a drum in my ears.

When I reach him, he's curled half onto his side, one arm clutched tight against his ribs.

"Mav?" My voice cracks on his name.

He smiles up at me, crooked and bloody-lipped. "Guess that beast's got some fight in him."

He thinks he's being funny. He always thinks he's being funny.

But his eyes are glazed, and he's pale under the sunburn, and his breath comes too short, too shallow.

"Don't move," I whisper, dropping to my knees beside him.

He still smells like dust and sunshine and that stupid soap he always steals from Colt.

I press my hands uselessly against his chest like I can physically hold him together, like I can keep him from falling apart if I just try hard enough.

"It's just a bruise, Cal," he says, but there's a wobble in his voice he can't hide.

"I'm fine."

He's not fine.

Neither am I.

Because all I can see, all I can hear, is my father's body lying broken in the dirt.

The roar of a crowd that didn't know he was already gone.

My vision blurs.

I curl over Maverick, breathing in his warmth, anchoring myself to the steady, stubborn beat of his heart.

I don't know how long we stay like that, locked in a silent battle against the fear trying to tear me apart.

Eventually, Colt jogs up, cursing under his breath when he sees Maverick on the ground.

He kneels beside us, throwing an arm around my back without thinking, steadying both of us.

"We're gonna get him up, okay, Cal?" he says quietly. "Gotta trust me."

I nod, but I don't let go.

Not until they pull him away from me, carefully, gently, carrying him toward the truck, where someone's already calling for ice packs and Tylenol.

I stay kneeling in the dirt long after they're gone, my hands trembling in the empty air where Maverick had been.

Something breaks inside me then.

Something fragile and desperate and beyond fixing.

Because I realize, in that moment, no matter how much I love them...If I stay here, someday, I'll lose them too.

Just like I lost him.

And I won't survive it.

That night, while they're still laughing about it over burgers and soda, I start looking at boarding school applications.

Chapter 37

Colt

Something's felt off all day. A twitch in my fingers. A tension in my gut I couldn't shake. The kind that clings to your ribs like a storm coming. And it doesn't go away when the gate swings open. If anything, it slams harder into me, riding shotgun with instinct, warning me I'm already too late.

Within two seconds, the bull twists left when I'm braced for him to go right, and I know instantly that I've fucked up. The momentum throws me off balance, my weight sliding off his flank. The ride's a bust. I've lost my seat. I swing my leg over, ready to dismount, but just as I lift into the air, the bull's hips snap upward with a violent buck.

The impact sends me flying a good two feet, spinning mid-air. I reach for the rope, my only lifeline, but as I come down, my shoulder wrenches outward, and the tension snaps tight. The coarse fibers bite into my skin, locking me in place. The same rope that's supposed to keep me safe is now the thing chaining me to eight hundred pounds of fury.

I jump in rhythm with the bull, doing my best to rotate my body and free my hand. My feet scramble to keep pace. Every time I miss his rhythm, the jolt rips through my shoulder and up into my neck.

I've trained for this. Spent years learning the rhythm of chaos, how to move with it instead of fight it. But there's no balance to find this time. No timing, no groove. Just blind instinct and the crushing reality that this might be the one ride I don't walk away from.

Four bullfighters close in. I hear them shouting, but their voices are muffled, drowned out by static in my ears.

If eight seconds *on* the bull is dangerous, eight seconds *hung up* is fucking terrifying.

I just have to hold it together until they get me out.

Hands grip my back, hauling me upward. I'm inches from freedom when the bull senses it. He whips toward the inside, veering directly at the bullfighter trying to save me. The guy's forced to let go, or he'll be gored.

His grip slips from my vest, and in the next second, I'm airborne again. The rope snaps taut, my hand still pinned beneath it, trapped against the top of the bull's flank, where it cuts across my palm like a vise.

My body whips forward, feet nearly parallel to my shoulders, joints screaming as I'm slingshotted into the dirt. I hit hard, and pain detonates through me.

My arm yanks with the full force of my weight, the

stretch tearing at every tendon, every socket. My legs drag behind me, boots scraping trenches in the arena floor, but there's nothing to catch. No leverage. Just the churn of hooves and dust.

I can't get my feet under me.

Can't lift myself.

Hooves crash down inches from my thighs, kicking up a storm of grit that blinds me and burns in my lungs.

The bull twists again, savage and sudden. My shoulder tears open with white-hot pain, and then he rears.

All that weight comes down on my leg, the sickening crunch reverberating down my shin.

A guttural scream rips from my throat, but even that pain feels distant, muted by the sheer chaos flooding my brain.

My body's being slammed over and over. The hooves are still too close, and with every buck, I'm jerked skyward, then slammed down like a rag doll.

I'm going to die like this.

The realization doesn't hit like fear. It hits like grief.

I always thought I wasn't afraid to die. I thought I'd stare it down, cowboy up, go out hard and fast.

But this isn't that.

This isn't courage or peace or pride.

This is devastation.

I want to scream. I want to fight. I want to claw my way out of this. Beg. Plead. Bargain with the devil himself if it means I get one more shot. One more breath. One more second to make things right.

Everything I shoved down, every feeling I tried to bury, is breaking through the cracks now. All that time I wasted pretending I didn't care. Pretending it didn't matter. It's unraveling around me, and I'd give anything to rewind it. To get it back.

A flash of copper in the haze, Callie's hair, maybe, or my mind playing tricks. Maverick's voice, faint like a memory, yelling my name.

I see their faces, and it's like getting kicked in the chest all over again. Because that's what hurts most. Not the pain. The loss. The not-getting-to-go-back.

If I could just have one more chance, just *one*. I'd get it right.

I'd hold on to the people who matter and never let go.

I'd tell Maverick that I want more, more than friends, more than rivals.

I'd tell Callie she was the only thing that ever made this life make sense.

I'd fight like hell for them, not for a buckle or a title, but for the pieces of my heart I never should have handed away so carelessly.

I'd figure it out with Mav, because who the hell cares what happened or *why* it happened? I should've fixed it a long time ago. I should've said something. I should've fought harder. I should have chased after *her*.

God, just give me one more chance. One. That's all I need.

I won't waste it. I swear to God, I won't waste it.

Then hands. Grabbing my vest. Hauling me up and flipping me over.

The rope slips free, and for one glorious, weightless second, I think I'm okay. I think maybe I'll walk away from this. Then the bull turns. Fast. Brutal.

And I don't stand a goddamn chance.

I collapse, not strong enough to stand, and he's on me before I can move. His weight crashes into my ribs, stomps over my legs. The ground disappears beneath me, and I'm sucked under him.

My face is shoved into the dirt, lungs scraping for air, breathing in sand with every gasp.

Pain swallows me whole.

Not from the crush. Not from the bruises or broken bones.

But from the raw, agonizing *unfairness* of it all.

A crack rings through my skull, jarring straight down my spine.

And as the world blacks out, my final thought follows me into unconsciousness:

I never told them I love them.

Chapter 38

Callie

I don't watch the rides.

Not anymore.

So I stay in the back tonight, tucked behind the trailers, pretending I'm too busy brushing down a horse to care about what's happening out there. Maverick teases me when I make up the excuse, but he doesn't push. Colt doesn't either. There's this quiet understanding in his eyes, like he knows exactly what I'm running from.

But then I hear it.

A different kind of noise, too quiet, too sharp. It slices straight through the noise of the night and lodges somewhere deep in my chest.

And I run.

I don't think. I just take off, boots pounding across concrete, cutting between fans and staff and fences until I'm at the edge of the arena. The dust cloud is still settling, and the bull is already being wrangled away.

Colt's not standing, waving his hat at the crowd like he always does.

He is on the ground.

Limp in a way no person should be.

The scream that rips out of me doesn't sound human. I shove past two security guards, one of them trying to hold me back. I duck under his arm and throw myself toward the chute, dropping to my knees beside Colt just as the medics reach him.

"Don't touch him!" I shout, my voice shrill, splintering. "Don't... don't touch him until I know he's..." My breath breaks mid-sentence. My hands shake as I reach for his.

His shoulder is twisted. His leg is bent wrong. There's blood in his hair.

He's not waking up.

"Be okay," I whisper, curling over his hand. "Please, be okay."

"Callie."

Maverick's voice cuts through the noise, low and close. I barely register him until he's crouching beside me, one hand curling around my wrist.

"Cal." He's softer now. Steadier. "They need to take him. You have to let go."

"No." I shake my head, tighter around Colt's arm. "Don't make me—Maverick, I can't—"

He doesn't argue. Doesn't tell me to be strong or calm down.

He just holds me tighter and lifts me off the ground,

one arm around my back, the other beneath my knees like I weigh nothing.

I don't even fight it. I'm too broken to care.

The crowd is still roaring, announcers scrambling to keep things moving, but it all fades behind us as Maverick carries me away. Past the gates. Past the medics. Past the arena.

He finds a shadowed corner near the far side of the trailer row, behind one of the livestock holding pens. Quiet. Secluded.

And that's where I break.

He sinks down onto the concrete with me in his lap, arms still around me like a fortress, my sobs shaking the both of us.

"She begged him," I gasp, curling my fingers into his shirt. "My mom begged him to quit. Over and over again. And he kept saying, 'Just one more ride.' Then he died in the fucking dirt."

Maverick holds me tighter. His jaw is locked, face pressed into the side of my head like he's holding himself together for both of us.

"I know," he says. It's ragged, almost broken. "I know."

"I can't," I rasp.

I can't do this again. I can't. "I thought I could handle it, but I was wrong. I was so fucking wrong."

He pulls me tighter against him, and we just sit there, pressed together in the shadow of the arena. I can hear the crowd buzzing, the announcers trying to fill the air with noise again. Like Colt's blood isn't still drying in the dirt.

Like he didn't almost die right in front of me.

"I should've stayed away," I whisper. "I never should've come back."

Maverick doesn't let go. He just rests his chin on my shoulder, his voice rough in my ear. "You did come back. You're here. We're all here. And you're not losing us, Callie."

Not yet.

Chapter 39

Colt

THE BEEP of machines cuts through the fog first, slow, steady, too calm for how my chest aches like it's been torn open.

I blink, the scratch of the hospital sheets rough against my fingers, and for a second, I'm not sure if I'm still dreaming.

There's a weight against my side. Warm. Familiar.

When I turn my head, sharp pain slices down my neck, and I find Callie curled against me, clinging like she's afraid I'll vanish if she lets go. Her hand fists my side like she's anchoring me to the earth

Maverick's here too, slouched low in a chair, elbows on his knees, his head bowed like the weight of the whole goddamn world is pressing him down.

He's watching me like he never once looked away. His sharp gaze softens on mine, his shoulders slumping inward as he takes a deep breath.

"What time is it?" I ask, voice rough.

"Around 3:00 a.m." He looks down at his clenched fist in his lap. "Jesus, man. You scared the shit out of us."

"Callie." I can only manage one word, but he knows what I'm asking.

"She didn't calm down until she could hear your heart," Maverick says, voice low and gutted.

I glance down at Callie, at the pale cast to her face, at the way her knuckles are white from holding on to me in her sleep.

"She looks worse than me," I manage to rasp, trying for a joke that lands somewhere short of funny.

Maverick doesn't laugh. The red rims of his eyes tell me he doesn't find any of this funny either.

"What's the damage?" A part of me doesn't want to know, well aware this could end my season.

"Dislocated shoulder. Shattered collarbone. Several broken ribs. Bruised tibia," Maverick says flatly.

"Hey, at least my leg isn't broken."

"Yeah... you're totally fine..."

Sarcasm drips out, and then he's just... broken.

"Fuck, Colt..."

He can't look at me. His fingers tear through his hair, like he's trying to rip out whatever's eating him alive.

"I thought..." His voice splinters. He fists his hands in his lap, shoulders shaking under the strain. "I thought we were gonna lose you."

"Nah, I'm not that breakable," I joke, but the pure anguish carved into his face has a gnawing guilt ripping into my chest that has nothing to do with being trampled. I can't keep doing this and expect them to stay whole.

Heavy seconds stretch between us, his gaze devouring me like he's trying to hold me here with sheer fucking will. I want to break the tension, joke around and wash that look from his face, but the pain is catching up to me fully now.

The throbbing in my shoulder has spread up my neck, until it pulses in my temple. The simple act of breathing feels wrong, too shallow, like my ribs are cracking all over again, an echo of every individual fracture as if they're yelling at me for what I did to them.

Exhaustion's heavy in my bones, but I can't stop looking at them, taking in every detail. Callie is crushed against my side. Even in her sleep, she's holding me like she's afraid I'll disappear if she lets go. Maverick shifts closer, close enough I could reach out and touch him if I tried.

She shivers, a soft sound breaking through her lips, and lightning bolts of pain travel down my side as I attempt to lift the blanket to cover her, the fabric falling from my too weak fingers.

It's humiliating in a way nothing else has been.

Maverick notices, stepping in without a word to adjust the covers for me, moving slow like he's afraid I'll shatter.

And maybe I already have.

I grit my teeth, too broken to hide the pain anymore.

"You should've told me it was this bad," he says, immediately getting up and calling the nurse. Their muffled voices come from the doorway as he asks for more meds.

I hate morphine. It makes me itchy and nauseous, but right now, I'll take anything that provides any sort of relief.

"Don't," I croak when the nurse walks in, eying Callie, and it's clear that she's going to intervene.

"It's against hospital policy."

I try to give her my signature-winning smile, but all I manage is a slight curl of my lips. "Please, I need her."

She softens, exhaling a long sigh. "Fine. I'm the only one here right now, but she'll have to move before my shift is over."

The machine attached to my IV beeps as she pushes a series of buttons, the coolness of the medicine crawling up my vein.

"Next time, don't wait so long to call me," she chastises, but there's no heat to it. "You let me know if he wakes up again."

Maverick nods, a seriousness taking over.

She flicks the overhead light off on her way out.

My eyes grow heavy, and I sink into my pillow, waiting for it to kick in. Flashes of being dragged, crushed under hooves, play behind my eyelids. As the reality that I was going to die fully sank in, all I thought about was them, not bull riding, not winning... *them*.

The pain dulls.

My body grows heavier, looser, my vision blurring at the edges.

I want to say something. God, I want to, but the words claw at my throat and die there.

I'm too fucking tired, and it hurts too much.

I tighten my grip on Callie first, her heartbeat steady against my ribs. Proof that I'm still here. Still breathing. Still not too late.

Then blindly, desperately, I reach out again and find Maverick's hand.

His fingers jerk in shock, but only for a second before he laces them through mine, clinging so tight it almost hurts.

I force my eyes open, fighting through the haze.

His face swims into view, blurred but still achingly familiar.

His throat works as he leans closer, rough knuckles brushing my jaw.

"Rest, Colt," Maverick breathes, voice hoarse.

He says something else, words breaking apart in his throat, but I'm already slipping under, too far gone to catch them.

Too far gone to answer.

I fall under with her heartbeat against my ribs, with his hand wrapped around mine, and the weight of everything I should've said dragging me down with it.

Chapter 40

Maverick

Colt's breathing is steady now. Slow and shallow but steady.

It's the only goddamn thing keeping me sitting in this chair instead of losing my mind.

He looks rough, bruised all over and bandages peppering his skin.

I shift forward in the chair, elbows on my knees, fists clenched so tight they're going numb, but I can't look away. Every shallow rise and fall of his chest feels like a goddamn miracle.

And every pause between those beeps on the heart monitor?

Like a knife sliding in slowly.

It's mid-morning, and I finally convinced Callie to leave.

Not because I wanted her gone, but because she needed to take care of herself.

She'd been curled up in that bed for hours, head tilted at a brutal angle, barely sleeping.

When she woke up, her eyes locked on Colt like she could keep him alive through sheer stubbornness.

She was furious when I told her he'd woken up during the night.

Furious I hadn't shaken her awake.

But she needed the rest.

And when she finally went still beside him, her hand tucked into his hospital gown like it was the only thing tethering her to earth, and I couldn't bring myself to break that.

I couldn't touch the way Colt seemed to breathe easier with her there.

I rub my thumb along Colt's forehead, brushing back a strand of sweat-damp hair.

The cut near his temple is red and angry, a thin line of stitches holding him together by a thread.

Too damn close to where that hoof could've stomped straight into his skull.

The thought makes my stomach lurch. I don't know if it's relief or fear rattling in my chest, but I've never hated a hospital bed more.

Colt grumbles softly in his sleep, shifting toward my hand.

He blinks, groggy and confused, fighting through the fog. His eyes slowly find mine, brows knitting like he's not sure how he got here.

He tries to sit up.

"Hey. Easy, Colt." I press a steady hand to his good shoulder, keeping him grounded. "You're okay. Just breathe."

He makes a sound, half groan, half laugh, and winces through a crooked smile. "You look like shit."

It comes out strained, like he's aiming for cocky but can't quite hold the weight of it.

I choke on a laugh, relief crashing through me. "Yeah, well, you're not exactly winning beauty contests."

Talking to him last night felt too much like a dream to offer real comfort today. I need to see it with my own eyes, need to *feel* that he's really here.

Without thinking, I brush my knuckles along his jaw, then down the bruises on his neck, careful not to hurt him.

His skin's warm, solid, *real*. And I don't realize I'm shaking until I feel it in my hand.

Colt closes his eyes for a beat, then opens them again.

His gaze sharpens and lands right on me.

"Mav..." His voice is barely a whisper, torn and raw. "I'm sorry."

Hell no.

I shake my head. "No. You don't get to say that first. You don't get to fucking apologize to me."

The words crack something open inside me. A tremor builds in my chest, crawling out to my fingers, until I'm gripping the edge of the bed like it's the only thing holding me up.

"I should've grabbed you by the collar and forced the truth out of you. Should've made you yell, cry, hit me. Whatever it fucking took. Anything but silence."

I drag a hand down my face, hard, like I can wipe the guilt off with my skin. My chest's too tight. My throat burns.

"I should've *known* better." It hits me then just how much I failed him. "You disappearing like that? Shutting down? I should've seen it for what it was. Not anger. Not jealousy. It was pain. And I missed it."

I swallow hard, my throat thick. "Should've followed you to the hospital back then. Screw the ride, screw the rookie buckle."

I look at him, *really* look.

"Because if I'd followed you... maybe we wouldn't have lost all that time. Maybe you wouldn't have had to carry all that shit alone."

My throat tightens, but I force it out anyway.

"I chose wrong, Colt. And I've regretted it every damn day since."

Colt's mouth parts slightly, but no sound comes out.

Shock, disbelief, a hundred different emotions flicker across his bruised face.

"I bailed on my ride last night," I say quietly. "When you went down... I didn't even think. They called my name, but I was already running after you."

I rake a shaking hand through my hair. "And I'd do it again. Every damn time."

I lean in, close enough that he can't look away.

"I should've done it back then," I whisper. "Should've chased you the second you fell. Followed you to the hospital. Who the fuck cares about the championship when it cost me *you?*"

My voice breaks.

I swipe at my eyes, rough and useless, because the tears are already falling.

"I've been dying on *should-haves*, Colt," I breathe. "For years. I let you believe that winning mattered more to me than you did."

I shake my head. "Points. Titles. None of it fucking matters if you're not here."

My chest caves as I force myself to meet his eyes.

"I'm so fucking sorry."

Colt shifts weakly, reaching out.

I catch his hand without thinking, lacing our fingers together.

His grip is weak, but it's there. Solid. Fierce, in its own way.

Like he's holding on to more than just me.

His brow pulls, eyes flicking away, then back again like he's not sure he heard me right.

"Mav..."

"I needed to be the best," I confess. "Because if I was the best, you'd want to stay by my side. You'd be right there with me. Like always."

The truth tears out of me, ugly, cracked wide open.

"And when you pulled away... I didn't know how to fix it."

Colt's hand flexes weakly in mine, and for a second, I think he might let go.

But then he holds on tighter.

The shell he's protected himself with cracks, revealing something raw and vulnerable underneath.

"I thought you left me behind," he whispers.

The words gut me, sharp and brutal. No armor between us now.

Just blood, bone, and everything we never said.

A tear overruns his lashes, and I catch it, wiping it away with shaking fingers.

"I thought... you didn't think I was good enough to stand next to you."

He might as well have punched through my ribs and squeezed my heart bare.

"*Fuck.*"

I choke back a sound and bury my forehead against our joined hands, squeezing his fingers tight.

I don't care if it hurts him.

I don't care if it hurts me.

I just need him to feel it. To know it. To believe it.

"You were always enough," I whisper against his skin. "You are enough."

Slowly, carefully, I lift my head. My grip tightens around his hand. I bring it between us and press a kiss to his knuckles.

He gasps, chest heaving, but he doesn't look away.

"You're the best goddamn thing that ever happened to me, Colt Lawson," I rasp, my voice torn to shreds. "You've always been enough," I repeat, driving it into the space between us like a stake in the ground. "I was just too fucking stupid to tell you."

Colt's breath hitches, his lashes fluttering like he's trying to blink back the sting in his eyes.

"I hated you," he says, voice splintering in half. "And I hated myself more."

I don't say anything, just give him space.

My thumb traces soft crescents against his wrist, the only comfort I can offer.

"I watched you win everything," he grits out, a tear escaping down his cheek, "and I was proud. I was so fucking proud, but I hated you for not needing me."

I bite the inside of my cheek until I taste blood.

"I always needed you."

The silence stretches heavy between us, thick with all the things we never said when it might have made a difference.

And now... now, it's bleeding out of both of us, slow and messy and unavoidable.

"You're my best friend... you're more than that," I say fiercely, squeezing his hand. "I would've been lucky to have you by my side all these years. And as far as I'm concerned, you're the best damn rider out there. Your instincts are unreal. You move with the bull like you belong up there. Like you're reading its mind."

Colt exhales a jagged, shaky breath.

"And I never wanted to beat you," I admit. "I always wanted to be next to you. Sharing every moment of it. Because what's the fucking point if you aren't there with me?"

"Maverick."

His lip wobbles, the first crack of hope breaking through all that hurt.

"If you want my spot, you can have it," I say, leaning closer, my voice steady now. "I'll give it up. I'll throw rides. I'll step back, and you can have the goddamn buckle."

"No," Colt breathes, fierce, even in his brokenness. "I don't want you to give it to me. I want to earn it."

Pride stirs hot and raw in my chest, the kind that threatens to undo me all over again.

Because that's Colt. That's the boy who used to race me across pastures, laughing like the whole damn world was ours.

That's the man he became while I wasn't looking.

A weight lifts in my chest like sunlight cutting through the goddamn clouds.

I give him a small, crooked smile, wiping my face and then his with the edge of my sleeve.

"Then I'll help you. You already have everything you need."

Colt rolls his eyes, but there's a glint behind them now.

A grin spreads, crooked and cocky, all too familiar, like he knows he's just won something.

"What are you so smug about?" I mutter, narrowing my eyes.

"Would you really give up the championship for me?" he asks, half-joking, half-serious.

I don't even hesitate.

"Yes."

Colt's throat bobs. A flush crawls up his neck, spreading over his jaw, painting his cheeks in pink.

He shifts awkwardly, mumbling under his breath, "Never mind."

Humming, I lean back, giving us both some space to breathe.

Colt watches me with something new in his eyes, careful, tentative... hopeful.

I don't push. I don't tease.

Because I mean it.

Every damn word.

He slumps deeper into the bed, exhausted but faintly smiling.

I rest my head against the edge of his mattress, feeling lighter than I have in years.

Warmth curls in my stomach, and I have to bite back a whimper when his fingers stroke gently through my hair, so soft, so careful, it undoes me completely.

We stay like that, wrapped in a bubble of silence broken only by the slow, steady beep of the monitor.

There's a soft giggle from the doorway.

A small voice cuts through the quiet. "You two are idiots, you know that, right?"

Both of us whip our heads around, startled.

Colt blinks at her like she's a hallucination.

I gape at her.

Callie's standing there, beaming, a tray of coffees balanced in her hands, her copper hair tousled and wild, cheeks still flushed from crying earlier.

"Have you been here this whole time? When did you get back?" Colt croaks, hesitantly hopeful that she didn't hear everything. It's embarrassing enough between just the two of us.

Callie grins mischievously. "Maybe," she teases. "Maybe not."

"Did you hear everything?" Dropping my head, I grumble into Colt's arm, my voice muffled.

Callie shrugs, taking a slow sip of her coffee.

"Define *everything*," she says innocently.

Colt groans, dragging his good hand over his face.

"I hate you," he mutters weakly.

"No you don't," she chirps.

Colt lets out a choked sound, half a wheeze, half a laugh, and clumsily pats my shoulder like I'm the idiot here.

Callie crosses the room, setting the coffee tray on the little table with a soft clatter.

She's a mess.

Her hair's pulled up in a lopsided bun, her sweatshirt stretched off one shoulder, her eyes still red-rimmed from crying.

And she's the most beautiful fucking thing I've ever seen.

Colt's hand tightens on mine briefly.

When I glance up at him, he's staring at her too, the same awestruck look written all over his battered face.

Yeah.

We're both so fucking gone for her it's not even funny anymore.

Chapter 41

Callie

Colt's grumbling under his breath, wrestling the blanket off his legs one-handed while the other stays strapped tight across his chest.

Maverick halts mid-pace like he's physically pained just watching. "You stubborn—" He sighs, crossing the room. "Do you have any idea how exhausting it is trying to keep your ass alive?"

Colt glares at him. "I can move a damn blanket."

"Sure," Maverick says, smoothing it into place anyway. "Right after you win a slap fight with gravity."

I bite back a grin from my spot in the chair, watching them with a kind of fond exasperation. Honestly, they're one forehead kiss away from starring in their own slow-burn romance novel.

Maverick even flattens the corner of the blanket like Colt's a fussy toddler instead of a grumpy six-foot-two man.

"You're lucky you're pretty, Lawson," Maverick mutters.

"Didn't hear you complaining the other night," Colt fires back, but his voice cracks halfway through it, and his face goes beet red.

It's so fast and so fierce that I snort before I can stop myself.

Colt sinks lower in the bed, looking betrayed at both of us like we're the ones embarrassing him.

Maverick just grins, all lazy menace. "Aw, is someone blushing?"

"Shut up," Colt growls, turning his head to the side so we can't see how red his ears have gotten.

Maverick's grin only widens. He leans down close, deliberately ruffling Colt's hair until it's sticking up wildly.

"Goddamn, you're cute when you're cranky," he says, voice low and shamelessly fond.

Colt groans, dragging the blanket up over his face like he's hoping it'll swallow him whole.

Maverick just chuckles and pulls it gently back down, uncovering Colt's furious, burning cheeks.

"Don't hide from me, sweetheart," Maverick says, smoothing his palm across Colt's hairline with a ridiculous amount of tenderness. "You're my favorite thing to look at."

Colt makes a noise that can only be described as *a strangled whimper*, his hand flailing half-heartedly like he wants to shove Maverick away but can't work up the strength.

I am *not* helping because I've pulled my hoodie up over my face like that'll stop the full-body giggles threatening to escape.

Colt stares at the ceiling like he's praying for divine intervention. His whole face is fire-engine red.

"You're not gonna survive being loved properly, are you?" Maverick teases, voice soft and smug.

Colt mumbles something about *"inhumane treatment"* and *"filing a complaint."*

Maverick just leans back with a pleased little hum.

I swear to God, this man is thriving. Absolutely thriving. On Colt's suffering.

And honestly? I've never loved him more.

Thankfully, the universe must take pity on Colt because the door swings open, and in walks the doctor, chart in hand, radiating the exact energy of a man preparing for battle.

"How's the pain?" the doctor asks, raising an eyebrow like he already knows the answer.

"Manageable," Colt lies through his damn teeth.

The doctor doesn't even blink. "Sure. And I'm a ballerina."

Maverick chokes back a laugh. I don't.

"Right," the doctor says, flipping the page like it personally offended him. "Dislocated shoulder's back in place. Tibia's just bruised. But that collarbone? That's shattered. If you want a clean heal, you're looking at surgery."

Colt stiffens. Maverick goes still.

"Time frame?" Colt asks, too casually.

"Six months. You'd miss the rest of the season."

The temperature in the room drops five degrees.

"No surgery," Colt says flatly.

The doctor exhales, visibly unimpressed. "You'll lose mobility. You'll be in pain. It might rebreak."

Colt doesn't flinch. "Still ridin'."

A quiet pressure builds in my chest. Not anger just that familiar ache that comes when I remember exactly what this life costs. The risk. The hurt. The fact that even now, he wouldn't choose differently.

Maverick scrubs a hand down his face.

The doctor mutters "idiot riders" like a prayer and leaves, the chart snapping shut in his hands like a gavel on his way out.

I don't blame him. I kind of want to shake Colt myself.

A knock sounds on the half-open door.

Luke's shaggy head pops in, grinning. "Hope you're not naked. I brought company."

Maverick groans. Colt smirks. "No promises."

Luke saunters in like he owns the place, taking in the room with an exaggerated whistle. "Damn, you're lookin' halfway human already, Lawson."

Colt grins at him, and it hits me how different he looks. How different they *both* look. Nothing like they did when I first rolled up at the start of the season, all cold shoulders and old grudges.

This... this feels like breathing fresh air after years underwater.

They joke. They laugh.

Colt rolls his eyes when Luke flops dramatically into the visitor chair, making it squeak. Maverick pretends to throw a pillow at him. Luke, unfazed, reaches for the tray of untouched hospital food and pokes at it with a plastic fork.

He recoils instantly. "What even *is* that?"

Colt looks at the mush like it personally offended him. "Torture."

Luke nods solemnly. "Can confirm. I'm getting sympathy hunger pains just being in the same room."

Maverick, who's been leaning against the wall with his arms crossed, hasn't said much, just watches. But the second Colt shifts a little too fast and flinches, his whole expression changes.

His arms drop. His jaw tightens. He clocks everything. Colt's wince, the tension in his shoulders, the way his smile falters when he thinks no one's looking.

Without a word, Maverick pushes off the wall and steps toward Luke.

"Out."

Luke startles. "Wait, what? I just got here."

"You're gonna rile him up," Maverick says, already steering him toward the door. There's no heat in his voice, but there's no budging either. His tone is all quiet command and simmering worry.

"I haven't even insulted anyone yet!"

Maverick gives him a look that could peel paint.

Luke throws his hands up. "Fine, fine. I'll leave. Want

fries?"

Colt perks up like a kid. Maverick groans. "Stop encouraging him."

Luke vanishes into the hallway, still laughing, and Maverick sighs, dragging a hand through his hair before grabbing his keys from the counter.

Colt watches him, amused but glassy-eyed with exhaustion. "You don't have to—"

"Don't finish that sentence," Maverick mutters. "You're pale, you're hurting, and you haven't eaten more than three bites. I'm getting you something you'll actually eat."

He doesn't say it with softness. But he doesn't have to.

He's already halfway out the door before Colt can argue.

And I'm left here blinking back this rush of affection like it might knock me flat.

Because Maverick notices *everything*. The pain. The cracks. The wear Colt tries to pretend isn't there. He sees the wince, the fatigue, and that's it. That's all it takes. One look, and he's already moving like protecting Colt is the only thing that's ever made sense.

The door clicks shut behind him, and the ache in my chest lingers as Colt turns to me with that quiet look I'll never recover from.

He shifts, wincing, then pats the narrow space beside him with his good hand.

"C'mere, sweetheart." He pats again, one brow lifted. His eyes soften, silently pleading.

Carefully, I toe off my shoes and climb in, mindful of the IV and his bandages. I settle on my side, facing him, close but careful.

His hand finds my hip under the blanket, gentle but insistent. Steady. Like he needs the contact as much as I do.

I don't mean to cry, but the tears come anyway. Silent and sudden. Relief and terror tangled so tight I can't tell which is which anymore.

I press my forehead to his chest, breathing him in. The scent of antiseptic can't quite cover the familiar warm skin beneath it. I try to memorize this. *Him alive, breathing, smiling at me.*

Colt kisses me first.

Not soft. Not sweet.

Desperate.

And I kiss him back, fingers curling into his hospital gown like I can anchor myself to him.

There's no plan to it. No soft build. Just this overwhelming need to feel him, hold him, breathe with him.

Like maybe if I stay close enough, the rest of the world will stay quiet a little longer.

At some point, he pulls me fully against his good side. I stretch out beside him, tucked carefully into the curve of his body. My leg hooks gently over his.

We don't speak.

We just breathe. Together.

His thumb strokes idly at my side, and the quiet

stretches long and golden. We must stay like that for twenty minutes. Maybe more.

The hospital room buzzes low with machines. The hallway hums faintly with movement. But here, with him, the world feels still.

Colt shifts slightly, his hand tightening on my waist.

He looks at me like maybe, just maybe, we could have it all.

The door creaks open, and I jerk, cheeks going hot.

Maverick steps inside, a paper bag in one hand, a drink tucked under his arm.

He freezes when he sees us tangled up together.

His gaze lands on my flushed face, Colt's possessive grip around my waist.

Then he looks at me. Really looks.

His eyes go dark with something deep and familiar. Something that makes my breath catch.

Then, without hesitation, he crosses the room, sets the bag down, and leans in.

His hand cradles my cheek, his thumb brushing away the tear tracks I didn't realize were still there.

And he kisses me too.

Slow.

Steady.

Grounding me.

Like telling me without words that he's here too.

Colt's hand never leaves my hip.

I kiss Maverick back, my fingers fisting his shirt.

And when he finally pulls away, breathing uneven, he presses his forehead against mine for a second longer, one heartbeat, two.

Colt watches us.

Doesn't let go.

The three of us are knotted up in a tangle of bruised hearts and broken pieces trying to fit together.

And for one perfect second, it feels like we actually could.

I don't realize I'm crying again until Colt brushes his thumb over my cheek.

"Sunshine," he murmurs, soft and full of everything he doesn't know how to say.

But beneath all of it. Under the sweetness, under the desperate hope. The dread is still there.

Buried deep but clawing up my throat.

Because Colt getting hurt cracked me wide open.

Brought every memory of my father's accident roaring back.

The frantic medics.

The sound of my mother screaming.

The empty house afterward.

The wreckage my father left behind.

Colt telling the doctor he wouldn't get surgery because it would cost him the season?

It confirms what I already know.

They love bull riding.

It's stitched into their bones.

And I can't ask them to stop.

I won't be the girl who begs someone to give up the thing that makes them feel alive.

But I also can't survive waiting for the call.

Can't survive another casket.

Another funeral.

Another promise broken.

I love them.

God, I love them so much it hurts.

But I already know I won't survive staying.

Not forever.

Maybe not even through the end of the season.

The thought splits something inside me so viciously I have to shove it down hard.

Swallow it.

Tonight is supposed to be happy.

Tonight, we're supposed to breathe.

Colt shifts, brushing a kiss against my forehead, his fingers still curled tight around my waist like he can sense I'm slipping away inside.

Maverick nuzzles into the side of my neck, from his spot on the chair, his hand slipping over Colt's.

Their weight. Their warmth. Their stubborn, reckless, perfect hearts.

I let myself drown in them.

Just for a little while longer.

I pretend this moment could last forever.

I love them both fiercely with everything I have left to give.

Even knowing I won't stay.

Even knowing I wasn't built to survive this kind of love.

Chapter 42

Colt

THE TIRES CRUNCH over gravel as we roll up the long drive, and for the first time in weeks, I feel like I can actually breathe.

Porch light's on. Wind chimes still hang from the rafters, jangling in the breeze.

Same rocking chair. Same busted step.

The house groans like it's been waiting on me.

I've got Callie. I've got Mav.

For the first time in years, I want more than just the next ride.

I shift to open the door, but the second my boot hits gravel, Maverick's already there, a crutch in hand.

"I've got it," I mutter, even though we both know I don't.

"You've got a shattered collarbone and a bruised tibia," he fires back, already unfolding the crutch. "What you've got is a one-way ticket to landing flat on your ass if you try and play hero."

I glare at him. He doesn't flinch, just holds it steady.

I hate needing help. Always have.

I let him slide the crutch under my good arm, brace my elbow, and swing my weight forward, climbing down from the truck one stiff, awkward inch at a time.

He doesn't make a show of it. Doesn't gloat. Just mutters under his breath, "Stubborn cowboy," and stays close enough to catch me, like he always has.

It shouldn't make my chest feel like this.

Tight. Warm. Seen.

We don't even make it to the front door before it opens and my mom comes barreling down the steps, apron still on, eyes already wet. She wraps me up in a hug like she's afraid I might vanish if she lets go. I grunt when she squeezes too tight, but I don't stop her. Not this time.

"You scared the hell out of us," she mutters into my hair. "You boys never do anything halfway, do you?"

"No, ma'am," I say, smiling into her shoulder. "We sure don't."

Callie gets her own hug a second later, just as fierce.

"And you, young lady, you owed us a visit a long time ago. You didn't forget about us, did you?" That same tightness I used to hear when I was in trouble, but she didn't want to yell. She knows what Callie's absence did to all of us. She wasn't just a visitor in this house; she grew up in it. My folks didn't treat her like a guest back then. They treated her like she was a daughter.

"I could never forget you. You still make the best damn peach pie in the state," Callie says, trying to keep it playful, even as her eyes shine. And just like that, it hits me. I wasn't the only one who lost something when she left. We all did.

"You're right, and I'm sorry. It's been way too long," she says sincerely, squeezing my mom one last time before letting go and stepping straight into one of my dad's bear hugs.

He wraps her up tight, feet lifting off the ground. "Well, you're home now."

Warmth settles in my chest like it belongs there. Like this is how things are supposed to be. I wish I could see Callie's face to know if she's feeling it too. She hasn't said anything about staying.

Still, the way she's looked at me these last few days... after everything we've been through...

I've got hope.

Hope that maybe she's not ready to walk away.

Because I'm sure as hell not ready to let her go.

I can't lose her again. I won't.

Maverick trails in behind us, bags over one shoulder, and accepts a kiss on the cheek from my mom. She grabs onto his arms and doesn't let go.

"And you? What's your excuse?"

He ducks his head, all sheepish, like he's fourteen again. "I don't have one, ma'am. I should've come back long ago."

Those words hit harder than I expect. After everything we said at the hospital, it still guts me. All the time we lost. All the silence we didn't have to suffer through. But we can't change the past. And I'm not about to let it mess up our future.

"Leave him be, Ellie," my dad chimes in, crossing his arms. "We both know our boy's just as damn stubborn. And just as guilty."

I expect Maverick to brush it off. Throw out some smart-ass comment to deflect the heat. Instead, He just squares his shoulders and looks my mom in the eye, voice low, steady.

"No. It was me."

He holds there. Doesn't flinch. Doesn't look away.

Then, almost like he can't help it, his eyes flick to mine.

"I'm the one that fucked up. I should've tried harder. I should've come back sooner."

My fingers curl reflexively on the crutch handle.

That's enough.

My parents share a look, then both turn toward me with matching smirks.

Just how much did they know back then?

Apparently, more than we did.

Maverick grabs our bags, lifting them over both shoulders, and hovers behind me as I take the stairs one at a time. Those four steps nearly do me in. Callie's on my other side, brows drawn tight with concern. Then she rushes ahead to the door, reaching to open it for me.

I walk in, and the smell of my mom's homemade cooking hits me like a memory I didn't know I was starving for. Nostalgia floods in, heavy and warm. Having Maverick and Callie here, too, just makes it clearer how much I've missed this.

"Your cooking smells amazing. Thank you for having us over, ma'am," Callie says, ever the politest out of the three of us.

My mom gives her a warm smile, welcoming her without words. "Well, I'd ask you for help, but everybody here knows how that would turn out."

She's not wrong. Callie's an awful cook. Her ability to burn rice has been a favorite story of mine. Still, she didn't need to be so harsh about it.

Callie just laughs, knowing it's all in fun, and turns to look up when Maverick wraps an arm around her back, resting it on her shoulder. His eyes are hooded, gazing at her. I'm sure he'd like to do more, but none of us is sure how to explain it to my parents, so we all agreed to be on our best behavior.

"I'll help you, Mrs. Lawson," Maverick offers, making his way to the kitchen, rolling up his sleeves, revealing his thick arms. And I have to force myself to look away before I start drooling.

"That's right," Mom says. "You're all grown up now."

There's a sadness in her voice that sneaks in at the edges, like she feels the weight of all the years we lost.

My dad claps his hands together, breaking the

moment, and looks at Callie and me. "Alright, you two. You may be awful at cooking, but you sure can set that table."

"Yes, sir," Callie says with a nod and a smile, heading off after my mom and Maverick.

He holds me back with a firm hand on my arm, his gaze searching mine. "I'm happy for you, son."

I startle a little, caught off guard, not sure how he's read the situation, but he lets me go, giving me a firm push on the shoulder. I stumble forward, crutch snagging on the ground, and he catches me before I tumble.

"Oh, right," my dad says, like he's just now remembering I'm here to recover from my injuries. "Go sit down—but don't think you'll be able to use this as an excuse for everything." His words are rough, but his tone is warm. He's always been a softie underneath the bark.

It's not long before the long wooden table is filled with dishes that smell so good my mouth waters. Pot roast, homemade bread, pie in the oven.

I go to dig in, but Maverick, sitting to my right, slaps my hand and raises a single brow.

Ah, fuck. I forgot. We may not pray in this family, but there's still a rule. Nobody eats until we give thanks.

Looking between Maverick and Callie, sitting on either side of me, I try to pour the truth into my words, quiet but clear, meant just for them.

"I'm grateful to have found what I lost. To feel that hollowed-out part of me finally filled."

My voice cracks, but I push through.

"I've been walking in the dark for a long time... and it finally feels like the sun's coming up."

I take a long, steadying breath and hope they hear what I can't say out loud. Not yet. Not here.

"I'm grateful to be surrounded by the people who matter most. That feeling of invincibility that I can do anything, so long as they're beside me, is finally back."

Maverick doesn't look at me, but his hand finds my thigh under the table, wrapping around it tight. The tremble in his grip travels straight through me.

He's saying everything without a single word.

Callie's hazel eyes are locked on mine, wide and shining. A soft pink blooms across her cheeks, and her chest rises a little too fast.

God, I'd give anything to pull her into my arms and never let her go.

Across the table, I catch the look on my mom's face.

She's already picturing holiday dinners and baby showers and probably sewing a damn quilt.

"Let's dig in before it gets cold and all your mom's hard work goes to waste," Dad says, scooping up a big spoonful of mashed potatoes.

Callie covers her mouth as she chews, eyes bright. "I'd never let her cooking go to waste. I'm pretty sure I dreamed about this."

Conversation picks up fast, everyone talking over each other. Laughter echoes through the room, the kind that settles in your bones and stays there. A warm, easy buzz hums around the table.

Then my parents share a look.

Dad clears his throat. "We've been thinking about selling the farm."

The words hit harder than a kick to the ribs. I choke on nothing, fork frozen halfway to my mouth.

"It's a hard decision," he says gently. "We're getting older. It's just... too much work now."

Callie and Maverick both go still. Their faces say it all, like they're losing something that belongs to them too. But they stay quiet.

This land runs through me. Dirt under my nails, sweat in the wood beams and floorboards.

No way in hell I let someone bulldoze it for condos or strip malls.

The pot roast on my plate turns to ash in my mouth.

"May I be excused?" I ask, already pushing back from the table. I can't sit here and act like this is just news.

Like it doesn't feel like the floor just dropped out from under me.

My dad doesn't lift his eyes, just gives me a silent nod.

I push back from my chair and head for the door, doing my best not to stomp or let the mess of feelings inside me show.

I know they wouldn't bring this up unless they had to.

And I know they're not trying to hurt me.

But still... fuck.

The night air hits like a slap, cool against my overheated skin. I suck in a breath, lungs filling with the scent of hay, dirt, and worn leather. The smell of my childhood.

I rest my hands on the porch railing and stare out into the dark. The fields are shadowed now, barely visible. The barn looms in the distance, still standing. Still mine. That was my kingdom once. I used to sneak up into the rafters and nap for hours, sunlight on my face, nothing but time to kill.

So many summers lost to harmless trouble and wild dreams.

The door creaks behind me, and I half expect Callie. Or Mav.

"I told them to stay back," my mom says softly, stepping up beside me. "I wanted to talk to you alone."

She's a freaking mind reader, always has been, never been able to get away with shit. "Your father and I have mulled this over for years. We wouldn't have told you if we didn't know this was the best decision. I know it'll be hard to let this place go, but with no one else to run it, this is the only way your father and I can settle down."

"I'm not letting this go. I'll figure it out. Loans, sponsors. Whatever it takes."

She hums low in her throat, not acceptance or denial, then asks the thing I knew she would.

"So Callie's back." She's not one to tiptoe around something. So this is proof. She knows how delicate this topic is.

"She told me she's just here for the summer. But I'm not letting her walk away. Not this time," I say.

"Good. She's always been what's best for you. They both have." My mom places a warm hand on my shoulder, then walks back inside, leaving me out here with my thoughts. Her words ring in my ears, confirming what I already know.

She's always been it for me. Even when I didn't have the words for it.

And Maverick... he's always been part of that too.

It's not just her. It's *them*.

They're the ones who make me feel whole.

And I think, no, I *know* we could be everything if I can just prove we're worth staying for.

By the time I come back inside, dinner's long over, and the dishes are already washed and put away. I find Callie in her room two doors down from mine, and she greets me with that quiet smile that's been undoing me since we were kids.

She wraps her arms around my waist and leans in, her cheek pressed to my chest like she can hear every storm still raging inside me.

And somehow, just standing here with her makes it a little quieter.

Losing the farm feels like losing the last piece of who I was before everything broke. But holding her like this? It reminds me that some things can still be mine.

"You smell good. Like outside. Like memories and trouble." She nuzzles her nose into my chest, squeezing a little bit harder. Her own sadness shows in the way she holds me tight.

"Hm... not as good as you," I say truthfully. She still smells like citrus and pomegranates, soft, warm, like she's already curled herself into this house without meaning to.

I make a mental note to steal the name of whatever soap she's using. The only thing better would be her smelling like *me*.

"Stop sniffing me," she grumbles, giving me a shove, but there's no force behind it.

I don't let go. My hands settle on her hips, firm and steady, keeping her close as I lean back enough to look into her eyes.

"You're one to talk. You had your face buried in my shirt a second ago."

She shrugs, trying for casual, but her voice betrays her.

"Yeah... but that's 'cause you smell like home."

The words hit like a strike to the chest, instant, deep, permanent.

A ripple shoots through me, all the way down to my heels. The way she says *home* like she means it, like she *wants* it sets something warm and dangerous spinning in my gut.

Lately, I've started to think maybe knowing what she wants isn't the problem.

Maybe it's just giving her a reason to believe she could have it.

This time, I let her go when she pulls away and take a seat on her bed. I watch her run a brush through her long copper hair, the strands glowing in the dim lamplight, each stroke making it shine a little more. There's peace in the mundane.

I can picture it so clearly, sitting like this every night. Her in my room. Us getting ready for bed.

Slowly, a pink flush takes over the skin at the nape of her neck, not immune to my attention. My gaze doesn't stray.

She huffs and turns, waving the brush at me. "Why are you staring at me?"

I shrug, a loose smile tugging at my lips. "Just makin' sure this isn't a dream."

She crosses the room and leans in. Her kiss is soft, reverent, and I sink into it like something I've needed for years. She pulls back but just barely. Her breath brushes my skin.

"It's not."

Barely a whisper, but it still runs straight down my spine, leaving goose bumps in its wake.

Does she know?

That I'm already picturing a life she doesn't believe we can have?

Her in this house. Our kids running wild. Maverick fixing fences while I wrangle horses.

It's the sweetest goddamn dream I've ever had.

I already know I'm not strong enough to let it go.

The part that guts me most?

She might be strong enough to leave it behind.

She kisses me again, deeper, needier. My arms go around her, anchoring her to me. Her mouth moves against mine, and I swear I feel her shaking. A low groan escapes me, unfiltered.

Then she pulls back.

Something flickers in her eyes, something distant.

Like she's already slipping out of it.

Already pulling away from the fantasy.

Chapter 43

Callie

Hard to believe we leave tomorrow.

Two weeks at Colt's family farm, gone in a blink.

We head back for the next ride in the morning. Maverick's in. Colt's still sidelined, no matter how much he hates it.

The round pen isn't much anymore, just weathered rails and half a gate hanging off its hinges, but the moment I see it, something in my chest pulls tight. I wander closer, boots dragging through dry grass. We must've ridden a thousand circles in this pen growing up, but I was barely old enough to tie my own shoes when I climbed into the saddle first. Back then, we were only allowed to ride with our parents watching, but I snuck in anyway, daring the boys to follow.

Colt and Maverick climbed the fence rails, wide-eyed and hollering advice like they knew better. But they didn't dare climb in until I did. I still remember the look on Colt's face when I took off at a trot, equal parts terrified and impressed. Maverick followed the next day, jaw set like he had something to prove. And after that, it was always the three of us.

Colt trails behind, his crutch slowing him down, but he's steadier now, moving better than he was even a week ago. He tossed his sling a week out of the hospital, stubborn as ever. Determined to ride in the championship, whether he's ready or not.

Maverick walks beside him, close enough to catch him if he stumbles. The air between them isn't tense anymore. It's warm. Quiet. Full of something unspoken. Lingering glances. The kind that say more than words ever could.

I climb onto the lowest rail, arms stretched wide for balance. The wood creaks beneath me, but it holds.

"Remember when you tried to rope that bale of hay and ended up tying yourself to the fence?" I grin, tossing the memory over my shoulder.

Colt groans. "You gonna bring that up every time we're near this place?"

"Yes," Maverick answers flatly, stepping onto the bottom rail beside me. "Because it was hilarious."

Colt snorts, brushing a hand through his hair. "You try learning to dally with a rope twice your size."

"You were seven," I tease.

"And convinced he was already a rodeo champion," Maverick adds, voice lighter than I've heard all day.

We fall into silence, each of us taking in the space.

The dirt's cracked, weeds creeping through in places, but the bones of it are still there. Solid. Familiar. Like the three of us, maybe older, rougher, but still standing.

A breeze kicks up, carrying the scent of dry grass and storm on the wind. I glance toward the sky, dark clouds, bruised and low. "We should probably head back."

Too late.

The first fat drop hits my arm. Then another. In seconds, the sky opens up like someone flipped a switch.

"Shit!" Colt laughs, already trying to tuck the blanket back into the basket we brought, but he's fumbling with one hand and a crutch, moving too slow.

"Go!" I take them from him, already half running toward the shelter just past the edge of the field.

I barely make it a few steps before my boots slip in the wet grass, and suddenly, Colt's no longer behind me.

"Don't—" he starts, but Maverick's already there, cutting him off with a curse.

"Save it."

In one smooth motion, Maverick hauls Colt up into his arms like it's nothing.

Colt lets out a strangled sound. "I swear to God, Mav—"

"Complain later," Maverick grits out, already jogging after me, rain soaking his shirt. "Or you can break the other leg too."

"I hate you."

"Sure you do."

They catch up fast, and we duck under the rusted

metal overhang just as the rain really lets loose, thunder rumbling low as the rain pounds down in silver sheets. It's not much, just a wide-open space with one wall half caved in, but the roof holds, and it's dry.

Colt's scowling when Maverick sets him on his feet, muttering something about dignity and how he could've *managed*, but his cheeks are pink, and his eyes are lit up in a way I haven't seen in years.

I don't say anything. I just smile and lay the blanket out while they catch their breath, drenched and grinning, the ease between them as natural as breathing, like no time has passed.

The wind howls just outside, pushing sheets of rain sideways through the open bay. But in here, it's warm, cozy in the way only something old and familiar can be.

Colt eases down onto the blanket, groaning as he shifts to stretch out his leg. Maverick stands nearby, shaking the water from his hair, his shirt stuck to his chest, dark with rain. He glances at me, then down at Colt, like he's checking both of us before finally settling beside him.

It's quiet for a moment. Just the sound of the storm and my heartbeat.

"I forgot how good this kind of quiet feels," I say softly, brushing damp hair out of my face. "Like the world's finally minding its business for once."

I glance between them, both soaked, both beautiful in completely different ways. The kind of beautiful that aches a little to look at. Maverick's gaze is steady, guarded like always, but there's warmth there now.

Colt grins. "We still got those strawberries?"

I reach for the picnic basket, peeling back the damp towel covering the food. "A little smushed, but yeah." I lift out the container and a can of whipped cream.

Colt lets out a dramatic sigh of relief. "Thank God. I was about to think this day couldn't be saved."

I plop down between them and pop the lid. The strawberries are definitely bruised, but still red and sweet-smelling. I hand one to each of them, then grab the whipped cream.

Colt leans in, his eyes dark with mischief, but there's a low hum beneath it now, something heavier. "You gonna make it fancy?"

I arch a brow, pulse fluttering. "You want me to serve you?"

He grins, slow and lazy, like he already knows the answer. "I mean... you could just put it straight in my mouth."

My heart skips. I cover it with a smirk, but my fingers tighten on the can. I swirl the whipped cream onto a berry, slower than necessary, watching his gaze follow every movement like he's starving.

"Open up, cowboy."

He does. No hesitation.

I lift it to his mouth. Colt leans in, lips parting, and wraps them around both the berry and my fingers, sucking them into his mouth with a slow, deliberate pull.

The heat is instant, spreading between my thighs, dampening my panties. I feel the wet flick of his tongue, the soft scrape of teeth. It's too much and nowhere near enough.

My fingers slip free with a soft pop, and his eyes fall shut as he bites down on the berry. "Hmmm," he hums, voice gravel-thick. "Tastes good."

A shiver runs through me, goosebumps erupting along my skin as Colt's tongue catches a drop of cream at the corner of his mouth and licks it clean, slow and unhurried, like he knows exactly what he's doing to me.

Across from us, Maverick hasn't moved.

He's watching every breath, every shift. His posture is rigid, jaw tight, like he's barely holding himself together. His eyes are hooded, unreadable, but the way he looks at us is anything but calm.

I reach for another berry.

He stops me.

His hand circles my wrist gently, but firm enough that I freeze. My pulse spikes as his fingers slide down to my palm, guiding it toward him with deliberate care.

His gaze holds mine. Dark. Hungry. Pupils blown wide.

Then, softly, almost reverently, he brushes his lips across the tips of my fingers.

There's a pause. A breath suspended in time. The current arcs between us, wrapping around my ribs, my spine, winding me so tight I could break open.

Then he leans forward, and his tongue flicks out, swirling over the tips of my fingers, catching the sticky sheen of strawberry juice. But it's more than that. His mouth lingers. His eyes stay locked on mine.

And it hits me. He's licking Colt too.

The berry. The whipped cream. My skin. His tongue. Colt. It's all connected.

The thought shatters me. Delicious and dangerous.

A full-body flush blooms through me like wildfire, liquid heat coiling low, spreading out until my skin feels too tight, too sensitive.

Outside, the rain picks up, hammering the roof like it's got something to say. Thunder cracks again, loud and deep, but it barely registers.

Because inside this shelter, the world has shrunk.

Just us.

Just touch. Just taste. Just the heat of those ravenous gazes.

Colt sits up behind me, his thighs bracketing mine, my back to his chest. His hands land on my hips, pulling my ass against him, hard, sure, claiming every inch.

I shiver under the weight of it.

"You know..." he murmurs near my ear, voice lower now, rough with intent. "We could make this a whole lot messier."

The rasp of it slips under my skin and curls in my gut, a dark ripple of need growing.

I laugh, but it breaks halfway. A sound caught between a moan and a whimper.

And I don't pull away.

Maverick's eyes are locked on mine, pinning me in place, dark and unreadable, like storm clouds gathering.

Colt's hands glide up my spine beneath the hem of my shirt. His knuckles brush bare skin, and I inhale sharply, the cool air against my stomach only making me more aware of how warm he is. He slides them higher, slow enough to make me tremble.

Maverick cocks his head, lips parting slightly as his eyes roam over me. Then he moves, spreading my knees to make room for himself. He takes the hem of my shirt from Colt, lifting it until the pink lace of my bra is revealed.

Colt cups me through the fabric, thumbs brushing over the peaks, and lets out a ragged exhale against my shoulder. My spine arches, a helpless sound slipping from my throat.

"Good girl," Maverick murmurs, voice like smoke. Then he lifts the hem to my mouth.

"Bite."

I do. My teeth sink into the fabric, and my chest heaves under their hot gazes.

Every heartbeat feels counted. Every inch exposed as the air between us crackles, hot and waiting.

Maverick leans forward, plucks a strawberry from the basket, and circles my navel, the pink juice dripping down my stomach.

Then his tongue is there, hot on my skin, licking the path he made.

He and Colt exchange a look over my shoulder, some silent command passing between them.

Then my bra's snapping open.

Colt lifts my back from his chest to slip it off, and the new angle shifts me closer to Maverick.

He doesn't hesitate, swirling the berry around my nipple before sucking it into his mouth.

He groans, low, teeth scraping gently at the tender peak before letting go with a pop.

"Sweetest thing I've ever had."

Colt replaces Maverick's mouth with rough fingers, rolling my nipple between them as Maverick continues his torment.

The barest graze skims over my other breast, cool liquid turning warm against my fevered skin.

I ache for his mouth. For more.

Maverick presses his nose into my collarbone, a low growl rumbling from his chest.

"So fucking delicious. We're going to eat you up."

He guides Colt's hands until he's cupping both of my breasts from below, long fingers bracketing my nipples. I moan when Colt pinches them.

Maverick stares at me, grin a slash across his face, hunger radiating off him in waves.

Then he runs his tongue along my nipple again, this time sucking Colt's fingers too. The slick sound of his tongue sends shivers down my spine. Watching him take Colt into his mouth undoes something inside me.

Colt groans behind me, fingers flexing, hips jerking.

The sound punches through me like a pulse, a deep ache blooming low and sharp.

Then Maverick runs that damn fruit over Colt's fingers, lifting his hand and sliding two of them deep into his mouth, a low rumble vibrating in his throat.

Colt grinds his cock into my back, hard and desperate. I feel every inch of him, hot, insistent, and perfectly pressed against me. My pulse skips, then races.

Maverick's mouth leaves my breast with a wet pop, and he leans back just enough to look at me, eyes blown wide, lips slick, and jaw tight with restraint.

He hooks his thumb into the waistband. "Take these off."

His voice is deep gravel, not a request. A promise.

I nod, but Colt beats me to it. His hands slide down my sides, fingers hooking into the waistband of my shorts and tugging them down my hips. He pauses, glancing to Maverick like he's waiting for approval.

Maverick nods once. "Nice and slow."

The fabric drags along my thighs, cool air kissing new skin. My breath shudders. I lift my hips, letting them strip me bare. When they're gone, Colt's hands trail back up, palms warm, reverent, stroking over my knees, the inside of my thighs.

Maverick hands anchor me, firm and possessive, as he spreads me wider, hooking my legs on the outside of Colt's. I feel completely exposed, but never safer.

Then his mouth is on me.

A cry bursts from my lips, high and raw, as his tongue slides through my core, purposeful and slow. He licks me like he's tasting something he's craved for years. Like he's memorizing every reaction.

Colt shifts behind me, cradling my back against his chest. One hand wraps around my ribs; the other returns to my breasts, fingertips circling, teasing, pinching just enough to make my hips jolt.

"Fuck, you're perfect like this," he whispers, voice ragged.

Maverick groans into me. The vibration tears through my core, and I moan loud, needy, falling apart with every stroke of his tongue.

He doesn't rush. He works me over, licking, sucking, then flicking that spot again and again until I'm trembling, my thighs closing around his head, my hands clutching at Colt's arms for something, *anything* to ground me.

Colt presses kisses to my neck, murmuring in my ear. "That's it, baby. Let him make you feel good. Let us take care of you."

The words melt through me like honey. My hips rock without meaning to, chasing every bit of friction.

Maverick doesn't let up.

His mouth is devastating. He licks into me like a man possessed, slow and deep one moment, relentless and precise the next. When he slides two fingers inside, curling just right, I break.

My cry echoes through the shelter, swallowed by the rain hammering the roof. My body bows, locked tight, heat exploding through every nerve.

Colt holds me as I shake apart in his arms, his breath

ragged, his hand still teasing my nipple, gently now like he's grounding me. Worshiping me.

Maverick licks me through the aftershocks, slow and lazy, until I whimper from the sensitivity and try to pull away.

He looks up then, mouth glistening, and gives me a wicked smile.

"Told you we'd eat you up."

Chapter 44

Colt

I'M STILL HALF OUT of my damn mind from watching Maverick devour her.

My head's spinning, every nerve lit up, and I haven't even been touched yet.

Then Callie turns, hair wild, lips kiss-swollen, eyes dark and glassy with want.

Her gaze drops to my lap, then lifts again, deliberately. "Take these off."

It takes a second to process, my brain short-circuiting from everything that's just happened. I glance down at my jeans. My cock strains painfully behind the zipper, and suddenly, I can't get them off fast enough.

I grunt, shifting to work the button open one-handed, but it's clumsy with the brace, the angle, and the lingering ache in my leg.

Callie bites her lip like she's trying not to laugh. "Need help?"

"I've got it," I mutter, even though I absolutely don't.

I get the jeans and boxers halfway down my thighs.

Maverick leans forward from where he's sitting behind her, expression unreadable, voice dry. "Don't be stubborn, princess."

"Fuck off," I say, but I'm smiling, and they both know it.

He reaches over and tugs my boxers and pants the rest of the way off, slow and unapologetic.

And now I'm bare, cock flushed and hard, aching in the cool air between us.

The second I'm free, Callie shifts forward on her knees, hair spilling across her shoulders. One hand curls around the base of me, warm and sure.

She peers through her lashes. "Can I?"

My voice breaks on the inhale. "Please."

She lowers her mouth, and I swear to God, the second her lips wrap around me, I stop breathing.

The heat. The suction. The way she moans like I'm the best thing she's ever tasted.

My head knocks back, and I clutch the blanket beneath me, every muscle in my legs locking tight.

She takes her time licking the tip, swirling her tongue, teasing on purpose.

Maverick watches from behind her. Silent. Still. Hungry.

Callie's mouth is heaven, hot, soft, eager, but when Maverick moves behind her, everything changes.

She pulls back, lips glistening, and turns toward him like she already knows.

He leans in, first kissing her slow, filthy, tasting me between their mouths.

Then his gaze lifts, locking on mine. His hand wraps around my cock, sure, steady, like he's done it a hundred times in his head.

His thumb swipes over the tip, slick with spit and precum, and then he lowers.

The first touch of his lips fries my nerves.

My back arches like I've been struck by lightning. A raw, choked sound punches out of me, part gasp, part moan.

"Fuck," I hiss, but it doesn't sound like me.

He takes me slow, mouth so warm, unreal, tongue curling with a mix of reverence and hunger that makes my head spin.

Maverick.

Maverick is sucking my cock.

And it's not soft. Not tentative.

It's greedy. Devastating.

He sinks deeper, dragging a moan from my chest I didn't know I was capable of.

My hands fly to the blanket, clutching it like a lifeline, trying not to come undone.

My hips twitch.

My vision whites out.

Jesus Christ.

He groans around me, deep, vibrating, and the world

goes fuzzy around me. It's too much. Too good. And worse, he knows exactly what he's doing. How to tease. How to pull. How to hollow out his cheeks and take me so deep I swear I hit the back of his fucking throat.

Callie shifts beside me, close enough that her bare skin brushes mine with every shaky breath. Her hand finds my chest, palm warm over my pounding heart. She leans in, kissing my jaw, my neck, whispering something soft and sweet, but I can't process the words.

Not with Maverick's mouth still on me.

Not when I can see him.

He's between my legs, shoulders broad, back flexing as he works me over like he wants to ruin me from the inside out. His lips are wet, cheeks hollowing, throat taking every inch I give him. And fuck, the way he looks, eyes half-lidded, focused like this is what he's meant to be doing. It's obscene. Beautiful.

Callie's hand drifts lower, tracing my ribs as Maverick sucks harder, deeper until my hips buck off the blanket.

She can't look away, and neither can I.

Him. On his knees for me.

His mouth on my cock.

He grips my hips tighter than they need to, like he wants to own every second of this.

The sight of him like that, lips stretched, spit-slick and messy, eyes locked with mine and so damn hungry nearly shatters me.

"Oh my—fucking hell, Mav—"

My voice breaks. My thighs shake. I'm coming apart, and he's not stopping.

His pace only picks up, throat working around me with practiced ease, like he wants to ruin me.

And God, he is.

Every stroke strips me down further.

Like I've waited years for this without knowing it.

And now that I have it... I'll never want anything else.

Maverick pulls off with a slick sound that leaves me gasping. My cock twitches in the cool air, spit glistening at the tip. My hands curl into the blanket beneath me, searching for something to hold on to.

Then Callie's mouth is on mine.

Soft. Familiar. Steadying.

She kisses me like she's trying to anchor me to the earth, like I'm coming apart and she's the only thing holding me together. I taste myself on her lips and groan into her mouth, everything inside me unspooling.

Maverick's hand wraps around my cock again firm and possessive, like he owns every inch of me.

He strokes me slow and tight, palm dragging over the sensitive head until precum beads and spills, trailing down the side.

It's slick and messy, a mix of spit and precum coating every inch as he works me in an unhurried rhythm that makes me hiss through my teeth.

Then his fingers dip lower.

I flinch at the first brush of them against my rim, the sensation so new it knocks the breath from my lungs.

"Breathe," Callie whispers, her forehead pressed to mine, her palm cradling my face like I'm something fragile.

Maverick circles again, patient and deliberate as he presses in with a wet glide that makes my spine bow.

The burn is sharp. But it's the pressure. The sheer gravity of it. It shreds through whatever defenses I had left.

Then his tongue is there.

Warm. Wet. Unforgiving.

He licks me like it's something he's craved. Like he wants to carve the memory of this into both of us.

He eases them into me, slow but insistent, until my thighs shake and my body forgets how to resist.

Callie's lips move over mine again, and I suck in a broken breath as Maverick works deeper.

"Fuck," I whisper, voice shredded. "What—what is he—"

She kisses my jaw, my cheek, my mouth. "He's making you feel good. Let him."

My brain's static. My body's fire.

Maverick moans into me like he's the one losing control, and it punches straight through me.

He circles, then fucks me deep enough to short-circuit everything I am.

It's too much.

Too fucking good.

I'm not even sure who I'm holding on to, but my hands are in someone's hair, and my back is arching off the blanket like I'm going to split apart.

His mouth doesn't stop. Neither do his fingers.

Maverick pushes a second, and the stretch hits like lightning.

My hips jerk before I can stop them. It's instinct. Chaos. Need.

A groan claws up my throat, raw and helpless. I grab at him, his shoulders, his hair, grasping for anything solid because the world's tilting sideways, and I'm not sure I'll survive it.

I'm shaking now. My thighs. My arms. My fucking soul.

Between my legs, his mouth closes over my cock again, and I swear I shatter.

He sucks hard, tongue swirling until I'm gone.

Pressure slams through me like a freight train.

I can't breathe. Can't think.

"I'm going to—" I gasp, desperate, voice cracking open with a warning. "Mav, *move*."

Maverick groans deep in his throat and tightens his grip.

He takes me deeper, swallowing me whole, fingers never stopping as they stretch me open from the inside out, and that's it.

That's the end of me.

I detonate.

My hips buck helplessly, fucking into him. My body seizes, every muscle locking down as I explode, hot and hard, wave after wave crashing through me.

He takes all of it, moaning like he's starving for it.

I'm wrecked. Ruined. Gasping. My body trembles like I've never come before.

And when I finally collapse back, my heart's pounding, lungs barely working as Callie kisses me, soft and slow, like I didn't just lose my mind.

I blink at her, dazed. "Was I—" My laugh hitches on the breath. "Am I the bottom?"

She grins down at me, smug and sparkling and utterly in love.

"No," she says, brushing her lips over mine. "You're the lucky one."

Maverick rises to his knees, jaw clenched, eyes locked on her like he's already claimed every inch.

He doesn't speak. He doesn't need to.

His hand finds Callie's hip, then slides lower, wrapping around her thigh. She shifts automatically, moving with him, and he guides her over me with confident, unrelenting pressure.

I'm still catching my breath when she's suddenly above me, thighs bracketing my ribs, heat pulsing against my skin.

Her hair falls forward as she braces her hands beside my shoulders, searching like she's trying to read my mind.

Maverick's not done.

He plants one hand between her shoulder blades and pushes, not hard, but firm, until her chest lowers to mine, her back arching with the motion.

My hands land on her hips instinctively, steadying her.

His hands grip the sides of her ass, spreading her open. *Fuck.*

His mouth parts, tongue out, and he lets it drip.

My cum. Onto her skin.

Between her cheeks.

My hips twitch, already stirring.

A low sound rips from my throat.

The sight alone, his cum-slick lips, the glisten on her flushed skin, the possessive way he holds her, has me spiraling.

He glances up, catches me watching.

And he fucking smirks.

Callie's breath hitches, sharp, and uneven as she cuts crescents into my shoulders like she's holding on for dear life.

Her hips jerk when he touches her.

It courses through me.

Every tremor. Every broken breath. Every desperate shift as she rocks toward his hand.

Behind her, Maverick growls, voice thick with possession. "You're so fucking tight."

Callie whimpers, her forehead dropping to my chest. I slide a hand up her back, up and down in smooth motions, trying to soothe her.

I watch the tension ripple through her as Maverick works her open, one hand gripping her ass, the other... lower. Deeper.

"Relax for me," he murmurs. "Let me in, Callie."

She lets out a long, broken breath. Her thighs quiver.

"Good girl," he breathes. "Just like that."

Her whole body shudders as he presses deeper.

"That's my girl." His growl is rough, reverent, completely undone.

He's taking his time.

That obscene, wet slide. The way she moans. The way she arches.

The way she reaches for it has me tearing at the seams.

Maverick chuckles, dark and low. "You like it when I stretch your pretty ass, don't you?"

Callie whines, rocking her hips back into him. She's panting our names like a prayer. I can hear how good he's making her feel, stretching her, finger by finger.

Maverick's voice drops to a whisper, but every syllable hits like a brand. He's stroking his cock with one hand, positioning himself with a low, appreciative hum.

"Can't wait for this ass to clench around me."

She arches above me, taut with tension, breath stuttering against my cheek, as he presses into her. She's shaking, and her nails dig into my chest as she tries to steady herself.

What I want, what I *need* is to watch Maverick sink into her. The way she stretches around him. My cum still glistening, slicking his way in.

I picture it anyway.

His hands on her hips, thumbs spreading her open. Her body gives way, inch by inch, like it was made for him. The flushed pink of her skin. The tight heat of her taking him deeper and deeper.

My cock twitches, hard again, the ache nearly unbearable.

Callie's cries are soft and broken, and fuck, it's the hottest sound I've ever heard.

"Good girl," Maverick groans, voice low and ragged. "You feel so good."

She shifts, hips jerking, trying to breathe through it. Her head drops to my shoulder as whimpers escape, and her whole body quivers with the stretch.

Maverick pauses, fully seated deep inside her, and leans forward. His chest brushes her back as he sucks on the soft bottom of her ear.

"You feel that? The way your body's gripping me? Like it knows I belong here."

I slide my hands up her sides. I can't move. Can't breathe.

Watching them. Feeling her. Being here. It's almost too much.

And still, I want more.

"Colt..." Her voice is barely a breath, but she says my name, and it sounds like a plea, and it lands straight in my chest.

"I need—"

"I know." My voice cracks with it.

Maverick lifts his eyes to mine over her shoulder. There's fire there. Possession. Hunger.

But there's something softer too. A flicker that says this matters. That he's not just doing this for her.

He's doing it for all of us.

He drags his mouth along the line of her spine as he reaches between us. His fingers wrap around my slick and pulsing cock and line me up beneath her.

"Ready?" he rasps, voice thick.

I nod. Or moan. I'm not sure. My whole body's buzzing, strung tight with need.

"Then let's give her everything."

And then he's guiding her down.

Her body sinks around me, hot, tight, impossibly wet. Every inch of her stretches as she takes me, slow and aching, until I'm fully seated inside her and she's gasping, nails digging into my chest like she's trying to hold on to something real.

Above us, Maverick groans, hips flexing as her body clenches around us both.

Holy fuck.

She's full, breathless and unraveling, caught between the two of us, and so am I.

Every breath is a battle now.

Because nothing—nothing—has ever felt like this.

Maverick moves first, a slow pull of his hips, barely more than an inch, but it ripples through her. The drag of him inside her tightens everything around my cock, and I swear I see stars.

Callie moans, clenching down, and my head thumps back against the blanket, breath torn straight from my lungs.

Then he thrusts again, deeper this time. Controlled. Deliberate.

The friction is unreal, shared and all-consuming. His cock presses against mine through the thin wall of her body, like he's fucking me too.

Callie whimpers, mouth brushing over my jaw as her body rocks between us. "God... I—"

"You're doing so good, baby," Maverick murmurs, voice ragged, reverent. "Taking both of us like you were made for it."

He thrusts again, and the sound she makes splits me open.

Her hips move on instinct now, down onto me, then back against him, trapped in a rhythm of want.

I match her, hips rising to meet every stroke, and fuck...

Maverick's hand slides around her ribs, hauling her back against his chest as he drives into her harder. Each thrust pushes her deeper onto me.

His voice drops to a growl. "You love this, don't you? Being ours. Being full."

Callie can't speak. She just nods, whimpers, body shaking as she reaches behind her for him.

He catches her hand, entwining them, holding her steady as he fucks her deeper. Faster.

Every motion of his hips drives her down tighter around me. She's hot, wet, pulsing.

I realize I'm not going to last.

Not with her clenched so tight.

Not with Maverick fucking her like he owns her... *me*.

Not when every nerve is lit up and begging for release.

Callie's thighs start to quiver in uneven jerks as her body begins to give out. Her nails bite into my chest again, and her breath spills out in broken gasps.

"Maverick—Colt—oh my God, I'm—"

She clamps down, seizing around me.

Then the sound.

Half sob, half scream, as her orgasm hits her.

Her whole body locks. Her mouth parts in a silent cry as she shudders between us.

Maverick groans behind her. "That's it. That's our girl. Come for us, just like that."

She pulses around me again and again, and I arch, hips jerking without thought, chasing the high she just lit like a match to dry grass.

Maverick's hand slides down, stroking where we're both buried inside her. His fingers press just above the root of my cock, palm rubbing tight circles over her clit as she rides it out.

That pressure, his hand, her body, the heat, sends me careening toward the edge.

"Shit." I gasp, fists tangling in the blanket, teeth gritted as my body jerks. "I'm gonna—"

He just growls, "Give it to me."

And then I'm gone.

My body bucks, hips slamming up as I spill inside her.

Callie's still shaking around me, moaning as she collapses onto my chest, breath hitching in my ear.

My vision whites out at the edges, everything else dissolving except for her... and Maverick still inside her.

His pace falters.

Once.

Twice.

Then his head drops, and a sound tears out of him, half growl, half moan, as he jerks, fist wrapped tight around the base of his cock.

I watch, dazed, as he spills across her back in thick, hot ropes, groaning through his teeth as he empties himself.

Callie shudders on top of me, still full of me, her muscles fluttering in the aftermath.

We're blissed out, riding the high of pleasure.

All of us.

Maverick's chest heaves, one hand braced on her lower back, the other resting heavily on his thigh, breath dragging in and out.

Then he leans and presses a kiss to the base of her spine. Then another.

Soft, reverent kisses press into the back of my hand where it's still curled around her waist.

Our bodies are still tangled, sticky with sweat and cum, skin flushed and trembling, but no one moves to fix it.

No rush to clean up.

Just soft breaths and the sound of rain still pattering outside the shelter.

Callie's cheek rests against my chest, her hair damp where it sticks to my skin.

I run a hand through it slowly, untangling the strands.

Her breathing is steady now. Calmer.

But she hasn't let go of me.

Maverick lowers himself to the blanket beside us, his arm curling around her waist from behind. His other hand finds mine.

No words, just a squeeze.

That old ache in my chest swells again, but this time it's something good. Something solid.

I glance down, and Callie's looking up at me, her eyes sleepy, sated, and soft.

"You okay?" I murmur, brushing her hair from her cheek.

She nods, but her voice is barely a whisper. "Better than okay."

Maverick shifts closer, pressing a kiss to her shoulder. "You were perfect," he says, and his voice catches just slightly, making something hot bloom behind my ribs.

Callie smiles, eyes slipping closed again. "You two really know how to wreck a girl."

"Pretty sure it's the other way around," I say, her laugh vibrates through my chest.

We stay like that for a while.

No more teasing. No more games.

Just tangled limbs, quiet touches, and the steady thrum of three hearts beating in the same rhythm.

Chapter 45

Callie

THE RAIN'S STILL FALLING, soft and steady against the tin roof.

I'm boneless, melted between them like my body doesn't belong to me anymore.

Colt's chest rises beneath my cheek, slow and sure, his hand stroking absently through my hair. Maverick's arm is around my waist, warm and solid, his breath at the nape of my neck.

For a minute, no one moves.

The air smells like skin and sweat and rain. The rise and fall, like we're synced now. Like something clicked into place and decided to stay.

Then Colt shifts. "You okay?"

I nod, or I think I do. "Sticky."

Maverick chuckles behind me. "We've got wipes somewhere."

He rolls away and rustles through the duffel bag in the

corner. When he comes back, his touch is gentle. He cleans me first, quietly, carefully, then Colt.

"Better?" he asks.

I hum and curl back between them. "I don't think my bones work anymore," I murmur.

Colt grins. "That bad, huh?"

I don't say anything after that. I just breathe.

Let my guard drop.

Let my heart settle.

Let myself stop thinking about what comes next.

For once, I don't brace for goodbye.

I just let myself be here.

Held.

Wanted.

Home.

Chapter 46

Maverick

It's early. That pale, gray-gold kind of dawn that doesn't give a damn if you're not ready.

I slam the tailgate shut and rest my palms on the edge of the truck bed, letting the silence settle around me. There's not much left to pack, just a few last-minute things Callie's grabbing from inside, but I don't move. Don't talk. My chest is too full.

Colt's next to me, adjusting a ratchet strap. I watch him out of the corner of my eye like he might fall over. Like if I blink, he'll vanish altogether.

We spent our childhoods here, barefoot summers and bruised-up winters, secrets traded under porch lights and fireflies. It's quiet now. Different. But in the kind of way that settles into your bones instead of sliding off your back.

Two weeks. That's all it was. But fuck, it changed something.

Colt nudges me with his shoulder. "You good?"

"Yeah," I lie because I'm not sure how to explain what this place feels like now. Like coming home to a version of myself I didn't know I missed.

He doesn't push. Just nods and turns back to the strap.

Behind us, the front door opens. Callie steps out with her hair twisted up and a duffel slung over one shoulder. She looks like summer and heartbreak. Like every good thing I ever thought I couldn't have.

Colt's mom meets her at the bottom of the steps and pulls her into a hug so tight it makes my throat close. "This will always be home, you know," she says, quiet but not casual. Loaded.

Callie doesn't say anything right away, just hugs her back and nods into her shoulder. When she pulls away, her eyes are a little glassy, but her smile's easy.

Colt's dad clasps my hand in that no-bullshit way he always does, then gives me a look like he already knows. Like he's waiting for me to figure it out too. "Come visit, anytime," he says, then glances at Colt and Callie like he's drawing a damn map for me.

I nod, jaw tight. "Thanks."

Callie tosses her bag into the back seat and slides into the passenger side, her bare foot hanging out the window before the door's even shut.

I take the driver's seat, adjust the mirror, and sit there for a second with my hands on the wheel. Gravel crunches under Colt's boot as he walks around and climbs into the back seat. His hand settles on the console, and she takes it, like it's second nature, like they've done this a hundred times before

I turn the key, and the engine hums to life.

The rearview mirror catches the porch one last time. Colt's parents stand there like a postcard, his dad with an arm slung around his mom's shoulders, both of them waving, both of them watching us go like they know something we don't.

Something in my chest shifts. A slow, hard tug behind my ribs.

We pull away. Tires crunch against the gravel. The house gets smaller, and unwanted memories start to replay.

The hospital.

That stink of bleach and panic.

Callie's voice cracked as she fought to stay calm speaking with the nurse.

Colt too pale, too still, blood streaked on his brow.

And me...standing there, pretending I wasn't fucking terrified.

There's no such thing as easy in this sport. One bad second is all it takes.

I used to live for the rush. Now, it's the fastest way to lose them both.

The high doesn't thrill me anymore. It guts me.

Because now I've got more to lose than just myself.

Callie glances over at me, her sunglasses sliding down her nose. "You okay?"

I nod. "Yeah."

She doesn't ask again, just lets go of Colt's hand and threads hers with mine.

It's that quiet kind of love, that knowing kind. It hits hard.

The two weeks felt like a piece of heaven. Cold beers. Fireflies blinking lazily in the dusk. No words, just Callie's head on my shoulder and Colt's foot nudging mine and that deep, impossible peace.

Everything's different now. That part of me that chased chaos just to feel something, it's quiet for once. This place did that. The slow mornings. The way she looks at me. The way *he* does.

There's something better than adrenaline. Something steadier.

That's when it hits me.

I used to think bull riding was everything. That nothing else could match the way it made me feel free, wild, infinite.

But now?

Now I know better.

I don't want the ride. I want the landing.

I want the after.

The hand on mine. The porch light on. The kind of love that doesn't burn out the second it gets hard.

The truck hums beneath us, the road wide open ahead.

And for the first time in a long time, I'm not chasing the ride.

I'm chasing them.

Chapter 47

Callie

We've been back on the road for a few days, from one small town to another, but this morning moves slowly. Warm. The kind that stretches and yawns before it ever thinks about starting.

I wake up smushed between Colt and Maverick, one of Colt's arms draped across my ribs like a seat belt while Maverick's thigh lines my right side. The motel AC is doing its best impression of a dying animal, barely rattling out any cool air, so we're all a little too warm. A little sticky. But I don't mind. Not even close.

Colt groans into my hair like he's in pain. "Coffee or death," he mutters.

Behind me, Maverick chuckles low, amused, already awake. Probably been up since dawn, scrolling the news or checking ride stats. He shifts behind me and reaches one long arm over my shoulder, helping Colt, who won't admit his shoulder is still sore, sit up. Maverick passes over a mug to the half-asleep Colt, who grunts his thanks.

They think they're subtle, but come on, Maverick refilling Colt's travel mug before the man even opens his eyes? That's not friendship. That's a damn love letter.

I wriggle free from under Colt's weight and pad barefoot toward the counter, stretching out like a cat. Maverick's already crouched by the motel's sad little coffee station, brewing more of what Colt calls "real coffee" and what the rest of us call motor oil.

He glances up at me with a resigned expression. "He better appreciate this."

I smile. "He won't."

He shrugs, like he expected as much, and goes back to stirring. There's only enough drinkable coffee for one more cup. I really freaking want it, but I'm not so shameless to steal it from him.

Mav pours it into the mug, and I watch, trying not to sigh. Now I'll have to wait until Colt drinks his sludge before I can make more.

"You're pretty cute, you know that?" Maverick says in that easy, peaceful tone I'm still getting used to.

I look down at myself, wearing one of their shirts. My hair is what I'm sure is a rat's nest of a bun, and I haven't brushed my teeth yet. "I think we're going to have to examine your definition of cute."

He stirs the coffee, adding the perfect amount of creamer and sugar. "Well, the way you were pouting silently over this was definitely what I would consider cute." Then he holds it out for me. "It's already yours. I made sure there was enough left for you."

Bubbles pop as they fill my chest. This new lightness is something I've been trying to get used to. This man's love language is acts of service, and it's freaking working.

I hum, taking a cautious sip of the hot liquid. "You're pretty cute too."

The pink flush across his cheeks just proves my point.

That low, constant current between us crackles to life.

Colt strides out of the bathroom, shirtless, leg brace in one hand, towel slung dangerously low on his hips, and reaches between us for his own mug. "You two look intense."

He's halfway done with his drink before I've had a chance to really start mine.

"You're welcome," Maverick mutters.

Colt grunts and takes a long sip, trying to look annoyed. He's not. He's smiling around the rim.

"Thanks."

Maverick turns to me, hoodie in hand. "Cold this morning," he murmurs, then pulls it gently over my head. It smells like him soap and cedar, and I melt a little on the spot. He presses a kiss to my temple without thinking.

My heart? Does that stupid flutter thing it's been doing for weeks now.

Colt drops onto the corner of the bed and starts fumbling with his brace, trying to fasten it one-handed. Maverick doesn't say anything, just crouches down and straps it into place, movements fast and familiar. Colt doesn't move to stop him, having given up on this particular argument weeks ago.

It hits me in the quiet between their banter how much I love this. Not the chaos. Not the fame or the arenas. Just... this.

The three of us, tangled and half-dressed in a too-warm motel room, moving around each other like we've done it a hundred times.

I've just thrown my hair into what I'd say is a semi-decent ponytail when Maverick calls from the front door. "Let's go, you two."

Colt grins conspiratorially at me and purposely slows as he finishes brushing his teeth. I swear these two will do anything to get under each other's skin.

"Come on, Princess." The rumble of Maverick's voice is thick in the small bathroom

Colt chokes, his own blush happening. Not quite used to this new form of attention from his former nemesis.

He finishes brushing his teeth, sighing. "Let's get this over with."

"You're acting like you're heading to the gallows."

"I might as well be. I'm going to a press conference while injured, only one ride away from the championship. The reporters are going to go for blood."

We stop for gas just off the highway, one of those half-abandoned places where the pumps are sun-faded and the ice chest outside is held together with duct tape. Colt hops out to start fueling up, his ball cap tipped low over his eyes.

Maverick climbs out too, grabbing a squeegee, and starts scrubbing bug guts off the windshield with the intensity of a man avenging his family.

I leave them to their manly nonsense and head inside for slushies and Twizzlers, the kind of fuel *I* actually care about. The air-conditioning inside is working overtime, the cold biting after the sun, and the floor sticks a little under my sandals as I make my way to the candy aisle.

I'm halfway through the checkout when I notice the shift. I smile at the cashier after finishing paying and head out, pausing just a few steps outside with my bag of snacks, sipping my slushie like I've got all the time in the world, watching the whole thing unfold with the kind of calm that comes from dating two incredibly hot idiots.

Three girls hover by the pumps now, trying for casual but giving themselves away with every wide-eyed glance and whispered nudge. I clock the recognition the second it lands before they've even made it halfway across the lot.

They're cute. Confident. The kind of girls who know how to turn heads without breaking a sweat. Crop tops and glossy lips, denim shorts and practiced ease. Not a single one of them looks flustered to be standing in front of Colt and Maverick.

I don't blame them. They're both stupid hot. It's practically unfair.

But when one of them steps forward, all lit up with excitement, and lays her hand on Colt's arm, *that's* when something in me tightens.

I'm not the jealous type. I swear I'm not.

Still, the way she leans in, lashes lowered, full of soft-lipped flirtation... yeah. That's the exact moment every molecule of my girls' girl energy ends.

"You're even hotter in real life," she says, her voice going up half an octave.

Colt blinks, startled. He shifts his weight and glances around like he's trying to be polite about it, but I can already see the tightness in his neck.

Maverick spots me over the hood, frozen mid-swipe, his eyebrows hitting his hairline. He tilts his head like, *You seeing this shit?*

I lift a single brow. *Handle it.*

Oh, he does.

He drops the squeegee with a *clunk*, walks straight across the lot like he owns the pavement, and before I can even breathe, he's got a hand curled around Colt's neck, pulling him in.

The kiss is... emphatic. Slow. Territorial in a way that's not even a tiny bit subtle.

Colt's eyes go wide for half a second, and then his whole body sinks into it, hands fisting in Maverick's shirt like instinct. Like home.

Gas pump forgotten. Flirty girls officially invisible.

I make my way over, enjoying the view, and place myself between them and my guys.

A shocked gasp bubbles up from behind me. "Wait... are they dating?"

I turn, lean against the wall, and take a long, loud sip from my straw. "Jealous?"

The girl startles, blinking like I've caught her shoplifting. "Uh. Yeah."

"You're out of luck. He's super taken."

Maverick finally pulls back, breathing a little harder, and Colt, God bless him, is red from the neck up but still dazed enough that his lips part like he might go back in for another.

I stroll up and hand over the bag of snacks to Maverick, ignoring the girls who are now staring wide-eyed with mouths half-open. One of them is, unsurprisingly, filming this play out. They'd better saddle up because I'm about to give them an even bigger show.

I step in close and tug Colt down by the front of his shirt. His lips are still warm from Maverick's, still parted like he's caught between a breath and a laugh.

I kiss him slowly, like he's mine to claim.

He exhales against my mouth, one hand finding my hip, holding me close.

Then I shift toward Maverick, slide a hand into his curls, and pull him in next. He doesn't hesitate. He kisses me deep, with that kind of anchored certainty that still undoes me, even now. His thumb brushes my jaw like he's grounding both of us.

When I pull back, they're both looking at me like I hung the stars and handed them the moon.

A soda can clatters to the pavement. Someone gasps loudly enough to draw a few stares of their own.

"Oh my God. Are all three of them?"

"Did she just kiss both of them?"

"Wait. Are they, like... together?"

Maverick slings an arm around my shoulder, deadpan as ever. "Think we broke 'em."

I sip my slushie. "Good."

One girl blinks at me, stunned. "I mean, wow. Are you... like... is that a thing?"

"Apparently," I say, breezing past her and back to the truck. "And it's a damn good one."

Colt exhales a laugh and rubs the back of his neck. "Y'all could've warned me."

"You needed the reminder," I say, popping a Twizzler into my mouth.

"I so did not need a reminder. Hell, I can promise you that I will *never* need a reminder." He huffs, but he's grinning now, wide and unrepentant, then winks. "But feel free to give me one anytime."

Once the dust settles and the fans disperse, we climb back into the truck. We left Maverick's at Colt's parents' house in favor of the fold-up center console making a bench seat that works perfectly for us.

I climb into the middle. Colt passes me my slushie without looking, Maverick slides the aux cord into my lap, and our hands find each other without even trying. It's second nature now.

Colt's thigh presses against mine, warm and steady, and none of us says anything for a while.

The engine hums low, gravel crunching beneath the tires as we pull back onto the road.

"We're a little obvious, huh?" I say finally, glancing out the window at the open stretch ahead.

Colt chuckles, low and smug. "They'll get used to it."

Maverick smirks, rubbing a thumb across my knuckles. "Or they won't. Doesn't change a damn thing."

The gas station fades in the rearview, slushies half-melted in the cup holders, Twizzlers passed back and forth between bites of protein bars and road trip silence.

Maverick's hand is still in mine, Colt's thigh pressed warm to my other side. The windows are down. The wind tangles my hair. We don't say much.

But it's not quiet.

Not really.

Because Colt hums low to the music, and Maverick's knuckles brush my thigh. Because this truck smells like leather and sweat and the sweet, syrupy mess I spilled earlier, and somehow, it smells like home.

I glance over at them, Colt squinting into the sun, Maverick stealing a Twizzler from my lap, and my chest aches with how easy it all feels.

Chapter 48

Colt

The press tent buzzes with the usual noise: camera shutters, caffeine-fueled whispers, the hum of too many voices pretending to be polite.

It smells like dust, leather, and nerves. I lean into it like always.

Rolled sleeves, soft-worn jeans, brace still visible under the denim.

I take my seat behind the mic, flashing that dimpled, easy grin they all eat up. Country-boy charm dialed just right. Enough cockiness to remind them who I am, who I *still* am, even if I haven't been on a bull in weeks.

This weekend will be the second event I've missed since we got back from the ranch, and it's eating me alive.

No one here needs to see that though.

Like sharks smelling blood in the water, they start in, not wasting a second before they take a bite.

Are you worried about reinjury? Do you think your riding style contributed to the injury? How's the leg?

I answer with the same charm I've always used to keep the media happy.

"Aww. You worried about me?" I lean into the mic, voice smooth as butter. "Leg's not as bad as you all seem to think."

"You've been out for a while. Will you ride again this season?"

"I'll be ready for the championship," I say, letting my voice curl into a confident drawl. "That's what matters, right?"

What if I'm not ready? The thought weighs on me less than I thought it would.

The next question turns the tide, really going for blood now, aiming for the kill shot to get that juicy headline.

"What about Maverick Kane pulling further ahead while you've been benched? Considering your... history, that's gotta sting."

I stiffen before I can stop myself, but I school it quickly, raising a brow, sitting back like I've got all the time in the world.

"Mav's always been a strong rider," I say evenly. "He deserves the lead, but you better believe I'm going to take it from him."

"Last question," the marketing coordinator says, holding up her hand.

Tension eases from my shoulders, grateful for the save. Don't think I could take much more of this.

Displeasure rumbles through the crowd, but they know the rules, and they know what happens if they break them.

She points at our reporter from *Rodeo Weekly*, and I have to fight against clenching my teeth. He's always been a little weasel.

"You say that, but your odds are mighty slim now. That's got to be getting to you." His smile is cutting. He knows exactly what he's doing.

Fucking asshole.

I take a beat, then lean into the country-boy bravado on the outside, shoving down the fury underneath.

"I wouldn't bet against me just yet. We all know the championship is where it counts."

There are enough points in that one tournament that leads are won and lost every year. Someone can come in as a favorite and not make it out on the other side.

I search myself for the ruthlessness that's always burned hot. The drive to take Maverick down, no matter the cost, and I find it missing.

My gaze sweeps the crowd, landing on Callie. There's no sweet sunshine in her now. She's staring down the reporter like she's ready to take him out and hide the body somewhere out back.

A genuine smile hits my lips at the gleam and fire in my girl's eyes.

If looks could kill, he'd already be six feet under.

The attention shifts to where Maverick's sitting in

front of a mic, being interviewed by a different circle of reporters.

He's giving his standard stoic, no-bullshit answers in that short-clip tone of his, the kind that doesn't waste a single word, but when my name comes up, his voice cuts across the space like a damn whip crack.

"He's not out of the race," Maverick says, loud enough for everyone to hear. "Not even close. You don't write off a man like Colt Lawson. Not unless you're ready to eat your words in front of a stadium."

The air shifts.

Maverick's always been calm, unshakable in front of the press. Now, there's an edge to his voice, and the tendons in his neck stand out.

A brave reporter speaks up. "You've got to admit, you've got this in the bag whether he comes back or not."

Maverick just looks straight into the cameras like he means every damn word. "If I want to be the best, I have to compete against the best. There's not a man in this tent I'd rather face in the arena," Mav replies. Sharp. Calm. Fiercely loyal. "Because when Colt rides, the rest of us are just trying to keep up."

It's not a sound bite.

It's a statement of fact.

The words hit me harder than I expected. Not because they're flattering, but because they're *real*.

Maverick's not just backing me.

He just declared his respect. *Publicly.*

He just showed everyone that if anybody wants to take me down, they'll have to go through him too.

I meet Callie's eyes. She's biting the corner of her lip, giving me an all-knowing smirk, like she's known this version of Maverick all along.

I sigh and shake my head, because of course she has.

She's been pushing us together since the day she came back.

They finally give the signal that Maverick's done, and the reporters thin out.

I make my way toward him, trying to keep my cool, but my throat's thick with emotion, slurring my words.

"What the hell was that?" I say with fake indignation.

I'm sure happiness is written all over my face.

Maverick keeps his voice low, just for us. "Had to set the record straight."

I look away as the heat crawls up my neck, flushing my cheeks. I mumble, "Appreciate it."

He shifts, stepping into my line of sight, gaze locking with mine like he's trying to brand the words into me.

"You're not out of this, Colt. I meant everything I said."

It's a rush. A tidal wave. An electric current snapping straight through my chest.

Every doubt I've been dragging behind me disappears under the weight of that stare.

"Yeah?"

"Yeah."

Callie's shoulder bumps into mine. "You two done flirting? I'm hungry."

Suddenly, I'm starving, and it has nothing to do with lunch.

Maverick darkens, his thumb running along his bottom lip.

He's thinking the same thing I am.

"Fucking ravenous." Lust drips from my tongue.

Callie swallows hard, her cheeks a pretty pink. "Oh."

"Yeah." I wrap my fingers around her waist and tug her closer to me, dropping my mouth to her ear. "Yeah, *oh*."

Chapter 49

Maverick

CALLIE's already taking off her shirt by the time the motel door clicks shut behind us.

No words. No pretense. Just her, standing at the foot of the bed, hair wild, mouth pink from kissing, eyes full of challenge, fucking electric as she peels off her top inch by inch and tosses it aside. My mouth goes dry as she runs her hands slowly down her bare stomach, like she knows exactly what she's doing.

Colt makes a noise low in his throat. "Holy shit."

Every curve, every movement, slow and deliberate. She unbuttons her jeans, slides them down her legs with a little shimmy of her hips, and we both follow the motion like she's got us on strings.

She's doing this on purpose, showing herself off like this body is a gift, and we'd be fools not to fall to our knees and worship it.

Jesus Christ, I want to. I want her on her back, on her

knees, on my tongue. I want her dripping and trembling and pulling Colt apart while I lose my mind watching.

Colt's already pulling his shirt over his head, eyes locked on her like he's half-wild.

She's still in her bra and panties, barefoot, flushed, eyes flashing with wicked intent. Her hands drift over her own hips. Sin incarnate, all bare skin and flushed cheeks as she tilts her chin toward us.

"You're driving us crazy." Colt lets out something between a groan and a prayer.

I mutter my agreement, yanking my shirt off in one breath and kicking my boots free, Colt a mirror image of me as he strips down.

Callie grins. "That was the plan."

I'm not sure who groans louder, Colt or me.

My hands twitch with the need to touch her, but I don't move. Not yet. My girl is having fun, and I'm not going to stop her.

She reaches behind her back and unclasps her bra, letting it slide down her arms. Her nipples are already peaked, and my cock jerks just watching her drop the bra on the floor.

Colt's halfway to her already, drawn in like gravity, but he waits.

Callie hooks her thumbs into the waistband of her panties, eyes flicking between us. "Well?"

I move.

She doesn't flinch as I close in, just lifts her chin, daring me.

I grip her hips, run my palms down her thighs, then back up again, slow and possessive. "Touch me."

She does.

Her hand wraps around my cock, hot and confident, and the second her fingers close, I hiss through my teeth. I'm already hard as fuck, and the way she strokes me steadily, firm, teasing the head with her thumb, knowing exactly what I like, has me pulsing in her grip.

Colt's behind her now, naked and wild-eyed. His hands settle on her waist as he leans in to kiss her neck, and she turns her head to meet him, mouths crashing.

It's messy. Hot. Her other hand dives into his hair, fisting it tight, like she can't get close enough fast enough.

She's sandwiched between us, my cock in her hand, Colt's mouth on hers, and she's moaning now, helpless against the way we both press into her.

Colt growls when she tugs his hair. "Jesus, Callie..."

"I want both of you," she begs.

My hand covers hers on my cock, guiding the rhythm for a few more strokes. "Get on the bed."

She crawls backward onto the bed, knees wide, then lies back, one leg bent.

"Fuck," Colt breathes, staring at her like she's already ruined him. "Look at her."

I do. And it damn near brings me to my knees.

She's spread out for us, flushed and panting, one hand between her legs like she doesn't know what else to do with the need that's taken over her body.

Her other hand reaches for me, fingers curling around

my cock, and I swear to God I almost lose it right then. Colt lowers himself between her thighs. His shoulders press into her as he kisses up the inside of her thigh, and I feel her shaky exhale as her grip on me tightens.

I kneel on the bed, guiding her closer.

"Good girl," I murmur, brushing my thumb over her chin before lining myself up above her lips. "Open."

Her lips close around me, drawing a deep rumble of approval from my chest as I thread a hand into her hair. She takes me deep, greedy, like she needs this too, and the sounds she makes while Colt licks into her are enough to short-circuit my brain.

She moans around my cock when Colt sucks at her clit.

My hips jerk forward, and her hand flies, nails digging in just enough to hurt.

Colt growls something I can't make out, but the way her whole body trembles says she felt it.

I shudder at the sensation. Her lips suction harder as Colt works her over, my cock muffling her cries. I wrap her hair around my fist and fuck into her mouth slow and deep while her whole body arches for more.

The sight of her like this, her mouth full of me, thighs shaking, and Colt buried between her legs, is enough to break something open inside me.

God, I've never seen anything so fucking beautiful.

Her hips buck off the bed, and I know exactly what Colt's doing to her. The rhythm of her throat, the way her legs tense and shudder. She's right on the edge. I push deeper, her lips stretched tight around my cock as her cries vibrate through me.

"That's it," I growl. "Come for us."

She cries loudly and desperately, back arching clean off the mattress as her whole body goes taut. I swear she nearly chokes on me as she breaks apart. Colt devours her through her orgasm, stretching it out until he's licked every last drop.

Fuck, I'm close. Too close.

I ease out of her mouth with a hiss, both hands curling tight in her hair as I pull back just enough to let her breathe. Her lips are swollen, spit slick across her chin. She blinks up at me, dazed. Ruined.

"Why'd you stop?" she whispers, voice hoarse.

I lean down and kiss her, rough and claiming, before I murmur against her lips, "Because I'm not done with you. Not even close."

Then I glance down at Colt, whose mouth is glistening, eyes dark with want. "Get on the bed," I tell him, voice still low, still firm.

He obeys, breathless, muscles tight with tension, half propped up by his bent forearms. I grab Callie by the hips and guide her to straddle his waist, back facing him, her knees on either side of his hips.

"Now, watch," I say to them both, heat coiling deep in my gut. "Because this is mine."

Colt's breath stutters as I stroke his cock, slipping the head through her folds, sensitive and soaking, drawing out her gasp. She's trembling from her orgasm, hand steadying herself on my shoulder, as I tease her entrance, circling it with his wet tip.

He lets out a needy whine, the sound gritted through clenched teeth.

"You ready for him?" I ask, voice low.

She nods, biting her lip, already sinking down inch by slow inch. The stretch draws a moan out of both of them. Her head falls back against his shoulder, his hands flying to her hips like he can't help himself.

"Fuck," Colt breathes. "She's so—Jesus, Callie."

I grab the lube, flip the cap, and pour some over my fingers. Colt's too distracted by her to notice, until I skim them along his ass, running between his cheeks. His hips jerk, nearly lifting her off him.

"You like that?" I murmur.

He nods, dazed, jaw slack.

Callie's still rolling her hips, riding him slow, and sweet little whimpers spill from her mouth as she leans forward, grinding down harder.

I circle a lubed finger around his rim, waiting until his breath catches again.

"Let me in," I say. "I've got you."

He doesn't hesitate, just nods, one sharp jerk of his head. I start slowly, one finger pushing in, then two, working him open while Callie fucks down onto him, one hand still on my shoulder, like she can't get enough.

"You're doing so fucking good," I whisper, leaning closer as I scissor him open. "I can feel how bad you want it."

Callie's trembling again, clawing at my chest for balance, lost in the sensation. She looks down, eyes wide as she sees my fingers moving in and out of him, the base of Colt's cock slick and glistening.

"God," she breathes. "Maverick..."

"I know," I rasp. "Just wait."

I add a third finger, and Colt moans as his hips twitch up, lifting her with him. She gasps. "Holy shit."

I slow them both down with a firm hand on Callie's hip. "Not yet."

It's not until Colt's panting and open and begging beneath her that I pull my fingers free and slick myself up.

Because now. Now I'm going to fuck him while he's buried inside her.

I position myself behind him, dragging his ass over the edge, pressing his knees up and wide, spreading him open. He's panting, glazed over, and completely undone, and I haven't even gotten inside him yet.

"Breathe for me," I murmur, dragging the head of my cock over his hole. "You're ready. I know you are."

His fingers dig into Callie's thighs. She's still seated on him, still clenching around him, still trembling every time his hips twitch. Her eyes on me are blown wide, lips parted, awe struck across her face.

"Fuck him," she pleads. "Maverick... give it to him."

She doesn't have to ask twice.

I press forward, slow and steady, every muscle in my body clenched with the effort it takes not to lose it too fast.

He's hot and tight and gripping me like he's never letting go.

Colt groans raw and loud as I slide in, until I'm buried to the base. His head drops back, mouth open.

"Jesus," he chokes out. "I—fuck."

"Yeah," I growl, adjusting my grip on his hips. "You feel that? That's mine."

I pull back and thrust in again, the angle pushing him deeper into her. She gasps, arching her spine, her nails cutting into my shoulders as the force of it rocks her too.

"Oh my God," she breathes.

Colt bucks beneath her, helpless now, caught between us.

"That's it." One hand holds him firmly in place, the other tangled in her hair. "Let us ruin you."

The rhythm builds fast. Colt fucking up into her, me driving into him, her body caught in the middle and shaking with each thrust. We're a tangle of breath and skin and friction and heat, and there's no space between us anymore.

No air. No past. No future.

Just this.

Them.

Us.

My mouth finds hers, and I swipe my thumb across Colt's lips, pushing it deeper when he opens because I fucking need both. Their moans mix with mine, ragged and breathless and desperate.

"I've got you," I promise again. "Both of you. Always."

Colt's hands claw at the sheets, teeth sinking into me. Callie's eyes close, her cries ragged.

"You're close," I grit, my hand sliding around his waist, stroking him in time with my thrusts. "I can feel it."

He whimpers, actually fucking whimpers, and Callie nearly shatters on top of him.

"Mav—" she gasps, eyes fluttering. "I'm gonna—"

"Then come for us, baby," I growl, pounding into Colt harder now. "Come all over his cock while I ruin him."

She cries out, her whole body locking up as she splinters apart. Colt shouts, hips jerking as he spills into her, and I don't stop, don't let up, riding them both through it, every muscle in my body straining.

The sight of them, undone, shoves me right over the edge.

"Fuck—Colt—" I slam in deep one last time, burying myself in him as I come, heat flooding through me, eyes squeezed shut as the world whites out.

I collapse to the bed, taking Callie with me, sandwiching her between us.

We're a pile of limbs, sweat, and shaking breath as I press my forehead to Callie's, one hand still gripping Colt's thigh.

For a long moment, no one says anything. We just breathe. In and out.

Colt groans weakly. "I don't think I can feel my legs."

Callie lets out a choked laugh and leans forward to press a kiss to his jaw. "Pretty sure Maverick broke you."

"I'm okay with that," Colt mutters, boneless.

I smile and press a kiss between her brows. "You're mine," I say quietly.

Callie cups my cheek. "Yours."

I kiss her, all the heat stripped back to something deeper. Something that feels permanent.

"You two wreck me," I whisper.

Own me.

Colt murmurs sleepily, "You're one to talk."

I close my eyes. Let the quiet settle in. Let myself believe it's real.

Because it is.

Because we are.

And nothing else matters.

Chapter 50

Callie

THE CROWD IS DEAFENING. The kind of roar that makes your bones vibrate, even from the safety of a VIP seat. I haven't watched a single ride in over a month, but this is different. This is the championship. This is for the buckle. Everything they've been working for culminates into one event.

Excitement glints in the riders' eyes. That feeling like anything is possible. Some of them are still gunning for that buckle, while others are just excited to be here. Unlike the usual small-town setups where it's just bulls, riders, and bleachers, this arena's enormous. The dome ceiling is sealed above us, making the noise twice as loud.

I watch as the top five riders are announced one by one, each stepping forward to the center of the dirt. Smoke cannons blast. Indoor fireworks spit sparks ten feet into the air behind them. Colt's got that cocky mask on, the one he saves for moments like this, when everyone's watching and he wants to remind them exactly who the hell he is.

Maverick's the opposite, storm clouds and laser focus, jaw tight.

Even from here, I can tell they're searching.

Their gazes sweep the crowd, sliding past VIPs and cameras and the hum of the arena until they find me.

Just like that, the act drops.

Colt's grin shifts to something real, crooked and boyish.

Maverick's scowl breaks, just a fraction, his mouth twitching like he's fighting a smile he doesn't want the cameras to catch.

The world zooms in like the noise dims and the crowd fades, and for one breathless second, it's just us.

Possessiveness hits hard, fast and unforgiving. Because these boys are mine. Whether I deserve to call them that or not. Somehow, in some way, they've always been mine. And they'll always be mine, no matter what.

Eight years apart taught me I needed closure, or I'd never stop thinking about them. This summer was supposed to be about making peace and saying goodbye. I was so naive to think I could show up here, spend a little time, and not give them a piece of myself. One that'll rip me apart when I leave.

While I'm lost in my head, the riders disappear back into the tunnels, back to the chutes to get ready.

A few rides go by. Some good. Some bad. A lot of dirt gets eaten. At least no broken bones yet.

Anxiety skitters across my skin like static, crawling and everywhere at once. My heart punches at my ribs in uneven beats, like it's trying to claw its way out. My fists clench in my lap, trying to breathe through it. In. Out. In. Out. But my lungs feel too tight, like the air can't reach the bottom.

Maverick's name blares from the speakers, and every nerve in my body lights up like a struck match.

I knew this was coming. It's why I'm here. But that doesn't stop the tremor that starts in my head and rolls all the way to my toes. The cheer that erupts is deafening. Maverick fucking Kane. Untouchable, unshakable, sitting on top of the leaderboard, but he'd be the first to remind everyone not to count Colt out.

God, that interview. Watching him defend Colt, hearing the quiet fury in his voice, the loyalty... undid me.

His face appears on the jumbotron. It's at least fifteen feet tall and twenty feet wide. The camera zooms in until I can see his lashes, the creases in his sun-tanned eyes. He's calm, steady, breathing in an even rhythm. I match it without thinking.

I can almost hear him, that low promise against my skin: "You're okay, Wildflower." And when he holds me like that, I believe him.

He runs through his checks. Strap. Glove. Grip. Each movement precise. Controlled. He's doing everything he can to make this safe, even though it never is. Not really.

My hands fly to my face, pressing to my eyes like I can

block out the whole world, like maybe if I can't see it, I can't lose him.

Eight seconds stretch into eternity.

The announcer calls out the end of the ride, but my palms are still glued over my eyes, like if I lift them too soon, I'll see something I can't unsee.

A calm, warm voice beside me cuts through the panic. "He made it through just fine."

I turn to the woman. I've been too busy freaking out to notice her until now and blink at her in wide-eyed surprise.

She's stunning.

Golden waves tumble over her shoulders, and her eyes are a clear, bright green. There's something about her. She's calm, grounded, welcoming. Like she knows exactly what it's like to be in my shoes and isn't in any rush to make me explain it.

She offers me a water bottle like we've known each other for years. "Here. Drink. Helps more than you think."

Her tone is low and even, the kind people use when they don't want to scare something skittish.

I accept the water with a muttered "Thanks" and take a long sip. The coolness is a shock, but so is the way my panic starts to dull around the edges, like her voice is smoothing out all the ragged parts of me.

"First time watching someone you love ride?" she asks, still in that even, reassuring tone.

I huff a quiet laugh. "If only it were that simple."

She tilts her head, clearly curious, but she doesn't

press. Just nods, then pivots to something easier. "I'm Mia."

"Callie." I shake her hand, awkward and too aware of how tightly I'm still clutching the water bottle.

She doesn't seem to mind, just smiles and keeps talking, like this isn't strange at all. "So, who are you rooting for?"

"Colt and Maverick."

Her brow lifts, and her lips twitch. "The rivals?"

I twist my fingers in my lap, the heat crawling up my neck. My brain immediately floods with memories that have nothing to do with rivalry. Maverick's hand gripping Colt's thigh, Colt's low moan echoing against my neck, the way they moved together until I couldn't tell where one of us ended and the other began. My face ignites, heat crawling up my neck until I can feel it all the way up to my ears.

Mia watches me closely, then grins. "Oh. So it's like that."

I open my mouth. Close it again. Try to find the words, but they scramble. "I mean—sort of. Yeah. We're... together."

"First time saying that out loud?"

I pause. "Technically second. If you count a group of girls in a gas station parking lot."

She laughs, and the sound is light, not mocking. "These two," she nods toward the men seated beside her, "are mine."

My brows rise, reaching for my hairline. "Wait. Seriously?"

"Seriously," she says brightly. "This one's River." She pats the thigh of the dark-haired, brooding man beside her. "And this charmer with the dimples is Alex."

Both men glance over at me, curiosity in their expressions, but their attention never strays far from Mia.

"I've never met another throuple before," I admit, still a little stunned.

She giggles. "And isn't that a shame?"

I choke on a laugh because... yeah. It kind of is.

She chirps happily as she introduces them, telling me how they're here to cheer on a friend who switched from hockey to bull riding. How they both play in the NHL, that they've been together for several years, and that she couldn't imagine life without them. It's all said so casually, like love like that is the most natural thing in the world.

The way Mia says it, like love that big isn't rare or reckless, makes my chest ache.

I shift in my seat, pulse still fluttering beneath my ribs, but it's not fear anymore. It's the weight of wanting something I'm scared I don't deserve.

"How did you make that work?" I ask, no filter. But Mia just smiles, easy and unbothered.

"Lots of talking. And a little stubbornness." Her expression turns soft. "I cared about them so much I thought protecting them meant letting them go. Turns out, love doesn't need protecting when you accept it for all that it is."

There's something about her open honesty that's grounding. Even though we're strangers, it makes me feel like I can tell her anything.

For some reason... I do.

The words pour out before I can stop them. Every worry that's been stacking in my chest this summer spills out of my mouth in one breathless rush. The fear. The guilt. Everything that happened with my dad. The way he never chose us. No matter how many times he promised. The ache of knowing I'm falling, or let's face it, *fell*, in love with two men whose first love will always be this sport.

Who would risk everything for the ride. Who have risked everything before.

Mia doesn't interrupt. Doesn't flinch. Just listens, her gaze steady on mine. She nods along, gives quiet hums of understanding, like she's holding space for every jagged piece I hand her.

When I finally stop talking, my lungs feel tight, but my shoulders are lighter.

She places a hand over my wrist. "So let me get this straight. The three of you were best friends until your dad died in a bull riding accident. That trauma made you terrified to get close to anyone who rides, so you disappeared for eight years. You came back because staying away hurt too much, and you needed closure, needed to say goodbye. But somewhere along the way, the friendship turned into something more. And now you're scared to ask if they'd ever give it up for you."

Well, when you wrap it up that way... I nod, biting the inside of my cheek.

Then her boyfriend Alex leans forward. "Your dad was a fucking asshole, if you ask me."

"Alex." River elbows him, a sigh in his tone like this is regular behavior that he's learned to put up with.

"What? It's true. He promised he'd quit and then died doing the one thing he swore he wouldn't. Sounds like selfish bullshit to me."

My brain stutters, and I have no idea how to respond. No one's ever talked about my dad's death without romanticizing it. People love the notion that he died doing what he loved, like it somehow made it all okay.

Alex doesn't take his side and doesn't sugarcoat exactly what he thinks of my dad. Finally having someone understand, to acknowledge what he cost me, twists my gut, sending a wave of nausea up my throat. Ever since that day, I've never dared hope that I was worth choosing.

"See?" Alex says, looking smug. "She gets it."

"Not sure that look means she gets it," River mutters, but Mia continues like she's heard it all before.

She squeezes my wrist gently. "So now you're here, and leaving feels like tearing your own heart out, but asking them to choose you over the arena feels like stepping off a cliff and they'll jump off with you."

My throat tightens. "Exactly."

"Are you ready for some tough love?"

No... "Yeah."

"Why?" Her question is blunt.

It cuts sharper than I expect, and I lay it out there for her to dissect. "Because bull riding isn't just something they do—it's who they are. It's in their blood, their bones. It's the goddamn sun they've built their whole world around since they were kids. What kind of selfish idiot would I be to ask them to walk away from that for me?"

Mia doesn't miss a beat. "Don't you think it's a bit selfish not to give them that choice?"

Stunned, all I can do is blink.

"From the way they both lit up when they saw you up here?" Mia's voice is gentle, but her words land sharply. "I'd bet everything they love you. That kind of love—real love—it doesn't come around more than once."

She glances toward the men beside her with tenderness.

"You know that, don't you? Isn't that why you came back?"

She gives me a second just long enough for the weight of it to settle.

"I say jump. Take that leap off the cliff, and give them the chance to catch you."

God, I want to, but every time I inch toward believing it, my dad's voice slips in, filled with easy confidence, full of promises he never kept.

I'll quit next after this championship. I just need one more shot. One last ride.

He was like a gambling addict, but instead of money, it was his life on the line and the future I didn't get a chance to have with him.

"My dad loved us." My voice breaks, unsteady. "I know he did, but he still didn't choose us. It wasn't enough. *I* wasn't enough. How am I supposed to believe anyone else ever could?"

"If you don't ask, you lose either way," she says gently.

I swallow hard. "What if they don't?"

"What if they do?" she counters, her voice still calm, still kind.

I look down at my hands, clenched tight in my lap. "It's complicated. They love riding."

"Callie, listen to me. Wanting to be with someone *with people* who don't risk their lives every time they go to work? That's not selfish. That's valid. This isn't about asking too much. It's about knowing what you need. You've spent so long treating your boundaries like they're flaws, but they're not."

She leans in, voice steady. "Everything you're afraid of could still be true. They could love the sport more. They could say no. But it would *still* be worth asking. Because not asking? That guarantees you lose."

I sit there, breath caught as my lungs compress. Hope is a dangerous thing, but for the first time, that flame my own father snuffed out flickers back to life.

"Believe me, I understand. Fear almost cost me everything," Mia says. "I'll be damned if I sit by quietly and let that happen to someone else."

Alex squeezes her knee, River presses a kiss to her temple, and all I can think is:

I want that.

Chapter 51

Colt

I ROLL MY BAD SHOULDER, and it gives a dull throb in return, like a warning shot, reminding me that every time I told Callie I'm fine, it's been a lie.

The wood-paneled wall is hard against my back as I work my palm into that constant ache. "Come on, man. Get it together," I mutter, not that there's anyone around to hear it.

The back hallway echoes with the noise of the arena. Everyone's out front, either riding, getting ready to ride, or watching. The excitement is fucking palpable on every single one of them.

That should be me. I should be out there, running scenarios through my head, meticulously going through each step of my process. I definitely shouldn't be back here hiding, but every time I try to walk up, a weight compresses my chest, growing heavier with each step I take.

This isn't something I'm used to. I've always run head-first into challenges, not giving a damn about the consequences, just craving the high of the win.

I was born with that "I can do anything" attitude. The type that encourages irrational confidence, but hell, it hasn't let me down yet... at least, it hadn't.

I rake grooves through my hair, fisting the ends. That confidence broke somewhere under those stomping hooves, and I'm reminded every time my leg aches or my shoulder throbs just how close I came to not making it out of there.

This shit has never been a problem before. I've ridden through plenty of injuries, just a part of the job, but this is something different, something dug into the back of my brain that's hard to shake off.

I need to get myself together before I blow it all. I've already fallen behind in the ranks taking the last two rides off. I'm lucky I still have a shot at winning at all.

Making the finals practically a winner-takes-all was a special type of genius. Who doesn't love a good underdog story, taking the top spot in the final showdown. As far as entertainment value, nothing has this beat.

It's one bad ride vs. one great ride. Winner takes the buckle.

So fucking this up is not an option.

No championship. No comeback. Just another almost.

The thought is a stone in my stomach, doing nothing but weighing me down.

Riding through pressure has always been half the fun.

Nothing like a good comeback to get your adrenaline going. So why does it feel like a stone has lodged itself deep in my gut? Where's that all-encompassing need to win that's always burning white-hot, driving me toward the win?

No matter how deep I search, there's something missing, something different that's holding me back in this hallway.

I'm one ride from my dream. This is my shot.

Footsteps come up from behind me, and I dip my hat low so whoever it is can't see my face. The brim blocks out my vision so completely that I don't notice the man in front of me until he's gripping my shoulders.

I snap up, ready to shove whoever it is off me, and freeze.

Maverick. Steady. Confident. Wearing a look that strips me bare. His eyes darken as he searches mine, reading every one of my thoughts and doubts like an open book

"Come here," he commands, voice low, as he drags me into an empty tack room. The air is stale, the dim casting Maverick's face in sharp shadows, and it's so hot my clothes instantly stick to my skin.

"What the hell are you doing—" I don't get the whole question out before Mav pins me against the wall.

His mouth crashes down on mine, taking it like he owns it. Teeth sink into my lower lip until I open for him. No warm-up, no hesitation. Just hunger and devotion.

Maverick's touch burns through every thought until I'm all needy hands and sweat-slick skin.

I moan deep in my throat when he shoves his thigh between my legs, and I buck against him, his low hum of satisfaction vibrating against my neck.

It's my undoing.

"Want you." I rip the hem of his shirt out of his pants, greedy, until I can press my palm to his abs, dragging a sharp inhale from his chest.

I explore every hill and valley, tracing along the lines until I've memorized every inch of him, not stopping until his grip trembles where it's still holding me in place.

It's a heated, messy kiss, none of his normal smooth control. We've devolved into pushed-up clothes and roaming hands, urgently covering every inch of each other, but it's not enough, never enough.

I lift my chin and run my teeth along his jaw, nipping at the hard line as I dip my fingers beneath the edge of his jeans. His groan is deep and guttural. Heat floods through me, so fast and sharp it feels like a match striking bone.

"Fuck." I hiss through my teeth, patience evaporating, needing to hold the weight of his cock in my hand, needing the high of knowing I'm the one making him this way.

I've got his button undone, zipper halfway down, when a voice calls out from the hall.

"Hey, anybody see Lawson? He's up in three."

There's no answer, because of course there isn't. The

only two people here are Maverick and me, and we're not saying shit.

Maverick's lips curl in a slow, wicked grin, giving me a glimpse of his tongue tracing the edge of his top teeth. Just fucking ravenous.

I crush my mouth to his, devouring that smile, relishing the fact that it's all for me.

One hand curls around my hip, the other on my chest until I'm flattened against the wall, and I search for Maverick's mouth when he pulls back, needing just one more taste.

He chuckles low in his throat, pressing his forehead to mine. Both of us are panting, our stifling breaths mixing between us.

It's brutally hot. Dust kicks off the floor, filtering the air, but I don't push him off. Instead, I close the distance as much as his grip allows and brush my lips over his.

All those things that used to drive me to win are screaming at me to stay right here.

Black pupils take over brown eyes as he says through gritted teeth, "You better win this."

I'm still dazed from the kiss, brain not firing on all cylinders. "Huh?"

His fingers grip my jaw, locking me in place. "I said, you better fucking win this."

I huff out a laugh. Nothing about that makes sense. "You know that means you'll lose, right?"

That wicked grin is back. The one he reserves just for

Callie and me. The one that has my dick hardening just by looking at it.

"That's right. Fucking perfect," he says, still not making any sense. He doesn't speak again until the fog clears from my mind.

"Ride like hell for me, Princess." Maverick's voice starts as a caress then morphs into that low command he uses while he fucks us. "Show me how good you are."

I twitch as shivers run down my spine all the way to my toes.

"Okay." I nod, stunned dumb.

He pushes off me, gaze focused on where his thumb traces the edge of my mouth. "Go. Win this fucking thing. Then get your ass back to me. I've got plans for you."

My limbs tremble as I make my way to the chute, but it has nothing to do with nerves. That was the best goddamn pep talk I've ever heard.

I close my eyes as they get ready to open the gate and hear his voice again.

Ride like hell for me.

The gate slams open, and everything goes quiet. No noise. No fear. Just instinct. My grip holds, legs locked, body moving with every violent twist beneath me. I ride like I've got something to prove, like I've got something to lose. Eight seconds of muscle and grit and the sharp, electric certainty that I was made for this.

They shout my name over the speakers. The words "perfect ride" and "best score of the decade" ripple through the air as people rush toward me, clapping me on the back.

Photographers, staff, other riders, all trying to grab a piece of my attention, but all I want, all I've wanted this whole damn time, is to find them.

My vision tunnels in on Maverick and Callie in the stands. Both of them are beaming, eyes bright, smiles wide. The next thing I know, I'm running, jumping until I catch the railing and pull myself toward them. Maverick hooks an arm under my good one, steadying me, as Callie wraps around me. Her mouth is open slightly, and I don't hesitate to take it.

There are whistles, hoots, and hollers, but I don't let go of her mouth, even as Maverick guides me over the rail so I can stand between them. His chest presses into my back, pulling us into a hug that lasts long enough to spark questions I'm more than fine answering.

Hell, give me a mic and I'll scream it at the top of my lungs. The stress, the pressure, that overwhelming feeling of conflict I felt before my ride drains from me, and I just lean into them, soaking in this moment like it'll last a lifetime.

The thing lighting me up inside has nothing to do with that gold buckle and *everything* to do with them. The world starts to clear as I realize who I've actually been chasing all along.

Chapter 52

Callie

THE CROWD IS GONE, but the dust still hangs in the air, catching in the rafters like it doesn't know the show's over.

They've turned off the bright lights, leaving only a few at the corners that cast the arena in a dim glow where I stand at the center. The last time I'd been on the inside like this was Colt's accident. And the time before that was before my dad's death.

These buildings represent competition, adrenaline, and living high on life, but for me, for a long time now, all of my pain has been wrapped around this dirt.

I bend over and scoop some up with my hand, letting the grains slip through my fingers.

How can something I've let hold so much power over me, something that's haunted me... be so simple?

It's the same dirt you see in the parking lot, just a little finer, a little deeper. Nothing special. Nothing sacred. Nothing to fear.

Yet I've been hiding from this dirt, and everything it represents, for over eight years.

I close my eyes and take a deep breath through my nose, filling my lungs as I tip my head back, face tilted toward the sky.

This isn't the arena where my dad died, but it was one just like it.

The image of him is still too clear. One I haven't been able to shake.

My throat itches to scream for everything this place has taken from me... and everything it's still holding on to.

It would be easy to run. To walk away and never look back.

Mia's voice keeps echoing through me. Even without knowing me, she managed to cut bone-deep, like she saw a part of herself buried in me. Like a mother warning her daughter not to take the same path.

I inhale again and loosen my fist, letting the last of the dirt fall to the ground.

No matter how I turn her words over in my mind, they always land the same.

This sport may have taken from me, but right now, *I'm* the one choosing to give them up.

I've been letting the image of my mother falling apart beside me dictate every decision I've made since. Letting the memory of my father and all his broken promises shape who I am.

A quiet laugh slips from my lips.

Maybe Alex is right. Maybe he really was just an asshole.

All my fears, everything I've built my life around. The fundamental belief that for bull riders, the sport comes first. You don't risk your life day after day for something you're only halfway in on. That kind of wild, obsessive love, the kind you'd sacrifice anything for, is unbreakable. No matter what anyone says, everything else comes second. Their wife. Their kids. Their body. Their life. Nothing matters as much as that buckle.

It's something I've understood my whole life. Something I've seen with my own eyes and felt with my own heart.

I don't know when that certainty started to crack. Somewhere this summer, a hairline fracture formed, and Colt and Maverick chipped away at it slowly, steadily until the break was wide enough to let the light in.

Waiting on the other side of that crack was a question I'd never dared ask:

What if I'm wrong?

What if everything I believed was built on one imperfect man's mistake?

Coupled with Mia's words, it's damn near mind-altering.

"Everything you're afraid of could still be true. They could love the sport more. They could say no. But it would still be worth asking. Because not asking? That guarantees you lose."

I open my arms wide and try to breathe in the bravery that feels stitched into the bones of this place.

There's a voice in the back of my head screaming at me to run. Telling me staying here is a mistake I won't walk away from.

But my heels dig into the same dirt I used to fear, done letting ghosts control me.

Footsteps crunch behind me, and Maverick's familiar voice calls out. "What are you doing out here?"

It's hesitant, laced with concern. I can practically feel the love rolling off him in waves.

"Waiting for you." My smile wobbles as I roll up every ounce of courage and clutch it tight. Whether this ends in heartbreak or hope, I'm not leaving.

Not until I tell them why I left and what I need to stay.

Not until they look me in the eye and tell me I'm not worth it.

"Woah." Colt's boots thud across the arena floor, closing the distance in a few long strides. His hand is on my face before I can say a word, thumbs brushing at the tears I didn't even know were falling. "What happened?"

Nothing.

Everything.

Maverick's beside him now, scanning me like he's checking for wounds, like he's trying to read me in one long look.

I take a step back, needing space, needing to stand on my own for this.

Colt's blue eyes follow the motion, worry etched across his face.

"I... we need to talk."

"You're still leaving? After *everything*?" Colt says it like the words rip straight out of him.

Maverick grips his shoulder, steadying him, but there's no less hurt in his eyes.

"That's... that's not what I'm saying. Although you might wish it was by the time I'm done."

"Not possible," Maverick replies without hesitation.

My mouth twists into an ironic smile. "I can only hope you're right."

Colt reaches for me but flinches when I take a step back.

"Just let me say this. I won't be able to take it... if you have to let me go."

Both boys still.

"What is it, Wildflower?" Maverick asks, voice low. "What's so bad that we can't even touch you?"

A bitter laugh coils in my chest because that's exactly what I'm trying to find out.

"After this summer, I owe you some explanations." My fingers knot together, restless, before I shove them into my back pockets. "That's not quite right. I've always owed you this."

"It's okay, Callie. You don't have to explain," Colt says, nodding toward the arena. "It's fine. You're here. With us."

"It's not okay. It's never been *okay*. I need you to really listen. Can you do that for me?"

"Say what you need to say. We're not going anywhere." Maverick says softly.

His reassurance helps prop me up, and even though my voice shakes, I don't look away. "You know a lot about me, probably more than anyone. But the things you don't know? They're just as big."

Silent, they wait for me to continue.

"Once I explain, I hope you understand why I can't compromise on this."

"Whatever it is... it's okay." Colt's words hit like a balm and a blade, hurting and healing all at once.

"Losing my dad was devastating. Watching it break my mom was worse." My voice is low, rough as I push through. "I never told you, but my mom hated the fact that my dad competed. She begged him. Begged him to stop. Every season, every event, every ride... she was frozen in fear. She didn't want him to get hurt. She didn't want me to grow up without a father."

They move to speak, but I hold up a hand.

"He never told her no. Never called her selfish. He just... promised over and over that he'd stop. That he understood why she was afraid. Why she was asking something like this of him. He said he'd always put us first. But he didn't mean it. Not really." I clear my throat. "I didn't understand why it mattered so much to her until the day he died. Then I understood all too well. Way too late."

My gaze drops, voice growing quieter. "A week after his funeral, Maverick got hurt. It wasn't even bad, less than half the injuries you'd had before. Nothing out of the ordinary."

I look at them both, eyes brimming.

"But for me? It was like getting electrocuted. Like being thrown back into the moment I watched my dad bleed. That same fear. That same helplessness." A tear slips free, but I don't wipe it away.

"I knew deep in my bones that I couldn't do it again. You loved it so much I knew I could never ask you to stop, but I couldn't watch you ride either. So, I ran."

My tears fall freely now, my voice cracking all over the place, but I keep going. If I stop now, I might never find the courage again.

"Eight years. Thousands of dollars in therapy, and I still couldn't let go of this place. I came back to tie up all the pieces I'd left behind. I thought a few months would be enough. A few smiles, a few laughs, and I'd be okay."

I press a shaking arm across my chest like I can physically hold myself together.

"But you two... you made me fall in love with you in a thousand small ways. You respooled the thread that unraveled when I left and used it to sew the broken pieces of me back together."

My breath shudders.

"I've lived believing that even the men who love you will never choose you over the sport. That even asking them to is selfish. I've treated that like an unshakable truth. A rule written in blood. Even my own *dad* didn't choose me."

A pause, then a softer admission. "Then I spent this summer with you... I started to wonder... what if it's different with you? What if it's okay to be just a little bit selfish?"

My hands tremble, but I keep my eyes on theirs.

"You've done so many things to make my heart believe. Even when I've been too scared to admit it."

A single breath. One last beat, and I slice myself open, leaving me bare.

"And just as much as I'm sure I love you, I'm equally sure... I can't stay if you're going to keep competing."

I brace myself for the silence. For the pity. For the heartbreak.

"So this is me choosing you. Asking you to choose me."

"There has never been another option," Maverick says, his voice low and steady. "You've always been the only choice. No ride, no win, certainly no damn buckle will ever compare to how I feel about you. I will always choose you. I will always choose us."

"Honestly, I'm a little insulted you didn't know that," Colt says with a shaky laugh, his eyes damp as he opens his arms and catches me when I crash into them. Maverick's breath is warm on my neck, grounding me, while Colt supports my weight like he's never letting go.

"You don't think I'm being selfish?"

"So what if you are?" Colt strokes a crescent over my cheek. "Be selfish."

"Circling back," he murmurs, voice lighter now, "did you just say you love us?"

"Uh... yeah."

"Say it again."

"I love you."

Colt kisses me. "Again."

"I love you."

"Again."

I laugh, my chest finally loosening. "I love you. Both of you. I think I always have. Maybe not in the same way, but just as deeply."

It feels a little awkward, the air thick with everything we've said and haven't said. "Are you... do you have anything to say to me in response?"

Maverick arches a brow. "You mean besides saying 'fuck bull riding'?"

"Let's be together forever," Colt adds.

"Please don't leave us. You mean besides all that?" Maverick grins.

"Ah... when you put it like that..."

Colt laughs and dips me backward, whispering, "I love you," against my lips before kissing me senseless.

By the time he lets me go, my vision is blurry again, but this time, it's not from crying. "I love you, Callie Harper," Maverick says, pulling me into his arms, voice rough with emotion. "Thank you for choosing us."

"Hey, what about me, asshole?" Colt cuts in.

"I love you too," Maverick grumbles, and I snort.

Colt flushes bright red and mutters, "Alright, whatever... you too, I guess,"

Maverick leans in to kiss him over my head, all teasing gone. "I love you."

Colt breathes out like the words knocked the air out of him. "Damn. When you say it like that... I love you too."

Colt looks between us and exhales, slow and sure. "Come on," he says softly. "Let's go home."

I blink at him. "What about the championship party?"

He squeezes my hand. "They can celebrate without me. I've already got everything I want."

Chapter 53

Callie

The dust is finally starting to settle.

Literally. The last of the bulls have been loaded, the gates dragged closed, and the thrum of post-championship adrenaline has faded to a hum. Most of the riders are packing up their gear, their trailers rumbling over dry gravel as they pull away one by one. The season's over.

I sit on the tailgate of Colt's truck, legs swinging, boots tapping together. The metal's warm under my thighs, sun-baked and steady. Colt's beside me, one arm looped loosely around my waist, the other balancing a water bottle between his knees. Maverick leans against the open tailgate, sunglasses perched on his nose like he's hiding from the world, but I know better. He hasn't stopped watching me since we sat down.

It's quiet here, but not empty. Just... done. Like we made it to the last page of something that mattered.

Colt nudges my knee with his. "You thinking about running again?" he teases, voice low.

I huff a dry laugh. "Nah. Might just take a minute to believe it's real."

Maverick drops his sunglasses down his nose, eyes glinting with amusement. "Better get used to it."

Behind us, someone whistles. Luke ambles over, tossing a pair of gloves into the bed of his truck and giving Colt a look that's equal parts fond and exasperated.

"You three look like a damn movie poster," he mutters. "You planning on riding off into the sunset or just sitting there long enough to make everyone jealous?"

Colt smirks. "Little of both."

Luke claps him on the back, nods once at me, then tips his hat toward Maverick. "So is it true? You two done?"

"I wouldn't put it that way. I'd say things are just beginning," Maverick says, his tone even, but the corner of his mouth twitches.

"Can't say I'm complaining. I think I've finally got a shot next year." He winks as he walks backward and leaves us with parting words. "Glad to see you finally getting over your bullshit and settling down."

Just like that, it's the three of us again. I bite my lip, but Maverick still catches the hint of my smirk.

"Think that's funny?"

"You guys really were drowning in your own idiocy."

"That's only because we didn't have you." Colt kisses my temple, then rests his head against mine. "You're ours now."

Warmth settles in my stomach, the kind that warms you all the way down to your bones.

The truck bed creaks as I shift, curling my fingers around the edge of the tailgate. The sun's dipping lower now, stretching golden light across the lot like it's trying to hold on to the day a little longer.

"I need to go back," I say quietly.

Colt's arm stiffens slightly around my waist. Maverick's head turns, slow and sharp.

"Not like that," I add quickly. "Not to leave. Just... my stuff's still there. My whole life, really. I have to pack it up."

Colt exhales, the kind of breath that carries weeks of tension. "Good," he says. "'Cause I was starting to get real sick of pretending we were gonna say goodbye again."

I nudge his thigh with mine. "You weren't pretending all that hard."

"I was trying, damn it."

Maverick snorts.

A beat passes. Just enough for the weight of the future to settle in.

Colt leans forward, forearms resting on his knees. "I've been thinking," he says, tone quieter now. "About what comes next."

I turn to him, heart thudding. "Yeah?"

"I got the prize money from the championship. It's a hell of a payout." He looks between us. "And I've been talking to my folks. They'd sell us the farm."

I blink. "Sell us the farm?"

He nods. "We'd have the space. Privacy. I know it's not the same as what you planned. Slow compared to the city…"

"It's perfect," I say before he can finish. "I never belonged there anyway."

Maverick shifts around to face us fully. "You serious?"

Colt's eyes are steady. "Dead serious."

Something swells in my chest. It's not just relief but recognition. Like the three of us have been circling the same truth from different sides, and now we're finally speaking it out loud.

"We could build something there," I whisper. "Something real."

Colt reaches for my hand. Maverick folds his fingers over mine from the other side.

For the first time in a long time, there's no fear clawing at my ribs. No uncertainty in my chest.

Just peace.

Just them.

The lot's mostly cleared now. Trucks are pulling out, trailers rattling behind them, kicking up dust and leftover adrenaline. Somewhere, someone calls a goodbye. A horn honks twice.

"We should go," I murmur, but none of us moves.

Colt's eyes drift toward me. "We really doing this?"

"Try and stop me," Maverick replies, helping me down from the tailgate.

Colt tosses the last duffel into the bed. Maverick opens

the truck door for me, and I climb into the middle seat where I belong between them.

I reach for the aux cord, brushing my fingers over the dial. "Same road," I say, glancing at them both. "But we're not who we were at the start of it."

Colt leans across me and kisses Maverick's jaw. "Thank fuck for that."

Maverick starts the engine, and the hum of it vibrates through my ribs. Colt's hand settles on my thigh. Mine stays in Maverick's.

The dust in the rearview mirrors fades.

All I can think is that I'm not afraid anymore.

Not of staying.

Not of love.

Not of being chosen last.

Because they will always choose us, and I will choose them right back.

Chapter 54

Colt

THE SUITE IS TOO CLEAN, too quiet, like it doesn't know we just walked in on the high of a lifetime. Crisp linen, polished wood, glass everywhere. Floor-to-ceiling windows give us the entire skyline, lit up like a goddamn celebration.

It's not the city I'm looking at.

It's her.

Callie's standing at the window, still in the clothes she wore to the arena. Hair wild. Backlit by the lights, like something untouchable. Beautiful in a way that guts me.

Maverick steps behind her, hands skimming low over her waist, undoing the button of her jeans with practiced ease. I move to her front, sliding my fingers into her belt loops. Together, we lower the denim inch by inch, slowly and reverently, until they hit the floor. She steps out, and Maverick tosses them aside.

I kiss her before she can catch her breath, fist her hair,

tilt her head back, and devour her mouth. Then I move to her neck, dragging my lips over the curve of her throat, biting hard enough to leave proof that she's mine. She shudders in response, and I swear I feel it echo in my bones.

I grab the hem of her shirt, lift it over her head, and drop it without looking where it lands.

Her bra stays on for exactly three seconds before I'm tugging the cups down, exposing her to the city. My mouth closes over one breast, sucking hard, then swirling my tongue over her nipple until it's tight and pebbled. I switch sides, dragging my teeth over the other, and her moan rips through the quiet like a shot.

Maverick's behind her, brushing her hair aside, saying something low and dark that makes her eyes flutter shut as he rolls her nipples between his fingers, making her gasp, hips pressing forward, and back.

I kiss my way down her body, trailing my lips over every stretch of skin I can reach. My knees hit the carpet, and I graze my knuckles up the backs of her thighs, slow and hungry.

I circle my tongue around her navel, then bite gently at her hip bone, reveling in her sharp gasp. I'm right where I've wanted to be all goddamn day.

Maverick's hands slip beneath the waistband of her panties and tug them down, revealing every inch of her. Bare, blushing, and breathtaking.

My mouth hovers, hot breath against her core, raising goose bumps across her skin. I take my time, wanting her desperate for my touch, grazing my nose along the seam of her thigh, inhaling her scent as I brush her clit with my lips. She moans, hand digging into my hair. The sting of her grip sends sparks straight to my weeping cock. Everything about our girl is perfect.

Callie's thighs tremble under my hands as I lick a slow stripe through her, tongue pressed flat and filthy, her sweet taste filling my mouth and clouding my brain. I groan against her, grip tightening on her ass as I bury my face deeper.

"Shit," she gasps, hips jolting forward.

Maverick's hands slide up from her wrists to her biceps as he gently, but firmly, presses Callie forward until her bare chest meets the cool glass. Her palms splay flat on the window above her head, breath fogging the pane in quick bursts.

"You like being on display like this, Wildflower?" he murmurs, voice dark silk behind her. "City out there doesn't even know what they're missing."

She moans in response, and I feel it ripple through her thighs.

"Look at her," Maverick says, like he's talking to himself. "Dripping for us."

I lap at her, slow and indulgent, letting my tongue circle her clit before flicking it just the way she likes. Tight, fast, controlled. Her legs nearly give out, but I hold her steady.

"Colt—" she pants.

Maverick slides one hand down her front, dragging

over her stomach, holding her still as I suck harder. Her hips jerk, thighs clenching.

I pull back, and she whines in frustration, but Maverick holds her firmly in place as he presses his cock between her thighs. Slow at first, dragging it through the slick mess I'm making of her, then harder, deeper, until the tip bumps my mouth with every thrust.

My dick aches, and I grip it through my pants, opening my mouth, alternating between sucking her clit and taking his thick, hard, leaking tip into my mouth as he rocks forward again. Swirling my tongue around the slit, I taste the mix of his salt and her sweetness.

It's fucking delicious.

"Fuck—Colt," he grits out, his voice raw as he thrusts again, sliding between her legs until the head nudges into my mouth and I open for him. He pulls back through my lips, wet and throbbing, with a slick pop. I work Callie's clit with deep, steady licks while I reach between her legs, grip the base of Maverick's length, and angle him toward her entrance.

She moans, long and broken, the second he bumps her, her hips pushing back instinctively.

"Hold her," I rasp, voice rough from the taste of both of them coating my mouth. Maverick's hands flex around her waist, locking her in place. She's shaking between us, wild and needy, as I guide him forward.

The head of his cock breaches her slowly, so fucking slowly, and her whole body tenses, a sharp gasp escaping her throat.

"So fucking good," I whisper against her clit, and she shivers.

Maverick groans low and vicious as he pushes deeper, his thighs slamming against the backs of hers.

I dive back in mouth greedy on her clit while Maverick fucks her in long, deliberate strokes. The wet sound of it, the scent of sex. I can't get enough. I want to stay here forever, buried in the taste of her and the weight of him.

Her legs nearly give out, but I hold her steady.

"Please—" she pants.

I hum, "Come on my mouth, baby. Let me taste it."

Maverick's hold on her tightens as he fucks into her. She cries out, shattering against my tongue, and I don't stop until her moans fade into whimpers.

Maverick strokes her back, grounding her. "That's it, Wildflower."

She twitches when I kiss the inside of her thigh again, a little too sensitive now. I press a final kiss just above her clit and drag my mouth away, chin slick.

We're not done.

Not even close.

Maverick lifts her back so it's pressed into him, still buried deep inside her, his hands spanning her hips like he never wants to let go.

I stand slowly, wiping my chin with the back of my hand, savoring the taste still lingering on my tongue. My knees ache, but I don't care. She's radiant, trembling and breathless, and I want all of her.

Maverick meets my eyes over her shoulder, something sharp and primal flickering between us. I undo my pants and shove them to the floor, kicking them aside, ripping my shirt off with one hand.

His voice is rough when he says, "Bend for him."

She lets out a soft, shaky breath and obeys, one hand pressed against the window for balance, the other trailing down to brace against my thigh. Her lashes lift, eyes shining.

I grip the base of my cock and stroke it once, twice, before tapping it against her bottom lip.

"Open," I murmur, watching her pupils dilate.

She does, hot and eager, taking me into her mouth with slow, deliberate pressure. My hand finds the back of her head, not forcing, just guiding, fingers tangling in her hair.

Maverick groans behind her, hips rocking as he thrusts in again, deeper this time. The movement nudges her mouth forward on my cock and a moan vibrates around me.

A guttural sound rips from my throat. She's caught between us every breath and movement shared, matched, multiplied. Her mouth goes deeper, her tongue swirling around me, cheeks hollowing as she sucks.

I thrust, slow at first, then deeper as her eyes flick up to meet mine, tear-lined and full of that same desperate hunger. She pulls me closer, wanting more, always more.

She's taking us both. And loving every fucking second of it.

Chapter 55

Maverick

Callie's moans go straight to my cock, needy, ragged little sounds that vibrate in my chest and settle low in my gut.

She's stretched out between us, so fucking perfect I could lose my mind.

My cock slides into her again, slow and smooth, glistening. Every time I pull out, I watch her grip down, greedy for more, like her body's begging me not to stop.

Fucking her with deep, steady thrusts, I slide my fingers down to her entrance, feeling where she stretches around me. Then, carefully, I press the tip where she's wrapped tightly around my length.

She chokes on a moan, still latched around Colt's cock, but doesn't let go.

God, she's a dream.

Her spine's hot against my palm as I run it in soothing

arcs, waiting for her to settle before adding a second finger.

I want to see how much she can take. I want to push her until she's crying on both our cocks, until her pretty pussy takes us together.

She's stretched wide, taking my every thrust, and I damn near come when she rocks back into them.

"Holy fuck." I have to clench every muscle to keep myself from spilling into her.

With each of our thrusts, her moans turn louder, greedy, needy sounds as she rocks between us.

"You want him buried inside of you, don't you, Wildflower," I rasp. She whimpers, pussy clenching around me.

"Colt," I say, taking my time thrusting in before continuing. "You hear our girl? She wants your cock."

Colt's eyes go molten. He lifts her legs around his waist as she clings to him, her face buried in his neck. I slip free when he shifts, but I don't mind, not with what comes next.

He kisses her in easy, languid motions like he has all the time in the world to devour her. I nuzzle her neck, licking a path up the column and kissing the sensitive spot behind her ear as I anchor her with a firm grip on her waist.

Colt lines himself up, and she gasps, nails biting into his shoulders, and I can see it. All of it. The way her face morphs with pleasure. The way her whole body trembles like she's seconds from breaking.

We're just getting started.

Colt thrusts up into her once. Twice. Her breath catches, a soft whimper leaving her lips, her thighs twitching around his waist.

I grip her ass and guide her up, giving him room to pull out. He does it slowly, his cock dragging against her walls.

I press in behind. I drag my cock through her slick folds, nudging against her opening where she's still quivering and wet from taking him.

She gasps as I enter her, twice, three times, before pulling out. Colt's already there, cock burying itself into her in one smooth thrust. She takes us one by one as we take turns fucking her.

Her back arches, and she mutters a strangled "Please—God, please."

Colt leans his forehead against hers, keeping his length deep inside. "You want both of us, Sunshine?"

She nods, wild and desperate. "Yes. Please. More."

Her need cuts through me like a blade as I begin to push in alongside Colt.

"Fuck," I grit out, inching deeper, feeling him right there with me, our lengths rubbing together inside her. She lets out a sobbing moan, caught somewhere between pain and bliss.

Her walls clamp down, greedy and tight.

"So fucking perfect," I hiss, hips working in slow, measured thrusts until I'm fully seated.

Colt's eyes are squeezed shut, holding her up like he's the only thing tethering her to earth.

She's trembling, gasping, tears streaking her cheeks as she grips his shoulders like she'll fall apart if she lets go.

We're not moving yet. Just breathing. Adjusting.

Together.

Callie's trembling between us, so full she can barely speak, but the sounds she's making, soft, broken gasps, say everything.

"Breathe, Wildflower," I murmur, voice low against the shell of her ear. "You're doing so good."

Colt shifts beneath her, his hands steadying her hips, his jaw clenched like he's barely hanging on. She whimpers when he flexes upward, the small movement forcing her to take us both a little deeper.

"God," she gasps, nails digging into his shoulders.

"That's both of us, Sunshine," Colt grits out.

I start to move, slow at first, just a shallow rock of my hips, feeling the thick pressure where we're both inside her. Her body tightens, fluttering around us like it's too much, but she's still begging for more.

"You take us so well," I whisper, kissing her shoulder. "So fucking perfect like this. Made for it."

She moans, long and high, her back arching, and I thrust again, deeper this time. Colt holds steady as I fuck into her, his eyes locked on mine over her shoulder.

She's crying now, not from pain but from the kind of overwhelming pleasure that breaks people open. Her walls pulse around us both, and she sobs as her orgasm hits hard, wild and beautiful.

"Oh my God," she gasps, trembling. "Oh my God, I—I can't—"

"You can," I growl, fucking her through it. "You're perfect. You're fucking perfect."

Colt chokes out a broken noise and jerks up into her, and I feel it. Feel him. Feel her. Feel us.

That's what undoes me.

I slam into her one last time and come hard, thick and hot, buried inside her, buried against him.

Colt lets go right after, a low groan tearing out of his throat, his hands clutching her tighter as his hips twitch.

We breathe like we've been drowning, mouths open, chests heaving, our bodies still locked together.

Callie's shaking between us, sweat-slick and glowing, and I press my lips to her spine. Colt strokes her thigh, murmuring her name like a prayer.

When I finally ease back, I slide out with a wet sound and watch our cum leak from her, thick and messy.

I gather some on my fingers and push it right back in. "No spilling a fucking drop," I say softly.

She nods, dazed and trembling, and Colt kisses her jaw, brushing her hair out of her face.

We hold her there, pressed between us, until her heartbeat slows, until our breath evens out, until there's nothing left but the quiet aftermath and the three of us, tangled and undone in the best fucking way.

Epilogue

Callie

THE BRUSH GLIDES over the wall in a wide arc, sage green softening the old farmhouse drywall, still patchy with spackle in some corners. I tuck a coppery strand of hair behind my ear, squinting at the uneven edge near the window trim.

"Dammit," I mutter under my breath, leaning closer to fix it.

Somewhere in the background, the screen door creaks open, followed by the sound of boots on hardwood.

"You missed a spot." Colt's voice is a teasing, low drawl from the hallway. I don't turn. I don't have to. I can feel his grin.

"Unless you're volunteering," I say, "maybe keep that brilliant commentary to yourself, cowboy."

I hear him move closer. Feel him, even before I catch

his reflection in the window, arms crossed, T-shirt damp with sweat. His hat's off, hair a mess. "I'd volunteer," he says, voice lower now, "but I'm enjoying the view."

I finally turn. That's when he sees it.

The thick swipe of green paint streaked along my bare shoulder.

I follow his gaze, groaning. "Don't start."

"You look like a forest sprite," Colt says solemnly. "A very sexy, mildly unhinged forest sprite."

"I swear to God," I warn, raising the brush like a weapon, "if you make another joke—"

Too late.

He crosses the room in two long strides and grabs my waist, hauling me in like he's got every right. Like I'm his home base.

"You gonna threaten me with that brush?" he murmurs against my cheek.

I nod.

He kisses me anyway.

Colt's mouth brushes mine, warm and easy, in no hurry until a sudden sharp whistle cuts through the air.

We both turn.

Maverick stands in the doorway, arms crossed, eyebrows raised, wearing that exasperated half smile.

"I leave you two alone for five minutes," he says, "and you're already making out?"

"She started it," Colt says without missing a beat, arms still looped around my waist.

I jab my elbow into his ribs. "You're the one ogling me like I'm some kind of mural."

Maverick steps closer, eyeing the paint on my skin, grinning as he inspects me. "You've got paint on your neck, your arm, and somehow," his fingers swipe down to my thigh, "your jeans."

"Unreal," I say, voice dry. "I'm being hazed by the tidy one."

"Not hazing," Maverick says, dipping the corner of a cloth into the water cup on the side table, "just trying to keep my girl from blending into the walls."

He slides it over my shoulder, his fingers lingering, and my breath stutters under his touch.

Colt lets out a long, satisfied sigh from behind me. "This is the kind of teamwork I was promised when we moved in together."

Maverick stands again, gaze flicking between us. "We should all stop flirting and finish this damn room before nightfall."

Colt presses his face into my neck, pretending to groan in agony. "You got it, boss."

"You'll thank me when we're not tripping over paint cans in the dark," Mav mutters.

I lean back into Colt and smile over my shoulder at Maverick. "You love us messy."

He doesn't argue. Just picks up a roller, dips it, and starts on the opposite wall like he has more than one reason to rush to get done.

Colt nudges me toward the tray. "Come on, Sunshine. Before he paints this whole house without us."

Maverick

Steam curls in the air, softening the edges of everything. Callie laughs as Colt yelps, water bouncing off her hands where she's just flicked it at him. There's paint smudged on her neck, a soft sage streak we didn't quite manage to scrub off. I reach over and swipe it with my thumb, but all I do is smear it further.

"You are ridiculously bad at painting," Colt mutters, but his eyes are lit with the kind of fondness I used to think was reserved for fairy tales.

She nudges him with her hip. "You love me."

"Unfortunately," he deadpans, then grins when she shoves him again. It's light, easy, familiar in a way that hits me straight in the chest.

I watch them for a beat. His hand on her waist, her body melting into him without a second thought, and something in me exhales. I've loved them both for years, but this... this is more than I ever thought I'd get.

Their laughter fades when they turn to look at me. My breath catches.

Callie's cheeks are flushed from the heat, hair slicked back, eyes bright with that wild spark I can never resist. Colt stands behind her, one arm still around her waist, water running down his chest, catching in the valleys of muscle and scar. They're both so fucking beautiful it almost hurts to look.

They're mine.

"Are you going to come over here or just stand there looking like you forgot how to breathe?" Colt teases.

I step forward, the tile warm beneath my feet, and slide my hands around them both, one at her back, the other curling around Colt's neck. Their bodies press into mine like puzzle pieces. It's easy. Right.

"I'm just..." My voice comes out rough, and I shake my head. "I'm really fucking happy."

Callie's face softens. She leans up and kisses my jaw. "We're happy too."

Colt tilts his head, brushing his lips against mine. "Even if we are stuck painting for the next week."

"I'll paint for a month if it means I get to come home to this."

Water patters around us, a quiet rhythm as our mouths find each other in turns. Callie's lips, then Colt's, then both of them pressing kisses to my jaw, my shoulder, my chest.

The air is thick with heat and citrus-scented soap, but all I feel is the weight of them against me. Warm and safe. Real.

My hands slide over Callie's hips, tugging her closer,

and Colt's fingers tangle with mine where they rest on her skin.

I don't need to say it out loud. They already know.

This is everything.

And it's ours.

The End

If you liked this book, please take a second to drop a rating. It helps *so* freaking much.

Reviews are amazing, but even just hitting those stars makes a huge difference too.

If you're in the mood for more MMF, Bi-awakening, Sports Romance, go check out **Rules of Our Own**. It's not a sequel, but it's got the same vibes: one girl, two boys, and a whole lot of heart(Smut). Mia, Alex, and River are featured in chapter 50.

Thank you for reading **Reckless Hearts**. You have no idea how much it means to me that you gave these three your time and love.

Thank you

This book would not exist without the wild, wonderful, supportive people who helped bring it to life.

First, to **Aly Beck**—my chaos wrangler, pace-keeper, and all-around writing wizard. I'd be lost (and probably still on chapter five) without you.

To **Nicole, Sierra, and Catherine**—my brilliant alpha readers. Thank you for screaming in the margins, and catching my chaos.

Becca, Clary, and Maggie—working with you is pure joy. Thank you for making this book sparkle and helping me shape it into something I'm proud of.

To my editing dream team, **Sandra and Geissa**—you are queens. Thank you for polishing every page with your magic touch (and your ruthless red pens).

And lastly to **you.**

Yes, *you* reading this.

Your love for these characters has changed my life in

Thank you

more ways than I can count. Thank you for every message, every reread, every time you screamed "JUST KISS ALREADY."

Your support means the absolute world to me.

Here's to messy love, found family, and stories that stay with you.

With all my heart,
   Jessa

READ MORE

MMF - Male ✦ Male ✦ Female

Rules Of Our Own

MMF - Not a a sequel to Reckless Hearts, but it has the same vibes. If this book has left you craving more, than Rules Of Our Own is the way to go. Mia, Alex, and River are featured in chapter 50.

READ NOW

Blurb:

Somehow, I've landed myself a do-over and this time we aren't screwing it up. This time, I don't want her all to myself. This time we're going to share.

Mia:

The second the Boston Bruins star forward steps out of the villa bathroom, looking like a god in nothing but a

READ MORE

low slung towel...I should turn around and beg for a different room.

When his tall, dark and broody teammate walks in offering to share the villa...I should run.

And when they offer me one weekend of no strings attached fun...I should absolutely say no.

But I've never been good at doing what I'm supposed to.

Alex:

Three nights wasn't enough. Not when I still wake up dreaming about her. About them.

Imagine our surprise when our new neighbor ends up being the girl we've both been obsessing over.

This time, we won't lose her.

This time, things will be different.

This time...we're ready to share.

River:

They're mine to own, possess, consume. They just don't know it yet.

READ NOW

MFM - Male - Female - Male
Gifted To His Dad
Smutty Christmas Novella
READ NOW
Blurb:
When my boyfriend Cole invited me to celebrate Christmas at his step-dad's cabin. Nothing could have prepared for what would happen next.

Griffin's nothing like I pictured. Instead of a typical middle-aged man. I'm faced with broad shoulders, a muscular chest and a jawline sharp enough to kill.

Spine tingling grazes, and heated glances that last too long have me feeling guilty about how my body's reacting.

That is until my boyfriend asks to share me with his step-dad

After the steamiest Christmas holiday of my life, everything feels perfect.

Note: All characters meet as **ADULTS.**

READ NOW

Hockey Romance:

Rule Number Five

Rule Breaker Interconnected standalone Series. (Can be read on its own.)

READ NOW

I had my whole life planned out… until I met a hockey player obsessed with breaking all of my rules.

My 5 simple rules for hooking up keep me from being distracted. And now I'm so close to landing my dream internship. Nothing is going to make me break them.

Even a protective hockey player with clear grey eyes, a sharp jaw, and a body that makes my breath catch.

Until Jax wins a bet and one kiss has me breaking them all.

TROPES:

READ MORE

- Slowburn
- He Falls First
- Friends with benefits
- Jealousy
- Mutual pining

Rules Of The Game

Rule Breaker Interconnected standalone Series. (Can be read on it's own.)
READ NOW

He's the star hockey player, my brother's best friend and the boy I've been in love with since I was 7.

The problem? He wants nothing to do with me.

Then why does he sneak into my room when I have a nightmare?

Gets jealous when I go on a date?

And has a tattoo of my birthday on his ribs.

Lucas Knight's a lot of things. He's possessive, jealous and overprotective. And he just might be in love with me.

Angst filled, heartbreaking and kick your feet in the air giddy inducing.

Rules Of Our Own

Rule Breaker Interconnected standalone Series. (Can be read on it's own.)

MMF - Not a a sequel to Reckless Hearts, but it has the same vibes. If this book has left you craving more than Rules Of Our Own is the way to go.

READ MORE

READ NOW
Blurb

Somehow, I've landed myself a do-over and this time we aren't screwing it up. This time, I don't want her all to myself. This time we're going to share.

Mia:

The second the Boston Bruins star forward steps out of the villa bathroom, looking like a god in nothing but a low slung towel...I should turn around and beg for a different room.

When his tall, dark and broody teammate walks in offering to share the villa...I should run.

And when they offer me one weekend of no strings attached fun...I should absolutely say no.

But I've never been good at doing what I'm supposed to.

Alex:

Three nights wasn't enough. Not when I still wake up dreaming about her. About them.

Imagine our surprise when our new neighbor ends up being the girl we've both been obsessing over.

This time, we won't lose her.

This time, things will be different.

This time...we're ready to share.

River:

They're mine to own, possess, consume. They just don't know it yet.

Dark Romance:

A Tempting Arrangement
READ NOW

Marry or lose his inheritance? That's the ultimatum billionaire Damon Everette faces. There's one problem. The woman he craves is his sunshine PR rep...who wants nothing to do with him.

Ruthless, arrogant, cold-hearted are some of the words I would use to describe my a**hole of a boss, Damon Everette.

That doesn't stop the goosebumps from rising along my neck every time he says my name, or the way my pulse races when his stormy gray eyes pierce mine.

So, when he coerces me into a fake marriage to uphold his family's tradition, I can't resist pushing his buttons.

He's a walking red flag, and I should run the second this arrangement ends. But the very thought of losing him is suffocating - a dangerous addiction that I can't seem to break.

Is this really love or just a twisted desire to own me? And deep down, do I secretly crave to be possessed by him?

READ NOW

A Twisted Arrangement
READ NOW

You might say my obsession has become a

READ MORE

compulsion in the way I need to know everything about Scarlet Laurent.

Even though I've taken a step into the background, I could never look away from my Little Sparrow.

She's a sliver, buried under my skin, a constant reminder of her presence, with no way to dig it out.

Staying away from her for the last ten years has been a brutal form of torture.

Her times run out and when the clock ticks midnight on her 25th birthday, I'll tie her to me forever.

After all, I can't kidnap what's already mine.

Cozy Obsession Interconnected Standalone. Can be read on its own.

READ NOW

A Devious Arrangement
READ NOW

She broke in, thinking she could leave. I kissed her. Claimed her. Now she's mine.

Anastasia:

Posing as my older brother, I infiltrated the most dangerous gala of the year, hell-bent on stealing a legendary tiara and saving my family. I slipped past guards. Navigated hidden passageways. Made it all the way to the vault.

And for one glorious second, I thought I'd gotten away with it.

Then he caught me.

READ MORE

Bash Everette.

Heir to the society I'm robbing.

Too powerful. Too pretty. Way too perceptive.

He doesn't call for help. Doesn't even blink.

He just pulls me into the shadows, pins me with a smirk...

And kisses me like he's been waiting his whole life to do it.

A cover, he says. To protect my identity.

Liar.

Then he makes me a deal: fake-date him, and he'll help me steal the crown.

I should run.

But his kiss still lingers, and the way he watches me like I already belong to him makes it impossible to say no.

Getting caught was never part of the plan.

Neither was he.

Bash:

She broke into my world wearing a stolen name and a reckless smile.

I kissed her. Marked her.

Now she's mine.

I wasn't supposed to be there that night—wasn't supposed to catch her slipping through the shadows, dressed in lies and ambition.

But I did.

And instead of turning her in, I dragged her into the dark with me.

She thinks I kissed her to keep her secret.

READ MORE

To protect her.

How cute.

I kissed her because I wanted to see how fast she'd fall.

And how hard.

Now she owes me.

One fake relationship. One dangerous heist. One crown to steal.

But the moment she said yes, the rules changed.

Because I don't share. And I don't let go.

She doesn't know it yet, but I'm not helping her escape.

I'm luring her deeper.

Twisting the game until she begs me to finish it.

Getting caught was never part of her plan.

But being mine?

That was always inevitable.